CLIPTON SECRETS

MARIE THOMPSON

iUniverse LLC
Bloomington

CLIPTON SECRETS

This is a work of fiction. All of the characters, names, incidents, organizations, and dialogue in this novel are either the products of the author's imagination or are used fictitiously.

iUniverse books may be ordered through booksellers or by contacting:

iUniverse LLC
1663 Liberty Drive
Bloomington, IN 47403
www.iuniverse.com
1-800-Authors (1-800-288-4677)

ISBN: 978-1-4917-2759-1 (sc)
ISBN: 978-1-4917-2761-4 (hc)
ISBN: 978-1-4917-2760-7 (e)

Library of Congress Control Number: 2014904477

Printed in the United States of America.

iUniverse rev. date: 05/22/2014

For my children, Karen, Guy, and Scott, who captivate and bring so much joy.
For my sister and brother-in-law, Trish and John, whose unconditional love and support keep me warm.

CHAPTER ONE

My marriage to Geoffrey became a listless meandering. Like so many wedded couples, we gave the impression of riding a tandem in sync, yet we pedaled two independent bicycles, albeit along the same road. Geoffrey and I were devoted to each other, certainly; as the years passed, we became more comfortable with each other, but it was a lazy compromise. We were like a cosy sweater—a bit frayed around the edges, yet still valued for its warmth. I hadn't realised how well we fitted until it was too late. My widow status over the past two years had brought wrenching loneliness and an overwhelming sense of loss. Living without him was like having a clamp around my lifeline that made me gasp for every breath—at least until 2 May 1983. While resting in my usual stupor in bed that morning, for the first time in a long, long time, I felt a violent shudder of energy within, a seismic jolt that crushed my ennui. Just out of the blue, my mind and body had apparently concluded they were sick of listening to the internal tale of woe wherein I laid on self-pity, to the point of suffocation. I don't know who or what screamed, "Enough!" but I obediently pushed back the bed covers and stepped into life again.

I discovered Clipton St Marks when Reg, my chauffeur, took me for a jaunt out of London on a breezy Sunday afternoon. The small Buckinghamshire County hamlet is less than forty miles north-west of London, and lies nestled among rolling hills and the beech-clad Chilterns, a chalk escarpment that runs for miles throughout magnificent countryside. Imposing Georgian houses are incognito behind giant oaks, and thatched cottages cluster around vegetable plots and perfumed rose gardens. On the outskirts, a meticulously tended green is at the ready for a cricket match on languid summer afternoons.

"Of course, it would be a Sunday when no garage is open!" A petulant Reg kicked the deflated tyre with his shoe. A stocky man with close-cropped red hair and freckles, Reginald Wills had been with me for six months. He had been the third of four men who answered my advertisement for a chauffeur. His confidence and dry wit gave him an energy that I needed in my secluded life, and I had hired him on the spot. His usual relaxed manner was markedly absent lately, since his wife had served him with divorce papers. I made allowances for his dour attitude, not only because of his ability to manipulate my Bentley through London traffic, quite simply it was because I liked him.

"Can't you take care of it, Reg?"

"I have to, don't I?" Making no effort to hide his aversion for the job ahead, he took off his jacket and started to roll up his shirtsleeves. My own dander began to rise at his boorish manner. "This will take a while, Mrs Campbell." Mumbling unintelligently, he rummaged noisily through a tool bag in the car boot. "Why don't you take a look around town instead of waiting here?"

"Good idea." Of course, he was really warning me not to get under his feet.

The car was stopped only yards from a perfect retreat where mallards and a couple of black swans coasted lazily on an oval pond. I watched for a few moments before turning to the quiet, twisting streets, and wandered aimlessly. No city traffic disturbed my thoughts; no noisy crowds pushed by—just the soothing sounds of nature. I strolled contentedly along a narrow road that took me beyond the outskirts of town. Fields stretched into the distance on either side, and I stopped for a moment, drawing in the peace and the sun's warm rays.

I continued a little farther and came upon a neglected but impressive half-timbered house set back from the road. Curious, I pushed through the overgrown hedge and strolled up the driveway. My knocking on the heavy door several times received no response. Spitting on a handkerchief, I was able to rub off a patch of grime covering a leaded window, and revealed an interior with high ceilings, stained wall coverings, and the curve of a graceful staircase. Utterly fascinated, I meandered onto the derelict grounds. Leggy geraniums and wild privet hedges rode roughshod over unkempt lawns. On a paved patio, I found a long-forgotten deck chair and sat down to contemplate the span of land before me. In a distant field, lethargic Jersey cattle were sheltering from the heat under a protective canopy of sweeping elms. No such luxury for a border collie in the adjacent meadow rounding up peripatetic sheep . . . their indignant bleating carried aloft in the humid air.

I found myself at peace as I breathed in the sweet scent of an abandoned rambling rose; its flowers carpeted the soil below in a layer of yellow petals. The oasis of calm was salve to those remnants of grief over the loss of my husband that still continued to churn deep within me. I looked around, making mental pictures of what the property once had been and could be again. My imagination began to awaken. I could breathe life back into the old place. This could be the challenge I needed, the mission to fill my life so there was no room for loneliness. *Why not?* I felt almost drunk as excitement swept over me, and I laughed aloud. *I'm making progress, Geoff.*

Geoffrey Campbell and I were married in 1968, during his internship at St George's Hospital in London. In the thirteen years we were together, I never quite got used to being his wife. Mrs Campbell did not fit me, somehow. When our children Tim and Julia came along, our friends thought we were the perfect family. It seemed that way on the surface, but I felt like an observer rather than a participant as our lives played out. Oh, I was deeply in love with Geoffrey. He was as good a husband and father as he could be, but his allegiance went first to his patients. They loved him, too. Eventually, the physically drained and impotent man returning from the disinfected corridors of authority was simply not able to relate to the mundane lives of his spouse and offspring. I discovered emotional distance could be both a relief and extremely painful. He died at the age of forty-eight after being run over by a number 30 bus at Hyde Park Corner. Although only yards from the prestigious hospital where he practised unconditional devotion, he was unable to be saved. His death brought me an unrelenting heartache, and insurance benefits of several million pounds.

We had met in a coffee bar in Earls Court Road, where I lived in one of the hundreds of bed-sitters in that energetic cosmopolitan area. I was working during those days in Wilson's Fashion Centre, a corner dress shop in Hammersmith, and attending landscape design classes at night. It was spring break, and I was eager to get out for a bit of fun with Rita, a classmate.

"Did you see the way he looked at you?"

"Who?"

"That chap over there—the tall, blond one. He practically stripped you with his eyes!"

"Don't be silly!" I tried to turn my head to get a look at him without being obvious. He caught my eye and smiled. I blushed beet red.

"Oh, he's coming over," Rita said.

"Evening, ladies." He sat down in the chair next to me. "I'm Geoff. My friend Nigel and I wondered if we could buy you two girls a cup of coffee." He leaned into me. I could feel the pressure of his shoulder against mine. "How about it?"

"Of course, Geoff. Tell Nigel to come on over."

"Rita!"

"What?" She widened her eyes in overstated innocence. "There's no harm!"

I relaxed. Of course there was no harm. Having a cup of coffee with two men, even if they were strangers, was perfectly all right. Girls did it all the time, especially in Earls Court, a neighbourhood of five-storey Victorian houses that had been converted into single-room rentals, complete with sparse furniture, a gas ring for cooking, and a sink. Bathrooms were shared. Rents were cheap and comforts limited. The majority of tenants were students from the British Commonwealth, mostly Australians, West Indians, and Pakistanis. You knew you were heading towards the area because the whiff of spicy curry tantalised your nose. It was one of the two bargain-priced dishes served by the multitude of coffee bars along Earls Court Road, the other being spaghetti bolognese.

We had a good time that evening. Nigel and Rita took off together, and Geoff walked me to the doorway of number 51 Cromwell Road. I gave him my telephone number without hesitation after his passionate kisses made me feel weak in the knees. A first for me, and my heart was beating very fast as I brushed my teeth later that night.

My parents liked him at once and were impressed that I was of interest to a future doctor. It was a bit embarrassing, though, when my mother complained about her arthritis and then the ache in her back. Geoff tried to tell her he was far from being qualified. I think her opinion of him was changed somewhat by the time that important information eventually sunk in. My parents lived in a ground floor flat in Fulham . . . not a very nice flat. It had been home to the Sullivan family for years. I felt a bit sensitive about taking Geoff there the first time, since it was small and rather shabby, but my father's magnificent garden made up for any concern. It had been his focus long before his retirement, and the result proved it. It was when Geoff enthusiastically complimented my father's efforts that I started to fall in love with him.

Dr and Mrs Campbell Sr did not take warmly to me when we met at their beautiful country house—not that first time, not ever. I didn't really care. Geoff had become my world, and nothing was going to stop us from being together. I believed that then. Our wedding was a simple service in our local Presbyterian church; it was for convenience, really, as neither of us held much belief in formal religion. My parents had no money for extra expenses, so I paid most of the bills myself with my saved wages and a hundred pounds borrowed from the bank. Getting a ten per cent discount from Wilson's shop meant I bought my dress there, and even an outfit for Mum—a navy-blue wool suit. I was too happy to care about Geoff's mother's disapproval of the rather stingy reception. As is the custom, his family paid for the car rentals, and the street was briefly brought up a peg or two by the immaculate Daimlers parked on the kerb. Because Geoff was tall, I wore a short white taffeta dress, thinking it made me look taller standing next to him, but I have always regretted not choosing a full length. About the only chance a girl like me gets to wear a long dress is on her wedding day. I have never worn one.

Our honeymoon in tropical Majorca took persistence. It wasn't the island's fault; it was spectacular. For some incomprehensible reason Geoff assumed I was sexually experienced, and had only deflected his passionate advances to increase his libido before my total submission. He soon learned differently. After all, a respectable girl raised by upright parents is supposed to be a virgin until her wedding night, right? My mother's talk had been brief and quite useless to me. Geoff's own experience was limited to a few romps in the bushes with trainee nurses. It took a while before we finally found our way, and joyfully discovered each other with escalating excitement and passion. We needn't have gone abroad at all, as we only left our room to eat. Naively, we thought our happiness would never end.

Because of Geoff's schedule at St George's, we did not see much of each other those first years. He would be away for days. His eating and sleeping schedule went by the wayside. When he was home, he was so dog-tired he fell asleep immediately—frequently alone. His appetite never matched my own, so I stopped cooking dinner, and we just snacked. I felt miserable and resentful of the endless days and nights alone but tried to keep my feelings to myself because, as Geoff reminded me, it would not be for ever.

"Why don't you give up that god-awful shop job and go back to school full-time? We don't need the money, and it'll give you something to talk about when I'm home." He was right, of course. My salary contributed little, and I knew I bored him with my limited world. It was understandable. While he was cutting into people's chests, I was putting dresses on hangers.

Fully committed, I gave my notice at Wilson's and again enrolled in landscape design classes. I was a quick learner and approached my studies with dedicated determination.

Landscaping had been an outgrowth of helping my father with his beloved garden. He was a good teacher. As my interest grew, he recognised I had talent and encouraged me. I began to dream of becoming a head gardener for one of the parks or royal estates. My father made me think I could really do it, although a female reaching such a position was unheard of at that time. I look a lot like my dad with my blue eyes and black hair. Dad thought it champion when I told him I was back at school, this time as a full-time student. "You'll do well, luv. I've always regretted you gave up before. Of course, I know why." Mum did too. While living at home, my dream had been overwhelmed by the need to help reduce the financial struggles of the Sullivan household, and I had learned to be somewhat content as a sales girl at Wilson's. It helped knowing my parents appreciated my sacrifice. Eventually, they seemed to manage better, and I moved out.

When Geoff got home from the hospital, I was busy with my own studies and left him in peace. Poor Geoff. It is a terrible thing to be with someone out of duty, but soon I could tell his attitude towards me was changing. I'm sure my going to school saved my marriage. "I was looking at some of your drawings. They're pretty good." He sounded awkward. I knew he was learning to talk to me all over again. "When we have our own house, you must plan the grounds for us." I said nothing, just smiled happily to encourage him.

In the end, Geoff Campbell became a heart specialist, and I added CLA—Certified Landscape Architect—after my name. My husband and my parents were very proud, and so was I. I had proved to them and myself that I was equal to anyone. I no longer felt inferior to my husband or in-laws, and my new straightened back and look-'em-in-the-eye attitude suited me just fine. I was losing my less-than-refined accent, too. Well, when you have a degree, you have to sound educated; otherwise people will think you've forged it or something.

"There you are, Mrs Campbell!" In my daydreaming stupor, I had completely forgotten Reg. "I've been driving all over the place looking for you," he scolded.

"Sorry, Reg. When I found this marvellous place, I lost all sense of time. I hadn't noticed I'd strayed so far. Next time, I'll leave a trail of breadcrumbs," I said flippantly. He was not amused. We walked to the car in silence.

We drove back to Main Street, stopping at Clipton's one hotel, the Retreat, where I enquired about taking rooms for an indefinite period.

"If you don't know how long you'll be staying, may I suggest reserving a room for a fortnight to begin with?" The elegant receptionist was very polite. "You won't find a more beautiful region anywhere in England." She gestured to a rack of coloured brochures. "I'd be happy to arrange a tour of the area for you."

"Thank you, that's unnecessary; my objective is to investigate the current status of a house I came across just outside the village. It looks abandoned. Perhaps you know the place?"

"Yes, you mean the rectory."

After I thoroughly reassured Reg his job was not in jeopardy, he remained in London while I moved into the comfortable hotel a couple of weeks later. I quickly settled in, spending long hours poring over architectural plans and photographs of restored National Trust buildings, and taking leisurely strolls around this charming yet decidedly uncongenial community. It was a lonely, isolated time for me. Clipton residents are close-knit, sceptical of newcomers until the intruder, having proved neither thief nor foe, is accepted without fanfare. The shopkeepers took my money stoically at first, but eventually a cheery "Mornin', miss" greeted me. The thaw was confirmed when I received a casual wave of the hand from the milkman making his rounds as I took my early-morning walk. Those simple gestures gave my confidence a boost; interest in my venture was stirring. It had taken a while.

The renovation work needed on the rectory was not modest, and would, indeed, be very costly; however, I felt driven to bring the dilapidated building back to its full glory. Convinced I could bring it off, I began to search out the talents of local craftsmen.

"The place has been abandoned for years. It's still officially church property, but Clipton has no use for it now there's a new vicarage in the centre of the village." Ted Nyby reviewed the blueprint flattened across the bench table. "It was a private residence in the old days. The church bought it to house the vicar and his large family before realising it was a bit far out of town. At that time, there were only dirt roads, so when the weather was bad, he was stuck . . . and that happened a lot! Eventually, it was given up as a lost cause. I think you'll get it for a good price, but it'll cost you plenty to bring the old place back, Mrs Campbell—if you want to do it properly."

"The church commissioners accepted my offer last week, Mr Nyby, and I can afford to do it properly." His frown changed to a look of respect, something I had seen before when I mentioned I had money. "I want to create both a beautiful home for myself and a historic building for Clipton. I came to you because you have a reputation as a master builder, and you know local contractors and suppliers." Regrettably, I heard the pleading edge to my voice. "I can't do it alone. I need someone with your experience to be my partner."

He rubbed his fingers across his chin while contemplating my petition; the grey stubble reverberated like coarse sandpaper. My anxiety grew as I waited for him to break the silence. After a minute or so, he faced me. "Well, if you've got the money to pay for it, then I'm the man to make it happen." He held out a well-worn hand, the first two fingers of which were the colour of tanned leather, presumably from smoking. I grabbed it thankfully.

"You won't regret it, Mr Nyby!"

"I'd better not! I'm putting my good name on the line." Nonetheless, I caught a flash of humour in his eye.

Joyfully, I returned to the hotel. I knew I had accomplished a great deal in acquiring Ted Nyby's expertise for the job. He came well recommended, having renovated historic buildings throughout Southern England to the highest standard. My vision was going to become a reality. Would it also be the new personal beginning I hoped for?

CHAPTER TWO

Mr Nyby was true to his word, and we met for a walk through the rectory a few days following our initial meeting.

"The whole roof needs replacing," he said, leading me into the library. He looked apologetic as his hand swept around the oak-panelled room. "And this wood is rotten, so it'll all have to come out, Mrs Campbell. By the time we gut this place, there's not going to be much left. Are you sure you don't want to rebuild?"

"Absolutely! I'm counting on you to save whatever you can." Large pieces of panelling had been ripped off the walls and lay in crumbling disarray on the dusty floor. "We can make the rectory really grand again, Mr Nyby." I felt excitement as I walked over to the carved fireplace and ran my fingers over the beautifully grained piece of wood adorned with leaves and acorns. "Whoever did this work must have put his heart and soul into it. How old do you think it is?"

"Well over a hundred years . . . more. Oak is a tough wood to carve . . . would have taken scores of hours and blistered fingers to create such work. You'd rarely see such dedication nowadays."

"Can nothing be done to save it?"

"I know it's not what you want to hear, but no—it's full of worms and ruddy falling apart!"

I looked at my palm. It had an imprint of an oak leaf where I had rested my hand against the carving. "I understand this isn't a Grinling Gibbons masterpiece, Mr Nyby; all the same, it is wonderful craftsmanship."

"Believe me, if it was anything close to Gibbons' work, it wouldn't be rotting away in this shambles. The church people would have saved it before they moved out. Gibbons was a master carver commissioned by kings."

"Nevertheless, I don't want you to touch it until I make a few calls to London, all right? At least let me try." I was not about to discard this gem without a fight.

I watched Mr Nyby walk away. He was a tall, thin man with a stern manner that affected my confidence. My ignorance of the realities of what could or could not be saved left me at a great disadvantage, and I struggled not to give in to his propensity to clean sweep the whole house. The mantelpiece, however, was a different matter. I was determined to stand my ground and would start my research that evening. Feeling quite apprehensive, I went into the garden. Sitting down on a rickety bench, I tried to mollify my racing thoughts. Had I taken on more than I could handle? There were so many details to consider, so many decisions that I, alone, had to make. Each day seemed to bring its own crisis.

My daughter, Julia, stayed at the hotel with me for a few days, and it was a welcome timeout to be with her. She looked so pretty, and so much like Geoff. Each time I looked at her, I was reminded of how much I missed him. I was sorry when the time came to put her on the train back to London, where she was a pre-med student at St George's Hospital, proudly following in her father's footsteps. It was good of her to take the time to visit me. I felt the warmth of her soft cheek against mine well after we hugged goodbye.

Serious work started on the old building almost at once; even so, it took more than two years to fully restore the rectory, including the fine mantelpiece. Mr Nyby and the contractors were as proud of the finished house as I was. It had been a true partnership; they did the work, and I paid the bills. It worked most of the time, but we had flared tempers and hostile silences a lot, too. These were not the type of contractors who laid concrete paths or put in new sinks and faucets; these were craftsmen in the true sense of the word—skilled, proficient; all showing artistic temperaments that matched my own in our struggle for autonomy and control. Initially, they felt uncomfortable having me working alongside them with their outbursts of profanities, but when they heard I could give as good as any of them, we got along just fine. Their acceptance helped to ease me further into the community, and there was much satisfaction in hearing congratulations from the last holdouts at the small celebratory reception. At last, I was one of them.

It was a fine house; beams of preserved timber stood out against walls washed in white, and the leaded windows gleamed welcomingly. Now it was time to make it a home, and choosing furnishings required the help of an interior designer. I chose Ethan Gilbert, whose beautiful interiors graced many glamorous architectural magazines. He waved his hand confidently as he followed me from room to room.

"Just leave everything to me, Mrs Campbell. I'll change this glorious house into a magnificent home with a heart." His protruding Adam's apple increasingly rose up and down as his excitement grew.

"I want it to be a real home, Ethan. The furnishings are to be in light, neutral colours—and lots of rugs. I like rugs."

"Your wish is my command, my dear." His steps were short as he crossed the room, holding one hand out as if he were balancing a tray. I don't think he would have made a good waiter, though. He was true to his word, and I was indeed proud of the finished result. He followed through on all my wishes; the drapes and soft furniture were in natural linen, and brightly woven rugs lay over the parquet floors. The lighting was restful yet bright enough to draw out the colours and warmth of my collection of paintings, similar in style to the Impressionists. The walls of the three guest rooms were lined in cream silk and decorated with Georgian furnishings purchased by Ethan through the trade. Two additional bathrooms were created from the maids' quarters. My own room, with its canopied bed covered in pale green and lavender chintz, was very pleasing. I had a real home of my own creation at last. I was glad to have Reg back with me. Together, we gussied up the guesthouse and made comfortable quarters for the now single man. The next and final project was my true love—the garden! I rubbed my hands together with delight.

CHAPTER THREE

"My goodness! You startled me!"

"I didn't mean to." The tall man came towards me. A red MG was parked outside the gate. "Simon Belsky." He held out his hand. I took off my gardening glove and held out my own, aware of the dirt under my fingernails. He did not seem to mind and shook it rather vigorously. "I was on my way to the McKinleys' and saw this." He gestured towards the house. "I remember how it used to be. I've been watching you for some time. You look as if you know what you are doing." He smiled and flashed white, even teeth. "Would you object to me taking a walk around?" My frown must have told him I did not like unexpected intrusions, for he hesitated.

"The house is fully renovated, but as you see, everything out here is in such chaos. I can't imagine what you find interesting in the grounds at this stage."

"If it's not convenient, perhaps I can come back another day? I'll be in Clipton for the week."

Reluctantly, I gave in. "No, it's all right. You're welcome to have a look. Take your time." I turned back to clipping the overgrowth off the box hedge. It was a warm day, and the exertion soon caused sweat to soak my shirt. I became so absorbed in shaping the hard yellow wood, I totally forgot the stranger until his wave caught my eye as he departed through the gate.

"Of course you must come. Stella, you need a break. That garden is taking over your life!"

"Not enough to put up with the boring small talk in your drawing room, Beverly." I chuckled. "You just want me there to keep you from going bonkers yourself!"

"That's not so! Although this small town doesn't lend itself to electrifying conversation, I must admit. Nothing happens here," she groaned. "Say yes, Stel. Help me out! It'll only be the Dawsons."

"You'll owe me big time, Beverly. I'll come, but once Robert starts on his week in the big-city oratory, I'm making my getaway."

"He says he commutes to London each day to give the children and me the pleasure of living in the country. What bloody rot! He can't wait for Mondays to escape from so much pleasure! I wish I could go with him!"

"Why don't you move back to London?" We'd gone through this conversation many times before, and I knew what was coming.

"It would break his heart if he couldn't play the country gentleman."

Beverly Petersen and her husband, Robert, had become my closest friends in Clipton. A few years younger than I, Beverly was like a sister, and we bared our souls with absolute honesty. Robert was fond of me but was mostly grateful I was around to take Beverly off his hands. Their grey stone home was very grand, and I had the pleasure of designing a formal landscape for them that included an arboretum and rose garden. Prominent in the community and hosts to well-to-do weekend guests from London, the Petersens never lost a chance to endorse me whenever the graceful results were admired, and gradually, I began to build a clientele and make a name for myself.

The long mahogany dining table had eight formal settings. "Everyone's here now, so we can be seated."

"How could you, Bev? You said nothing fancy!"

"Well, it's not really. Robert met the McKinleys and their houseguest Simon Belsky in the pub. At least we'll have fresh blood," she whispered back, her lips unmoving like a ventriloquist's. "As much as we adore the Dawsons, they are a little limited in their dinner dialogue." I agreed but was irked I had been deceived, because I would not have dressed so casually.

Simon smiled at me when we took our places at the table. He was seated to my left, the McKinleys across from me. Beverly offered the platter of slices of roast beef to him as I helped myself to the delicious salad the cook had especially prepared. "Stella's a vegetarian, Simon. Didn't I tell you she was peculiar?"

"Actually, I eat egg whites and dairy, so lacto-ovo-vegetarian would be more accurate."

"Sounds like she's got a dreadful disease, doesn't it?" Robert winked at me as he added a large portion of the rare flesh to his own plate.

Simon barely participated in the trite conversation that followed; the McKinleys made up for him, however. They were dears, really . . . attractive in their own way, although a little eager for the spotlight. Cynthia was about thirty-five, with blond hair and brown eyes, and not a hint of makeup. She was quite an accomplished academic in her own right, apparently, having published a number of important papers. Michael looked to me to be the epitome of a college professor—very tall and thin, with a goatee that made his face seem leaner. Keith Dawson and his devoted wife, Fay, were middle-aged locals who lived very comfortably from well-established investments that put their names among the wealthiest in the county. They eased their consciences by donating considerable sums of money to several charities. Understandably, they were on many hit lists.

I was unusually quiet that evening. The hot summer days were not conducive to shovelling and muck spreading, and I had certainly done a lot of both over the past month. Every muscle in my body complained, and my skin was the colour of toast. I must confess that was only part of it; I was embarrassed at seeing Simon again. Not long after his walking tour of the rectory grounds, I had gone to take a hot bath, and caught a glimpse of myself in the mirror before it misted over. I looked like a raving banshee! My long hair stood on end, starched by sweat and grime. Streaks of dirt ran down my cheeks and—oh, the very worst—my nostrils were caked in a black crust. I shudder to think of it, even now. The only way I could bring myself to face him again was to reassure myself he probably hadn't noticed. After all, he was interested in the rectory improvements, certainly not an aging country bumpkin.

"Have you never eaten meat, Stella?" He leaned towards me, as if grateful for the opportunity to talk on a subject beyond banking or the ever-increasing cost of illegally imported Cuban cigars.

"Not since I was fourteen."

"She couldn't see the difference between animal flesh and human flesh. Right, Stel?"

"Yes." I began to think about those black nostrils again, and avoided looking up.

Beverly reached over and patted my hand. "She's got a tender heart—that's really why. Can't bear to think about killing the cows and things." She caught the butler's eye. "Blanchard, we'll have dessert and coffee on the terrace."

Simon followed me out, making agreeable small talk. He intended to make brief visits to Clipton over the next year, but did not elaborate.

I was in a pensive frame of mind when I walked the quiet lane back to the rectory that evening. I hardly noticed when an owl swooped passed, fanning the air like a whisper. It had become apparent to me the life I was living was not enough. I did not want the highlight of my week to be dinner at the Petersens'. There had to be more. Courting bullfrogs noisily deflating their ballooning membranes broke the silence. I pulled my coat collar up. A storm was gathering energy on the horizon, and an occasional flash of lightning silhouetted the trees like a dramatic backdrop for a production of Macbeth. I reached the rectory and closed the front door with relief.

My deepening loneliness was the impetus I needed to become more involved within the community, and I began attending church fetes and meetings of the town council. For a small village, local politics were very active. I enjoyed the heated debates, and was careful not to take one side or the other. The blatant *I'll-scratch-your-back* attitude was fascinating. I must have been caught with my mouth open on more than a few occasions because the mayor, Albert Burr, took me aside one evening before the start of a public meeting of the town council. He made it quite clear an unreadable facial expression was an essential qualification for any official office—most particularly when there was a public meeting.

"Doesn't do to let anyone know what you're thinking, Mrs Campbell. You must learn to play your trump card without giving it away first."

I wasn't clear about what he had said until halfway through the meeting. At that moment I knew being an observer wasn't enough anymore. It appeared Mayor Burr had shrewdly recognised the aspiration in me. I wanted to make a difference—a difference that would benefit the community in a real way. Right then and there, I decided to run for the vacancy on the planning commission, and determined I would definitely not scratch anyone's back. With what I hoped was an unreadable facial expression, I remained in my seat amid the rowdy audience, and concentrated on my plan of action while the commotion continued at the podium.

Being a female in her early forties proved to be no handicap, for I won the election easily and became one of the five planning commissioners. My pride was stroked by this considerable honour. The inspiration behind my campaign was the belief that I really could make a difference, and bringing the rectory back to life had enhanced my standing in the community. I began my pitch. "My success with the rectory is only the beginning. Clipton has too many crumbling historic buildings that could—should—be brought back to their full grandeur. We can give this lovely hamlet a soul again." The applause was thin but encouraging, and I made promises I intended to keep.

The first planning commission meeting I participated in as a commissioner seemed a farce; four tweed-garbed men in their middle years and I faced a well-informed and verbal audience in the formal setting of the council chambers. The renovation of public buildings was the first item on the agenda that evening. I think a lot of the rhetoric was for my benefit, and I was baited mercilessly.

"What do you know about Clipton, Mrs Campbell? You're a Londoner, a city woman. You can't relate to what we want in our village." The speaker's face hung in synclinal folds, and looked an unhealthy purple in the artificial light of the council chambers. Terence Murdock may have had good standing in Clipton, but he was not going to make a fool of me.

"Don't be absurd, Mr Murdock. The people of this community elected me because they believe my platform."

"And just what is that platform, may I ask?" His tone was mocking, and I resented his jeering smile.

"Why don't we talk after the meeting, Mr Murdock? We are running a public hearing at the moment." I fought back the anger that brought a flush to my cheeks. I turned to the chairman, hoping he would back me up. Instead, he grinned and winked at me. A few folk in the audience observed him, and sniggered. I nearly lost it then.

"If the commission approves the plans, and they can be done without going over budget, then you've got my vote." The man had a slight Scottish brogue. About fifty with a shock of graying hair, he looked straight at me. "I'm Joe Blake, farmer. If you fail, I'll have your guts for garters." He displayed no pleasantry, just got up from his chair and faced the audience. "Well, we haven't got all bloody day. Pull your fingers out of your arses, and let's get on with it. All those in favour say aye." His hard-nosed demeanour dared anyone to oppose him.

Slowly, hands went up in support of the project, and I breathed easier when the vote was unanimous. "Thank you, ladies and gentlemen. You will have public buildings you can be proud of," I promised.

The meeting adjourned at seven thirty without Mr Murdock demanding further sparring time, and I caught up with Joe Blake as he was about to get into his truck. "Mr Blake. You saved the day." I held out my hand. "Thank you." Ignoring my hand, he started up the vehicle, revving the engine loudly. I stepped out of the way quickly and stared through the exhaust fumes as he sped away. "Rude bastard!" I pretended not to notice the heads turning in my direction as I walked briskly down the street.

"Good evening, Mrs Campbell." I waved happily in response to Dr Levinton's greeting, and crossed the road to the newsagent's shop. My mood remained positive after the commission meeting. As it was a warm evening, I decided to treat myself to an ice cream. Joe Blake stepped back to allow me to enter the shop. He paused, and then turned to me.

"I'm sorry about before. I had a lot on my mind, but there is no excuse for my behaviour." He smiled and offered a hand.

"That's exactly what I was thinking, Mr Blake." I ignored his hand.

"I deserve that." To my surprise, he chuckled. "When you can forgive me, please call me Joe." He turned, and was gone before I could think of a response.

The first major project sanctioned through the planning commission was the renovation of the town hall, originally built in 1835. The lovely red brick school and library were to follow. I was officially designated as project supervisor. My first action was to solicit the help of Mr Nyby, and together we held a public meeting with local craftsmen and contractors.

"You'll not be using your own money this time, Mrs Campbell, so they'll be watching every penny you spend. Mark my words."

"Actually, I'm making a loan. I'll be advancing funds from my own account, yes—but all the money I put up will be reimbursed from Clipton's Building Society's trust fund. That's why we've got to keep to the budget, Mr Nyby. Not one penny over, or I'll have to answer to my banker, the trustees, and the planning commissioners." My reputation was in the hands of the dozen men seated around the table. The silence was heavy. "Well? Can I count on you?"

"Aye, I'll go along with you, Mrs Campbell. It'll mean work for the men, and the village will benefit by having a decent place to hold meetings and for the youngsters to hold their functions. It'll be the beginnings of a real civic centre."

"Thank you, Mr Derby. Your ideas for a children's sports centre will be needed as soon as you can draw them up." I waited quietly for further comments. An unpretentious but firm voice caused me to look up.

"I think Mrs Campbell has made a very reasonable start on her promises. The town hall will be a credit to Clipton." It was Joe Blake. He must have arrived late, as I had not noticed him earlier.

"Thank you, Mr Blake. It is just the beginning."

"One step at a time, Mrs Campbell." He seemed to be teasing me. My insecurity allowed me to feel like an inexperienced girl, and I retreated somewhat for the rest of the meeting. I was thankful when the meeting adjourned. The council chambers emptied quickly. When I saw Joe Blake making his way through the foyer, I decided to confront him.

"That's the second time you've spoken up for me and then acted like a bloody swine!"

"You know, you're not the lady people think you are."

"You're damn right!"

"Mrs Campbell—Stella—I'm not your enemy. I suppose I've been a bachelor for so long I've forgotten my manners." He put out his hand. "Truce?"

In spite of my anger, I shook his hand. "Truce."

"Good." He was close enough that I could smell the tobacco from the pipe sticking out of his jacket top pocket. I became aware he was still holding my hand; blushing a little, I quickly pulled away.

"Are you in a hurry? I was going to stop for a drink. If you'd care to join me, I'd be happy to drive you to the rectory after. I noticed you rode your bike to the meeting."

"I don't want to put you out."

"Not at all. It's on my way." He suddenly laughed. "We are civilized—such polite conversation."

I smiled back. "I'd love a drink, thank you."

I quickly learned Joe was not trying to take advantage of a woman alone. We talked easily together that evening. He had lost his wife to cancer several years earlier. There were no children. To make up for the void, he had turned his attention to Tythe Farm, acquired five years previously. Two hundred and seventy acres of rugged terrain were a challenge to be tamed into a manageable moneymaking business. With a single-track mind, he set out to establish one of the most successful dairy farms in Buckinghamshire. By the time he dropped me off at the rectory, it was as if we had known each other for a long time. Without knowing why, we had connected.

We both took risks that first evening, perhaps he more than I. As we sipped our gin and tonics, a realisation that neither of us wanted anything from the other allowed us to relax. I found him to be entertaining and full of wit. I studied him over the rim of my glass. He was a man of average height and average looks, his thick greying hair needed a professional cut, and his shirt collar curled up, but it was his hazel eyes that held my attention. They revealed sensitivity and awareness. Although our relationship was just beginning, I vowed never to take advantage of him. Joe Blake had become my friend.

I was on the phone with my mother, a regular Saturday-morning routine, when the doorbell rang. "There's someone at the door. I'll call you back, Mum. Yes, as soon as I can." I was being chided for not visiting my parents enough, and was relieved to terminate her complaining. I hurried to see who was at the door. It was Simon Belsky in a tan linen jacket and beige slacks that complemented his blond hair. He looked very attractive, and I was pleased my cotton dress was exactly the blue of my eyes.

"Hello, Stella. I'm returning to York this afternoon. I came to say goodbye."

"It's nice of you to take the time." I stepped back to let him pass.

"I regret we didn't get to know each other better. I would like to have talked to you about the changes you made to the house." He looked around the sitting room with obvious pleasure. "You've done a marvellous job."

I smiled. "I should have given you the grand tour."

"Yes, indeed. I would have liked that. I've a professorship in architecture at York University. I came over from Canada a couple of years ago."

"I had no idea. You never mentioned it at the Petersens'."

"No, I didn't. I hope you won't hold that against me and I'll get the VIP treatment next time I'm in Clipton." He glanced at his wristwatch. "I'd better be going. I've got quite a drive ahead of me." I smelled his aftershave as I followed him to the front door, and waited until the MG disappeared from sight.

It was because of the success of the rectory that I was becoming integrated into Clipton. Of course, being a planning commissioner played its part, too. I began holding dinner parties once a month. They worked wonders to get me in with local high society and important residents in our lovely village. Lucrative landscape design contracts came my way; then again, such parties had benefits for all. We were able to gossip under the pretence it was for the social good of the community, and even got to know what went on beyond the façade witnessed in the boardrooms. The women's fashion parade was something to behold. The little black dress was no longer in vogue; flowing, full-length organza prints competed with form-hugging vibrant silk shifts. Local interest increased as work started on the town hall; benches placed opposite the site were often occupied. Overgrown, insect-infested ivy was torn away, uncovering the rich russet colour of the original brick. In due course, an elegant building began to emerge from behind the scaffolding. When I walked along the narrow streets to meetings or shopping, friendly nods and smiles came my way. *It's a good start, but you've seen nothing yet,* I pledged silently.

CHAPTER FOUR

"You're not going over to Joe Blake's again, Stella?" Beverly shook her head. "People are already talking, you know? Have you no shame, you hussy?" She giggled like a sixteen-year-old.

"Let them," I replied, and continued loading the back of my newly purchased Land Rover. The boxes contained cleaning solvents, brushes, and rags—tools needed for my new venture, the restoration of the more-than-a-century-old slaughterhouse on Joe's farm. The two of us decided it was important enough not to be allowed further deterioration, and it had become our joint project. I got into the driving seat and put the key in the ignition. "Will you and Robert come to dinner on the seventeenth of next month? Miller Owens is coming for the weekend. I want him to take a look at the brook. If something isn't done soon, we'll have a blocked, stagnant stream."

"Ladies and gentlemen, let me introduce Ms Stella Campbell, champion of many causes." Beverly bowed low, mocking me. "You're becoming our conscience, dear. Be careful on whose toes you tread. Not everyone will thank you."

"Does that include you?" It was a serious question.

"Absolutely! It's my father's factory upstream that's part of the problem. If you succeed in closing him down, my loyalty is with him."

"Understood." I leaned out of the Rover's window and kissed her on the cheek. She waited until I reached the bend in the road before starting back to her own home.

Joe and I had spent several weeks working in the dilapidated slaughterhouse, a square brick building with a small paned window on each side. Our priority was to clear the roof of its overhang of rancid moss that infused the surrounding air with a stench that made us gag. Next we dragged out the rotted remains of the narrow stalls where livestock once awaited slaughter. In those days, there was little support for the humane handling of animals, and I cringed at the thought of the fear and brutality they had endured before ending up as someone's dinner.

"There were likely a lot more vegetarians back then than there are now—not through choice like you, Stella, just lack of money. The poor only got scraps, if they were lucky. The farmer didn't make much selling to the locals, so he was living hand-to-mouth, too."

"Well, I'm glad you keep to dairy farming, Joe," I told him.

"What do you think happens to the cows when they stop producing milk?" He smiled, not unkindly. "Meat doesn't appear on grocery shelves by magic, you know."

A thick layer of dried, blackened blood had preserved the fine local slate floor. We scrubbed and sweated trying to remove the decades of grime with industrial cleaners, but a sticky coating obstinately clung to the surface. With hands raw and cracked, our enthusiasm began to wane, and put us on the brink of abandoning the idea.

It was Robert Petersen who suggested we use hydrochloric acid. Joe and I had gone for a ride, and were resting the horses under a flowering chestnut tree. It was one of those perfect English spring days. Fluffy cumulus clouds sailed as shadows across an ocean of green velvet, and cowslips, primroses, and daisies grew in profusion among the hedgerows. Too comfortable to speak, we lay side by side on the sweet grass and listened to the frantic din of the insect metropolis.

"You two have the life o' Riley!" I squinted up at Robert's hefty figure.

"Come off it, Robert. You're already chomping at the bit to get back to London. Poor Bev. She was counting on having a week alone with you. I thought you were going to have a romantic break without the children. What stopped you?"

He laughed good-naturedly. "She'll be glad to see the back of me. All my good intentions to take her away for a couple of days seemed to fizzle out. We just couldn't leave the kiddies behind, but did manage to have some amorous moments." Grinning, he sat down beside me. "Beautiful, isn't it?" He was quiet for a moment, taking in our surroundings. "Hey, Joe! How's that clean-up job coming along?"

Joe propped himself up against the tree. "Not so well. It's proving to be a bugger, actually!"

"How d'you mean?"

"We've run into one problem after another with the slate floor. The muck covering it is sodding impossible to move." He ran through the list of cleaners we had used.

"You need something that will dissolve it."

"Can't seem to get anything strong enough."

"What about hydrochloric acid? I've got some at the house . . . use it to keep the swimming pool healthy. Can be bloody lethal stuff if not diluted, though. You have to be careful around it."

"Excellent idea, Robert. I should have thought of something like that."

"Seems awfully dangerous, doesn't it, Joe? You know, an acid?" I did not like the idea at all.

"Not if we're cautious, Stella. We've done so well with the building, I hate to be done in by the floor." Joe put his hand on my arm to reassure me. "Don't worry, lass." But I was worried. I looked down at my hands and groaned. Acid could really make a mess of them.

Joe couldn't wait, and drove over to the Petersens' later that afternoon to pick up a sample. "It's amazing stuff, Stella. I tested a few feet and it ate the crud right up." He sounded excited over the telephone. "Would you be a good girl and get us our own supply—the strongest Fred carries? Okay?"

"Be careful, Joe. Make sure you wear gloves and things."

"I will. Don't be so concerned, there's nothing to worry about. It'll do the trick all right!"

Joe was waiting for me when I drove up and parked the Rover at the side of his truck. He was unshaven and dressed in baggy cords and a navy pullover, his mucking-about getup. "Of course, you'd arrive just when the kettle boiled."

"Aye, yer know your tea has a reputation in these parts, laddie." I mimicked a Scottish accent. "A wee cup of char will hit the spot."

He put his arm around my shoulder as we went into the kitchen. "Sit yourself down, lass. Did you get everything on the list?"

"Yes. Fred keeps hydrochloric acid in stock in a molarity of ten—takes up less space, and if someone wants any, he just dilutes it to the strength they need. He said it's used mainly in swimming pools, so the water needs to be tested regularly to maintain proper pH and keep swimmers comfortable. I got the most concentrated formula his shop carries; however, he was adamant we should be very careful working with it." I poured milk into the two cups on the table. "I'm really uneasy about the whole idea, Joe."

"Don't worry. We'll take every precaution." He added the amber tea to the milk, filling both cups to the brim before handing me one. "Be careful, it's hot."

"Miller Owens accepted my invitation for next month." I blew on my cup and took a sip. "Told you so!"

"Well, I have to admit I'm impressed. I suppose the name of Stella Campbell has some pull, after all."

"If anyone can open the eyes of these dinosaurs to what they are doing to the environment, the chairman of Save Our Waterways should."

"Feeling pretty chipper, eh?" He brushed the hair out of my eyes. "You should tie that hair back. Can't see what the heck you're doing."

"Don't be such a mother, Joe!"

We donned wellington boots, coveralls, and thick rubber gloves before entering the old building.

"Here, Stella. Put these on." He held out a pair of goggles and a surgical mask. "Can't be too careful." He then tied a rubber apron around my waist.

Fully garbed, I burst out laughing.

"Well, you did nag me about taking precautions," he protested. "Don't fool about now. This is serious stuff." His voice was stern, but I did hear a stifled chortle.

The building smelled dank. Although we had whitewashed the brick walls, spores of mildew were developing into black patches again.

"Better leave the door open all the way, Stella. We'll need as much ventilation we can get." Joe plugged the industrial fan into the electric generator, and set it to full capacity. Frowning with concentration, he carefully unscrewed the gallon container and slowly tipped it to pour a few drops of acid onto the slate floor. "Stand back, lass!" It hissed and smoked on impact, turning the slime into a mass of exploding black bubbles.

"Won't it eat the slate? It's strong stuff, Joe."

"Don't know. We'll control it. Do a bit at a time, then hose it off." His voice was muffled behind the mask.

"I don't like it, Joe. It's jolly dangerous."

"Don't be daft, girl. It's practically the same stuff you've got in your gut," he refuted with authority.

"Are you serious?"

"Well, almost . . . your gut also has a couple of enzymes to help break down your dinner." He laughed. "And this is breaking down another gourmet fare." He was enjoying himself—a schoolboy again who'd discovered both the horror and fascination of pouring salt on a slug, and watching it dissolve into a frothing mass before his eyes. We became excited as the beauty of the blue stone began to be revealed from under the coagulated filth. He bent over to get a better look. "It's working like a bloody miracle." He poured a larger amount of the acid, and the bubbles increased in size. As they exploded, tiny droplets projected into the air and caught him off guard. He drew back in alarm, and almost lost his balance.

"You are a fool!" I shouted. "Don't get so close!"

"Listen, Stella, if you want to go, just go." He turned to me and removed his mask. "I'll be a nervous wreck with you standing over me like that." He started to cough as he breathed in the fumes.

"Idiot," I protested. "Put your mask on! You're not playing with a toy!"

"I know that, and I also know I can't work with you in this state."

"At least dilute it with water." I gestured to the ten-gallon plastic bucket against the wall. "Please, Joe."

"Go home, Stella. I'll phone you later." His gaze was steady. I turned away, surprised to find myself dismissed so easily.

Driving back to the rectory, I regretted panicking. I should have known better. Joe was not going to take any notice of a hysterical female. I had already learned to approach him in quite . . . yes, I'll admit . . . *conniving* ways in other circumstances. If I wanted him to give up the idea of using the acid, I needed to use a different approach. I turned the Rover into the rectory driveway, and rehearsed what I would say when Joe telephoned later.

"Stella. I shouldn't have spoken to you like that."

"I deserved it, Joe. I could have caused a serious accident getting so agitated. Anyway, you're quite right. It's best if I leave the floor up to you."

"You're being very understanding. Thanks, lass."

"Of course." I replaced the receiver. I could have made a prediction. When the telephone rang again two hours later, I knew who it was.

"Stella, I've been thinking. The slaughterhouse was our project from the beginning. We should see it through together."

"Joe, I'm not trying to boss you around, it's just I won't touch that dangerous stuff." I chose my words carefully.

"Why don't you pop over tomorrow, and we'll talk more about it?" He was coming around.

"I don't know what there is to discuss, Joe. I'll not change my mind."

"I know that, lass. Maybe we can get a couple of the farm lads to give us a bit of a hand." He paused. "The truth is, I miss you. There's no satisfaction doing it on my own. I need someone to brag to, to share the excitement with." I could hear the smile in his voice. "Stella, this is the closest you'll get to an apology from me."

I was happy. "I'll come over after lunch."

"Good."

Fighting against the wind, I pushed hard on the bicycle pedals to stay balanced. I chastised myself for setting out on such a turbulent day; however, when you live under the English climate, you learn not to allow the depressing elements to infringe on your plans. My plan to visit Joe at Tythe Farm was being thwarted by elements impossible to ignore. The fields and sky were blanketed in a dark mist. My face was stinging and every muscle aching by the time I arrived. "Joe!" I knocked loudly on the stout door. "Joe! It's Stella." I listened for a reply above the whine of the wind. Damn! He knew I was coming over. Grumbling under my breath, I walked over to the large barn. Standing at the entrance, I peered into the damp gloom. A large rat ran across the straw, startling not only me but also a speckled rooster keeping warm in a pile of folded sacks. My mood continued to worsen as I went around the back of the barn towards the slaughterhouse. "What the blazes has got into you? I've not come all this way to play hide-and-seek." I spat the words out furiously. "It's not funny, Joe!"

By the time I reached the old building, my boots were caked with mud. The solid wooden door was difficult for me to manoeuvre, and I applied every one of my hundred and thirty pounds to the effort until I managed a partial opening. I poked my head around the gap to find out why the door was not opening completely. Horrified, I saw a man sprawled on the filthy floor. "Joe?" *Ohgod-ohgod!* I pushed against the door with all my strength until the opening was wide enough for me to squeeze through. My knees almost gave out with relief as I saw the man was shorter than Joe. A distinct odour coming from him irritated my nostrils, and I sneezed. Struggling to turn him onto his back, I tugged at the man's shoulder, and his head swung around. My body recoiled in shock at the bloodied eyes staring at me from a hideous swollen mass; salt-like crystals covered the nose and lips. Panic stole my breath, and I stumbled from the building, gulping greedily for fresh air. Mustering the little energy I had left, I somehow got back to the farmhouse and mounted my bicycle.

"What is it, Mrs Campbell? You look as if you've seen a ghost!" My housekeeper and I collided as I rushed through the front door of the rectory.

"I've got to call the police, Alice. There's been a dreadful accident." I was shivering uncontrollably.

"Oh, Mrs Campbell. Whatever's happened?"

"I can't talk about it now. I have to call."

"Let me help you, dear." She eased me out of my soaked Burberry and led me to the warmth of the fire. "I'll bring you something hot to drink."

"No, I need milk—lots of it. I've breathed in some strong fumes. Please hurry, Alice!" My throat felt like a really bad bout of tonsillitis. I stumbled to the telephone, and was relieved to hear the efficient, friendly voice of the local constable. "Now, calm yourself, Mrs Campbell. I can assure you someone will be over right away." Alice brought a tray with a pitcher of milk, and I gulped down several glasses. A few minutes later, I found comfort in a cup of warm sweet tea while I tried to focus clearly on what I had seen at the farm. What was Sir Ralph doing there? I didn't know he was acquainted with Joe Blake. My temple throbbed. How did such a horrendous accident happen? Where was Joe? Was he safe? I struggled to gain composure as my heart raced.

"Mrs Campbell, a police inspector and sergeant are here."

"Thank you, Alice. Show them in."

She returned with a tall, well-dressed man who was followed by an older man wearing a crumpled raincoat. "Mrs Campbell, I'm Detective Chief Inspector Gailbrath. This is Detective Sergeant Ball."

"Do sit down." I gestured to the chairs opposite.

The detective chief inspector took out a notebook and referred to some scrawl. "I understand you discovered a body at Tythe Farm. Would you please go over what you saw while my sergeant makes notes?" I glanced at the sergeant, who remained silent, but I saw his eyes were alert to everything. I absently thought he looked a lot like Britain's previous prime minister Harold Wilson, but with more hair.

I talked for what seemed an hour, trying to describe what I had seen without concentrating on the gruesome details. The detective chief inspector's biting questions, however, kept probing until he got what he wanted.

"Were there any containers? Did you notice any odours? Was anything out of place?" He kept up the pressure, his words pulsating in my brain.

"I've told you everything I remember. I got out as quickly as I could. I'd gone to see Joe Blake, but he wasn't there." Then, nervously, I confessed. "Sir Ralph smelled of chlorine. Joe and I'd been using hydrochloric acid to clean the slate floor of the slaughterhouse. There weren't any containers because we always put everything away each time we finished for the day." My voice gave out, and tears started up again. "How could such a terrible thing happen?" The inspector waited patiently for me to collect myself, and then announced I must accompany him to the farm.

"I don't think I can, Detective Chief Inspector. Not now. I've told you everything I can remember. Please, don't make me go back today."

"I'm sorry, Mrs Campbell. We need to go while it is still light. By the way, *detective chief inspector* is quite a mouthful. I can live with just inspector." Both Alice and I were grateful for that.

Police wearing wellington boots and yellow parkers beset the slaughterhouse. Looking like a giant spider's web, yellow tape was wound around the building and surrounding area. An ambulance waited in the driveway, its engine running and lights flashing, ready for a run, presumably to the morgue. The inspector stopped the car at the farm gate and spoke with a pudgy-faced officer wearing coveralls and a navy-blue raincoat. The drenched man touched his rain-sodden cap in a half-hearted salute, and quickly strolled off to a van. He returned with two large torches, and handed them to the inspector through the car window.

"Here you are, sir. The coroner is just about finished."

The inspector turned to me. "I know this is very hard on you, Mrs Campbell. Let's get it over with as soon as possible." He reached over and opened the car door for me. "We'll have to go the rest of the way on foot. The area within the tape is a designated crime scene, so please don't touch anything." Dusk was falling fast. He handed me a torch. "Constable! Get that umbrella over here."

I put on the paper-like booties over my shoes as instructed by the inspector, but hesitated to enter the open doorway. He took my arm and led me inside. Light from several high-voltage lamps lit up the room, and industrial fans were working, I assumed to clear the air of possible contaminants. Someone had placed a red hospital blanket over Sir Ralph. Several men wearing what looked like paper coveralls and blue booties were busy collecting samples from around the body or taking photographs. They communicated between themselves in subdued voices. A couple glanced up as the inspector and I entered, but paid little attention to us.

"Mrs Campbell, can you tell if anything has been moved or changed since you were last here?"

I shrugged my shoulders. How could I possibly know if anything was different when there were a dozen men walking around?

"Is this where you found the body you identified as Sir Ralph Hughes Young?"

"Yes."

"Will you please look again, so I can witness your identification?"

A man wearing latex gloves folded back the blanket, exposing Sir Ralph's head. Whatever he'd been doused with had continued to eat away at his face, and I looked down upon a monstrosity beyond anything my imagination could create. The inspector steadied me as I felt the room move around me. From a far distance, I heard my voice. "From his clothing, size, it's—it's Sir Ralph. Those are the clothes I saw him wearing this morning." This morning? Was it only this morning? It seemed days ago. My voice broke as I remembered his wife, Margot, commenting in earlier days how he looked the epitome of a country squire in his cap and tweeds, and the pleasure he took in such a getup.

"Thank you, Mrs Campbell. I won't detain you any longer. I'll have this officer take you home. Walker, take Mrs Campbell back to the rectory."

A thought came to my mind, and I turned to the inspector. "It was very convenient that you and the sergeant were in Clipton. I was expecting our local bobbies to take care of things."

"Yes, we've been in town a while," he said, walking away.

As the police car pulled up in front of the rectory, Beverly Petersen came to the window. "Stella! What's happened? What's wrong, my dear?" The policeman opened the car door for me, touching his cap respectfully. I thanked him and then turned to my friend.

"Bev." I bit my lip as the nightmarish image flooded my mind once more. "It's Sir Ralph. He's dead!" I covered my face with my hands, trying to block out the horror. Gratefully, I let Bev lead me into the house.

She sat on the couch next to me, her arm looped through mine. "I needed to get out of the house, and thought I'd pop over for a before-dinner sherry. Alice said you were out. Just like that! No explanation at all. I thought her rather rude, actually, and told her so." She rubbed her hands together. "I'm sick of this frightful weather."

"Beverly! Didn't you hear me? I said Sir Ralph is dead! How can you think of Alice's manners at a time like this?"

"What are you talking about? Of course I heard what you said. And I'm sorry! What do you want me to say?" She stood up and spread her hands in front of the log burning in the grate. "That's better. I'm like ice." She turned to me. "Don't look at me like that, Stella. I hardly knew the old bugger. By all accounts, he had a good life. How old was he—seventy-five or so? That's a pretty good innings, I'd say."

I glared at her. "I can't believe your callousness."

"Really, Stella, I think you're overreacting. I'm not going to pretend I feel something for the old man when I don't. Needless to say, I'm sorry he's dead."

"He didn't die of natural causes."

"What do you mean?"

"He . . . he was killed . . . murdered."

"Good heavens!" She sat down heavily next to me. "I really need that sherry now."

By the time I relayed what I had discovered at Joe's farm, Bev's initial reaction had changed considerably. "How could such a brutal thing happen?"

Weariness was fast overtaking me. "I saw him this morning, before the storm. It was around eleven. He was walking the dogs."

"How did he seem?"

"Just his usual self." I shook my head. "Said nothing . . . just waved."

"You say his face was unrecognisable?"

"Yes, acid of some kind had been used. That's why the police must suspect foul play."

"How did you know it was him?"

"His clothes."

"Do the police know who did it?"

"Too early, I would think." I stared off into space. "No one in their right mind would drink something like that unless forced to. The poor, harmless old man. I hope to goodness it's not the stuff Joe and I used on the slate floor."

"What a terrible way to go. I suppose Margot knows by now?"

"Oh, Bev. I hadn't even thought about her. How dreadful. I'd better go over there right now." I got up and went into the hall for my coat.

"Do you mind if I don't come with you, Stella? I'm not the type you want around in this kind of situation." She smiled sheepishly.

"If you promise to call Robert to pick you up. It's dark now, and still raining." I looked at my watch. "Six thirty. He must be wondering where you are." I opened the front door to a blast of freezing air and drew my coat tightly around me. "You owe Alice an apology before you leave."

"I give you my word."

I stepped out into the darkness, and rain immediately cascaded over my umbrella. Walking quickly, I was aware of the echo of my footsteps, and the rustling trees unnerved me. For the first time since moving to Clipton I was afraid for my safety. Yes, I had discovered a terrible scene, but I had not connected myself to its horror until then. Now every shadow, every muffled sound caused my heart to race.

Although the Hughes Youngs' splendid home was only a mile or so from the rectory, that evening the walk seemed much farther. I rang the bell anxiously. I was not surprised to see a female police constable when the door opened.

"Mrs Hughes Young is indisposed at the moment. Is there a message?" The officer was polite enough, but I knew she was observing everything about me.

"I'm Stella Campbell. I discovered Sir Ralph this afternoon."

"Sorry, miss, I didn't recognise you. I know your name, of course. You'd better come in, although I don't think she wants to see anyone just now."

"Poor Margot. I'm not sure why I came, really. I thought she might have some questions . . . would want to, you know, hear what happened." I paused, suddenly unsure of myself. What was I doing there? I didn't know what happened. The poor woman should be left alone. I turned to leave.

"Stella, don't go." The voice was high, childlike. I stepped passed the constable into the hall and looked into the tormented mask of Margot Hughes Young. Her eyes were red and swollen. "Thank you for coming, Stella." I felt awkward and lost for words.

"Can I do anything? Anything at all, Margot?"

"Joe's here. He's taking care of everything."

I looked up and saw Joe Blake. He acknowledged me with a curt nod of his head. "You must be cold." He took my umbrella and placed it in the stand by the front door. "Would you like a drink?"

"Thank you." He caught me off guard. I did not want a drink. I wanted to get out of there, and quickly. Instead, I followed him into the lounge with my arm around Margot, and sat next to her on the deeply cushioned sofa. He handed me a glass of something. "Thanks."

"You were the one who found him, weren't you?" Margot did not look at me.

"Yes. I had an appointment with Joe. When he didn't answer my knock, I went looking for him." I took a sip of the warming liquor. "I found Sir Ralph in the slaughterhouse." I looked questioningly at Joe. He stared back without reacting.

Margot put her hands over her face and started to sob. "Who could have done such a thing? Why? My Ralph wouldn't hurt a fly."

"Mrs Hughes Young, excuse me." The female constable looked exceptionally young for such a job. I wondered who would want her responsibilities. "The chief detective inspector's here, madam, and would like a few words with you." Inspector Gailbrath stood behind her; his face was drawn with fatigue.

I stood up and placed the empty glass on the coffee table. "If I can't be of help, Margot, I'll be on my way. I'll come back in the morning, if you like?"

"Yes. In the morning, dear."

I bent and kissed her damp cheek. "Joe, will you see me out?"

"I'll walk you home."

I nodded.

He touched Margot's shoulder. "I'll call you later, my dear." His tone was full of kindness, and I felt a surge of affection for him as I closed the door behind us.

"You said to meet you at the farm. What happened?" My surge of affection was quickly overwhelmed by fury. "Where the bloody hell were you?"

"Where was I? Right where you told me to be!"

"I told you? What are you talking about? You told me to meet you at the farm!" My voice was shrill with accusation.

"Yes, yes . . . earlier. Then you left a message on my answering machine. You said to meet you at three o'clock in the café. Said something came up and you had to go into the village."

"I what? I never called you," I spluttered. "If I bloody well had, do you think I would traipse over to your place in a gale?"

"I know that now, lass!" He put his hands on my shoulders. "Someone sounding very much like you did call and, at three o'clock, I was in the café ordering tea for us both. I waited for more than an hour, and then went back to the farm. The rest you know."

"Didn't you wonder when I didn't show up at the café?"

"I just thought you'd been delayed with whatever you had to do in town. I did call the rectory once; there was no answer."

"What does it all mean, Joe?"

"Someone wanted me away from the farm when you got there. What time did you arrive?"

"Probably around two thirty. Do you think they wanted me to find Sir Ralph? Why me?" I looked up at his strong face. "None of it makes any sense." We started to walk towards the rectory, and I was glad to have his company.

"Stella, don't go out on your own for a while. Let the police do their job, and then everything can get back to normal."

"Surely you don't think I'm in danger?"

"No, no! There are questions that need to be answered." He smiled, trying to reassure me. "I'm just saying be cautious, that's all."

"You too, Joe." We arrived at the front door. "Shall I drive you home?"

"No, lass. I'll be fine. The walk will give me time to think." He waited until I closed the front door against him, and I heard his sturdy step fade away into the night.

CHAPTER FIVE

It seemed as if the entire town turned out for Sir Ralph's funeral. There was an inquest, of course. Although we knew in our hearts it was murder, it was still a shock to hear the official announcement that his death was attributed to foul play by a person or persons unknown. Robert and Beverly Petersen escorted his widow into the church. Margot Hughes Young was heavily veiled, and held a limp white handkerchief at the ready as she walked down the aisle on Robert's arm. I caught Beverly's eye and openly raised my eyebrow at her now devoted demeanour. "Atonement, eh?" I mouthed. Her returned stare was hostile.

It was a short, haunting service. The flowers were magnificent, and the sweet voices of the young choir remained as an echo clinging to the walls of the church sanctuary. I was unable to close my eyes, even in prayer, for the memory of what I had found was as sharp as ever. My only respite was a small pink pill prescribed by Dr Levinton. I regretted not taking one that morning, but I did not want to be woolly brained for Margot's sake. I had visited with her consistently over the past couple of weeks, and she had shown incredible courage. After the initial shock of Sir Ralph's brutal end, she seemed to gather strength, and directed much kindness to me. "What a dreadful experience for you to find him like that, Stella." Then the tears returned. "My dear Ralph. The agony he must have gone through."

They say misery seeks out misery. Well, we certainly proved that. I found myself in her sitting room almost daily. Because I discovered Sir Ralph, I felt responsible, somehow, and needed to share in her pain. Eventually, she came to accept her loss, while my nightmares continued. Alice called Dr Levinton on more than a couple of occasions. The image of Sir Ralph's ravaged face was stamped on my brain, and I awoke calling out and soaked in sweat.

After the service, Joe returned to the rectory with me. Neither of us had the slightest desire to attend the reception. He hovered over me like an expectant father. I didn't appreciate his attention. I felt stifled, and begged him to leave me alone.

"I'm concerned for you, Stella. I know you've had a terrible shock, but you should be getting over it now."

"Don't tell me what I should or should not be doing. It's none of your goddamn business. I don't belong to you."

"Stella!"

"Go away, Joe. I can't breathe around you!" I could see my spiteful words cut into him, but I could not hold them back. A desperate need to get away from Clipton was building up. I was in a dark tunnel, running recklessly towards an end I could not reach. I collapsed into a heap at his feet.

Dr Levinton closed his bag with a snap. "You're going to be all right, Stella," he said. He sat down next to me on the sofa and took my hand. "It's just taking a little longer than I would have hoped for you to bounce back. It might help if you saw someone."

"You think I'm losing my mind?"

"No—no, my dear. There are experts in this kind of thing who could help you, that's all. Make it easier for you. It would be foolish not to seek help if it's available." He got up to leave. "Will you at least think about it?"

I nodded. There was no fight left in me to challenge him.

"I'll be in touch, then. You really will be all right. I promise," he said kindly.

"What about Joe? I scared him pretty badly."

"Joe understands. He's agreed to stay away until you feel ready to see him. He's one of the best, Stella."

"Yes, I know, doctor. I just need some space right now—from everyone."

I decided to go to London for a while. It would be good to spend some time with my parents and see Julia and Tim. Having made the decision, I got a burst of energy and telephoned my faithful friend Rita with the news. She had married a wealthy advertising executive and lived in Knightsbridge. We arranged to meet in Harrods for lunch. I found myself actually humming as I looked through the entertainment section of the *Daily Express*.

"Inspector Gailbrath is here, madam."

Surprised, I looked up at Alice. "What does he want?"

"He didn't say."

"You'd better show him in." I had not seen him out of a soaked raincoat before. He looked like an insurance salesman in his three-piece suit . . . quite dashing, all the same.

"Mrs Campbell, I'm sorry to disturb you again. I hear you haven't been well."

"You don't sound so good yourself. I hope you haven't got the flu. I'd hate to catch it from you when I'm just about to leave for London."

I noticed that his eyes crinkled at the edges as he smiled. "No. It's just a cold that won't go away." He sniffed as if to prove his point.

"Do sit down. Would you like a cup of tea?"

He nodded appreciatively. "I would, thank you."

I went to find Alice. She agreed to come up with a couple of slices of cake, too. When I returned to the sitting room, the inspector was rapidly writing in a small notebook. He did not seem to mind being caught off guard. "I don't know what I'd do without this. Too many things to think about . . . have to write myself notes all the time." He grinned, and suddenly the strain left his face and he looked younger.

"What do you need with me?"

"As you know, we're still continuing with our enquiries, Mrs Campbell. I need to go over with you again where and why you bought the hydrochloric acid. I'm sure you heard it's been confirmed hydrochloric acid was used on Sir Ralph."

I could feel the panic rising in my chest. "Yes, I heard that. Well?"

"Well what?"

"Was it our acid that killed him?" My voice rose with anxiety.

"It appears to have played a part. The cause was strangulation, but the coroner found a pretty good dose was rammed down the old man's throat before his face was destroyed." He sounded a long way off as the room began to revolve around me. "Mrs Campbell?"

"You think Joe Blake and I killed him, don't you?" I looked into his eyes. "We didn't. We really didn't. We aren't murderers. Lots of people have that stuff for various reasons, mainly for their swimming pools. Right?" I was pleading.

"That's right."

"How can you tell it was our supply, anyway?"

"We know it was your batch by the strength, the container . . . actually, several reasons, but I'm here to go over a few other points with you." His words were deliberate.

Alice came in with a tray loaded with flowered china and slices of fruitcake. She looked round at the inspector as she put the tray down on the table in front of me.

"Really, Alice, you don't have to act as if I'm not here! I know you're making signs at him."

She flushed with embarrassment and anger. "I was only trying to tell him to back off, Mrs Campbell. You don't need him to hound you." Her tone was quite brazen. "I think you've had enough for a while."

"Well, thank you for your opinion, but I can take care of myself. You must forgive me, Inspector, I've become surrounded by mother hens, and I don't appreciate it one bit!"

"Someone's got to look after you."

"Alice!"

She left the room, slamming the door behind her.

"She seems to care a lot for you, Mrs Campbell."

"Yes, I know." I bit my lip, feeling miserable for being so short tempered. "I'll apologise to her later. I seem to be doing that a lot lately. I don't know why she puts up with me."

I answered the seemingly straightforward questions, but my anxiety increased all the same. The inspector wanted to know every detail about the conversation with Robert Petersen when Robert suggested the hydrochloric acid, where I bought it, and who decided on what strength. He asked for the receipts from the hardware store; I was going to have to search a bit for those. He even wanted to know what precautions Joe and I took in storing the container, and what protective clothing we wore when working on the slaughterhouse floor. He wrote everything down in his notebook and, almost predictably, licked the end of the pencil from time to time. I felt I was watching an actor on the stage and, at any moment, the curtain would come down and I would return to reality.

"I just remembered . . . Joe received a phone call telling him to meet me in town that afternoon. He thought it was from me, but I was at the farm."

"Yes, he already told me about that. You have no idea who it could have been?"

"No . . . except it was a woman, of course."

"Of course." He smiled and looked up from his writing. "You said you were going away. When do you plan to go?"

"I'm going to London in a couple of days to see my two children and elderly parents. I need a change of scenery."

"I'm sure the visit will do the trick. I will ask you to let me have a telephone number of where you'll be staying, and I'd like you to let me know when you get back to Clipton."

"Is that absolutely necessary?" My voice sounded small and filled with anxiety.

"It's just a matter of routine in case we need to get in touch with you." He put his pencil and notebook into his jacket's inside pocket. "Now, how about that cup of tea?" He leaned over to the tray and picked up the teapot. "Do you take milk and sugar?"

CHAPTER SIX

Before I left for London, I apologised to Alice for my outburst. I reminded her we had only been together a couple of months and were still adjusting to each other. It was an opportune time to define exactly my expectations of her: no mothering, private space, et cetera, and she was forthright in voicing what she expected of me: "I am not a lowly servant, and deserve respect." I assured her she did indeed, and the air seemed cleared of further animosity.

It was during her interview I learned she had never married or been previously employed. She had devoted herself to running her parents' home until both were deceased. They sounded like unique people with broad horizons. Flummoxed by her remark that she had plenty of money, I questioned why she was sitting in front of me asking for a job. "I want to feel needed." There was tension in her tone. "I'm intelligent, well-read, and keep accurate accounts. You'll not regret taking me on." When I said the job would tie her down again, she laughed and replied, "But I'll have time off . . . there'll be time for *me*." I hired her without a second thought.

It was a relief to be away from the rectory and Clipton. I stayed with my parents in their small flat in Fulham. I lay on the lumpy couch for several days, and thumbed through magazines without reading. My mother coddled me as if I were a small child again, and brushed away my tears with tender concern. I suppose I ate and talked somewhat, but I do not remember much of the first couple of days at all. My father began to get peeved with my inertia and announced I had sat around long enough. It was time for some action.

"Leave the darling alone, Stan. She needs the rest." Dear Mum.

"She needs to get off her bum and get on with her life, that's what. Come on, Stella, we're going to the pub for a drink. A good stout will bring verve back into you. Then you can call your kids. You do remember them, don't you?"

"Verve? Where did you get that word from, Dad? I'm pretty impressed."

"Oh, Stella, he learned it from the crossword and has been dying to use it ever since."

I looked at the sweet faces of my adoring parents and felt overwhelming love for them. No matter what happened, I could always depend on them. Thanks to Geoff's forethought, I had financial wealth with which to help them, yet they insisted on remaining in the small flat with the tired furniture. When I had suggested moving them into a house, I received blank stares and absolutely no enthusiasm.

"Not much point in changing things now, not at our time of life, eh, Dix?" Dad had said.

Mum had nodded in agreement. "We're just happy for you, dear. There's not anything we want that we don't have already."

What I could do was pay their rent and see that they had plenty of food in the refrigerator. Nonetheless, one treat they both enjoyed was a generous supply of quality scotch, and they had no problem in asking for more when the supply got low.

"Okay, Dad, the pub it is. I suppose I have sat on my duff long enough." I got up off the couch and stretched. "A pint sounds pretty good."

I telephoned my children and arranged to meet them the next day for lunch. I took care with my appearance. The olive-green two-piece suited me very well, and I put my shoulder-length hair up in a twist. Arriving exactly at noon in the Garden Room of the Dorchester Hotel, I found Julia and Tim waiting for me. I looked at my handsome son and lovely daughter, and my heart filled with pride.

We sat at a table facing the open doors that led onto a garden terrace. Hydrangeas were planted in white urns by the entrance, and the heavy clusters of pink blossoms danced in the fresh air. We ordered, and were served quickly and unobtrusively. The food was delicious, and we ate in silence. Tim eventually placed his knife and fork on his empty plate and turned to me.

"So, Mother, let's hear the truth. What's going on in Clipton to drive you away?"

"Absolutely nothing, Tim!" I insisted. "Why would you think such a thing? I wanted to come to London to do some shopping. The styles in Clipton aren't exactly from *Vogue* magazine."

"Mother!" Julia touched my arm.

"It's the truth!"

"You've always told us that we'd be honest with each other, no matter what. We've never kept anything from you. Now it's your turn."

She had me. "You're right, of course . . . it's all silly really, I don't know where to begin." I looked from one to the other. "There was a terrible accident, and an elderly man died at Joe's farm. There's an investigation. I found him in the slaughterhouse where Joe and I were working to renovate the building. It's all dreadfully depressing, and I thought I'd get away for a few days."

"An investigation? Why? What happened?"

"The police aren't exactly sure."

"The police! Do they think it's murder?"

"Tim, please. I really don't know anything and don't want to talk about it anymore. Tell me how the job's going." I turned to Julia, hoping to solicit her help in changing the subject.

"He doesn't know what work is. He's a lazy bastard!"

"Julia! That's no talk for a young lady."

"Lady? That's a laugh," Tim teased. The sun had bleached his blond hair during a recent holiday in Venice, and his face with Geoff's prominent nose and my blue eyes was tanned a honey brown. My son had already learned his looks were a great asset. "The solicitor's office is dull. I arrive at nine each morning and leave at five thirty, just like the rest of the poor sods who are bored to tears."

"Why do you stay there? I want you to do something that's satisfying to you, Tim. There's got to be something you'd like to do."

"I can't compete with our dearest Julia, a daughter we can all be proud of following in dear ol' Dad's footsteps." His tone was slightly scornful, and I didn't like it.

"It's not that, Tim. You just couldn't cope with the hard work. I study all night and work at the hospital all day. It's no fun, I can tell you." Julia sounded strained. "I'm scared stiff I'm not going to be able to make it through."

To my dismay, her lip trembled. "Julia! Darling! If it's too much, then you must stop."

"Oh, Mummy, how can I? I can't give up now, not after I've put so much into it."

I leaned over and took her hand. "Darling, I want you to be happy. If you don't want to be a doctor, then don't. It's that simple."

"I don't mean any harm, Julia." Tim put his arm around her shoulder. "I'm actually very proud of my little sister."

"So you should be," she retorted, her voice sounding lighter. "Mother?" She looked at me intently. "Grandmother Campbell phoned last week. She and Grandfather are coming to London at the end of the month, and want to get together with Tim and me."

"You'll go, of course."

"They are dears. I wish you could reach out to them, particularly now they are up in years."

"They walked away from me, Julia. When Daddy died, I ceased to exist. Because they never approved of me, there is no reason why you and Tim can't see them. They are good grandparents, and I know Daddy would be pleased you keep in touch." It was true.

"I'm always pleased to see Grandfather, the old fart, but Grandmother is a bit overly snooty for me."

"Tim!"

"What?"

"Never mind." I broached the question uppermost in my thoughts. "Is there any chance the two of you could take a break and come to Clipton for a few days? It's been such a long time. Tim, you'll be pleasantly surprised how wonderful the rectory is now. And you haven't seen it since it was finished, Julia. Could you come?"

"Not a chance for me, not for quite a while, I'm afraid," she said.

"I know you are under a lot of pressure, darling, but you don't have to prove anything. I couldn't be more proud of you, whatever you do. It doesn't have to be medicine, you know?"

"I could take a week at Christmas," Tim offered.

"Tim, that would be wonderful." I meant it. I glanced back at Julia. She looked tired, troubled. "You should be having fun at your age," I chided.

She smiled, bringing light into her large, dark eyes. "I'll be all right; just feeling sorry for myself. Everyone I know is in the same boat." She placed her hand over mine. "Don't worry, Mum. It's what I want." I could see her father looking back at me.

"I'll keep my eye on her. We see each other about once a fortnight and phone a lot." Tim looked at his sister. In spite of his facetious chitchat, he cared deeply for her, and I relaxed in that knowledge. As we walked through the restaurant to go our separate ways, we passed a table where actor James Mason was seated with another good-looking man. I was pleased I was wearing my olive-green outfit when he nodded politely to me.

CHAPTER SEVEN

Reg met my train. I felt detached peering from the car window as we drove through Clipton. I reminded myself I was making a difference, bringing the small hamlet back. I was doing something tangible, something that existed in a defined way. The town hall restoration was completed, and the building looked stately once again. Work was about to begin on the school, and I could see that lorries parked in the playground areas were causing much excitement for the youngsters on their lunch break. Not for long, though—staff and students would be moving to temporary quarters when the real work began. I smiled with satisfaction. As the car pulled up at the entrance to the rectory, the front door opened, and Alice emerged with a grin on her round face.

"Mrs Campbell, it's good to have you back." She wrung her hands with pleasure. "Lunch is just about ready."

I put my arm through hers, and we walked into the house together. She was my housekeeper but, foremost, was becoming my friend, and we both knew it. After lunch, I called her in to my office.

"Alice, it's time you called me Stella."

"I'd like that, Mrs Campbell—Stella." She laughed. "It's going to take some getting used to, I'm afraid." Her eyes became very bright. "You pay me a wage for working here, but you know I don't need the money . . . I am your friend, Stella. You can count on me for anything."

"I know that, Alice. I appreciate all you do in running this large house, but I want the rectory to be your home, not the place where you work. We are going to be happy here, together."

She blew her nose, nodding in agreement. I watched her as she turned away, leaving me to rifle through the mail. She was a matronly figure of medium height . . . pretty, with brown, naturally curly hair. In her fifties, she had moulded herself to a *plain-jane* image. I intended to change that.

I wrote cheques to pay a couple of bills included in the mail, but it was too glorious a day to remain inside. I went into the garden and sat on the terrace steps, allowing the noise of the city to retreat from my mind. I had enjoyed my trip to London immensely but was happy to be back in my own home. It was the end of September; the sun was losing its warmth and the days were shortening. I lifted my face to the pale sky and heard the birds once again.

"What the . . .!" A warm, fat projectile bounced against my leg, causing me to return to reality with a start. The bundle was an explosion of energy determined to reach my face with its slobbering pink tongue. "Where did you come from?" I tried to grab the puppy, but its wriggling was too much for me, and I surrendered. The large black nose nudged at me, daring me to join in its game. "Stop! That's enough," I commanded. To my amazement, the puppy became still and looked up at me with luminous amber eyes. I placed my hand on the top of its beautiful head and fell in love. Incapable of resisting any longer, I grasped the creature to me.

"I knew you were meant for each other."

"Joe!" His eyes held mine for a moment. "I'm so pleased to see you, Joe." I meant it. I got up from the steps, holding the wriggling puppy out to him. "Yours, I presume?"

"Well, yours really . . . a welcome-home present. I thought a dog would be good company for you."

"I never thought about it. You're right . . . thank you, Joe! It's—*she*'s beautiful."

"You'll have to come up with a suitable name."

I looked at the pup for a moment. "I need to put some thought into that."

He smiled for the first time. "How was London?"

"Come on into the house, and I'll tell you all about it." I was pleased to feel his hand on my shoulder as we entered the rectory together.

As I talked about London, I realised just how good the trip had been for me. My mind was clearer, and I felt refreshed. I brought up my concerns about Julia and Tim.

"Julia is doing what she wants, Stella. Tim's only sewing his oats. He'll settle down. Don't worry about him."

"I can't help it. He seems—well, unfocused. It would be better if he weren't so aware of himself. A vain man—or woman, for that matter—is not at all attractive. I don't want him to think he can use his good looks to get ahead, Joe."

"Could your father talk with him?"

"I already thought of that, and he promised to give Tim a call."

"Sounds like you've done all you can for the moment."

I looked over at the man who was very dear to me, and was glad of his company. "Joe, I'm sorry I was so mean to you before I left Clipton."

"Mean? When was that? I think it would be more in line to apologise to you, actually. I don't think wanting some space to get your thoughts in order is too much to ask, Stella. I shouldn't have needed to be told." He looked so serious; I felt a wave of appreciation for him. He was at ease in the armchair with the puppy sleeping on his lap. "I've got some news for you. While you were away, I sold the farm."

"Joe! So quickly! Why?"

"I've lost interest. I made it a success; now it's become a daily routine. Time to move on to other things, I think."

"Sir Ralph's death is what made you sell. Don't lie to me, Joe."

"It had an influence, yes, but I made the decision some time ago. When that happened, it just made it final for me."

"Who bought it?"

"The McKinleys." He looked at me steadily. "You can't bear to go back, so I'd better find a place where you'll visit me again. I'll take digs in town while I look around."

"You can stay here, Joe. To hell with the gossip."

"If I did that, you may find it hard to get rid of me, Stella. I think the Retreat will be better for both of us." He stretched and changed the subject. "Isn't it next weekend Miller Owens is coming?"

"Yes. Several have agreed to attend his lecture. What he has to say should shake up a few of our local offenders. Make them aware we know what they're up to."

"Don't push anyone too far, Stella. You won't win any medals for it."

"I won't. I just want to rattle their cages a bit, that's all."

The day began overcast with gusty winds; fortunately, by midmorning, the chilly autumn landscape was bathed in warming sunlight. An abundance of colour still remained in the garden for my guests to enjoy. I looked around the library with pleasure. I had arranged branches of yellow and russet beech leaves in tall vases. The beautifully restored carved mantelpiece now framed a log fire. I plumped up the gold brocade pillows on the sofa for the third time, and then, hearing the clock strike eleven, decided to get bathed and dressed for Miller's arrival at two o'clock.

Miller Owens and I met while I was earning my degree in landscaping. He was a dapper individual who always wore a spotted bow tie and a blazer embellished with the Royal Air Force insignia. His passion for the preservation of the British waterways became well known while he was a student in my irrigation class. I was in awe of his knowledge, and he was amazed over my naivety. We hit it off at once. He had since made a name for himself as a leading expert in the demise of the once-healthy waterways through industrial waste seepage. He became an enemy of the chemical industry, and wore the honour proudly. We had kept in touch since our graduation, and I endeavoured to read every paper he published. It was a feather in my cap to have him speak to local businessmen and my other weekend guests.

"Do you need anything, Stella?"

"No thanks, Alice. Mr Owens will be here soon." I checked my watch again. Ten minutes past two. Reg had left in plenty of time to meet the London train. I went to the window and looked out apprehensively.

"It's a half hour's drive from the station. Don't fret yourself; he'll get here."

"Thank you, Alice. Now I have your assurance, I can relax."

She fought the impulse to retort, and hastily turned away, bumping into the man standing behind her. "Oh, excuse me, Mr Owens. We were just wondering when you'd get here."

"And here I am. Well, Stella?"

"Miller!"

We giggled delightedly as we hugged each other.

"Let me look at you." He stepped back and squinted at me. "You are wearing well . . . don't look a day over sixty!"

"You're still a swine!"

"It takes one to know one."

"Help! You've only just got here. Truce, please!" I beamed with pleasure at seeing him. Except for a little weathering, he still looked like a young student. He had one of those square jaws that jutted out like a comic book superhero . . . even had a head of thick black hair complete with a cowlick. "Take your bags up to your room, and then I'll give you a tour of this eighth wonder. You'll be so impressed you won't be able to help yourself."

He picked up his expensive leather suitcase and garment bag. "Lead the way, rich bitch!"

We had an early dinner, and then, donning overcoats against the chill, sat out on the terrace to catch the last of the delicate daylight.

"Who's coming to our grand affair?"

"Steven and Elizabeth Lagerquist. You know them; they're the London husband-and-wife team who designed the interior of the town hall. Then there's Roger Spencer. He's been an immense asset in fundraising for the renovation of the town hall, school, and library. I admire him greatly."

"Fundraising? I thought you used your funds?"

"Well, yes, as a loan so things could start moving, but certainly not only my money. Clipton's Building Society has established a trust fund, and monies are drawn as needed. Investors'll get repaid eventually. Roger was the impetus behind raising most of the money, even arranged my meeting with the board of trustees so I could present my proposal. I was delightfully surprised that it agreed so quickly. Of course, the Building Society will be the beneficiary, taking ownership of all the restored buildings. It has its own established assets and will be a good steward, I'm sure." I paused for a moment, thinking how much the town owed Roger. "It's truthful to say without Roger the restorations would still only be an idea. I asked, and through his skill in manipulating people to use their chequebooks, I received."

"Does he support your latest idea?"

"That I'm not sure about. He agrees something should be done about pollution, but stops short when we discuss picketing the local factories. I'm hoping you can persuade him to see he cannot stand on the sidelines any longer."

"I'll do my best, Stella. It takes a lot of convincing to win over a political heart. One has to prove, above all, there is personal gain."

I shook my head. "I don't think that applies to Roger. Oh, he is a politician all right, but he genuinely wants a better world."

"I'm too fagged out to argue the point." Miller shivered. "I enjoy my baby-smooth flesh being covered in goosebumps from time to time, but it's bloody freezing out here. Would you mind if I hit the sack early and discover warmth again?"

"Of course not. I wasn't thinking." I got up, and offered my hand. "Come along—my friend and comrade in arms. I'm glad you're here, Miller. We'll show those buggers."

Steven and Elizabeth were the first to arrive from London. They quickly settled in and then set out for a stroll around the village. During their work on the interior of the town hall, they had become quite taken with Clipton. In fact, they were contemplating relocating from their classy Onslow Gardens town house to Clipton. Roger arrived in time for dinner. A man in his early sixties with a paunch and thinning hair, he was not what I would describe as attractive, yet there was a sense of power about him that made one notice him. Although he maintained a flat in the village, he had agreed to stay at the rectory. I was surprised when he arrived accompanied by a considerably younger woman, whom he introduced only as Fiona.

Dinner that evening was a lively affair. I was pleased to have the ice broken before Miller's lecture the following day. My guests' emotions were heightened by a delicious flaky sea bass that would have made many mouths water. The vegetable cutlet creatively wrapped in phyllo pastry that was placed in front of me was *not* envied. All, however, enjoyed the excellent sauvignon blanc. Conversation topics were light, mainly focusing on committing to preserving Clipton's architectural assets. Miller chose the moments following to persuasively make his case that everyone present would be invaluable in aiding the preservation of something beyond any structure. I saw him smile to himself . . . the smug sod.

I opened the folding doors to merge the library and lounge into one large room and was gratified to see the space filling with local dignitaries. To catch the eye of those entering the room, Miller had displayed enlarged photographs of streams and rivers at various stages of decline. Now there was no mistaking what he was about.

The audience of forty people was polite and barely moved during Miller's hour-long opening presentation. When we closed the drapes in order to show a short film, the restlessness began. Miller caught my eye, and signalled a refreshment break would be in order the moment the film was over. I understood; there was no use in riling the natives. The film began with footage taken around the soft hills of Buckinghamshire, and then closed in on the hamlet of Clipton. Children played in streams dappled with sunlight, their excited voices filling the otherwise silent room. A relaxed Ted Nyby appeared with fly rod in hand and basket over his shoulder. His waders splashed refreshingly as he made his way into a fast-moving expanse of water. I saw enjoyment on some of the viewers' faces. The camera began to travel upstream, coming to rest on an outlet pipe protruding from a bank of dead and dying vegetation. The lens zoomed in on the leaking runoff that emerged as a thick black sludge. With deliberation, the pipe was followed to its origin—Euston's Chemical Plant.

"What does that prove?" The provocative question came from a man with a trimmed grey moustache sitting in the back row.

Miller took a step forward. "What it proves is that we are going to have to make some critical choices. If we don't take a stand on the health of our waters, from a narrow trickle to the widest ocean, Earth is a doomed planet. There is no question about it. That one outlet pipe spews unfiltered metals into the waters that serve Clipton. You are drinking it; your children are drinking it. You spray it onto your vegetable gardens and wash your clothes in it. Those metals transfer from the polluted water into your bodies and stay there, building up over time. I challenge any one of you to take a blood test to prove me wrong."

The audience was silent no longer. A soft buzz developed, quickly turning into a roar. "What can we do about it?"

"You can join us in picketing Euston's in a couple of weeks. Notices giving details of the event will be delivered to every household." Miller continued, "We can't afford to stand passively by any longer. This county belongs to all of us, and we shall have our say." Sweat glistened on his brow. He knew he had them, and glory was showing openly on his face. High energy heated the room, and Alice had to raise her voice considerably to announce refreshments were being served. I was ecstatic.

The Lagerquists, Roger Spencer, his friend Fiona, Joe, and the Petersens joined Miller and me for dinner that evening.

"You should notify Euston officially, you know. Just out of common courtesy, if nothing else," Roger urged.

"Courtesy?" Miller fumed. "His factory is making children sick, and you suggest we treat the bastard courteously? I can't believe just how bloody civilized you are!"

"Miller! Please." I didn't want him and Roger to fall out before the battle had begun.

"Well, I think this afternoon was a huge success. I'll follow up with organising the signs and things," Roger said more agreeably. He was experienced in dealing with temperamental personalities in his fundraising capacity.

"You do understand it is a very difficult situation for Robert and me," Beverly said quietly. "After all, you're trying to destroy my father. I told you before, Stella, I would stand with him on this."

"Sam Euston's your father?" Fiona's large blue eyes widened. "How awful to have the whole town against him."

"Fiona!" Roger admonished.

"Beverly, all he's got to do is filter the runoffs," Miller said. "It will cost him, but how can money come into it? The factory is creating a danger to everyone, not only in Clipton . . . the towns below, too—anywhere the water runs. Don't you see?"

"You want to ruin him. Make him a laughingstock among his peers. He's a local man. Grew up here. Don't humiliate him," she pleaded.

"Hold on, darling. That's not what this is about."

"Don't tell me you're taking their side, Robert? How could you? Stella?"

I got up from the table and went to my friend. "Bev, let's take a walk in the garden."

She followed me quietly, and I felt much love for her in that moment. "I promise you, Beverly Petersen, I will do all I can not to humiliate your father. You and Robert must stay out of things until your father agrees to our demands."

"I don't want it to destroy our friendship, Stella."

"It never could do that, Bev."

Later, Joe, Bev, and Robert set off to their own beds, while the others remained at the rectory for the convenience of working on our plans.

The next day my guests insisted on amusing themselves, and I was greatly relieved to have some free time for myself. After one of Alice's hearty breakfasts, they all scattered. Roger announced he was taking a short walk and would soon return to rest after having such a late night. I noticed he smiled at Fiona who reciprocated warmly. Elizabeth and Steven borrowed a couple of bicycles, and rode into town to have lunch with Mayor Burr. I had much to do, and set out to reduce my list of responsibilities.

"What about you, Miller?" I asked. "How are you going to spend the morning?"

He stretched lazily. "I thought I'd take a look at the slaughterhouse. Joe told me about the hours you both put into trying to save it." He paused. "I suppose I can take a look?"

"What do you mean? It's just an old building, not of much interest at all to a lay person. Why on earth would you want to go there?"

"How can you say such a thing, Stella—I may not be an archaeologist whatnot, but I would find it very interesting to see where someone was murdered."

"You are a scoundrel, Miller. It's only speculative that it was murder. Nothing's been proven," I insisted, trying to dissuade him.

"Come on, old girl. I find it difficult to believe anyone in their right mind, no matter how thirsty they were, would drink acid or throw the stuff on their own face." He shook his head decisively. "Anyway, I had a chat with Joe before he left last night. He called this morning after talking with the new owners, and they generously gave permission, providing the police have no objection. As we've not heard that they have, he is going to meet me there." He yawned sleepily. "I could do with a bit of fresh air. Can I take the pooch?"

I watched him walk down the drive with Camrose at his side. She was pulling at the leash, and he was quite comical as he tried to control her.

Later that afternoon I went to my room and tried to take a short nap. I found it difficult to relax. Miller had not returned; presumably he had decided to have lunch with Joe. I closed my eyes. The nightmare of discovering Sir Ralph started up. *Oh, damn you, Miller!* Talking with him about the slaughterhouse had brought it all back again. Fortunately, when I went downstairs later, I was in better spirits. Roger and Fiona were in the library.

"Did you both have a good day?"

"Lovely, thanks, Stella." Fiona looked relaxed and happy. So did Roger, as a matter of fact. I smiled to myself as I entered the kitchen. Was true romance in the air?

"Tea for three for now, Alice. Miller will be in any moment. You can make a fresh pot then."

She turned to fill the kettle with water from the faucet and then paused. "I suppose it's all right to drink this water?"

"What?" I looked at her questioningly.

"Well, you were saying yesterday we are killing ourselves with it."

"Oh, really, Alice. The water is quite safe; it's filtered." My tone was relaxed, but my level of irritation was rising.

"So that's what the contraption is under the sink!" She laughed, seemingly relieved. I knew she was having me on. I wondered why I put up with her. We both knew why.

It was past six thirty, and still no Miller. I had telephoned Joe at his lodgings earlier but only got his answering machine.

"Do you want me to drive over to the farm, Stella? It'll only take a few minutes," Steven Lagerquist offered.

"Oh, please, Steven. I'd like to go with you."

"Miller and Joe must have lost all sense of time."

"You're probably right."

Real concern was eating away at my nerves as we approached the farm. Squawking black rooks flew over us, aiming for the trees in the distance. I shivered.

"Cold?"

"Just a little. The nights are drawing in quickly, now."

"We had a good summer though. Got a lot of cricket in!" Steven's jovial chatter did nothing to quiet my rising anxiety. "Hold on, I'll get the gate." He got out of the car, and I slid over to the driver's seat. He opened the gate, and I let the clutch out, moving the car through. "Doesn't look like any lights are on. Have the McKinleys moved in?" He got into the passenger seat, slamming the door forcibly.

"No. The place has been empty since Joe sold it to them." I stopped the car in front of the darkened house.

"You know, it's likely they forgot about the time and Joe's driven Miller back to your place. Don't fret yourself, old girl. You wait and see."

"There's only one road, and we didn't pass them. I'm going to take a look around." I got out of the car, leaving the engine running, and hammered on the door. "Joe!" Steven joined me, and we walked around to the back of the building. We could see little as time stole away any twilight.

"Want to walk over to those outbuildings?" Steven pointed to the slaughterhouse and barns.

"No," I said emphatically. Then, less forcefully, I added, "No, we'd better go back. You are probably right. They're sitting in front of the fire, drinking my whisky while we're freezing out here." I tried to sound blasé, but my pulse was racing.

"What is it, Stella? You look so troubled!"

"I'm all right. I just need to get home."

We got back into the car, and I locked the door, not understanding why. Only when I saw the welcoming lights of the rectory did I begin to relax. We entered the house to find Fiona alone in the hall.

"Any sightings of those rogues?" Steven asked.

She looked intently at him. "Who?"

I think only Steven heard me say "air brain" under my breath.

"Oh, there you are, darling." Elizabeth came down the stairs. "I thought I heard voices." She took Steven's arm.

"Miller didn't return, then?" I was feeling really worried now.

"No. Obviously, you found no sign of him."

"No. Nor Joe." Steven touched my shoulder. "Do you want me to drive into town to take a look?"

I wanted to say yes, but sensibility took over. "He is a big boy. He knows his way home." I smiled reassuringly. "How about something to warm us up."

"Good idea!"

I sat by the window of my room most of that night. Numbness had taken over my mind and body. I had to be dreaming, I told myself. Miller was really asleep in his room, and that was what I should be doing. I got back into bed and draped a blanket over me, but my aching eyes refused to stay closed. There was still no relief when dawn came.

The phone was shrill, and broke through my escalating panic.

"Good morning, lass." The normality of the voice startled me.

"Joe! Is Miller with you?"

"No. I haven't seen him since yesterday." He paused. "He isn't with you, I take it?"

I struggled to get the words out. "He didn't return." Then my fear erupted. "Oh, Joe! What could have happened?"

"Steady on, now. You're letting your imagination run away with you. I'll be right over."

I continued to hold the telephone to my ear for at least a minute after he hung up. Then, unable to collect myself, I called the police.

"You must wait twenty-four hours before filing a missing persons report, Mrs Campbell."

"It is twenty-four hours, Constable! I'm coming to the station."

I went into the sitting room. Elizabeth and Fiona were lounging on the sofa while listening to the radio.

"I have to go to the police station. This has not turned out to be the weekend I had hoped for. Forgive me! I'll return as soon as I can."

"Don't worry about us, we're just listening to Jimmy Young interviewing some bigwig." Elizabeth got up and put her arm around my shoulders. "Is there anything we can do?

"Thank you, no. But there'll be bloody hell to pay when Miller does turn up. You may be needed to protect him." I tried to sound flippant; it was a thin effort.

Joe came into the room. "Alice let me in. I'll round up Steven and Roger. We'll find Miller, Stella. I promise. There's bound to be a simple explanation." He was gone in a second.

Elizabeth walked with me to the Rover. "Try not to worry, dear; the chaps will find him."

"Easier said than done, Elizabeth," I said, releasing the hand brake and putting the clutch in gear. As I sped along the empty road, I was consumed with trepidation.

"Now, now, Mrs Campbell. Compose yourself. There's probably some simple explanation for all this. Perhaps Mr Owens forgot his manners and returned to London." The police constable tried to calm me.

"Don't be an idiot, Bill! His things are still at the rectory. He went for a walk with Camrose over to Tythe Farm." Then I remembered. "Bill, my dog! What's happened to her?"

"Come and sit down over here, Mrs Campbell. I'll get you a cup of tea." I felt his gentle touch on my shoulder as he guided me to a chair in a small side office. I stared at the grubby yellow walls. A wire basket on top of a battleship-grey file cabinet had overflowed, littering the floor. I heard a telephone ring in the distance, then my thoughts shut down like an electrical overload during a heat wave.

"Here you are, Mrs Campbell. Drink it up. It'll do you good."

I looked questioningly into a pretty young face—it seemed familiar. "What?"

"Your tea, Mrs Campbell. The constable will be with you in a moment."

"Thank you." I took the mug from her and sipped obediently. The British use tea as a universal comforter. No matter if the ailment is psychological or physical, tea is the prescribed miracle worker; the more serious the problem, the stronger and sweeter the dose. I put the empty mug down on the dilapidated desk covered in etched cuss words. I leaned over to get a good look at some of the more complicated doodles that were deeply scored into the cheap wood. My concentration was not adequate to decipher many of them, so I turned to biting my thumbnail.

"Stella." Relieved, I looked up at Joe. He knelt down in front of me and took my hands in his. "We found Miller."

"Oh, thank heavens! And Camrose? He took her with him, you know. I've got a few things to say to that gentleman." I struggled to get up from the chair, but my legs seemed to be detached from me. I noticed the young policewoman had returned to the room.

"Miller's dead, Stella. He's been murdered."

I wanted to laugh. Joe looked like a gawking fish with his mouth opening and closing. I heard no more sound after he said the word *murdered*. I heard that all right. Then the policewoman was pushing my head down between my knees, but the room didn't stop spinning around me.

No one could eat that evening, and the food was returned to the kitchen without any comment from Alice. Fiona elected to stay in her room. Just as we were having coffee, Alice announced Inspector Gailbrath and Sergeant Ball. As expected, the inspector was full of questions, most of which were directed to Steven and Roger. I participated, yet the experience was surreal, like an out-of-body experience where I observed from a distance. Miller's body had been found in a ditch not far from Tythe Farm. He had met with the same fate as Sir Ralph. I voiced my concern about Miller taking Camrose with him. The sergeant scribbled down every detail. I was aware of the pencil lead scratching on the surface of his notepad.

"By the way, the hardware store owner, Fred Bailey, confirmed your purchase of the hydrochloric acid. Where did you say you keep the container, Mrs Campbell?"

"I'll show you. Joe brought it over when we stopped working on the slaughterhouse." I regretted Joe had left the rectory earlier. I would have preferred he dealt with the inspector.

Steven volunteered to join us. "Feel rather useless just sitting around, Stella."

We strolled over to the garden shed in the moonlight. Steven held the door, and the inspector entered in front of me. He stopped abruptly, causing me to walk into him. He put out his arm to stop me proceeding farther. "Just a moment, Mrs Campbell!"

"What is it? What's wrong?"

"You own a young dog, a retriever, yes?"

"Yes!" I pushed him aside and stepped into the shed. My sweet, devoted friend lay on the straw; her beautiful head was smashed and bloodied. I grabbed onto the side of the tool rack for support. "Oh, Camrose," I called into the night.

"Mr Lagerquist, please take Mrs Campbell back to the house," the inspector said. "I need to look around the shed on my own."

I found myself in the house without remembering getting there.

Elizabeth looked up from reading the local newspaper as Steven and I entered the lounge. "Hello, you two." She looked closer. "Whatever is it?"

"Camrose is dead," I managed to squeeze out. I became aware of Steven standing quietly at the entrance to the room. The poor man looked devastated. He went over and whispered to his wife, "I need to be alone for a while." His voice broke with emotion. "All right?"

"Darling, do you need me to come up?"

"No . . . no! Stella needs you now. I'll be down in a bit."

After a while I was able to tell Elizabeth what we had discovered. The colour drained from her face, and her makeup became garish against its pallor.

"How despicable. You say the dog was beaten? Who could do such a wicked thing?" Then the afterthought: "Fiona will be dreadfully upset. She really took to Camrose . . . it's the only time

I've seen the girl show any emotion, actually. By the way, where is she? I haven't seen her for hours."

"I haven't seen her since Steven and I got back from the farm when we went looking for Miller. I believe you and I—and Steven, of course—are the only ones who know about Camrose, apart from the police?"

"Steven's dreadfully upset, Stella. He's so fond of animals. I should go up to him. Hopefully, he's feeling better and can join us. Will you be all right on your own for a few minutes?"

"Of course. Dear man . . . no one should see such a sight."

She looked at me, uncertain how to respond. "I feel utterly helpless. What can I do, Stella?"

"Your kindness and being here with me helps, Elizabeth." I tried to sound appreciative but really wished she would go to Steven.

Roger and Fiona came in. "Hello, ladies." He gave me a puzzled glance. "You look glum, old girl. What's up? If you're dwelling on Miller, he wouldn't thank you for it." He sat down next to me. "If the plans for the church were turned down, don't worry; we can always appeal."

"No, it's nothing like that, Roger. My dog—Camrose was found dead this evening."

Fiona looked shocked. "Dead! How? What on earth happened, Stella?"

I explained how the inspector had wanted to see the shed where I had stored the hydrochloric acid, and what we had discovered. I spoke the words, yet was too numb to feel any emotion.

"Only a monster would harm an innocent creature." Fiona blew her nose into a lace handkerchief.

Our discussion turned to Miller's death. "Anyone who would use acid to kill has a lot of hate in them," Roger said. We then speculated on who would have enticed Sir Ralph to Tythe Farm and why anyone wanted me to find him. The horror of the unspoken conclusion pounded like a hammer on all of us. Had the killer mistakenly attacked Sir Ralph? Why had Joe been directed away from meeting me there? Obviously, the phone call to him had been intentional. Surprisingly, it was Fiona who brought the million-dollar question to the surface. "Perhaps you were the intended target, Stella, and Sir Ralph saved your life." The weight of those words hung over us. Who could possibly want *me* dead? To what purpose? I had seen no one at the farm, other than my grisly discovery. Not even Joe. Elizabeth broke up the gruesome conversation, suddenly remembering Steven.

"My poor husband. It's been hours since he went upstairs. He must have fallen asleep." She made an effort to smile, but the conversation had depleted any warmth behind it. "Be back in a moment." Roger, Fiona, and I sat without speaking, thinking our own thoughts.

"Steven!" The single word pierced the silence, bringing us back with a start.

Roger was ahead as we rushed up the stairs. Elizabeth was standing outside the bedroom door, holding her throat. "What is it? What's happened?"

Her face was twisted in grief. She was coughing—choking. "Steven . . . fumes," she gasped.

Roger pushed open the bedroom door, and we were about to enter when we saw Steven. He was leaning over the side of the bed. His head was on one side, so we could see his face. It was frozen in agony; his fine, chiselled nose was now swollen, and a discharge was oozing from his once-generous mouth. An empty glass decanter lay on the floor. A small patch of spilled liquid was dissolving the fibres of the carpet. I'm ashamed to say that somewhere in the back of my mind I noted that I would need to redo the flooring.

"Go downstairs at once, all of you." To my surprise, it was the inspector. I had forgotten he had been checking the grounds at the rectory. He put on the latex gloves he had taken from his trouser pocket and closed the bedroom door. "No one is to enter this room. The police are on their way." He signalled to Roger. "Make sure everyone drinks lots of water."

Obediently, we waited in the lounge. "What the hell is going on? Why Steven?" Roger asked no one in particular. Fiona excused herself and left the room. Shortly, the inspector joined us.

"The crime lab crew are here, and will be for quite a while. I don't want anyone going upstairs until they say it's all clear, Mrs Campbell."

"It's hydrochloric acid again, isn't it?"

The inspector nodded. "Can you all go into the village for the night? You shouldn't stay here until everything is secure."

"I'll go and round Fiona up."

"Oh, she's gone, Mr Spencer. I saw her drive away a few minutes ago."

"That was awfully nice of her. Not even a goodbye." Roger looked upset. "Well, ladies, let's be off, then. I'll drive."

"Good man," the inspector said.

"Elizabeth? Come, my dear, we have to leave." She looked up at Roger, questioning. "What? What did you say?" He gently helped her to her feet. "Get her coat, please, Stella."

We were silent during the drive to the Retreat. The inspector must have telephoned Dr Levinton, as he met us at the hotel. At first Elizabeth refused a sedative but Dr Levinton's insistence prevailed. I don't think anyone else slept that night. I certainly didn't. The next morning, Sergeant Ball took statements from each of us. Later that day, we were allowed to return to the rectory; as expected, access to the room Elizabeth and Steven had shared was refused. A policeman was at the main entrance to the house, and another at the back. They gave little comfort. We were realising any one of us could be in danger. It didn't matter why. Elizabeth stared vacantly; grief had destroyed her beauty. She declined further medication, and no one blamed her; we had to be fully alert. Who knew what was next? Who was next?

Following the post-mortem, Elizabeth petitioned for an early release of Steven's remains for transportation to London. The coroner granted her request, and a modest service took place at

Mortlake Crematorium. Steven's ashes were later scattered over the ancient Thames, floating a while before disappearing beneath the rippling, murky water. Promising to call me as soon as she returned, Elizabeth went to stay with her parents in Italy. There was no objection from Inspector Gailbrath. I was back on the pink pills with a troubled Alice hovering over me.

"None of this is real, is it, Alice? I'm just imagining it all."

"Shhh, dear. Mr Blake will be here any minute. He'll blame me if you're getting all upset again." She fussed with a vase of crimson dahlias. "These are the last from the garden. There's a lot of work to be done out there. I'll give you a hand when you're up to it."

Yes, that was what I needed—to work in the soil, to get my hands back into the good earth. Autumn was almost over, and mulch should be in place before the first frost came. "I'd like to go outside now, take a look around." I got up out of the chair eagerly. "Will you come with me?"

"I'll get our jackets."

The smell of wood smoke was in the air, and I sniffed appreciatively. Neighbours were working in their gardens, burning the end-of-season debris, and preparing for the harshness of the looming winter. Migrating birds had already started their journeys to warmer climates, and prickly hedgehogs were on the lookout for snug retreats within which to slumber until spring. I held on to Alice's arm as we walked along the path. She was right; there was a lot to be done, and I was glad of it. We came to the tool shed. Propped up against the wall was a spade. Vivid orange rust had attacked the exposed metal. I examined the damage. "It's still got some life in it. I'll ask Fred to oil it."

Alice took it from me. "I'll put it into the shed. You wait for me here." I watched her go into the wooden building, and sadly remembered my innocent pup. After a moment, she appeared at the doorway with the spade still in her hands.

"Alice?"

"Stella. I just need to take care of something. Go back to the house for a couple of minutes."

"What is it?"

"Just go back, there's a dear. I'll only be a moment."

"What's wrong? Alice?" I pushed passed her and peered into the gloom. I could see nothing at first, and then my eyes adjusted and I saw the bloodied leash and collar. I just started sobbing as if I would never stop.

"She could come and stay with us, Joe. I'll take care of her." Beverly Petersen spoke in a whisper.

"I think she should stay with her parents. She'd also be close to her children," he replied.

"Whatever you think is best."

"Whatever you think is best!" I mimicked Bev. "How do you know what is best for me?" My throat was raw. Alice said it had taken a sharp slap from her before I quieted my wailing at the shed. "I am not going anywhere. No one's going to shove me around."

Joe smiled. "That's more like it, lass."

"It's stupid! She may be in danger, Joe. She can't stay here."

"Bev," I said slowly, "Steven, just like Sir Ralph and Miller, was doused with hydrochloric acid. Only a raving monster could do such a thing. I'll have nightmares for the rest of my life, but I'm not going to run."

"That's my point, Stella. Whoever it is, is sick. He could do anything . . . to anyone."

"I'm going to fight back, Bev. I'll get my strength from what I saw in the slaughterhouse, at the coroner's, and in my own home. I'm going to live my life in the open, not cowering in the shadows." Alice came into the room carrying a small silver tray with a glass of water and a brown plastic container. "You can take that away right now, Alice. No more pink pills. My head is clear at last."

CHAPTER EIGHT

Three weeks later, close to a hundred people gathered in the rugby field behind the school. Alas, the weather had turned against us, and a heavy downpour soaked not only bodies, but spirits too. A few stout hearts continued to hammer handles of plywood onto large placards, although the slogans printed in black ink were disappearing in the torrent.

"Forget the signs. We'll shout the words." I laughed at Megan Fleming's enthusiasm. "It is still on, right, Stella?"

"Of course, it's on. Let's get everyone loaded up."

With determination written on her cold, wet face, Megan hustled the picketers towards the vans and cars in the school parking lot. She had become one of my strongest supporters of the event after hearing of Miller's cruel demise.

We looked a sad bunch, but our voices were strong as we chanted outside the Euston factory. A couple of young men had climbed the fence and were running off into the mist. "They'll get themselves arrested, the bloody fools," a protester called out.

"It's one way to get the media's attention," Megan replied. But not a single reporter had turned up. I felt bitterly disappointed. I had telephoned the newspapers and television stations myself.

"It's this god-awful weather," Ben, Megan's husband, reasoned.

"No! I didn't make it interesting enough. Picketing one factory that's polluting our water doesn't make a headline. I should have told them Clipton's water is murdering children."

"Stella! Steady on," Ben warned.

"Harold Euston is responsible for the disgusting water in our village and, therefore, the failing health of our people. When someone intentionally takes the life of another, it is murder. In my opinion, he is potentially a mass murderer."

"Oh, come on, woman—he's a stubborn old man. Making such rash statements is not the way to persuade him to change his ways." Ted Nyby struggled against the wind to keep the hood of his yellow slicker over his head. "Be clear about your direction, Stella."

A group carrying banners was walking up and down the wire fencing, chanting loudly, "Euston's factory is killing our kids. Boycott Euston goods!"

"What they are saying is true, Ted. If we stand together, we have the power to fight him," I insisted.

"If it wasn't for that factory, many people in Clipton would be without a job," Dr Levinton joined us.

"We're not trying to close the factory down. We just want Euston to stop poisoning our water. It's not unreasonable, doctor. Of all people, you should support that."

"I agree, Stella! Don't misunderstand me. I support what you are trying to do; I'm just not sure degrading the man will get what we want."

"My friend lost his life because he was fighting for Clipton." My voice became hoarse with emotion. "This county is our home. I'll do whatever it takes to protect it." There was silence for a moment before Dr Levinton turned on his heels and walked away. "I thought a doctor who takes an oath to save lives would be with us."

Ted patted my arm. "He is, Stella. Don't count him out, my dear."

A voice called out in alarm. "Ruddy hell, here's a Black Maria. Run, everybody! Run!" The bedraggled crowd scattered as the large vehicle came to a halt and the back doors swung open. Several policemen clambered out and made a dash after the demonstrators. There was a grinding of brakes as a police car and a van drew up, unloading more men in uniform. A couple came up to Ted and me.

"You're both under arrest for disturbing the peace."

One grabbed my arms behind my back and handcuffed me. I could not stop myself from laughing. It was such a charade. I got a disapproving look from Ted as he was being led away. A number of police officers were close on the heels of demonstrators scampering through the wet bushes, while others led a small group to the Black Maria. Barking wildly, two overly excited Alsatian guard dogs ran up and down behind the fence to the plant. Then I saw Roger being led into one of the cars. *Good old Roger. I can always count on him as an ally*, I told myself.

"Watch your step, Mrs Campbell." A police officer offered his hand as I stepped down from the van. It had been a cheerful trip, considering. There were ten of us, and the short journey gave enough time for us to become more resolute in our commitment to win the battle, even if it meant prison. We were led in single file into the police station, read our rights, fingerprinted, and had unflattering mug shots taken. As I went down the concrete steps to a cell, I passed a familiar figure. He nodded in recognition. It was Inspector Gailbrath.

After an hour or so, I was led out of a holding cell and taken back upstairs. The £150 bail had been put up by Beverly Petersen. She stood at the front desk, looking tragic.

"Bev, I'm sorry. I don't want to hurt you."

"You're determined to destroy my father, aren't you, Stella? I've heard the rotten things you've said about him. How can you? You don't even know him."

"We've gone over it a dozen times. It's nothing personal." I slipped my arm through hers as we walked out of the building. "The whole matter would be over if he simply put filters on the outlet pipes. Goodness, your children are his grandchildren. I'm fighting for them as well, Bev."

"I can't go against him, Stella." She was close to tears.

"Bev, please don't!" I put my arm around her shoulders.

"Stella!" I looked across the street and saw Simon Belsky coming towards us. "Hello." He looked at Beverly and then at me. "Anything I can do?"

"No, thanks." I tightened my grip around Beverly. "We're on our way home."

We were silent in the car. She dropped me off in front of the rectory but not before giving me a hug. I waited until the car disappeared out of sight. The weight of hurting my best friend was heavy, indeed.

"I suppose you're proud of yourself being arrested." Joe arrived at the rectory a few minutes after me, his face flushed with anger.

"Of course! It was great fun. I have a criminal record on file now."

"Stella, it isn't funny!" He was seething. "You are making enemies in influential places."

"If I'm stepping on toes, then so be it. I'm not giving in, Joe. Miller gave everything for this. Do you think I'm worried about a few hot shots?"

"He was murdered, Stella. And Steven! The same horrific way Sir Ralph was killed! I want you to remember every detail. There were burns all over their mouths; their throats and lungs were destroyed."

"I know, I know!" Did he think I was an idiot?

"And we don't know if there will be more. Don't let one of them be you." He was almost shouting.

"Or you, for that matter!" Suddenly, my voice sounded a long way off. "Joe! Tell me I'm dreaming." He held me in his arms but I felt no comfort.

Miller's body was released to his younger brother. Grief-stricken, I watched as the train carrying the casket shunted out of Clipton's small station. My jury of one's conviction pummelled my throbbing head. *Guilty*! My friend's death was because of me. He had come so willingly to Clipton simply because I had asked him. A raw fury churned deep within me. A light snow covered the shoulders of my black coat, and I brushed it off impatiently. Clenching my teeth, I silently promised Miller I would take on his cause to the end.

"Can I give you a lift, Mrs Campbell?"

I abruptly became aware of others around me. "No thank you, Inspector. I prefer to walk." I passed him, and made my way stiffly through the few officials and others who had come to show respect by seeing Miller off.

My steps were muffled as I walked briskly along the narrow road. Snow was accumulating, and I had to pay attention so as not to slip. No cars passed, and I became cognisant of the silence that surrounded me. The cold was numbing. I trudged on, scolding myself for not accepting the inspector's offer of a ride. It was a relief to see smoke pouring out of the rectory's tall chimneys in the distance. I had about half a mile to go, and began to recite Lear's whimsical poem, "The Owl and the Pussycat," to keep myself company.

The road continued into a bend, and it was there that I heard a sound—a sound that was not made by the wind or by my own step. I stopped. Silence. I slowly took a couple of steps forward. Still nothing. Hedges that lined both sides of the road were still. Then a dry twig snapped from within the shrubbery to the right of me, sounding like a gunshot, and I took off running. My winter coat was heavy, and lashed against my legs, holding me back as panic escalated, and I stumbled blindly. My throat constricted as I gulped in frigid air, choking me. I could run no farther, and fell heavily onto the hard asphalt. I waited, certain I would succumb to the same fate as Miller, and covered my head with my arms in a pathetic attempt at protection. Seconds passed. I could stand it no longer, and chanced a look back at the road where my own footprints were stamped in the snow. Gritting my teeth, I pulled myself up. My stockings were torn, and blood oozed down my legs. "Fool! You bloody fool!" I shouted aloud and struck a fist against my head in disgust.

I limped the rest of the way to the rectory and shamefully knocked on the door. "Alice, don't say anything." I looked threateningly at her startled face. She stepped back without a word, and I hobbled passed.

"I was in the area and thought I'd see that you made it home all right."

"You can see I did."

"Yes." The inspector looked closely at me, and I did not like his scrutiny.

"Well?"

"Seems like you had a bit of a scare on the way."

"Bollocks!"

"What?" He stared in surprise.

"You heard! Been talking to Alice again, eh? How I wish you'd put the same energy into your investigation. Maybe you'd get somewhere!"

"Alice has nothing to do with it, Mrs Campbell. The plasters covering your knees are a giveaway," he quipped.

That got me, and my guard went down. "Stella. Call me Stella. Mrs Campbell makes me feel a hundred years old." I looked at him. "Are you allowed to?"

"I don't think the Yard will demote me for it." He started to pull on leather gloves. "I'd better be getting back."

I walked out with him to the police car parked by the gate. Our breath turned to vapour in the cold, and I shivered.

"Goodbye, Stella."

"Inspector." I turned back to the house.

"John."

"What?"

"John."

I nodded, and waited until the car disappeared behind the trees.

My daughter, Julia, was not able to get time off from St George's for Christmas. Happily, Tim kept his word, and spent all of four days at the rectory. My parents drove him down, so I had three of the most important people in my life with me. Tim helped Dad put up the tree in the lounge, where Alice, Mum, and I decorated it. We attended a moving candlelight service at St Michael's Episcopal Church on Christmas Eve, and returned home for a light supper. On Christmas morning, my mother felt so out of place not having a dinner to prepare that Alice took her under her wing and they tackled the goose together. Soon, delicious aromas wafted throughout the house and whetted our appetites. Two contented collaborators emerged from the kitchen several hours later, flushed faced and a bit unsteady after consuming a few glasses of wine in between the stuffing and peeling.

"You've never had such a tasty goose as this one, Stan," my mother boasted. "Alice has taught me so many things. Of course, we have your nuts and rice patties, Stella."

"It wasn't all one way, Dixie," Alice said. "Until you showed me, I'd not been very creative or comfortable with tofu. Stella will attest to that."

"I can, indeed!"

"Well, I intend changing that now. Just you wait. We'll be eating at seven sharp, if that's all right with everyone?"

"Fine, if we can hold out that long, Alice! We're feeling neglected . . . we need something to snack on," I complained. "Right, Dad? Tim?"

It seemed a variety of cheeses, crackers, fruit, and a bottle of port appeared out of nowhere. And then Julia telephoned. Thankfully, it was quiet at the hospital, and she had been able to get to the cafeteria and eat a turkey dinner with all the trimmings. We missed her when we gathered around the fire in the lounge, and exchanged thoughtful gifts. My parents were overjoyed with the fortnight's holiday I had arranged for them in Tuscany. Alice said little when she opened the slim box and discovered the pearls she had admired in the village jeweller's shop. There was little doubt what she was feeling from the delighted expression on her face, however. I sat in the warmth of the moment and counted my many blessings.

"Mother, I'm perplexed," Tim said slowly. "This cheque is for several thousands of pounds. I thought it was agreed I should learn to live on my salary?"

"We did. The cheque is for you to go back to school to get your degree. When you've accomplished that, I'll set you up in your own business. Is that a deal, darling?"

"I don't know if I want to be a lawyer . . . my experience of law school actually put me off."

Oh, stop bellyaching, Tim! I wanted to shout.

"The legal process is not equitable, Mum. Money is a factor, if not *the* factor . . . how much you can pay decides your fate too often. Equality under the law sounds good, but not everyone gets a fair shake."

"We keep going over this, Tim." The frustration in my voice was obvious. "If you really believe that, then get involved with legal aid. The degree will allow you to help those who can't afford a good lawyer."

"You're pushing me, Mother. Please don't. It's Christmas, for crying out loud." He was getting prickly.

"I'm pushing, Tim, because I don't want you to have regrets later when it could be too late. If you graduate, and then decide law is not right for you, I give you my word I will support you in whatever field you choose. I can't be fairer than that, can I?"

"Just let me off the hook for the holiday. I'll think about it and let you know before the new year. Deal?"

"Deal!"

"Now you've both got that out of the way, can we please eat? My stomach is talking to me," my father wailed.

We went into the dining room and sat at the table Alice had decorated magnificently with red poinsettias. China and glassware gleamed in the candlelight, and in front of each place setting was the traditional Christmas cracker. Of course, those were pulled apart straight away, and the silly jokes they contained brought much laughter. We donned our paper hats, made a toast, and then gleefully tucked into a meal that was fit for a king.

CHAPTER NINE

The yellow coat caught my eye as I wheeled my bicycle across the road to the newsagent. It was Fiona. She was talking urgently to an expensively dressed mature man as they entered the Retreat. I selected some stationery and a supply of Callard and Bowser's treacle toffee, and then made my way to the impressive red-bricked school, Clipton's latest project underway now the town hall was completed. I was horrified at the unexpected shambles. Lengths of tarpaulin were no longer tethered to the scaffolding, and billowed like giant sails fighting the wind. I made my way around portable cement mixers standing in streams of soup-like runoff that soaked through my canvas shoes. Grumbling, I propped my bicycle against a stack of wood, and set off to find the watchman. Being a Saturday, no one else should have been on site, so I was surprised to hear voices coming from the foreman's trailer. I could not hear what was being said, but one voice I knew well. I called out. I must have taken them by surprise, because the conversation ceased immediately. "Hello," I called again, and was just about to enter the trailer.

"Stella!"

"Hello, Margot!"

"What a surprise, dear. I hope you had a good Christmas. I was just passing and saw Mr Edwards. He's been ever so kind. Gave me a tour and showed the plans to me." She looked relaxed and quite youthful in a cream-coloured pantsuit. "It's always nice to know one's money is not being wasted. It is going to be a grand building when completed. Lucky children!" She beamed at me.

"Good day, Mrs Campbell." The watchman came out from the trailer and stood beside Margot.

"Good day, Mr Edwards. I was looking for you." I turned and gestured to the mess around us. "I thought it was understood the site was to be cleaned up each night, particularly for the weekends. Have you seen Mr Nyby?"

"Not since midweek, miss. I'll have a word with the foreman on Monday when he comes on. It won't happen again."

"If he gives you any guff, let me know."

He touched his check cap. "Aye, I'll do that, Mrs Campbell, but I'm sure it will be all right."

"You look so serious, Stella. Cheer up, my dear."

I did not like Margot scolding me in front of Mr Edwards. "It's a serious matter, Margot."

"Oh, I can't imagine why."

I looked at her, perplexed at her manner. Perhaps I had stumbled on her and Mr Edwards in a compromising situation, and she was trying to bluff her way out of it. It did not make sense; she looked a few years older. Then I heard a sound from within the trailer. I looked at them both, but they avoided my gaze.

"I must be off. Thank you for the tour, Mr Edwards." Margot held out her hand.

"Any time, ma'am." He shook her hand briefly, aware of me staring.

Margot passed by me and walked delicately across the path of wooden planks laid over the wet ground. It was then that I noticed her shoes. They were clean except for a light edge of mud. She had not toured around that site any more than I had jumped over the moon. Pensively, I walked slowly back to my bicycle. Blocked gutters and melted ice had created a shallow pond at the crossroad junction; the captured pile of twigs and debris would have been the envy of any otter. The sound of a car splashing through the standing water caused me to turn. It was a black Volvo. I knew the type because Roger Spencer had one.

I saw the white police car as soon as I rounded the group of pines at the side of the rectory. The inspector was climbing out and did not notice me at first. I rang my bicycle bell and was satisfied to see him jump at the unexpected clatter. He was not smiling when he looked at me.

"You are not a very nice person, Stella."

"I know. In fact, a really terrible person." I grinned at his serious demeanour. "Are you here officially?"

"Yes. I want a word with you. It's important."

"You'd better come in."

"No. It'll only take a moment. I must get back to London this evening."

I propped the bicycle against the wall and sat down on the porch step. "Let's have it, then."

"When you walked from the station after seeing Miller Owens' remains off, you said you didn't see anyone."

"Yes, that's right. No one."

He sat down next to me. "You should know we believe someone was following you. After I came by the rectory to make sure you got home without mishap, I went along that road. The temperature was cold enough to freeze the imprint of your shoes in the light snow."

"Then you saw there was only one set of footprints."

"On the road, yes. There was another set just behind the hedge, and followed the road for about a mile. We found car tracks back about that distance. Looks like your instincts were correct; someone saw you walking alone, parked their car, and followed you."

"Yes, but whatever for? It would have been decent of whoever it was to offer me a lift, especially as it had turned so cold."

The inspector shook his head. "It isn't funny, Stella. I think you were stalked."

"Stalked?" I looked at him. "You're scaring me, John."

"Good. I need to! Now maybe you'll start being sensible and not walk about the countryside on your own."

"Was it a man?"

"Looks like it from the size of the shoeprint."

I chewed my lip nervously. I had been successful at maintaining an apathetic front since taking over Miller's crusade, but John's words unnerved me. "I'm in danger?"

"Things are pointing that way. That's why I want you to give me your word that you won't take unnecessary chances. If you have to go out, go with Alice or a friend."

"What about meetings and things? I can't drag Alice around everywhere."

"You must do what you have to do, Stella. This is serious. I want you to give me your word you'll do as I ask."

"Oh, very well! I'm not quite that stupid."

"Not stupid . . . pig-headed, I'd say."

"By the way, I've just come from the school site. Margot Hughes Young was there and seemed a little overly friendly with the watchman. As I was leaving, I'm pretty sure it was Roger Spencer's car that drove away."

"Why shouldn't she visit the site? She's on the renovation committee . . . and Spencer certainly would; he has to report the project's progress to the trustees." John looked blank.

"I know all that; I just feel those two are connected somehow beyond their fiduciary duties."

"I don't think there's anything to be concerned about." He stood up and held out his hand to help me up from the step. I held on to it a little longer than was necessary.

"Have a good trip to London."

"I'll be back in a couple of days."

I did not want him to leave. "You do a lot of going back and forth. Can't you handle the enquiries locally?"

"No. I'm stationed at the Yard." He opened the car door. "I'll call when I get back." He paused. "If that's okay."

"Yes," I answered softly.

He did not drive off until I was inside the rectory, safe behind the bolted door. I waved to him through the window. It felt lonely looking out at the empty road.

I did not see Beverly for a couple of weeks. My decision to go ahead with picketing her father's factory had caused us to become estranged. It seemed wise to avoid each other for a while, but it was not. I missed her. When I caught her eye during the enthusiastic rendering of the hymn "Onward Christian Solders" in church that Sunday morning, I impulsively decided to invite her and Robert to lunch. Knowing they would have to pass me at the end of the service, I delayed my exit from the pew by fussing with my handbag. My timing was perfect.

"Good morning, Robert—Beverly."

"Good morning, Stella." Robert smiled encouragingly, and I knew why I was so fond of him. I fell in step beside them as we waited our turn for the traditional few words of wisdom from Kenneth Wickam Foxwell, Clipton's rather unconventional keeper of the faith, standing at the south door exit. The young vicar had his ear to the pulse of the town and missed little. His pleasure at seeing me with the Petersens was obvious. Shoulder-length black hair and steel-toed biker boots signified his rebellious determination to step away from the traditional isolation of his calling. The polished black Harley-Davidson roaring through the countryside did nothing to dissuade the deep affection this gentle-natured man had won from the community.

"Nice to see you, as always." He shook hands with each of us.

"Can you make the twenty-first, Ken?"

"It looks like it will work out. I'll call you tomorrow."

"What was that all about?" Beverly gestured back to Ken as we walked away.

"I'm going to hold a series of seminars at the rectory. The first one is about controlling Dutch elm disease. Then, bulb planting for spring colour, and, lastly, how to control American tourists." I was pleased to hear Bev's laughter again.

"Can anyone attend?" She smiled impishly. "I've always wanted to know about controlling the Yanks."

"Well, it is by invitation only, but I'll see what I can do."

"You're a cow, Stella Campbell!"

The ice was broken. Children came streaming out of Sunday school, and Robert waved to catch the attention of Robbie and Sarah. They came scampering up, throwing themselves at him.

"Hey there! Take it easy, tiddlywinks."

Beverly agreed to join me for lunch. Robert begged off. "Too little notice, old thing. Promised to take these two to the pictures. Next time, for sure."

"I'll go with Stella now, darling. All right?"

"Of course! Come along, midgets. We'll see Mummy later."

I took Beverly's arm, and we walked back to the rectory. Fred drove the car at a snail's pace behind us. The sun was hazy and rapidly losing warmth, even though it was only late morning.

In the comfort of the rectory, Beverly placed her handbag and hat on the coffee table, and settled herself on the sofa. "Whatever do you mean? Stalked?"

"Apparently, I was followed from the station."

"What do the police say? What are they ruddy well doing about it? I can't understand what's happening in our little village. The police appear to be impotent. Don't they have any leads? It's been months and months since this whole thing started."

"I know no more than you. The inspector seems to pop up all over the place, but he keeps tight lipped about everything."

"Are you getting sweet on him?" Bev looked at me steadily. She was serious.

"Absolutely not! What a question!"

"Well, you do have a certain look when you talk about him." She sighed, changing the subject. "You'd have thought they would have caught the bastard by now. I look at friends and people in town and wonder if it could be any of them!"

"We need that elderly detective Alice is always reading about. The woman gets results, in spite of her age," I said wistfully.

"Who's that?"

"Oh . . . Miss something or other—Agatha Christie's spinster sleuth."

"You can make light of it, Stella, but it's terrible suspecting everyone."

"It couldn't be a local. It has to be a weekender—a stranger. Perhaps that's why the delay in an arrest—they have to check on who was here at the time." I did not sound convincing, and changed the subject. "Joe gets back tomorrow. I can't wait to hear his news."

"I didn't know he'd been away."

"Yes, he went to Cumberland to look at some land."

"Cumberland? That's a long way to go. You won't be able to see much of each other with him up there."

"No, I shall miss him dreadfully. He's like a brother to me. I wish it were different. A woman couldn't ask for a better man." I was saddened by the thought of Joe going away, but I could not pretend a feeling I did not have. It would not have been fair to either of us.

"What about that chap . . . you know, the McKinleys' fellow who came to dinner at our place that time? He came up and spoke to us when I got you out of the clink. What's his name?"

"Simon. Simon Belsky. If you can't remember his name after having him as a guest in your home, he obviously didn't make much of an impression. Actually, I saw him again recently. I was surprised, although he did say he would be returning to Clipton from time to time. We didn't speak . . . I don't think he saw me. He was waiting to cross the road at the traffic light outside the library."

"What do you know about him?"

"Not much. He is very pleasant . . . a professor of architecture at York. He showed interest in what I've done with the rectory, and that's about it, really."

Alice announced lunch was ready, and we followed her into the cheerful breakfast room. I was hungry and did not speak again until the mushroom quiche had been washed down with a strong cup of Colombian coffee.

"Can I clear up now, Stella?" I looked questioningly at Alice, and then remembered it was Sunday. We had agreed for her to take a few hours off.

"Sorry, Alice. I didn't mean to make you late. Mrs Petersen and I'll take care of this."

"If you're sure?"

"Yes, yes, of course." She was gone before I could wish her a good afternoon.

"It's hard to know who runs this house, you or that old witch." Bev helped herself to a meringue.

"She's a rough diamond, all right." I was serious. "I don't know what I would do without her."

"Stella. Now we're alone, can we talk about my father?" There was a tinge of anxiety to her voice. She toyed with a fork, tracing the checked pattern of the tablecloth.

"Your father? Of course."

"He's going to go after you in a big way, Stella. Charge you with defamation of character, loss of business. Even endangerment."

"And?"

"You're not bothered?" Her eyes widened.

"I expected it. He can afford a good lawyer. How did he react to you putting up bail for me?"

"As you might expect. He was deeply hurt. His only child going against him."

I put my hand over hers. "It's a clean fight, Bev. All we're asking is that he places industrial filters on pipes draining toxins into Clipton's water supply. It's an absolutely reasonable request, and one I'm committed to."

"I went through all that with him. He's so stubborn." She shook her head. "You both are!"

"I don't understand why he just doesn't do it! He got his wealth from this community. He owes it a safe water supply."

"That's what I told him. And he does understand."

"What's the problem, then?"

"It's the way you went about it that's the problem. You humiliated him, Stella. He's been really good to Clipton. He donated a lot of the trust money you've used to renovate the school. Many of the books in the library were a gift in my mother's memory." She sat back in the chair. "You tarnished all that, and took away his good name."

"Nonsense! I don't care if he's your father or the man in the moon. He is responsible for poisoning our water—the water we all drink each day!"

"If you're going to get angry, I'll leave."

"Angry? I'm going to go stark raving bonkers! Doesn't he get it? He can make a greater contribution to this whole county and get his goddamn name back just by spending a few thousand pounds. That's what it boils down to, Bev. A measly few thousand pounds!"

"If I arranged it, would you talk with him face to face?"

"I'll do whatever it takes. For crying out loud—I'm fighting for his daughter and grandchildren's health, too. Doesn't he understand?"

"I'll ask him over for dinner. You could casually pop by."

"I could, but I won't."

"You see! You're as mulish as he is! Neither of you will budge an inch!"

"I'll come, Beverly, but not to ambush him. I'll join you for dinner."

She looked at me for a moment. "Done!"

"So? Tell me all about it," I demanded, leading Joe into the library.

"I missed you, Stella." He sounded glum.

A fire burned in the grate, sending gyrating shadows against the walnut panelling. I curled up on the couch and yawned.

"I won't take that personally," he said.

"Oh, Joe, forgive me. It's being cooped up in the house all day. The rain hasn't stopped! Want some tea?"

"I'll take something stronger."

"At three in the afternoon?"

"I need some Dutch courage, as they say." He toyed with his watchstrap.

"Whatever is it?" I felt concern at his nervousness.

"Well . . . I decided to buy the stud ranch. It's three hundred acres with a good solid house. Quite a grand place, actually, you know . . . modernised kitchen and bathrooms. It's been in the horse business for the past hundred years or so, and I'll continue in that line. Certainly, for the time being."

"Sounds wonderful, Joe. I'm sure you'll make it a huge success."

"Alston's not far from the Scottish border. It is very beautiful. I'd like you to see it."

"Oh, I will!" I replied enthusiastically, wondering why he was looking at me so intensely.

"I'd like you to stay."

"Stay? How do you mean?"

"Stay. Stay with me as my wife, Stella." I looked at him for what seemed an eternity. I could not think of anything to say. "It can't be that much of a shock. You must know I love you."

"I . . . didn't think it was in that way. We're such good friends. It never occurred . . . Joe, I'm so sorry. I hadn't any idea." I continued to splutter, hating myself for hurting this decent, wonderful man. I wished with all my heart I loved him back in the way he wanted.

He got up from the chair. "I'm sorry, too. I thought . . . had hoped . . . you might love me." His voice was heavy with disappointment. "I'd better go." I heard the front door close. The room was too quiet and seemed utterly empty without him.

Beverly put her arm around my waist as she led me into the sitting room where her father and Robert were relaxing over an aperitif.

"Daddy, this is Stella Campbell. Stella, my father, Sam Euston."

"So, we meet at last, Mrs Campbell," he said, standing up. He was an attractive man, taller than I expected, and tastefully dressed in expensive wool trousers and a black turtleneck sweater. His silver hair was cut to just below his ears, making him seem younger than his mid sixties. "I always like to see my adversary face to face; then I know who I'm dealing with. Being told only you're Beverly's friend didn't quite make it." His grey eyes studied me closely.

"Well, I am Beverly's friend; her best friend, I hope." I suddenly felt tongue tied and looked appealingly at Robert.

"Forgive me, Stella, you need something to drink. Come and sit by the fire. It's freezing outside. Did Reg drive you, or did you walk over?"

I gave him a grateful smile, and sat on the sofa. "I walked."

Beverly sat beside me. "Daddy, I asked Stella to join us for dinner because I want my best friend to get to know and like my father. Robert and I intend to leave you both alone so you can work out what it is that you each need from the other. Then we can all enjoy the delicious dinner I spent hours preparing. Robert?"

"Coming, darling."

They quickly left the room, and I found myself alone with the man I had come to hold totally responsible for Clipton's contaminated water supply. *Well, here goes*, I told myself. "Mr Euston, all we want from you is safe water. I've researched what it will take to bring that about, and it is quite simple. Filters! They are not extraordinarily expensive and can be fitted easily. I've talked with several engineers who are willing to take on the project. Should you be concerned about the costs, I am prepared to make a contribution towards those costs." My voice wavered slightly, but I got out what I needed to say—actually, quite well I thought. Beverly's father said nothing, just looked at me intently. "Mr Euston?" I began to fidget with my fingers. "Did you hear me? Have you anything to say?"

He leaned forward until his face was no more than a couple of feet from mine. "Yes, I heard you, Mrs Campbell—loud and clear. Now hear me! Who the hell do you think you are, telling me what I need to do, and then to have the gall to offer me money? I've heard about you and all your noble deeds in Clipton. Why don't you just carry on with those and leave my business to me?" He was furious. "There are plenty of worthy causes you can involve yourself in to fill up your time. It must be lonely in that big house of yours. You should get a dog."

I fought down my anger with everything I had so as not to give him the satisfaction of knowing he had provoked me. "Thanks for the suggestion—a dog is a good idea. However, so are filters. You may not care about the citizens of this town. Why should you? They are strangers—anonymous figures passing in the street—but what about your grandchildren and your own daughter? I suppose Robert is dispensable . . . he isn't blood, right?"

"Don't be so ridiculous, woman! I've done a lot for this community. What makes you the authority on this problem, anyway? Who says it's my factory that's putting out pollutants when there are many others along the waterways?"

"You are correct on that point; nevertheless, the major flow has been traced to Euston's outlet pipes," I insisted. "A special friend of mine was brutally murdered in Clipton. He came here because he wanted to help the community, believing everyone has the right to safe water. I made a promise when I saw his mutilated body that I would carry on the cause in his place. You see, Mr Euston, it's not about you or me. It's about doing the right thing. Your factory is destroying the quality of our water, and eventually someone will get very sick. Neither of us wants it to be a member of your family."

"You should have come to me, not demonstrated like a pack of mindless yobs! You tarnished my name, and I'll not forget it."

"I regret that. I should have come to you. I can't undo what is done and I am sorry, truly sorry, but I am determined to succeed in winning this, Beverly's father, Robbie and Sarah's grandfather."

He sat back in the chair and took a sip from his glass. There was silence for quite a few minutes before he spoke. "I will add the filters on the condition that everyone in Clipton knows I did it willingly and without outside pressure. You will need to do a very good public relations job, Mrs Campbell, because I want to come out of this smelling like the sweetest perfumed rose known to man. You understand?"

"Oh yes, I certainly do. Your good deed will get you a plaque in the church, I'll be bound." I thought of Miller. "Peace, Mr Euston?"

He took my hand and pumped it several times. "Peace! Now, let's get those two in here. Their ears must be aching, pressed against the door all this time."

Miller's cause was won, and I had gained the respect of Beverly's father. I returned home that evening feeling both elated and emotionally sapped. Sam Euston had been right about one thing: another dog was a good suggestion.

CHAPTER TEN

The piano recital followed a string quartet's interpretation of Dmitri Shostakovich's achingly tragic No. 8, Opus 110. Leafless willows moved gracefully in time to the Brahms' dream-like waltz in A-flat drifting across the gardens through the open windows. The weekend of concerts would be the last for the year. Winter was already upon us. My Friday evening guests drove off in clouds of exhaust fumes. Two couples were staying over for the weekend—Roger Spencer, again with Fiona, and Justin Rahn, the gifted pianist who played so magnificently, and his wife, Helena. Surprisingly, Elizabeth Lagerquist was back from Italy and begged to join us, not wanting to be alone.

"Isn't that a little odd, considering her nightmare began at the rectory?" Roger whispered to me.

"Shhh," I implored, turning away from him and addressing the others. "I would say it was a most successful evening. Thanks to you, Justin."

"Not entirely, Stella. The ensemble was superb," he replied modestly. I beamed with delight and led my guests into the lounge for a final nightcap.

"You are being generous, Justin." Elizabeth smiled. She looked very elegant in a silver grey empire line dress. Her long black hair was pulled back into a chignon.

"Don't you agree, Elizabeth? I thought the whole evening was outstanding." Roger looked at her questioningly.

"Oh, absolutely. I'm in total agreement, Roger. Really, I wasn't criticising—making a comment, that's all. I just thought Justin carried the program."

"Elizabeth and I were discussing Chopin earlier," Helena Rahn interrupted politely. "Chopin's mazurkas reflect his Polish heritage, don't you think? So full of the cadence and character of folk music." Helena was a mouse compared to Elizabeth, but she had snared a good-looking, talented husband. What she lacked in beauty she made up in intelligence, and that was very attractive to many males. Justin was one of them. He watched his wife like a man who counted the minutes until he could bed her, and she knew it.

Everyone seemed in good spirits when we parted company after breakfast the following morning, going our separate ways for the rest of the day. I was puzzled, however, as I detected a strain between Roger and Fiona when we converged for dinner that evening. Looking particularly lovely in a topaz-coloured dress, Fiona toyed listlessly with the food in front of her. Roger, seated opposite her at the table, glared openly from under a heavy brow. A silly tiff, I presumed. Ignoring them both, I decided to make every effort to keep the conversation light, and did succeed in enlisting Helena to elaborate on her opinion of the latest Bonnard exhibit at London's Tate Gallery. Her dark curls bounced as she became animated over a favourite subject. It was not long before Roger and Justin joined the deliberately contrived conversation, and any discomfort at the table dissolved. By the time other guests arrived for an evening of Gershwin music, amiability had returned as we gathered at the door to bid them welcome.

We awoke on Sunday morning to a heavy frost. Nature had brushed the landscape with a wash of silver, and the result was achingly beautiful.

"I'm awfully relieved we had the concert last night. The attendance would have certainly been down with this weather," I said, joining the Rahns and Roger at the breakfast table. Alice had done herself proud. A variety of freshly baked muffins and scones was heaped on a large dish in the centre of the table. The Danish bacon was crisp, and the scrambled eggs were fluffy. I looked up at her as she filled my cup with coffee. "Good morning, Alice." I gestured to the buffet laid out before me. "This is wonderful!"

"Morning, Stella." She caught my eye. Smug is how I would describe her.

I helped myself to a cheese scone. It smelled delicious, and I took a bite. "You must have been up very early to bake these."

"Yes, I was. We had company."

"Company? What do you mean?"

"I heard someone outside, so I phoned the station. Old Bill came over, but he found nothing. He was frozen riding that bike, so I made him a cup of hot chocolate. By the time he left, it was daylight."

The bitterly cold weather deterred anyone from venturing out—except Joe, that is. I heard him talking to Alice in the hall around two in the afternoon. "You're a glutton for punishment coming out in weather like this," I called.

"Ah, but what's a poor lonely bachelor to do? This is where the only action is. The village has shut down."

We all congregated around the fireplace to read or indulge in light conversation. Justin played Broadway tunes on the piano for a while, lifting our stupor. My conscience was relieved, as Joe seemed relaxed, and conversed easily with Roger. We avoided each other's eyes, acutely aware of the emotional void we were about to face when he moved away. How easy it would have been to give in to him and move up north, but I wanted more. He later drove Elizabeth back to town, and the Rahns soon followed. Roger and Fiona stayed one more night. Although I saw little of them outside of their room, I was glad to have their company in the house.

The clock showed three fifteen. I had lain awake for hours after a hideous nightmare. My tormented thoughts conjured up grotesque, inhuman images that chased me through a dark forest. I got up to make a glass of warm milk. It took some control not to cower to the hovering shadows that seemed to be waiting for me on the way to the kitchen. I reached the kitchen door and, to my surprise, heard voices, one of which I recognised as Roger's. Although the second voice sounded familiar, I was unable to identify the man with him. Rather than disturb them, I hurriedly returned to my room. When I later questioned Roger at breakfast, he denied being anywhere other than tucked up in his warm bed, leaving me to wonder if I had been dreaming again.

CHAPTER ELEVEN

Joe stopped in at the rectory on his last morning. The parting was extremely painful. As he drove slowly away in his fully laden vehicle, it took all I had not to run after him and beg him to stay. We telephoned each other regularly at the beginning; then, gradually, more and more time elapsed between the calls. He was not only making improvements to the ranch, but also getting word out about its new improved stud services. I never doubted he would make the venture a great success. At first I wanted to be a part of it, promising to visit just as soon as he was settled. I missed him terribly. When I learned he was waiting impatiently for a couple of mares to give birth, I could barely stop myself from flying up to Cumberland on the next available flight. It was everyday life that held me back, and opportunities passed without me following through. I told myself it was not the right time. Of course, I knew there would never be a right time. With my increasing commitments in Clipton, diminishing efforts to keep in touch gradually stopped altogether.

Occasionally, John Gailbrath's path crossed mine, and we exchanged polite small talk. He continued to avoid my questions concerning the lack of progress in his police work, and gave his usual glib answer: "Our enquiries continue; you can be assured of that, Stella. Sometimes these things take a while."

"Our killer has been on the loose for well over a year. I thought New Scotland Yard knew all kinds of tricks of the trade. Isn't it time you used a few of them, John?"

"I'm trying, really . . . in spite of what you might think." I found his grin most annoying.

Reg picked me up from the train station and dropped me off at Main Street. I was feeling restless after a quick visit to London to spend a few days with my family, and decided to walk back to the rectory. My parents were now at that time in their lives when many daily responsibilities were becoming cumbersome, and I tried to delicately approach the subject of assisted living. I could afford excellent arrangements for them, but wanting to keep their independence was not something I could fault them on. I am their only child and got a double dose of that trait. Tim and Julia promised to keep an eye on their maternal grandparents, and would immediately report to me should the situation deteriorate, however slightly.

I tucked my handbag under my arm and set out with a brisk step. The tree-lined street looked particularly lovely with intermittent planters of spring flowers strategically placed along the pavements. I gave in to the urge to stop at the garden nursery. The variety of plants was impossible to resist, and I joined others enjoying the show as they strolled unhurriedly between the aisles.

"Stella?" Simon Belsky was walking towards me, a warm smile on his tanned face. "I thought it was you. Long time no see."

"Hello, Simon. How are you?" I liked his easy presence. "What are you doing back in Clipton?"

"Actually, I've been here a couple of months. Been researching for a renovation project for a few of my students, and decided on an old slaughterhouse at Tythe Farm. It was right under my nose." His face lit up with enthusiasm. "It's a wonderful place, at least hundred and fifty years old. My sister and her husband . . . you may remember, the McKinleys . . . own the property—it took some convincing to get them to agree to my proposal." He made a face. "Apparently, something bad happened over there quite some time ago. They wanted to bulldoze it and let the pasture take over. The police have stopped that for the time being. You likely know all about the incident?"

"Yes." I did not elaborate. "Are your students with you?"

"No. They are waiting in York and getting as frustrated as I am. The police are reluctant to release the building and surrounding area until their enquiries are completed. Goodness knows when that will be, although they assure me it will be soon."

"Actually, *the something bad*, as you put it, was murder. We've had three in the village—one being in the slaughterhouse. It was a fearful time. The police have still not made any arrests—and most of us have become complacent about there being any accountability for the crimes."

"I'd heard comments about what went on, but haven't been involved other than listening to speculations. It must have been a terrible time for everyone." He looked at me questioningly. "They were people you knew?"

"Yes, close friends, actually." Too many execrable memories began awakening. I suddenly thought of Joe, and a pang of loneliness enveloped me. If I could have persuaded myself to go back to the farm after finding Sir Ralph's body there, Joe would still have been in Clipton. I needed to change the subject. "I thought you were related to the McKinleys. You had never said exactly how." I was surprised at my ignorance. "I haven't noticed a resemblance or your sister's Canadian accent. I didn't notice yours, until you pointed it out."

He laughed lightly. "To hear the accent, you have to hear me speak. We've not had very much to say to each other up till now." He paused. "Perhaps you'll give me the grand tour of the rectory grounds one of these days, now you've finished the work."

"Of course, any time." I smiled flirtatiously. "Just give me a call beforehand. I may have to return to London unexpectedly." I watched him walk away and then impulsively called out, "Perhaps we'll have a chance to talk over lunch." He nodded and waved.

I let myself into the rectory and leaned back against the closed door. So, Simon Belsky was going to continue what Joe and I had started. I tried to clear my thoughts and concentrate on Simon Belsky's good looks. It was a boost to my somewhat deflated ego that he had stopped to say hello. Alice had the day off, and I enjoyed having the kitchen to myself. I listened to the BBC's *Top of the Form* on the radio as I prepared a bean salad for dinner.

The quiz show had competing secondary school teams, and I was aghast at my inability to answer the most fundamental questions.

Beverly and I met at the Main Street Café. We hadn't had an opportunity to spend time together for a while. Robert had taken her and the children to London with him. While he worked at the office, they enjoyed museums and parks, and generally played tourists. By her account, it had been a wonderful three weeks. We caught up on small talk, and then got around to Simon Belsky, and his plans to excavate the slaughterhouse.

"I can't understand why everyone's so fascinated by that dreadful place."

"The slaughterhouse will be a good project for Simon's students. He's trying to get things organised, but keeps running into a lot of red tape because of police restrictions. Said his students were frustrated with all the waiting. I should think they are. Apparently, Cynthia and Michael initially wanted to destroy the building because of the murder."

"I agree with the McKinleys. The whole area should be razed, if you ask me." Beverly added another dollop of cream to her scone.

"Well, I didn't ask you! They bought the farm from Joe with full knowledge of Sir Ralph's death, so they must have thought it a good investment to go ahead with the transaction. I am rather puzzled why Simon should be interested in it, though. There must be plenty of sites in and around ancient York that would be excellent projects for his students to research."

"Where's he from?"

"York University."

"No, I mean originally?"

"Canada. Your mind is going, I've told you before. Cynthia's lost her accent. He still has a slight one."

"York is such a lovely city. Robert and I had romantic weekends there before the children came. Actually, Robbie was the result of one of those delicious weekends." I looked at my friend. She had gained a few extra pounds, and her face showed a particular kind of contentment. She was more relaxed than I had seen her in some time.

"You're not trying to tell me something, are you?"

"I am actually, darling Stella! Robert and I are having another baby, and we didn't even get close to York."

"Beverly Petersen, I am thrilled!" I got up from my seat and threw my arms around her. "It's about time we had some joyful news to celebrate."

Simon phoned a few days later, and I invited him to come for lunch the following week. Alice did me proud with an herb soufflé that was so light it practically floated. We took coffee on the terrace and were quiet for a few moments, taking in the surrounding beauty.

"You are very lucky having this place, Stella. Thanks for showing me around. I envy you. You've not only made a wonderful home for yourself but added a fine estate to the community."

"Believe me, I am truly aware of my blessings. Not a day goes by without me giving thanks." I told him how I had come across the rector, and the challenges it had presented to bring it back to life. "I can't imagine living anywhere else, now. What about you? Do you have a house in York?"

"As a matter of fact, I do. It's a small cottage that I gutted and then built on to the back. Driving passed, one would think it a typical yokel's simple cabin, but it sits on an acre of sloping timbered land. I extended the house by building into the slope, so it looks rather like a wedge from the side. I have three bedrooms and two baths, a large kitchen, and plenty of space for visitors to relax in. One of my students even put up a swing in one of the trees. Like you, I had a project that was a labour of love."

"I assume you did the drawings yourself. After all, you are an architect, right?"

"Absolutely! It is completely my work. Fortunately, I have good friends in the building business, and again, like you, have a handcrafted structure. I'd like you to see it sometime. Will you come?"

"Oh, that would be lovely. Of course, I couldn't possibly get away just now. There's still so much going on with the renovations in the village."

"Well, I don't intend selling any time soon, and I'll be on the slaughterhouse project for a considerable time. You'll be welcome whenever we're both free." He stretched his long legs. "I must be getting back. I've enjoyed spending time with you, Stella. I hope to do it again."

"Simon, why the slaughterhouse? I mean, there must be many opportunities for your students in their own area, surely?" I had to ask.

"Of course, but this is not an overwhelming or sophisticated project for them. It's reasonable in size, and by the looks of it, someone has already contributed towards its salvation. The kids will see quick results from their efforts. This is a beginning for them; they are very young and eager. I don't want to squelch their enthusiasm—not now, anyway. Larger, more complicated projects will take months before they feel an iota of satisfaction; those are far in the future." He gave one of those half smiles that jump-started my heart.

"I'm sure you will all have a blast! By the way, the previous owner of Tythe Farm, Joe Blake, and I were the earlier contributors. We did quite well except for the slate floor. We were just beginning to tackle it when Sir Ralph was murdered there. We lost interest after that, and Joe sold the farm to your sister and brother-in-law."

"So, you were the culprits? You did a good job. Where's Joe now? Perhaps he'll give me a hand to finish where you left off."

"Joe's in Cumberland . . . owns a stud ranch now. If he was still here, I think he'd take you up on that invitation. He thoroughly enjoyed the challenge." I meant it. "We did quite well restoring the building—you know, the walls, roof, and so on—and were starting to tackle the slate floor before we quit."

"That's when the murder took place?"

"Yes."

"Well, I don't blame you. I think I'll keep that piece of information from my students. It's not something they need to know." He looked at his watch and got up from the chair. "I must be going. Thanks for lunch, Stella. I'll be seeing you . . . soon, I hope."

The phone rang and rang. I was not in the best of humour, having slept badly again the previous night. "Alice? The phone!"

"I'm coming as fast as I can. Couldn't you get it for once?" She picked up the receiver and announced, "The rectory." She paused. "I'm not sure Mrs Campbell is here just now. Hold on a moment, please." She put her hand over the mouthpiece. "It's the inspector . . . wants to come over, if you're available. What do you want me to say?"

"No peace for the wicked . . . he can come later this afternoon. I need to go to the bank now."

"Inspector, how about four o'clock? Yes, yes . . . she is here but busy at the moment. All right, I'll tell her." She replaced the receiver. "He said it is very important he sees you today, and will be here exactly at four."

"I'll be back in plenty of time."

Reg drove me to the bank, and I made my way to the manager's office, where Walter Pearce was waiting for me.

"Thanks for coming at such short notice, Stella. Do sit down. I've some rather distressing news, I'm afraid." I sat in the chair offered in front of his impressive Chippendale desk—a copy, but all the same, most impressive. "Can I get you a cup of coffee—anything?"

"Walter, never mind the niceties, just tell me what's wrong. You sounded positively mysterious on the telephone."

"You're right. I'll come straight out with it! You are short £270,000!" His face was moist. "Much of the money you advanced to the Building Society's trust was repaid to you with bad cheques."

The words just didn't register. "I don't understand. I loaned that money to prevent delays in completing the renovation projects. I received reimbursements on a regular basis. You know that because you set the account up for automatic deposits. Walter, you have to be wrong. I mean . . . it's been several years since all this started. How has it only come to light now?"

"Everything was copasetic to begin with. The reimbursements came in regularly and were deposited without any problems. It has only been during the last year things haven't gone accordingly. Because each cheque was for several thousands of pounds, it took ten to twelve working days to clear. By the time it was discovered there were insufficient funds and the Building Society was notified, more time had passed. A new cheque was issued from the trust account—with profound apologies, I might add—but the replacement cheque bounced just as high."

"There has to be enough money, Walter! Gifts were received in all forms—securities, life insurances, real estate, and so on, as well as very generous monetary donations. I mean we're talking about a couple of million pounds. The money is there, I'm certain. Roger Spencer organised and ran the fundraisers. I was staggered by how successful he was. His campaign slogan was all about guaranteeing a future for Clipton's historic past, and emphasising the tax benefits for donors."

"There may have been money at one time, but the trustees are holding a special meeting this afternoon to find out where it has disappeared to. I'm sorry, Stella. Someone's been cooking the books, as they say, and the beneficiary, the renovation work, is the casualty. In other words, practically all the work that has been done on the school thus far has been done on credit or with your money."

"There has to be some mistake," I insisted.

"That was my initial reaction, too. Unfortunately, there is no mistake. Ted Nyby and I warned you not to co-mingle your money with the trust's. There was something not quite right from the beginning, but Stella Campbell couldn't—wouldn't—listen to sound sense from her friends, no matter how hard they tried."

"I don't need a lecture, Walter, not now. Who discovered the discrepancies and when? Why wasn't I informed at the beginning?"

"I should have done so earlier, but I wanted to do my own investigation before coming to you. It seems just as questions concerning the reimbursement transactions were being asked, we had a change of staff. Dennis McGraugh was the financial officer on the account from its inception, then he up and left the bank suddenly, saying his mother in Cornwall was terminally ill, and in need of his care. His supervisor believed him—that is, until he started to review McGraugh's bookkeeping. McGraugh, it seems, might have been the inside man."

I heard what my faithful friend was saying, yet I could not accept the words. "We must talk with Roger Spencer. He'll soon clear this mess up." I leaned across the desk for the telephone.

"That seems the logical thing to do, of course, but the police are involved. That Detective Chief Inspector Gailbrath insists on doing the contacting on our behalf. I think he is right, Stella. Let him proceed with his enquiries—let him do his job." Walter Pearce was an attractive man in his sixties who kept in shape by running several miles each morning. His demeanour acutely expressed his distress as he absentmindedly toyed with a paperclip, carelessly bending and twisting it into tormented shapes.

"Walter, I don't hold you responsible for a moment. Please don't blame yourself. It will work out. You have looked after my finances and looked out for me as a friend since I came to Clipton. Of course there is one question I simply must ask. Am I still financially solvent?"

"Yes, thank goodness! You still have plenty of money, my dear. Your investment portfolio has worked well for you." He leaned forward to take my hand. "You are quite right; we are friends, Stella, and friends are supposed to look out for each other. I have let you down, my dear. I will make it up to you, you have my word." We exchanged a nod of understanding.

"Yes, you will—and you can start off by getting that cup of coffee now," I demanded, smiling. I was pleased to see his shoulders relax.

Reg drove me back to the rectory while I reflected on my meeting with Walter. I now knew why Inspector Gailbrath was eager to meet with me. I looked forward to seeing him but acknowledged that, if his murder investigations were anything to go on, we had little hope of a speedy resolution of the trust problems. Alice led him into the drawing room precisely at four.

"It's good to see you again, Stella."

"Really, John? It seems I've given you more work to do."

His face lit up with a grin. "Oh, I don't mind that—another reason to see you."

Such a response was unexpected, but very pleasing. "So you're looking into my finances now? I hope you get to the bottom of what's happened before I go broke. I've still got financial security that will take care of my own needs; however, my responsibilities are very high so I'm at risk."

He nodded, his face suddenly serious. "I know you have little confidence in my ability to solve murders, but let me assure you, I will investigate the trust embezzlement very thoroughly. I don't give up, even when the trail has gone cold. I'm very methodical . . . I suppose *you* would say slow; however, I have a record that proves I get my man in the end. Have faith in me, Stella." He brought out his writing pad from his briefcase. "You know the procedure by now."

"Ask away."

His questions were precise concerning my relationship with Roger Spencer: how we had met, how well I knew him. "I feel Roger and I have a good friendship. I have no reason to believe he would cheat me in any way."

John meticulously wrote everything down in his notebook. At last, he closed it with a snap and put it back into his briefcase. "Thanks, Stella. I know you've had enough of my third degrees, but your answers are important to the investigation."

"Well, I'm glad it's over." I rang the bell for Alice.

"You want tea?"

"Please, Alice. We'll have some of those Cadbury chocolate wafer things. I seem to remember you like those, John. Yes?"

"I do indeed."

Alice winked at the inspector. "I made sure we had some if you came. When Stella gets her hands on them, they disappear like magic. I'll only be a jiffy."

I laughed. "I detect a little soft spot for you, John. You must have made an impression, because she isn't easily taken in."

"No, it's nothing like that; it's just she knows we both want the best for you." He looked serious, and I felt self-conscious under his gaze.

"Any progress on the murder investigation?" I asked, changing the subject quickly. "Surely you must have by now?"

"I'm not talking to you about it, so you may as well change the subject again."

We enjoyed our tea, chocolate wafers, and small talk together, and then he left. I found myself liking him more than I wanted.

I was just exiting the library when I saw Roger Spencer talking very intently to Margot Hughes Young. He had his car door open, and appeared to be insisting she get in. I took time putting my books into the basket on the front of my bicycle, hoping to eavesdrop; alas, they were too far away. Margot called out as she hurriedly walked towards me, "Leave me alone, Roger!" He responded by getting into the car and driving off at high speed.

"Good morning, Margot," I said pleasantly. She looked at me without responding. "Margot? Is everything all right?"

"Yes . . . yes! Everything is just perfect!" She crossed the road, oblivious of oncoming traffic. Fortunately, there was very little; all the same, some explicit words were sent her way by one infuriated braking driver.

"What's up with Margot? She's fit to be tied!" Fiona, looking as fresh and lovely as ever in a form-fitting navy suit and white blouse, caught up with me wheeling my bicycle along the pavement.

"I haven't any idea. You'd likely know better than I, Fiona. She was talking with Roger."

"Why would you say that, Stella? Roger and I are friends . . . well, maybe more than that, but I'm not his keeper.

Actually, I don't see that much of him—not during the week, anyway." She looked me straight in the eye, challenging.

"I thought you were seriously involved, Fiona. You come as a couple whenever you stay at the rectory. What else would I think? Anyway, it's really none of my business."

"You're right, it isn't." She caught herself and added, "I'm sorry, that was rude of me. It's just I don't like people speculating about me." I got onto my bicycle, making ready to ride off when she caught my arm. "Stella, things are not always what they seem." She stepped back to let me pass. "Take care of yourself."

"Is that a warning?"

"Not at all." I thought she looked a little downcast as I pedaled away.

"Roger, I must see you. You know that. You can't go on avoiding me indefinitely." His secretary had heeded my threat and put me through to his office. He would rebuke her later, I felt certain.

"Stella! I'm extremely busy, that's all. You've got it all wrong. I'm not avoiding you." I was not convinced.

"Then why haven't you returned any of my calls? I'm not giving up until you account for what's been going on. Walter told me the board of trustees met last week. What do you have to say?"

"I just don't have any explanation to give."

"You must have known I wasn't getting my advances reimbursed—you had to." There was silence at the other end of the line. "Roger, say something! I'm totally appalled you continued to accept funds from me knowing I was being duped." My frustration increased. "At the very least, you owe me an explanation, Roger."

"Stella, we are still looking into the situation. As soon as I know anything, of course I'll let you know. There really isn't anything to tell you just now."

"Losing thousands of pounds gives me the right to an explanation! You're mistaken if you think you can avoid me, because I shall keep pushing until I get one." I was practically shouting through the telephone. "I have my good name at risk. If there is anything amiss, I do not intend to be implicated in any way. It may be my money that is missing, but people have the habit of tarring everyone with the same brush."

"We'll try to keep you out of it, Stella. It's regretful the police are involved, because we would have had our own investigation and avoided all the publicity and speculation. Once we know the depth of the situation, we will act accordingly. You have my word on that, Stella." The line went dead.

CHAPTER TWELVE

Roger and I did not speak again, but I saw him at the gymkhana a couple of weeks later. I had been looking forward to the event for months, having taken riding lessons so as to enter in my first equestrian competition. Two fields of open land on the outskirts of Clipton were abuzz with activity. Several large tents were set up. Streamers and red and yellow pennants flapped playfully atop the largest tent of all. It was there caterers were setting up in advance of the delicious menu Beverly had created. Horse trailers were being carefully unloaded at a prefabricated paddock filled with fresh hay and troughs of clean water. Men, women, and youngsters dressed in formal riding attire were strolling among an increasing number of spectators. Ominous dark clouds were gathering on the horizon, and I begged silently for the rain to hold off. Reg had taken my mount Butterfly to the paddock, and was rubbing her down with the help of his two sons, Ben and Teddy. The boys were staying with their father while on school holiday, and seemed not to want to leave his side. Butterfly was a beautiful two-year-old chestnut filly that made me look good, in spite of my misgivings about being a horsewoman. Her mane had been braided and her tail clipped. Beverly had ribbed me mercilessly about taking up riding—said I was subconsciously preparing myself for a trip to see Joe at his stud farm. She was quite wrong. Joe was no longer a part of my life, although at unexpected moments I missed him.

"Here she is, looking the epitome of an Olympic champion." Beverly and Robert joined me at the show clerk's table where I was completing the entrance paperwork and liability release forms.

"Now you're all signed up and ready to show us what you're made of." Bev teased.

"I'm scared stiff," I confessed. "I should have more sense than getting myself into this. I'm no horsewoman. I'm being ridiculous!"

"You will do just fine, Stella. When you put your mind to anything, you always come out on top." Robert encouraged me, but my confidence did not improve.

I turned to see Fiona and Roger talking to a rider behind me. The announcement came over the speaker system that riders were to return to their mounts, and wait for their names to be called. I was grateful I had entered only in the dressage competition, which was the first item on the agenda. When I reached the paddock, Reg pinned the number 6 onto the back of my jacket.

"A good number, Mrs Campbell. It will soon be over."

"Thank goodness, Reg. I've never been so nervous." His sons seemed to appreciate hearing my declaration as they turned away in a fit of giggling.

Butterfly and I had practised diligently for months at Clipton's equestrian centre, eventually reaching a reasonable standard of ease and grace, which was what dressage was all about. We needed to demonstrate different paces and speeds, while going in both circles and straight lines, all with fluid movements. We hadn't practised enough to manage sidesteps smoothly, and this was our weakness; it could be our downfall—literally. I heard the determined chatter of the riders around me, and became even more jittery.

"Good morning, Stella." It was Simon Belsky. He held out a single white carnation. "I got you this for luck."

"Thank you, Simon—how thoughtful. I need all the luck I can get. I don't know what's happened to me. I've become a bowl of jelly." I sniffed in the spicy fragrance. "This is lovely." I broke the stem and pulled the bloom through my lapel buttonhole. "Thanks so much, Simon."

"You're welcome. I didn't think anything made you nervous, Stella Steelpants!"

"Then Stella Steelpants has you hoodwinked!" We laughed, comfortable together, and when my name was called, he reached up and squeezed my hand. "Good luck."

Butterfly felt composed under me. She seemed to know what was expected of her before I gave any command, and her performance was confident and on course. She eased her way into each move with only the slightest pressure from my heel against her flank and, to my delight and pride, even managed to stride sideways with elegance. It was over too quickly, and to my surprise I regretted Joe Blake was not present to witness our performance.

I rode Butterfly back to the paddock to find Reg and his sons waiting with big grins on their round faces. "Well done, Mrs Campbell. Your timing was right on." Reg took the reins, and his eldest son, Teddy, helped me down.

"I can't believe I did it, Reg—well, it was Butterfly, of course. I just went along for the ride." I was feeling particularly pleased with myself. "Give her a good rub down and some oats, Reg, then make sure you and the boys get some lunch. Mrs Petersen has set up quite a fare." I reached into my jodhpur pocket and took out a couple of five-pound notes. Handing one each to Ben and Teddy, I thanked them for their help. "Go and enjoy yourselves—I'll see you later."

"Thank you, Mrs Campbell!" They looked at Reg. "Can we go, Dad?"

"Okay. Don't wander far, though." He watched them walk away chattering excitedly.

"You've good kids, Reg."

"I know it, Mrs Campbell."

I wandered around the arena, watching the other competitors. One rider made a false start and had to begin again, giving me a heads-up on time. Other events were in full swing: youngsters racing long-tailed ponies to a distant marker, and border collies working small groups of sheep in accordance to the shrill whistle commands of their masters. It all seemed perfect. I was getting congratulations and accolades from both friends and townsfolk as I strolled around, but Joe continued to slip into my mind. It was his praise I wanted to hear, and the acknowledgment caught me off guard. My spirit was somewhat diminished when I entered the refreshment tent.

"Wow there, missy, there's still plenty left to eat."

I had walked straight into John Gailbrath. "I'm pleased to hear it. I'm starving."

"You looked a bit glum coming in . . . is something wrong?" He wasn't a detective for nothing. Taking my arm, he led me to a quiet corner where a couple of children were gulping down glasses of lemonade. "You can talk to me about anything. Trust me."

"Thanks for your concern, John. Really, I'm actually feeling pretty good." I smiled. "I think I did quite well after watching my competition. None of us are quite ready for the Olympics, it seems."

"Well, if that's the case, will you have dinner with me this evening? I know you're tired so we can make it early. What do you say?"

"I don't know what to say! You've taken me by surprise." The last thing I wanted just then was to be across a dining table making small talk with someone I hardly knew, even if I found him most attractive. I looked into his eyes and saw only goodwill. "All right, but I can tell you now I won't be much company. I'm really dog tired."

"I'll take my chances. Don't dress up; my wages can only cover a hamburger and chips. I know you're not a meat eater, so you can guide us where to go with that in mind."

"How do you know I don't eat meat? I've never mentioned it to you before."

"Oh, you'd be surprised what I know." His face lit up, and I found him irresistible.

He picked me up a little after seven. As directed, I wore casual jeans and a sweater. I was totally whacked after driving the horse trailer to drop Butterfly off at the stables late that afternoon, but extremely proud of the third-place ribbon we had won. James, the owner of the equestrian centre, added it to the impressive display of other ribbons in the office. By the time I had bathed and dressed, I had more energy, and was pleased I had agreed to see John after all.

"It'll do you both good to have time out from all that's being going on. The inspector is such a nice gentleman, Stella—so good looking." Alice's tone was full of kindness. "You'll have to reciprocate, you know . . . invite him to dinner here, perhaps?"

"Don't get carried away, Alice. We're just going to the local for a beer and cheese sandwich. He said my choice, and that's it. I don't think we have to play my turn–your turn."

I was tightening a scarf to hold my hair back just as Alice let him in. "Good evening, John . . . thought we'd go to the Boar's Head, if that's okay with you? Then we can call it an early night. I'm sure you must be just as eager to get into bed as I am." I heard a muffled laugh from Alice, and she left the room rather quickly, her hand over her mouth. "What on earth got into her?" I looked at John. He was also holding back laughter. "You, too? What is it?"

"We're just being silly, Stella. It's nothing. I think we had better be on our way if we are to get to bed early."

"Oh!" I blushed with embarrassment. "You knew exactly what I meant."

"Of course." His face was serious, but I could see it took a lot of control. "I'm looking forward to this evening," he said, helping me into my jacket.

"You are?"

"Yes, I'm starving."

The pub was busier than usual because of the gymkhana. We were lucky to find a small table in the corner of the saloon. John looked most attractive; he was wearing jeans with a blue sweater over a white shirt. From the way he kept glancing in my direction, I guessed he was having similar thoughts about me. We gave our order and began a rather stilted conversation. Our simple meal was tasty, and finished nicely with a pint of local cider. The noise level in the room was very high, and we found our energy waning under the effort of keeping our voices audible. By the time our empty dishes were replaced with coffee, we had given in. It was then I heard several familiar voices behind me. I turned away, trying to be discrete. John was one step ahead of me. "Looks like several members of the Building Society are celebrating with Mrs Hughes Young and Roger Spencer. Oh, there's Fiona. Quite a gathering, eh?"

"I hope they're not spending my money! I'm still waiting for an explanation from Roger. My banker is losing sleep over what's happened. Have you any news?"

"I know you're fed up with hearing me say the same thing, but it is true, Stella: I'm making my enquiries, and they are confidential. There is a lot at stake here, and I can't jeopardise making my case. You'll know soon enough." He looked so serious, I believed him.

"I won't pester you about it again, I promise."

"Oh, don't stop pestering me, please. I rather like it—just not about this investigation. I'll get you your money back; that I will say."

I couldn't help myself; I reached over and touched his arm. "I do have one final question, and then I'll keep my word. Are the murders and the missing money connected?"

His smile disappeared. "I think they are. I just have to prove it. In the meantime, I want you to make me another promise—that you will be cautious about who you spend time with. You are a popular woman involved with many people and causes in the community. You are connected to the three murdered men, and it is your money that has gone missing. I'm serious, Stella. Promise me."

"If I was in danger, there were many opportunities to harm me. Look, I'm here, all safe and sound." A small shiver ran down my spine, in spite of my outward bravado.

"Promise me, Stella!"

"Oh, all right. If it means that much to you, I promise."

"Thank you. It means that much to me."

We drove back to the rectory in silence. Alice had left the sitting-room lights on. The glow through the tall windows flooded the driveway. John did not come in, but helped me out of the car and walked me to the front door.

"Thank you for an interesting evening, John." I reached up to kiss him on both cheeks; before I could follow through, I felt his warm lips on my own. Suddenly, I was kissing him back. Slightly embarrassed, we drew apart. He touched my shoulder and then was gone, leaving me feeling dumbfounded.

I worked at my desk all morning, paying bills, sorting through a pile of mail, and working on a bid requested by Vicar Ken. The church now had a healthy budget with which to do much-needed landscaping around the preschool building, and to build a new playground. Although I had professionally designed only two, children's playgrounds were something I had focused on as part of my thesis. I paid a lot of attention to ensure a kinetic experience. The height of the equipment allowed for different sized youngsters, and various textures under foot included soft grass and multi-sized stones set in concrete. I incorporated ropes, chain ladders, and thick nets to climb, as well as the conventional slides and playhouses. The building materials needed to be strong, and not hold the heat from a summer day . . . brightly coloured, too. I spent numerous hours working everything out, and thought my proposal very fair.

It was good to have my mind occupied with matters other than the pleasure of John Gailbrath's lips on mine a week earlier. I also thought over carefully, not only what he had said during dinner that evening, but what he had insinuated. Was he in agreement with Joe's view that someone had wanted me at Tythe Farm alone, and that Sir Ralph had foiled that plan? That thinking didn't seem plausible . . . I was available to meet with anyone at any time. If someone really wanted my blood, they had every opportunity. John was on the wrong track; he had to be. I was an unremarkable woman who was most certainly no threat to anyone. Nothing made sense. My dog, Camrose, was totally innocent . . . why her? And how was Miller involved? He was campaigning for clean water, and his energy was directed against Euston Industries.

Then Steven . . . what harm had he done to anyone? My head began to ache with so many questions. We had a merciless, sick person at large, someone who thought nothing of harming man or beast whenever the opportunity presented itself. The murders were certainly not connected, and had nothing whatsoever to do with my missing money. That was my conclusion . . . I felt only a little better for it.

I had the bid ready for the church, and made myself a copy before joining Alice for lunch. When it was just the two of us, we often ate together in the kitchen, cementing our relationship even more. She had been looking a little strained lately, and I knew it was because John had asked her to keep an eye on me and those who came to the house.

"Please don't fret over me, Alice. I'm not stupid, in spite of what you think. I have many things I want to do in my life. I'll not do anything to jeopardise that," I tried to reassure her.

"You don't understand. You're more like the daughter I never had. I know I step out of line at times, but I always have your best interest in mind. I love you, Stella."

"Oh, Alice. I love you, you old goat! You know that! I don't know what I'd do without you. I rely on you for so much . . . you keep me in line, help me keep focused when my thoughts and behaviour become chaotic—even tell me what to wear, who to invite here, and when to wipe my nose." I put my face close to hers so she could see I was joking. She put her cheek against mine. "We're going to get through this, my dear. John is going to get to the bottom of what's going on, and then we shall all live happily ever after. All right?"

"All right."

I loved my mother, but Alice was the one person with whom I could be completely honest. She knew me better than anyone, and that gave me solace.

"Any chance of some leftovers?" John Gailbrath was standing at the open patio doors. I don't know how long he had been there; his face gave nothing away.

"Come on in! We weren't very hungry, so there is a crust of bread on Alice's plate and a couple of slices of tomato on mine. Will that do you?" I was so happy to see him. He came into the kitchen and sat at the table, lightly touching Alice's shoulder as he passed.

"I've got a couple of things I need to talk to you both about, so I'm pleased to find you together. You can keep your crust and tomato. A cup of coffee would be very acceptable, however." He took the cup Alice handed him and leaned back comfortably in the chair. "It was quite some time ago, but I need you both to try to remember where everyone was when Steven Lagerquist was found upstairs. We've already established his wife, Elizabeth, was in the lounge when you and he came in from the garden, Stella. What about Fiona and Roger? Do you know if they spent the afternoon and early evening together, or just came into the room together?"

"I don't know. I just assumed they were together the whole time."

"I did see Mr Spencer earlier." Alice paused. "He was alone, walking around the garden. It must have been around four o'clock. He didn't take tea that afternoon. I remember distinctly because there were leftover pastries, and when he's around, that never happens. He eats everything sweet in sight."

John took out his notepad and jotted down a few abbreviated words—a kind of shorthand, I supposed.

"He was alone in the garden?" I became chilled. "Do you think he had anything to do with Camrose's beating?"

"What about Fiona? If he was alone, then likely she was," Alice concluded.

"I need to establish where the two were between lunch and when you saw them again after discovering the dog in the shed. My notes tell me Mr Lagerquist came in from the garden with you, Stella, and then went up to his room. Mrs Lagerquist remained talking with you, right?"

"Yes. Steven was almost as distraught as I was after finding Camrose, and said he needed to be alone—Elizabeth went up later to check on him because he was gone for quite some time." I was silent for a few moments, remembering. I heard once again Elizabeth's cry when she discovered her husband, recalled seeing her standing at the top of the stairs, holding her throat, and my own scream when I saw Steven's tortured face. "Steven was killed by the same acid as Sir Ralph, I assume?"

"He was strangled first. The acid was added after."

"That was such a long time ago—well over a year now. Impossible!" I felt anger rising, and I turned to him. "For crying out loud, you keep giving your glib answer that you are investigating. When are you going to end this? When can this nightmare be put behind us?"

He looked straight at me but directed his words to Alice, too. "I'm with New Scotland Yard in London, and have to go through a lot of inconvenience to commute to Clipton. This isn't my only case, and I oversee your local police. To say they are Mr Plods is putting it mildly. All the same, they know this village, the people in high places, and who rubs shoulders with whom. Clipton's Inspector Rice and his sergeant have been invaluable to my own enquiries. There is a lot going on behind the scenes that you aren't aware of, Stella, but I can assure you and Alice we continue undaunted." He sounded quite pompous. "We are getting close, but we have to be absolutely certain before we can make any official move. I've already told you, I believe the missing trust money is connected to the murders." He turned to Alice. "You said you heard a noise the night of the Rahn concert and called the constable over. What kind of noise was that, Alice? Do you remember the time I'm referring to?"

"Oh, yes. Footsteps—I could hear them crunching on the gravel path—and I'm pretty certain a woman's voice. I couldn't hear what was being said to the man with her. I looked out of the window but couldn't see anyone."

"What time would that have been?"

"It was four thirty. I know for sure because that's the time the sprinkler system was set for the perennial beds around the house.

Whoever was out there must have got a surprised soaking." Alice laughed. "Serves the blighters right!"

John continued to scribble his notes. "Did you notice any wet clothing in any of the rooms the next morning? It was a very cold night, right? You made the constable hot chocolate."

"Fancy you remembering that! I didn't notice anything out of the ordinary that morning. You're right though; it was a cold night. Bill was frozen by the time he got here on his bike. I shouldn't have called him, but I got nervous after all the terrible things that had been happening."

"You did the right thing, Alice," I assured her.

"Did the constable look for footprints in the planters, do you know?"

"No, he went straight back to the station." She grimaced. "Sorry, Inspector. I suppose he missed a good opportunity with the soil being wet. Is it too late to make a casting after all these months?"

"You know about castings, Alice?"

"It's all those mystery books she reads," I interjected.

"Well, I'll take a look around later, but it's a pretty slim chance anything has survived." John replaced the top onto his pen. I hoped that indicated his enquiry was concluded.

"John, is there anything else? I've got a riding lesson in half an hour. I can cancel, if necessary."

"No, don't do that! I'll give you a lift, if you like." His eyes warmed when he looked at me.

"Now that would be nice, eh? I'll clear this lot up and will be going out myself." Alice started gathering the dishes. John stood up and helped her stack them on a tray.

"I'll run up and change then. Thanks, John. I was going to ride my bike; a lift will be nice."

I sat in the car feeling a little awkward after our previous meeting. Then I felt his hand take mine. "You're growing on me, Stella Campbell. So much so that I'm prepared to wait for you while you take your lesson; then I can take you back to the rectory."

"There's really no need, John. I can walk back," I said stubbornly.

"If you are being your usual obstinate self, then I'll ignore that remark, but if you don't want me to, then that's a different matter. Which is it?"

"I'm scared, John. It's been a long time since I had any romance in my life. Too long, perhaps, because I don't know how to react. Give me some time, please. I'll not lead you on."

"I'm risking my career, you know. We're not supposed to fraternise with anyone involved in an investigation, and here I am wearing my heart on my sleeve over an intriguing woman who is up to her neck in my case. I'm scared too, Stella. I haven't felt this way about anyone in a long time, either." He put my hand to his lips. "I'll take the risk though, willingly."

We arrived at the equestrian centre and parked the car as James led his powerful chestnut, Buddy, and my Butterfly into the paddock. I looked up at John. "Please wait for me." I was aware of him watching me as I walked over to James.

"There's coffee in the tack room, Inspector," James called. "We'll be an hour, okay?"

"Thanks, James." John got out of the car and made his way over to the barn.

I was grateful I could lose myself in the lesson, and listened attentively to James as he encouraged me to feel more comfortable in the saddle. I had the ribbon from the gymkhana as a testament to my improvement, but a residue of nervousness still hung around. "Butterfly knows you a lot better than you know her, Stella. That has to change, or you'll destroy her confidence in you."

"I don't know what's holding me back, James."

"It'll happen, although better sooner than later. Keep up with your lessons. It'll come."

We rode at an easy pace along a wide path with open countryside around us. Rabbits bounded out of our way, dashing for cover in the tall grass sprinkled with wild red poppies. My view took in Tythe Farm nestled between hillocks about a mile in the distance. How peaceful it looked, without a hint of the violence committed there. Territorial thrushes fussing in the trees brought my attention back to Butterfly and the task at hand.

James and I were hot and dusty when we returned to the stables. We rubbed the two horses down, filled their troughs with fresh water, and fed them each a treat of my home-grown carrots. John was sitting patiently in the shade of a large oak when James and I joined him.

"Thanks for your patience, James. I am trying to do better."

"Relax, Stella. You're making progress. I'll see you on Tuesday at ten." James nodded to John and returned to the stables.

John walked up to me and put his arm around my shoulder. We walked back to the car without speaking. I looked out of the window, desperately trying to find something safe to talk about. The silence was getting to me. "I made an offer to James to buy Butterfly."

"You're a good match. I neglect Vanguard, my two-year-old Arabian stallion, shamefully. This job doesn't allow me time for passions."

"I didn't know you were a horseman. Actually, I don't know anything about you."

"Well then, that brings up the question: do you want to know?" His face was serious. "I want to know all you will allow me to know about you. Will you give me a chance?" He looked over at me, and our eyes met.

"Yes," I whispered.

He pulled the car over to the side of the road. I am happy to say we fogged up the windows with little delay.

Alice knew right away; I never could keep anything from her. The joy I felt in being in love again was contagious, and we both became engulfed in happiness, and floated around the rectory. When John returned to London, we talked on the phone every day. I found myself depending on hearing his voice. He sounded strong and confident, encouraging me to believe the amorous words we exchanged were real. I went to my meeting with Walter Pearce at the bank with energy in my step. When I walked into Walter's office I was surprised to see Roger Spencer sitting by the desk. He looked as if he'd lost weight.

"Stella." He stood up as I entered.

"Roger." I looked questioningly at Walter.

"Please sit down, the two of you. Stella, I asked Roger to be here because what he has to say applies to your situation with the Building Society. There is one other person who has lost money in this debacle. I'm not at liberty to divulge whom without that individual's consent. Although invited, that person declined to join us today." Walter sat back in his tan leather chair and pursed his lips while he contemplated his next move. He took a moment, and then leaned forward and looked directly at Roger. "I think we should begin with your explanation of what happened to Stella's money, Roger."

"Um, well, yes." Looking exceedingly uncomfortable, Roger straightened himself in his chair and cleared his throat. "I did not deposit all your cheques into the trust account, Stella, so the Building Society was unaware of the total loan amount you made." His voice was monotone. He kept his focus on the top of Walter's desk as he went on. "My own accounts were frozen. I was in a dangerous situation over a large gambling debt, and my debtors were out of patience. I was desperate and facing ruin. All I could think about was saving my hide . . . then you came along with your chequebook. I only had to ask, and you filled in the blanks so willingly. At first, I made the deposits into the trust account, and then made withdrawals under the deception contractors needed paying for working on the school project." His customary air of arrogance was gone.

"How could you, Roger?" I stared at him in disbelief. "You don't steal from friends. If you needed money, you could have come to me direct." I could see he was sweating.

"Dennis McGraugh, the trust's financial officer, became suspicious and began paying attention to the finer details. He caught me out and threatened to expose me. I told him the monies were just a loan, and I would reimburse the account within days. He just laughed, said he was anything but stupid." Roger grimaced with the memory. "I knew the game was up and asked what he wanted. He had me write a statement admitting I had embezzled from both the trust and you, Stella. It was his hold over me until I paid him £50,000."

"Fifty thousand? Where did you get that kind of money?"

"From you . . . again. Didn't bother depositing your cheques into the trust account anymore." He recoiled with shame. "I just signed them over to myself." Walter remained silent, pensive.

"So the mystery is solved." My tone was accusing. "The trust ledgers showed entries where I had advanced funds, but totalled only a fraction of the true amount." I felt a weight in the pit of my stomach. Roger had been a welcomed guest in my home, had gained my confidence over the years, and was someone I considered a friend. He had betrayed me without a second thought!

"Yes. Over a period of time, I deposited four of the cheques into the main account so they would show up on the books. Then I transferred the money by small increments to the escrow account, and made copies of some invoices we had already paid. By changing the invoice numbers and dates, I added a few bogus purchases to the existing items, and they gave me backup for the money I could pay out to myself. It looked like I was going to get myself out of the mess. All the interest and most of the principal on my debt were paid off." He smiled without humour. "Then McGraugh confronted me."

Walter raised his hand to prevent Roger from continuing. "There is a lot to adjust to, and a break would be in order at this point, if you are both in agreement? I think we could do with some fresh coffee, yes, Stella?" He rang for his secretary on the intercom. Roger looked relieved, but I wanted to go on, to get the whole ugly story out into the open, and said so. Walter nodded. "If you wish, my dear."

"I must excuse myself for a moment, and then I'll gladly go on. My bladder is at bursting point." Roger rose heavily from the chair and made his way to the door of the private bathroom adjacent to Walter's office. He turned back to me before entering. "I'm truly sorry, Stella. I intended to pay every penny back, I swear!" He closed the door quietly behind him.

"How are you holding up, Stella? It's a lot to take in."

"I would never have guessed this of Roger." I was overcome with disappointment. "We've gone through a lot together . . . getting the Building Society to back the renovation projects, and then the public forums and presentations to the planning commission. He was always there for me, urging me not to give up."

"Yes . . . well, he has some redeeming qualities, of course."

"I had genuine affection for him, Walter. When Miller Owens and Steven Lagerquist were murdered, he was a great comfort." Sadness swept over me. "The question is, what do we do now?"

"I should point out Roger means drug addiction when he refers to his gambling debt. He thinks it sounds less sordid. My other client wants to prosecute, wants to see Roger in prison. My advice right now, Stella, is to give yourself time for it all to sink in. Nothing needs to be done at this moment. I'm pleased Roger has talked with you at last."

"How long have you known Roger was the perpetrator, Walter?"

"He came to me yesterday and confessed. I believe his remorse to be genuine. What happens next is really up to you."

Roger came back into the office just as the secretary brought in the coffee tray. "Will there be anything else, Mr Pearce?"

"No, thank you, Vera, just continue to hold my calls."

I saw Beverly as I left the bank. A wave was all I could muster, and she continued on her way. She looked tired, I noticed. The pregnancy was going well, but she was not the type of person to sit all day with her feet up. I resolved that when I had myself together I would phone her and tell her all about John. That would be just the tonic to energise her! I returned to the rectory and went straight to my room and lay on the bed. Thoughts raced across my mind like cars in fifth gear, and quickly gave me a headache.

I was eager to talk to John that evening to find out what he knew about Roger. He usually phoned around seven. I got up and paced around the room. How could Roger have betrayed me like that? Who was the other person he had stolen money from? I wanted answers.

"Stella, do you want your tea in your room?" Alice called up the stairs.

Four o'clock already. "No, Alice. I'll come down." I went into the bathroom and freshened up. The woman staring at me from the mirror had deep furrows on her forehead. I stared back, uncertain . . . uncertain about everything.

I picked up the phone on the first ring. "John?"

"Hey, sweetie, you sound tense. Is something wrong?"

"I had a meeting today with my banker and Roger Spencer." I relayed every detail without giving him a chance to interrupt. "I understand you can't talk about your investigations, but at least reassure me you're on top of things. I need to know . . . I need to feel I've someone on my side." My level of anxiety was increasing. "The ground is slipping from under my feet."

"Stella, give yourself a moment to calm down. I know this news has shaken you—would shake up anyone. You've lost money, yes, and I can assure you that will eventually be recovered. I do know about Spencer. I don't want to talk about anything on the phone. We'll go over it all when I see you this weekend." His voice softened. "In the meantime, as I've asked you before, stay around the house or have Alice go with you if you go into the village. I don't want you to be alone, okay?"

"Please don't worry about me." I paused, afraid to go out on a limb, but the words tumbled out before I could stop them. "John . . . I've missed you so. I wanted you here when I got back from the meeting . . . just to have you close. The weekend seems so far away." Thankfully, I stopped before I voiced the ultimate confession. I loved him.

"I've missed you. Only three more days, and then we'll be together. Stella, you didn't answer me about taking care. I want your promise."

"I promise," I sulked.

"That's my girl. When this is all over—well, let's just say I'm looking forward to us spending a lot of time together. Goodnight, Stella. See you Friday evening, and then we'll have the whole weekend."

"Sleep well, John." I hung up the phone, feeling alone and utterly wiped out.

That evening, Alice and I watched television. I do not remember the programme, but she laughed a lot at the comedians' antics. I had another restless night, finding it difficult to unwind. There were decisions to be made. James needed to know if I was buying Butterfly, bills remained to be paid, and I really should call on Beverly. The mental to-do list seemed endless and added to my mounting agitation. Top priority was to arrange a meeting with Walter during the next week. I thought about John and how happy I would be to see him. Soon, I told myself—only a couple of days more.

CHAPTER THIRTEEN

I watched the car come to a stop in front of the rectory. John got out and grabbed a bouquet of pastel-coloured flowers from the back seat. I swung the door wide and ran to greet him. He held me tight; we kissed passionately, in spite of Alice looking out from the drawing-room window. Her face was alight with pleasure when we entered the house.

"Let me take the flowers and put them in some water." She pressed her nose into the bouquet, breathing in deeply. "My, they are lovely, Inspector. I'll put them on the dining table for the time being. You can enjoy them while you eat." She trotted away to the kitchen, grinning from ear to ear.

"You know, that is one special woman," John said. "I think she approves of me."

"She is very happy for us, John. Wait until you see the meal she's prepared. It's taken her all afternoon." I stopped and faced him. "I am so pleased you're here."

"Me too. After we've eaten, though, we need to talk about what's been going on in Clipton. It's about time I levelled with you, Stella." He looked grave. Seeing my concern, he took hold of my arm and led me in to dinner.

We talked little, content to be in each other's company. John ate with gusto—the perfect *thank you* to Alice, who discretely disappeared once she had placed the food on the table. The ease between us soothed me. I snatched glances at the man who seemed oblivious to anything beyond his plate. I like men who enjoy their food, unlike Geoff who picked at everything. I do not think I saw him eat a complete meal during the entire time we were together. It's funny how Geoff pops into my mind when I least expect it.

"Why don't we take our coffee into the garden? It's such a lovely evening."

"Good idea." John placed the coffee pot, cups, and saucers on the tray and followed me out to the patio.

"You're getting domesticated, Inspector!"

Remnants of the day's heat remained. I took off my sandals to take advantage of the warmth in the patio flagstones. John put his feet up on the chaise and removed his tie. "Umm, this is the life." He reached over and took my hand. I loved the way he kissed each individual finger. I wanted to purr like a spoilt cat. We didn't talk; we didn't need to, and I found the silence relaxing. After a while, I noticed he had fallen asleep, and I, too, allowed myself to drift off. It was dark when I awoke and looked up at John bending over me.

"Time to go in, I think."

"I can't believe I fell asleep." I stretched lazily. "Must be the calming effect you have on me, Mr Policeman." I smiled coyly.

"We haven't talked about it, but where do I sleep tonight? I hope not on the sofa!"

"No, not on the sofa."

We came together that night with a passion I never knew with Geoff. I held back at first, self-conscious and shy, but John's insistent touch awakened those parts of me that had lain dormant, and my electrified body shuddered in ecstasy. It was some time before sleep overtook our exhausted minds and bodies.

John was already halfway through a vegetable omelette when I joined him for breakfast the next morning. He looked up at me as he buttered a piece of toast.

"Morning, darling."

"Good morning." I cringed at Alice hearing his greeting.

"Morning, Stella. Sleep well?" I felt as if her eyes were burning into me. "Would you like an omelette?" I knew she was having fun with my embarrassment. I had never had a man in my bed at the rectory, and had no aplomb to handle it.

"No thanks; coffee is fine." I looked across the table and saw the twinkle in John's eye. Feeling quite out of my depth, I filled my cup.

"I'll be in the kitchen if you change your mind." Alice gathered up my unused dishes and then placed a bowl of strawberries in front of me. "At least have some fruit in your stomach." She was forever my surrogate mother, and I appreciated her kindness.

"If you have no other plans, I thought we'd take a walk over to Tythe Farm this morning. There are a couple of things I'd like to go over with you, Stella." I looked at John in surprise. He sounded quite businesslike—the officer on duty again. "It's something I want to get out of the way, and then we have the rest of the weekend to please ourselves. All right, sweetheart?"

"Why do you want to go to that place? You know I haven't been there since Sir Ralph's murder!" I felt vulnerable. "I didn't know you were still on duty."

"Stella, that's unkind! I'll explain when we get there. It won't take long, and by the way, a policeman is never off duty." He was having fun with me, and I tried to be a good sport.

"Does that mean you will be writing a report on your investigations of last night, Inspector?" I asked primly.

We finished breakfast quickly and separated to find coats and comfortable shoes for the trek to the farm.

I held John's hand as we rambled along. Neither of us had walked any distance for some time, and we were soon out of breath with the effort. "I thought you were a robust country girl roaming among the corn and cattle, biking to town, and traipsing to and from the Petersens'. You certainly fooled me, Mrs Campbell!"

"You can talk, Mr Inspector! Well, actually you can't. Listen to you—you're too winded!" I started to laugh, and soon we were both holding on to each other, giggling like children. We were happy, and for a few moments nothing else mattered except the strength of our feelings for each other. By the time we reached the farm, we were regretting that we had walked instead of sensibly riding bicycles. It was farther on foot than anticipated, and we glumly contemplated the walk back to the rectory. I looked questioningly at John as we approached the slaughterhouse. "Well?"

"I want to go over the building. There's something not quite coming together. I know it's difficult for you, but I thought if you were here, it might trigger a memory or something you didn't think important to report." He began to lead me towards the entrance.

"Please don't make me go inside," I implored, holding back.

"I'm with you, Stella. There is no need to be afraid. It's just an empty building. We'll not be long." I clung to him as he pushed against the wooden door, which gave easily. I waited while he entered first, and then followed him to the centre of the large space, conscious of the pervading smell of mildew. In one corner was a stack of ladders, tarps, and buckets. Propped against one wall was a large board onto which a sketch of the slaughterhouse interior was pinned. Areas were circled, and on one side a list of names had been written. "Simon Belsky's students, no doubt."

"So he did bring them here. I haven't seen Simon for quite some time—thought he had given up on the project." I looked around. "It looks like they have just started."

"I'm not certain what they intend to do. Do you know?"

"Well, only what Simon said before. The students are beginners, and need to excavate something that's not very complicated. He made a point of wanting a project that would give pretty much instant gratification. I suppose that's what it's all about nowadays. Not many like you anymore, patiently jogging along to an end. They want it straight away." John put his arm around my shoulder. We silently stared at the building outline—a rectangle of four straight lines drawn to scale. I pointed to the dozen or so names. "I think you're right. Those must be the students working here."

"A lot of people for such a small project." John took out his notebook and copied the list of names. "I want to look around the walls. How are you holding up?"

"I'm all right with you here but, please, let's go soon."

We walked slowly along each wall. John took out a torch and meticulously examined the dry, crumbling grout between the bricks. "All the work Joe Blake and I put into this was for naught. We spent forever replacing that grout. Now look at it—it's as if we never did a bloody thing!"

"It still looks sound in some sections. Did you do the whole place or just patches?"

"We replaced most, and left the smaller areas that were in good condition. I would have thought the new material would have held up longer than this!" I gestured around us. "Just look! It's so disappointing."

John peered at a small area and then reached up and ran his finger between a couple of bricks. "This is interesting. Look, Stella, it's wet." He leaned towards the wall and sniffed. "It's paint!"

I looked over his shoulder. "You mean they aren't replacing the grout—they're just painting over it? That doesn't make any sense." I looked around and then walked over to another section of the wall. "The grout is true here, John—and here." I picked between the bricks with my fingernail, and the hard mortar remained in place. John walked back to the drawing.

"Can you show the areas where you worked on this diagram—just roughly, of course? Was it on this wall or that? What about the area we just looked at?"

"I can't remember—it was a long time ago, John." I felt the pressure mounting.

"Don't stress yourself, Stella. Just look around. Give yourself time and see if anything comes to mind," he encouraged. "Take as much time as you need."

What the blazes? Take my time! It was taking all my energy not to think about finding Sir Ralph. Now this raving lunatic wanted me to think about which bricks had been re-grouted years ago. Biting my tongue, I sat down on the floor. John sat down beside me and ran the light slowly around on all four walls of the building.

"Anything, Stella?" I did not reply. He had given me an impossible task. Each brick followed another, looking exactly alike. "It will save a lot of time if you can remember; otherwise, I'm going to have to examine each and every brick—a job I don't relish, my love."

"It would help me if I knew what you were after," I complained. "Tell me what's going on. You said you would!" He looked apprehensively at me as I went on. "I deserve an explanation; after all, I'm here helping you. You have my word I'll keep whatever you say to myself."

"You're right, of course, but the less you know, the better for you." He turned the torch off. "I believe this building is a hiding place—a hiding place for large sums of money and drugs. I think this is where one is exchanged for the other. It would appear, Stella, you were meant to be the victim, not Sir Ralph. I think you were set up, but he arrived unexpectedly and discovered—what? We may never know. Whoever phoned Joe Blake asking him to meet you at another location likely saw you as a risk. They must have thought you, and not Blake, had discovered something through the renovation work. It all seems . . . oh, I don't know." John's voice faltered.

I reached out to him. "You think the hiding places for the money and drugs may be behind some of those bricks? And it was going on while Joe and I were working here, right under our noses? Now you're making me afraid."

"I need to, Stella. Your recklessness has been foolhardy. I am hoping now you will take care where you go and with whom. Certainly, do not go anywhere on your own—make sure you have Alice or your friend Beverly Petersen with you." He squeezed my hand. I felt no reassurance.

"Why me? Being a threat is absolutely ridiculous. I'm oblivious to anything beyond my own little haven at the rectory. The slaughterhouse restoration was a distraction for Joe and me—a hobby." I remembered the hours of pleasure we had working side by side. "I admit my imagination is quite vivid, but not that vivid!" I placed my hands on my hips defiantly. "The bogeyman is barking up the wrong tree."

"Stella, for goodness' sake!"

"Do you think Roger Spencer is a part of this? In the meeting with him at the bank, he said he stole money to get debtors off his back. Walter Pearce told me Roger really meant drug suppliers."

"I think he is involved, but I don't think he is a murderer. What do you know about Simon Belsky and the McKinleys?"

"Very little about the McKinleys, and you know Simon is using this building as a York University architectural student project. I've talked to Simon a few times. Gave him the grand tour of my gardens and house, and even had him to lunch once. He was very impressed, I might add. If I hadn't already become smitten with you, I might have asked him over again." I smiled, trying to lighten the conversation somewhat. John laughed and hugged me. I felt much better. "I was surprised the McKinleys bought the farm from Joe after Sir Ralph's murder," I continued. "Later, Simon said they were going to put it on the market. He was able to persuade them not to sell until he'd completed the student project."

John shook his head. "As you keep saying, there are so many questions. Sometimes a few get answered, but there are always more that follow. Now you know why police work can take a long, long time!" He got up from the floor and held out his hand to help me. "Let's call it a day, Stella. We've got one heck of a walk in front of us, and I'm starving."

"I second that." I brushed the dust off my slacks and followed him out of the building. He pushed the door closed so it looked the way we found it, and we set out on a shortcut across the field towards the road. I liked the warmth of his hand over mine. We walked most of the way without talking, but the silence was comfortable. When we entered the rectory's front door, the aroma of coffee greeted us. Something to eat could not be far behind.

After lunch, the three of us sat relaxing in the atrium. Alice was working on a piece of embroidery while I read Grahame's

The Wind in the Willows. John jotted things down in his little notebook, staring off into space from time to time. I was in heaven. We did not bring up Tythe Farm again that weekend, not wanting to spoil the remaining time we had together. Too quickly, he was kissing me goodbye and driving back to London.

John was going to be gone for three long weeks, and I had another meeting at the bank with Walter Pearce. Thanks to its insurance policy, the Building Society would make up my losses, he assured me. Because the agreement was between us, not Roger, it had no choice except to cough up. I was delighted. My son, Tim, was back in law school, and I could now pay his expenses without concern.

After running errands, I went into the Main Street Café to grab a cup of tea. Roger was sitting reading a newspaper at a table. I had not seen him for several weeks. I went over and sat down in the chair opposite him.

"Hello, Roger."

He looked up, surprised and certainly guarded. "How are you, Stella?"

"Good, thanks." The waitress came up, and I gave my order including a pastry. Roger looked dismayed, realising I was not there just to exchange greetings. "I've been wondering how things are going for you, now you are no longer with the Building Society. You've heard it's going to refund my money?"

"Yes, I'm glad about that, Stella. I never meant to hurt you—to take advantage of a friend like that. Things just got out of hand, and I was at serious risk for a good beating."

"Would it have stopped there? A beating, I mean?"

"I don't want to think otherwise . . . I repaid the money, and they no longer have a hold on me. It's now the Building Society's turn to go after me, but I'll pay it back, too."

"Who exactly are *they?*"

"It's not your concern, Stella." His tone was not discourteous. "Of course, you know by now I had an unfortunate habit, but I've moved on. My focus is getting back on my feet. I'm most grateful you decided not to prosecute. I'm sending out résumés daily, but I'm concerned my tarnished reputation will prevent me from finding a decent job. I can't pay off my debt to the Building Society without a reasonable income." He shrugged. "It's not easy, old girl. I've been very close to falling again."

I was sympathetic up to a point but didn't respond to his self-pity. I had another interest. "Are you still with Fiona? I haven't seen her for some time, either."

"No—actually we weren't so much the couple as everyone thought. Friends, really—well, I'd have liked it to be more; she's a wonderful young woman. It was quite amazing how we got together." He looked rather wistful. "She approached me. I wouldn't have had the nerve—an old sop like me chatting up a beauty like fair Fiona." He laughed. "She thought I had money. I took full advantage of the charade and let her think on. She soon made herself scarce when the truth came out. Said she was offered a new job and would have to move on, but I know it wasn't as simple as that."

"Was she involved with drugs, too?"

"No—absolutely clean." He folded his newspaper and got up from the table. "I must be on my way. I can't say it has been a pleasure, Stella; however, I am glad we talked."

"Good luck, Roger. Let me know if I can help—I mean that." I watched him leave the café and felt genuine sadness for him. After all, I had lost only money; he had lost everything.

I was exiting the café myself when I heard my name called. It was Robert Petersen. He pulled his car to the kerb in front of me.

"Beverly insists you meet our beautiful new daughter." He was ecstatic. "She practically burst into the world before we reached the hospital early this morning. It was a ruddy mad house."

"Robert! How splendid! I'll be there first thing tomorrow. Do you have a name for the little angel?"

"Yes, Stella."

"Do you have a name?"

"Yes—Stella. That's what we've called her: Stella—after you."

I screeched with delight. "How wonderful, Robert. I don't know what to say!"

"Well, that's a first," he teased. "I'm about to phone the hospital. I'll tell Bev to expect you. She'll be so happy. I'm off to bed myself now—it's been a long day, old thing."

"Bye, and thanks for letting me know. I'm so honoured, Robert. Sleep well, my dear."

I found it difficult to sleep that night myself. There was another Stella in the world.

I visited Beverly and Little Stella at ten the next morning. I was pleased to see my flowers had arrived. The baby was beautiful, of course, and Beverly looked very proud.

"I think this is the last, Stella. The labour was short, but I don't want to go through the carrying part again. My legs were like balloons, and the stretch marks . . . well, there'll be no more bikinis for me after this, I'm afraid." She leaned closer and softened her voice. "I'm getting my tubes tied without saying anything to Robert. Not much he can do after the fact. Three children are enough, thank you very much."

"And lovely they are, too. Is there anything you need, Bev? When do you think you will be going home?"

"I need nothing, Stella. I'm crazy to go home; unfortunately it won't be for a couple of days because of the tube surgery. When I had Robbie, all new mothers had a ten-day hospital stay. Ridiculous. Particularly when you have other kiddies at home waiting desperately for their mummy."

Robert came into the room carrying a large basket of fruit and a bouquet of pink balloons. "My darling." He kissed Beverly passionately on the lips. "I'm off to the nursery. It's down the corridor, Stella, when you're ready."

"I've already introduced myself, Robert. She is the prettiest girl in the room."

"That little one has him wrapped around her finger already." Bev looked on adoringly as Robert disappeared through the door.

"I'll be off now Robert has arrived. As I'm not family, the nurse said I could visit for only a few minutes. Take care of yourself, my dear. I'll stop and see my namesake again on the way out. Call me."

"When I get home, you must come over and bring me up to date on all the gossip."

"That will take all of five minutes, I'm afraid. Not much going on in Clipton."

"Oh no? Come clean, Stella. You've been seeing that policeman. You're blushing, so I know it's true."

"I'll see you later, Mrs Petersen." She was quite right; my face felt as if I had been sitting in front of a heat lamp.

CHAPTER FOURTEEN

John telephoned that evening, and we found ourselves talking more and more about a future together. I knew my love for him was becoming stronger, and I was thrilled he seemed to feel the same way. Were we hedging around marriage? Was that what he wanted to ask me when he came to Clipton the next weekend? He hinted as much. I tried to think clearly, but excitement and his beloved face filled my thoughts. I decided to go for a walk to calm myself. I saw no harm in taking a short stroll alone. Anyway, Alice was visiting a friend, and Bev was still hospitalised.

Lush grass muffled my footsteps, a benefit of a wet winter. I rambled along the narrow path still used by the herd of Jersey cows once owned by Joe Blake. Without any prompting, they made their way each evening from the pastures to their new farm home in the distance. When their udders were at their heaviest, they knew that path took them to relief. I stepped around the cakes of manure with care, making a mental note to ask Reg to collect a supply for the rectory's rose garden. After walking for about a mile I rested under a giant field maple. The thatch was thick, filtering the sunlight to only a shadow that prevented even weeds from growing under it. I was too hot to care, and stretched out on the dirt, disturbing a couple of woodpigeons whose strong wings flapped noisily as they took off. I lay still; the canopy of leaves above me danced as dark silhouettes against a blue sky. It was heavenly, but then everyone knows the world seems a far better place when you're in love.

I became conscious I was no longer alone. Someone was rather hurriedly making their way along the cow path. Then I heard a shout. Keeping low to the ground, I hid behind the tree and dared to take a look. I was startled to see Margot Hughes Young stomping after Roger Spencer. "You'll have to talk to me sometime. This can't go on, you know," she shouted in anger.

He was a few yards in front of her before he stopped and faced her. "I'm warning you, Margot," he threatened. "Leave me alone."

She caught up with him and breathlessly shouted back, "You can't frighten me, you wimp. You got yourself into this mess because you have no backbone. You disgust me," she snarled. "Always acting as if you're better than anybody else, but we all know the liar and thief you really are."

Roger stepped forward; his hand was raised as if to strike her. "Watch yourself, old woman. If I go down, just remember I don't intend going alone. The police would be most interested to hear what I have to say."

She pointed her finger at him, her voice rasping with fury. "Be careful, Roger. Be very careful." I watched, stunned by the verbal exchange; then Margot turned and walked across the field towards Clipton. She had a powerful stride for someone of her age; she was not the docile widow I had thought. Roger had a formidable foe. By the worried furrow in his brow, he seemed well aware of that fact as he began walking slowly back along the cow path. I shivered. The sun was losing its warmth, and I was unprepared in my cotton blouse and shorts. After waiting for what seemed an eternity for Roger to completely disappear, I started back to the rectory. The goings-on in our small hamlet were obviously a lot more complicated than I had understood.

It was a relief to close the door behind me once I got to the house. I was confused. What had caused Margot to be so angry with Roger, and what was he holding over her? Naturally, I had no answers. I decided to tell John about what I had witnessed. He would be disappointed in me for going out alone, and I was sorry for that. When he phoned that evening, I got it off my chest. "John, I went for a walk along the old cow path today, and overheard Margot Hughes Young and Roger Spencer having an argument. It was quite heated—they were threatening each other.

Couldn't tell what it was about, exactly." I steeled myself for his reaction. To my surprise, he made no comment. He seemed only interested in what was actually said that afternoon, insisting I search my memory for every detail.

"You've got it all, John. There's nothing more to tell you."

"It's just another piece of the puzzle, Stella. I'm at a disadvantage not living in Clipton. I don't have the same opportunity as you to rub shoulders with individuals."

"Can you get transferred here? Our local bobbies are wonderful, but all come from the Mr Plod mould. A handsome detective—my handsome detective—could make a big difference, and you could live here at the rectory."

I heard his voice soften slightly. "I don't know if I could concentrate on my work if I did that." Then his tone reverted back to businesslike again. "You don't make things easy for me, Stella."

"You sound so stern."

"I'm serious! I've asked you repeatedly not to go out on your own. You gave me your word. For goodness' sake, what's the use? You're going to do whatever you want, no matter what I say."

"It was only a short walk, really," I protested. "Don't be angry with me, John."

"You're missing the point! You could be in danger, yet you insist on being flippant about it. I worry myself sick when I'm away from you. If harm came to you, I don't know what I'd do."

I liked hearing that. Of course I repeated my promise, and that time I really meant it. I was not going to wreck our deepening relationship by being foolhardy. I was head over heels for this man and wanted to keep him. To change the subject, we agreed to meet in London the following weekend. He would meet my train.

When I saw him standing at the entrance to Green Park underground, my heartbeat increased wildly. Without a word, he took my hand, and we walked out onto the crowded pavement like a committed couple.

"You've got a letter from the Building Society. Hope it's a cheque!" Alice handed me the envelope. I quickly tore it open and took out a single sheet of letterhead.

"No . . . just more red tape. The chairman of the board wants to personally hand the cheque to me. What a bloody fool. Just give me my money back, Mr Chairman."

"I hope you're getting paid interest."

"You bet I am. When I get it, I'll take you to any restaurant you like for a celebration dinner. Us girls deserve a little spoiling, don't you think?" I was about to phone James at the stables to arrange another riding lesson when I remembered my promise to John. "Alice, when I go into town to the Building Society's office, will you come with me? I'd like to make the arrangement for this week. Will that work for you?"

"I'm at your service any time."

"Do I get that in writing?" I was being facetious and did not expect her response.

"The inspector had a word with me. Because you won't do as he says, he is hoping I can have some influence on your stubbornness. Don't get cross now; you mean a lot to both of us, Stella. Hopefully he is wrong about the need to keep an eye on you, but it is better to be safe than sorry. Right, dear?" I reluctantly agreed.

Later that afternoon, Reg drove us into town—I needed to pick up clothes from the cleaners, and Alice wanted more silk thread for her embroidery. We were just about to return to the car when Simon Belsky turned the corner.

"Afternoon, ladies."

"Hello, Simon. How are you?"

"Good, thank you, Stella."

Enough of these niceties, I thought. "How's your slaughterhouse project going? Your students are here, aren't they?"

"They are, indeed."

"What are they doing, exactly?"

"You should join us one day and see for yourself. We're taking our time, making sure each detail is recorded, et cetera. It is very interesting. All the bricks were handmade, you know."

"Yes, I do know."

"The beams holding up the roof are full of termites, so they have to be replaced. A couple of students were horror-struck at having to evict a nest of white owls."

"Oh, they'll soon make their way back."

He nodded, ready to move on. "Call me when you want a tour."

"I may just do that, Simon. Thank you." I intended to take him up on his offer as soon as possible. I wanted to know about that strange grout around the bricks.

At the rectory, there was a phone message requesting I pick up my cheque the next day from the Building Society. I called back and confirmed I would be happy to oblige.

"You look very businesslike in that suit, Stella." Alice had on her good coat and hat for the occasion.

"Don't forget we're having a girls' night out. Just say which restaurant."

"I'd love a curry with all those exotic condiments. Could we go to the new place—I think it's called New Delhi Delight. It's only recently opened in Gerrards Cross, and *The Times* gave a rave review. Is Gerrards Cross too far?"

"Not at all. It's . . . what, forty minutes away? I'll make the reservation as soon as the meeting's over. We'll come back and change. Does Reg like curry? He can join us if he likes. What do you think?"

"I think he'd like that. Ask him yourself."

"Ask me what, Mrs Campbell?" Reg entered the room.

"Alice and I are going to try a new Indian restaurant in Gerrards Cross this evening. The New Delhi Delight. We'd like you to join us."

"Well, thank you, ma'am. I'd like that very much. Can't have any drink though, you know—I'm driving."

"I don't remembering saying anything about drinks, Reg—just grub, ol' matey. However, I might be persuaded to cover just one each since we're celebrating." I grinned. "Get your bag, Alice; we mustn't be late. By the way, Reg, do call me Stella. You can't go for curry with a Mrs Campbell." His smile lit up his whole face.

The traffic was light, and we arrived at the Building Society headquarters a few minutes before my appointment. Alice walked with me into the foyer of the building. We arranged to meet back at the car in an hour, giving plenty of time for me to take care of business. Mr Farley, the chairman of the board, was waiting to greet me at the entrance of his office.

"Mrs Campbell, a pleasure."

"Thank you, Mr Farley. I don't want to be rude, but I'd like to take care of this matter rather quickly, as I've someone waiting for me."

"Of course. Please take a seat, and I'll get my secretary to bring the cheque in." He indicated a comfortable chair. I sat down, and he gave instructions through the intercom to his secretary. I was civil in my small talk while we waited because it was certainly not his fault—or the Building Society's, for that matter—that I had been diddled out of thousands of pounds. I started to warm towards the poor man who looked quite uncomfortable.

"I am very grateful to the Building Society for making up my loss, Mr Farley. Of course, I know the trust account had a major shortfall, too. I presume you are going to prosecute?"

"I'm not at liberty to speak on the matter, Mrs Campbell. Excuse me," he said when a slim young woman carrying a blue envelope and wearing the highest heels I had ever seen entered the room. "Thank you, Sandra." He reached out his hand as she hesitated. "Sandra. I'll take it." Reluctantly, she handed the envelope to him. "That will be all, thank you. Close the door on the way out, if you please." As she passed my chair, she gave me a cold stare. I wanted to put my foot out and trip her over—see how she could handle those three-inch stilettos, then.

"I must apologise, Mrs Campbell. I don't know what came over the girl. I'll have a word with her as soon as our meeting is over. As we discussed, the total amount includes interest." He reached for a file and took out several typewritten sheets of paper. "I'll need you to sign each of these, if you please. Just the normal formality. You are absolving Clipton's Building Society of all future liability. Once signed, I will release the cheque to you, and the matter will be closed."

"Has Walter Pearce reviewed the documents?"

"Yes indeed. He was here yesterday and initialled his approval on each page." He pointed to where Walter had added his mark and the date. "I can assure you, Mrs Campbell, everything is in order." He handed me a Parker fountain pen.

I sat back in the chair and took a moment or two to look the documents over. It all seemed too easy. The Building Society never disputed Roger's dishonesty, and simply said it would make good my losses. No questions, no protest. I unscrewed the top of the pen and signed my name in the appropriate places. If Walter thought all was well, then who was I to doubt him?

Alice was waiting for me as I got off the lift, and we strolled to the car. "To the bank, Reg. I need to see Walter Pearce. If he says what I hope, I have quite a large deposit to make."

Fortunately, Walter confirmed he had approved the documents. "What is Mr Farley's secretary's problem?" I asked him. "You would have thought it was her personal money being given to me."

Walter laughed. "It's not just her problem, Stella. All the Building Society staff are feeling the pinch because they won't be getting a bonus this year."

"Umm, so it really is her money. Poor girl."

I did not hear from Simon Belsky, so after a couple of weeks, I decided to overcome my nervousness and barge in on him at Tythe Farm. If anything was going on at the slaughterhouse as John suspected, I might discover something. I compromised my promise to John to not go anywhere alone by making Alice fully cognisant of my intended whereabouts. Naturally, there was an argument, but I was determined not to take her with me. For one thing, she would look suspiciously out of place, I insisted. I cycled off and was at the farm in no time. A couple of vans were parked in front of the building, and bags of what looked like cement were piled in a wheelbarrow. I casually walked through the door; no one seemed to pay attention to me. A male student was whistling an accompaniment to a song coming from a small portable radio propped up against a duffle bag on the floor. The whole scene was laid-back, relaxed. A young woman wearing a blue anorak and woollen hat was putting out sandwiches on a table set up in one corner; several cans of soda were in an opened ice chest by her feet. I waited quietly, trying to take in anything that might look amiss. I was puzzled to see about half a dozen young men painting the walls with a whitewash. If they were architectural students, would they not be studying the slaughterhouse design, how the structure was put together, the materials used? It did not make sense they would be covering over such a treasure with paint.

"Hello, Stella." Simon Belsky put his hand on my shoulder.

Startled, I spun round. "Hello, Simon. I thought I'd take you up on your offer and see how things were going." I tried to sound casual.

"Of course, but I would have preferred you contacted me first. Not much is going on just now. It will be more interesting next week. The project will be finished, and we're having an open house to show our good neighbours what we've been up to. Why don't you come back then?"

"Oh, I will—thank you, Simon. As I'm here now—couldn't you give me the grand tour today?"

"We're about to break for lunch. You'd be welcome to join us if you like. It's just a sandwich." He guided me over to the young woman. "One more for lunch, Jackie." She smiled pleasantly at me, and stood back so I could help myself.

"Aren't the others joining us?" I asked. The male students were still at work.

"In a moment. They're almost finished. I'll join you though. I'm ravenous." He no longer seemed perturbed but relaxed, more like the charming man I was used to. He reached for a paper plate, loaded it with food, and sat down on the bench next to me. Jackie drifted away, taking a soda with her. We ate in silence for a while. The food was delicious—fresh from the Jewish deli in Clipton, according to the logo printed on the paper bags and napkins.

"What are those chaps putting on the walls?"

"Oh, it's just a preservative." Simon wiped his mouth on a napkin. "We want to keep this historic gem standing for many more years. You did a good job with your renovation; you just didn't go far enough. We replaced many of the beams because of termite damage." He gestured to the floor and swept a patch of dust with his shoe. "What do you think of the tiles now?" They were cleansed of decades of blood and grime and, at long last, the wonderful blue hue of the slate was exposed.

"How did you do it? It is beautiful, Simon."

"We got the grunge off by countless hours of elbow grease. That's one of the many advantages of having eager students."

"Joe and I had little luck with our efforts until a friend suggested hydrochloric acid; then we made some progress. It's frightful stuff though. Lethal. We had to use protective gear, including breathing apparatus. After Sir Ralph's murder, we lost our enthusiasm." I suddenly felt cold. "This is the first time I've been back here since then. It was our acid that was used to kill him, you know."

"I didn't. Not what you wanted to hear, I'm sure," he said kindly. He took a mouthful of soda. "What happened to this Joe?"

"Joe—Joe Blake. After he sold the farm to your sister and brother-in-law, he moved to Cumberland. Runs a successful stud ranch now. I believe I mentioned that before."

"Do you keep in touch?"

"At first, but over time . . . you know how it is."

The students joined us, grabbing sandwiches and sodas. They were full of energy and chattered excitedly about the project at hand. Simon made it a point to tell them that Joe and I had been the initial restorers. I liked their enthusiasm, and regretted having to make my excuses after a few moments, saying I had an appointment in town. "Thanks for the sandwich," I called to the girl in the woollen hat. Simon walked me to my bicycle. "I should have called you rather than just turning up, but I was testing myself. You know, coming back after the murder."

He looked down at me and smiled. "Weren't you here a couple of weeks ago . . . with the inspector, I believe?"

"I don't know what you mean." I looked him in the eye, praying he did not see me flinch.

"Michael, my brother-in-law, saw you. He was certain of it."

"He was mistaken." I smiled brazenly. "Let me know when you have the open house." I wheeled my bicycle through the farm gate, aware he was watching me. I turned and gave a friendly wave. "Goodbye, Simon. Thanks again." I quickly rode back to the rectory. My stress level had increased considerably, not with exertion but with the shame of telling a lie.

John telephoned a few days later and announced the Yard required his presence in Clipton for a week. I was thrilled. To do what, he never said and I never asked, although the question stuck in my craw. I concentrated on the fact we would be together again; nothing else mattered. When he arrived, I got a good dressing down about going to the farm. I deserved it, so took it on the chin. Once he got that off his chest, he turned his attention to what Simon had said and what his students were up to.

"It all seemed perfectly normal, John. Simon certainly didn't behave as if he was trying to hide anything. Actually, he was quite charming." Alas, I did not get any reaction to that comment. "I did feel awful lying about you and me being over there before, though."

"Don't worry about Belsky. It's his brother-in-law's word against yours." He shrugged. "You know more about preserving buildings than I, but painting over those bricks smells very fishy to me. I need to go back sometime to get samples of the wash and the new grout."

"I can show you where the work was done."

"No, Stella. I want to go alone. You stay here!"

I didn't argue but offered to walk part of the way and wait for him.

"No, I don't want you going anywhere near that place again." He got up from the sofa and stretched. "I think I'll take a nap, darling. It's been a long day, and the drive from London just finished me off. Would you mind?"

"Of course not! I'll awaken you in a couple of hours for tea. Alice serves at four o'clock sharp." I went up to him and kissed him full on the mouth.

Beverly and Robert joined us for drinks that evening. John and Robert talked about football while Bev and I escaped to the kitchen and got caught up on romance and babies. Alice returned from the cinema with Reg, and together they made a delicious supper for all of us.

John seemed in no hurry to get his samples from Tythe Farm, and we spent wonderful days together before he announced his plan on the last morning.

"I won't be long, Stella. I'll go straight in and straight out." I grimaced. "Now, don't look like that. It's better I go alone. I have less chance of being seen."

I conceded he did make sense but was deflated until his return hours later. He had taken my bicycle and a backpack in which to carry any samples. He sounded excited when he returned and called out to me, so I knew he had what he wanted.

"I'll take everything to the laboratory as soon as I return to the Yard tomorrow. I have my suspicions; the forensics division should be able to confirm one way or the other." He stopped being the policeman and smiled at me. "Well, my love, we have the rest of the day to ourselves. Do you still want to go riding?"

"I do. James is expecting us. He warned his mounts are nothing like your own Vanguard, but it will be wonderful for us to be out together."

"Let's go, then." He reached for my hand.

I moped around for days after John returned to London. It was getting more difficult for us to say our goodbyes, and we knew we were on the brink of a major decision. I knew I loved him deeply and in a different way to Geoff. I was comfortable with Geoff, and we eventually became more like siblings, but John . . . my heart pounded just thinking about him. If he proposed, I would not hesitate. He called during the week, and announced the results of the samples taken from the slaughterhouse had come through.

"I'll fill you in as soon as we get together."

"Why can't you tell me now, John? I'll go crazy waiting until then," I complained.

"Too bad, Stella. I'm not saying anything over the phone . . . just a precaution, sweetheart." I could do nothing but accept it. The rest of the week seemed endless.

As usual, I was waiting at the window watching the road for John's familiar white Jaguar. As soon as it appeared through the trees, I took up my spot at the front door. I had taken considerable trouble with my makeup and hair, and wore new black slacks and a matching cashmere sweater. I felt elated standing at the door waiting for my love . . . my future. My pulse quickened when the car came to a stop in the driveway and he got out. I ran straight into his outstretched arms.

After a scrumptious dinner of tofu burgers and chips with lots of tomato ketchup, we settled in the lounge. I could not hold back any longer and nudged his shoulder.

"Well, aren't you going to tell me?"

"What? Tell you what?"

"John, you know exactly what I mean—the Tythe Farm samples."

"Oh, those? I remember now," he kidded. "It's all very interesting, actually. I've got my sergeant coming here next week to do a little snooping. He is so inconspicuous, people won't notice he's around—a great asset, in many ways."

"The samples, John, the samples—what did the laboratory discover?" I persisted. "You can tell me about all your sergeant's wonderful attributes later."

"Okay, okay, darling. I've tormented you enough." He sat down on the sofa beside me. "I took scrapings from the grout between the bricks and from the new paint that the students had applied to the walls. I even photographed the chart and drawings. You were uncertain which areas of brick you and your friend Joe had repaired . . . well, the film I used in my camera was particularly sensitive, and the photographs show the grout on certain portions of the walls as quite distinct in a dark grey colour. That could indicate your work areas because the softer grout photographs lighter in tone." He stood up. "Wait a moment; I'll go up and get my briefcase, and show you what I mean."

I waited impatiently for him to return. I was on edge—perhaps what John had discovered would finally lead to a conclusion after all this time. Three murders, and no one so far had paid a penalty. I felt a lump in my throat at the thought of my friends.

"Here we are, darling." John put his briefcase on the coffee table and snapped open the locks. "There's a lot in the lab report I don't understand. It's a bit too technical for my simple mind, so I just take a look at the conclusion paragraph at the end. It appears the wash painted onto the walls is just a preservative, as Simon Belsky informed you." He sat back in the chair and shuffled through several sheets of paper. "The first sample of grout was unstable, well over a century old, and consists mostly of clay and sand."

"That would be the original used when the building was put up," I interrupted.

"Um, yes. Well, the second sample was solid and made from a formula that's been available for about ten years."

"That's Joe's and my work," I said smugly.

John nodded his head, smiling. "You are correct, Madam Sleuth. The third sample I took from an area that measures roughly twelve feet wide by four deep and shows recent activity. That compound was pliable, similar to soft putty." John's brow was furrowed in concentration. "In his statement, Roger Spencer said he got his supply of narcotics at the slaughterhouse. He didn't say how exactly, but it makes sense cocaine could be stashed behind the bricks where the grout remains soft."

"How do you know it is cocaine?"

"I took scrapings from the cavities behind a couple of bricks in that area, and the lab identified traces of cocaine." John absently pulled at his chin. "It seems the slaughterhouse is where all the action takes place. The deal is made, and a supply is placed behind a certain brick. Very simple, isn't it?"

"The drugs are picked up, and money is left in their place?"

"No—you pay up front, Stella. There's no credit in this business."

"How would the person know which brick to go to? Are they marked?"

"They are numbered. Perhaps it's the seller's security. He or she assigns a number to a buyer and then puts the supply behind that particular brick." He paused for a moment. "If only two people know the number, it would prevent any double-crossing—each would know it was the other. The seller is in control; he feeds the buyer's need, and the poor sod can't get the monkey off his back."

"That doesn't make sense to me, John. Either one could tell a third person, or someone could see something. And what about the money? Who would pay a large sum in advance for drugs that are not collected until later? The dealer could be well gone by that time."

"Because, my sweet, when you're hooked, you do anything to keep your supply coming. The dealer holds the cards. If he says jump, you ask how high if it means you get your fix." John paused for a moment. "Roger Spencer is a good example—you didn't know he used drugs. You didn't see any outward symptoms at all, because you don't know what to look for. However, he was willing to steal very large sums of money from his employer and you, a close friend, to feed the habit, knowing full well he would eventually fall."

"I didn't suspect a thing, John. I must be pretty naive."

"People you would least expect are users, Stella. The phrase 'drug of choice' is thrown around a lot. One would think it really is a choice, one harmless indulgence over another. Cocaine is widely used because many think it's socially acceptable, and they can control it. It's the *in* thing. Tragically, it quickly becomes your mistress and, once hooked, you will sell your very soul to have her."

"You seem to know a lot about it," I said quietly.

"Addiction leads to ruin. I've been close to it myself." He looked sharply at me, perhaps to catch my expression as I digested what he had just said.

I heard myself say rather lightly, "You were a junkie?"

"A long time ago, yes!" He added, "I stopped cold turkey when it killed my wife twenty years ago."

"John!" What was he doing? I did not want my nice safe life turned upside down. I didn't want to hear about someone else he loved. "You were married?" I mumbled.

"We've never really talked about the past, Stella. I know a little about Geoff . . . only because I checked him out when I checked you out. At the beginning, when I was first given this case, I had to check everyone."

"So you have all my gory details, but it seems I don't really know you at all." I wanted to scream at him. *Why? Why now, when things were going so well?*

"It was all my fault. I introduced my wife to cocaine . . . wanted her to join me on my trips to heaven. She loved me enough to try it. Just once, she said." His words were heavy with bitterness. "Once is all it took. I found her in the bathroom; she had choked on her own vomit."

I didn't want to—I wanted to stay far away from him—but his voice was so broken I found myself getting up and going to him. He grabbed on to me. "I wanted to die too, Stella. She was only twenty-five. Twenty-five!"

Later, much later, we held each other tightly. My maternal instinct was on high alert, and I struggled not to play the mother role. He told me he had been married only four years before his wife died. He put himself through rehab and, when he was clean, joined the police academy. "It wasn't easy proving to my superiors that I could be reliable. Eventually, I made the grade from pounding the beat for two years and then passing exams to become a detective. More training and exams got me through the ranks. It took a long while, but here I am, a fully fledged detective chief inspector. My chief superintendent keeps an eye on me, and I am tested regularly." I kept my questions to myself and just listened as he went on. "I've been on the Metropolitan Police Force for eighteen years, a DCI for the last seven. Because of my past, my assignments usually involve narcotics in one way or another. I knew that to be the case in Clipton from the beginning."

"But aren't you tempted, John? Recovering alcoholics fight their demons every day. Isn't it the same for people who have used drugs?"

"The temptation is always there, yes; remembering my wife keeps me clean."

"I wish you had told me all this before. You could have trusted me." I was bruised and bleeding emotionally, but my voice sounded calm, surprising me.

"Try to understand, Stella, I never wanted to mislead you. John Gailbrath's murky past cost him—cost him a lot. I just didn't know how to bring it up; I was afraid I'd lose you, my love."

"You can't get rid of me that easily." I tightened my arms around him, drawing him closer.

Our need intensified, but we took time to explore each other. Our tongues delving into crevices tasted the salt of sweat, the sweetness of deep kisses, and brought escalating excitement to the brink again and again. At the point of no return, we called out in sync as a shattering climax left our bodies writhing.

CHAPTER FIFTEEN

They say confession heals the soul. Maybe. It certainly deepened our relationship. We seemed more mature, more tuned in to each other . . . and we both knew it was for keeps. When John left for London, I did not feel so alone or clingy as before. I relaxed, confident we would again be together soon. Our telephone conversations were more than mere words; it was what was not said that I valued. We knew each was committed to the other, bringing solace to those days we spent apart.

"I'll get it, Alice," I called out and picked up the telephone receiver. "Hello?" I listened for a moment before hanging up. It rang again. "Hello?" I was not quite so polite the second time. "Speak up or stop wasting my time!"

"Who was that?" Alice came in carrying a vase of freshly cut white roses from the garden.

"Wrong number, no doubt," I said absently.

Unable to settle with a book or lose myself in my latest project—cross-matching dahlias—I could only think about John's young wife and what her loss must have meant to him. Both of us were exceedingly vulnerable, and I vowed not to take advantage of the situation. Later, when Beverly Petersen phoned to ask me to lunch, I accepted gratefully. I needed company.

I returned to the rectory around mid afternoon in a much brighter mood. Spending time with my sweet namesake and being given a warm welcome by her mother was the perfect antidote to my melancholia. Alice was at her book club until five. The house seemed abnormally quiet, and I decided to potter around the rectory grounds. Changing into overalls, I got my clippers and wheelbarrow from the shed, and began to tackle the labour-intensive dead-heading of the perennial borders around the patio. They had been a profusion of colour a week ago, but it was this back-breaking task that ensured such a display.

I was well into it before I felt, and that is what it was—a feeling, that I was no longer alone. I stopped clipping and listened. "Anyone there?" Only the chirping of a family of sparrows broke the silence. Admonishing myself for letting my imagination run wild, I continued working, but the sensation that someone had been watching remained. The uneasy feeling compelled me to bag up the cuttings and return the tools to the shed before the job was completed. It was a relief to return to the house, and I made sure the doors were locked behind me.

It was only when I heard Alice's key in the front door that the tension finally left me.

"The librarian nabbed me on my way to the book club. It seems impossible my books were three weeks overdue."

"You should stop checking out so many at a time." I gave her a moment to take off her coat before relaying my experience in the garden. "It was probably my imagination, but I felt someone was watching me . . . spooked me quite a bit, actually."

"I'm glad I came straight home. I almost stopped at the café to have a coffee to make up for having to pay a hefty fine."

"I'm glad you came straight home, too, Alice."

"You didn't stay out there, I hope?" She paused, thoughtful for a moment. "You know, that call earlier was a bit suspicious."

"What call?"

"The one you took this morning. Normally I would answer. Whoever it was may have known our routine, and when they heard your voice, thought you were home alone."

"Now I really feel spooked."

"I don't mean to frighten you, dear." She came over and sat on the arm of my chair. "I shouldn't have gone to the book club. It never occurred to me you might be in danger at the rectory. I won't leave you alone again, Stella." She was resolute.

"Dear Alice." I smiled weakly. "Let's change the subject."

With dinner over, we went into the lounge, our usual comfortable spot for the evening. It had been a trying day for both of us, and to make up for it, we indulged ourselves by opening a box of chocolates and gluttonously consumed rather too many. Feeling in a much better frame of mind but rather queasy after the sugar high, I turned on the television. "*Masterpiece Theatre* should be on now."

"Oh, good—my favourite," Alice mumbled through a full mouth.

Things continued uneventfully. Sergeant Ball and John arrived from London and settled into rooms at the Retreat. I decided not say anything to them about the episode of unease I had experienced in the garden, a couple of weeks earlier. I had no idea what John and Sergeant Ball were up to, but John stayed with me for three whole days, leaving the rectory bright and early each morning. We were in a routine now, and I had learned to accept his obligation to the Yard.

I would see Sergeant Ball occasionally when I went into the village for supplies or lunch with a friend. He didn't seem to be doing anything in particular, although he was in attendance at the next planning commission meeting. John was right about him; wearing nondescript clothing and a blank look on his face, he blended in as just another hound in the pack. I didn't see anyone speak to him or, for that matter, look in his direction. As I was leaving, he brushed passed me without saying a word. I made my way to the car, but Reg was nowhere in sight. I tried the car door and was relieved to find it open. I sat in the back and peered impatiently into the darkness. "*Come on, Reggie. I'm bushed!*" My watch showed I'd been waiting for more than ten minutes. I cursed my chauffeur of eight years. Another minute or so passed before he came up to the car, and was reaching to open my door. "About time! Where have you been, Reg?" Before I knew what was happening, a figure loomed up behind him, and pulled him away from the car. There was a scuffle, an exchange of some swear words, and then Reg took off running. Terrified, I shrank into the corner of the seat as the figure leaned in closer.

"Stella, it's me, Reg. Are you all right? Stella?"

"Reg?" I was fighting back tears like a frightened girl. "I thought you ran off."

"No, not me, but I gave the other bloke something to remember me by. I saw him hanging around the car earlier, so when the meeting was over, I went looking for you. Mr Nyby said you'd already left, so I ran back and saw that bloke at the car door. I only caught a glimpse of his face because of the dark, but he looked familiar."

"I might have been in real trouble if you hadn't come along just then." I shuddered, thinking what could have happened.

"I agree. He didn't seem as if he was up to much good." He patted my arm and closed the car door. It was a relief when the engine started up and we headed home. I thought again of the time I had discovered Sir Ralph's body at Tythe Farm. Was the intruder about to harm me in the same horrific way? Was I unknowingly privy to some information that caused me to be a threat, after all? I was safe in John's arms as soon as the rectory door opened.

"I assure you, darling, Sergeant Ball witnessed everything. He was well aware of the man hanging around your car, and had everything under control. Earlier, he asked the chap for a light for a cigarette, although Ball doesn't smoke. It was a good ploy, however, because it gave Ball a closer look, and he could check in the man's pockets. I'm pleased to tell you they were empty."

"Well, John, Sergeant Ball didn't do me much good, did he? I could have been killed. It was Reg who came to help me—not your bloody sergeant!"

"I was remiss, Stella. I should have told you Ball would be keeping his eye on you. He went to the planning meeting because you were listed on the agenda as a speaker."

"Did he identify the man?"

"Yes. It was Michael McKinley."

"McKinley? Simon Belsky's brother-in-law?" I was astonished. "What did he want?"

"We don't know—yet. If your devoted driver hadn't turned up when he did, we may have got it out of him."

"Thank god for Reg. No thanks to your sergeant, standing on the sidelines being entertained," I retorted angrily. "Where is your precious Ball now? Hiding behind the curtains?"

John laughed, and I did feel rather childish. "He's in the kitchen with Alice."

John took me in his arms, and I began to relax. "I don't know what to do about you, Stella." I did not reply. "I have to rely on you to be careful, but you seem to enjoy provoking me." He tightened his hold on me. "Certain people are becoming more agitated now. They've had things their way for a long time, and they don't like the fact that's beginning to change."

"Because of your enquiries, you mean?"

"Partly. The police are now able to put two and two together, and we anticipate a conclusion fairly soon. I'm concerned your relationship with me puts you at risk, because you are the chink in my armour." He kissed my ear. "Of course you are . . . you are my love."

"As you are mine."

"Stella, things are escalating, and it could get extremely dangerous as the police close in. Think about it, darling; we've had three brutal murders. Let's leave it at three."

I held on to him. "You have to take care of you. Promise me you won't take any silly chances, either. I've got a lot to lose, too," I begged. His warm lips on mine sealed the deal.

John returned to London, but Sergeant Ball began turning up at the rectory more often, unannounced and unexpected. I noticed it was not only to see me. He was showing personal interest in Alice, and I certainly had no complaint about that. We made small talk when necessary; however, I was aware his eyes took in everything, and I got a sense of security from that. Needing a break, I had Reg drive me to the garden centre, and he patiently waited at the entrance while I gathered flats of Iceland poppies. I wheeled the cart down the aisle, my mind occupied with the vast selection of plants on either side.

"Mrs Campbell, a word if you don't mind?" I wasn't sure if my ears were playing tricks, because the voice was so very soft. "Stella. Over here." I turned, and faced Michael McKinley half-hidden behind hanging baskets of English ivy. "Please don't be alarmed." He was obviously very nervous, more so than I. "I've been trying to find an opportunity to talk with you, and when you came into the nursery, the moment presented itself."

"What do you want with me, Michael? I understand it was you who tried to attack me in my car after the planning meeting." I wanted to sound strong, in control, but it was a poor performance.

"Attack you? Never, Stella. I meant you no harm—I wanted to warn you. Warn you to be careful."

"Careful—careful of what? Michael, what is this all about? What mischief can I possibly cause anyone? I mind my own business, and live quite a humdrum life."

"I, too, am trying to live my life. I have a degree in Asian studies and want nothing more than to continue teaching." I think he teared up. "I inadvertently learned that certain people believe you have discovered information that's detrimental to them." He hesitated. "I can't say any more than that, Stella." He kept back under the plants. I wondered if Reg had seen him.

"Aren't you at risk talking with me? Surely you are putting yourself in danger."

"Most assuredly, yes, but I'm willing to take the risk if you take precautions to protect yourself." His demeanour oozed intrigue. "Heed what I've said, Stella—you must be careful." He was gone in a second.

I picked out a couple of plants without any idea of what I had chosen, and hurriedly made my way to the cashier and paid for them.

"Here, let me help you with those."

"Thanks, Reg. By the way, I thought I saw Michael McKinley just now. Did you?"

"No. That bugger better not show his face near you again."
"Right!"

Beverly and Robert sent out invitations to Little Stella's baptism several weeks in advance. I was entrusted with the honour of being godmother, even though I knew no god. Having limited knowledge of what responsibilities would be involved, I called on our vicar for guidance. We spent a good hour going over how I was to oversee the baby's religious education, and I took what Ken said very seriously. There had never been any pretence about my own spirituality, but I would certainly support Beverly and Robert's wishes. I knew Beverly's favourite colour was lavender, so I stopped at the florist to arrange for the church nave to be decorated in flowers of that hue together with lots of white baby's breath. It was a busy, enjoyable day, and I returned to the rectory in high spirits. The next day, I caught an early train to London, and made a beeline to Harrods in Knightsbridge. I chose a full-length christening gown in ivory silk, complete with a bonnet and shawl. I was reminded of my own two children when they received the blessing of baptism in St Andrews, a gothic wonder close to our home. They each took their turn to wear the same gown, and it remains carefully folded in tissue paper, hopefully to be used by their children when the time comes. Geoff and I went through the ritual because of unyielding pressure from our parents. Both children's godparents were in name only. Nevertheless, Geoff and I were comfortable with our choices, for love and devotion to both children was always present. They received the traditional solid silver gifts without either of them being introduced to a god: Julia got a spoon and egg cup and Tim an ivory teething ring with a silver bell. I smiled, remembering as I made my way to my parents' home for a short visit before catching the train back to Clipton.

"You're becoming a stranger, dear," my mother accused. "Of course, I understand you are busy," she quickly added to appease me.

"I am busy, Mummy, but you are quite right; I do need to make more effort. When can you come to Clipton?"

"Once Dad gets his garden ready for winter, we'll be free any time. You know he can't rest until that chore is done."

"He'll be finished by October, right? Couldn't you come for the Christmas holiday? I hope to persuade Julia and Tim to join us—we see so little of each other. We phone often, of course, but it's not the same."

"No, it's not, my dear. Now you know how your father and I feel about you!" Her voice held only a trace of sarcasm.

Feeling encouraged, I caught the train back to Clipton. I had my parents' promise they would spend Christmas at the rectory. Now I had to work on my children.

The day of the christening turned out to be quite cloudy and humid. Little Stella was testy, and her two siblings were overly excited with all the goings-on. Beverly looked lovely in a dusky pink dress with matching jacket. Regretfully, the level of her anxiety was increasing and was displayed in her face.

"Stella, help me. These two are being brats, and Robert isn't here to take them off my hands."

"Where is he?"

"He stopped at the club to make sure things were in order for the luncheon. He'll be here any moment—at least he'd better be, or there'll be trouble tonight." She grinned. "He drives me crazy, but I so love him."

She handed me the baby and hurried off, calling to Robbie and Sarah to join her. I studied the baby's perfect oval face and long eyelashes. Soft curls, the colour of chestnuts, poked from under the silk bonnet. I rocked her gently as overwhelming love flowed through me.

"You make a delightful picture, Stella." Cynthia McKinley was holding her brother's arm. "The invitation says you are godmother. It's such a privilege to be responsible for a child's religious upbringing. If Michael and I had been blessed with children, we would certainly have brought them up in the Christian faith."

I answered that I did, indeed, feel privileged. Simon said nothing, and only nodded in greeting. He seemed somewhat subdued. Perhaps he was not pleased to be his sister's chaperone.

"Is Michael joining us?" I asked sweetly. "It's a short service, and there's a posh reception at the club."

"Michael is unable to attend. He . . . he's working," Cynthia replied rather quickly. "Those students keep him unreasonably busy; he never has a minute for himself." She turned to her brother. "Come along, Simon. We'd better get seated."

I had an uneasy feeling as I watched them enter the church. I was not convinced Michael was working. Had he been seen talking with me? I became aware I was holding the baby a little too tightly; her puckered lips were about to omit a protest, and brought me back to reality. I kissed her soft brow and straightened her gown. I was pleased I had chosen the more expensive one. She looked adorable.

Vicar Ken had helped me come up with a short, charming ceremony. Beverly, Robert, and I slobbered a little . . . and so did a few others when he held the baby over the font and blessed her with holy water. Robbie and Sarah were fascinated. As soon as the service was over, Bev and Robert dashed off to the club in order to greet guests as they arrived for the lavish reception. Reg took extra care driving with the baby, Robbie, and Sarah as passengers. When I glanced at him in the rear-view mirror, he looked glum. I put it down to him perhaps thinking about his own two boys.

I came out of the club cloakroom after freshening up, and almost bumped into Margot Hughes Young. "Well, well. If it isn't the Lady Stella herself. How are you?"

"I'm very well, thank you, Margot. And you?"

"I heard you had a bit of a scare a couple of weeks ago. Someone attacked you after the planning commission meeting."

"No, you're mistaken. My chauffeur was waiting for me, and we drove straight home to the rectory."

"Umm, that's not what I heard. Several people said they saw a man about to strike you." She stared hard at me. "Several people."

"Well, whoever those people were, they were quite wrong, Margot. Now, if you will excuse me, I must get back to the reception." I felt her eyes burning into my back as I walked away.

I enjoyed every moment of the christening event; even so, it was a relief to return to the rectory and kick off my new high heels. I wriggled my sore toes. "These feet are not happy anymore unless they're in wellingtons."

Alice chuckled. "You do exaggerate, Stella."

"I've become a country bumpkin. Goodbye, sophisticated city girl," I lamented.

"Oh, drink your tea and be quiet!"

I became serious. "That Margot Hughes Young gives me the creeps. She isn't the innocent dowager she appears to be."

"Oh, I've always had my suspicions about her, Stella. When her husband was killed, she mourned as expected, but she certainly recovered quickly. All that insurance money went to her head."

"What do you mean?" I had no idea Alice had such feelings.

"Well, some folk thought she had a fancy man because she was seen with him quite often. Caused a lot of talk—he was quite a bit younger, and obviously not well off financially by the way he was dressed. More like an ex-con, if you ask me." She laughed, shaking her head. "I don't know; the old girl must have something. It can't all be put down to money."

I sipped my tea thoughtfully. "I'm worried someone may know Michael McKinley warned me, and has put himself in danger. His wife seemed very edgy at the christening."

"Hopefully you're paying attention to what he said, Stella. If he is in danger, don't let it be for nothing."

"I won't," I answered soberly.

On the surface, Clipton seemed untouched by the problems of city life, but I had resided at the rectory long enough to know the small community was just as susceptible. Drug trafficking, murder, intrigue . . . Clipton had it all. Miller's campaign for clean water seemed long ago. How I wished he had seen the fruits of his labour. Beverly's father, Sam Euston, had followed through with his promise, and pressured owners of factories farther upstream to install filters on all their discharge pipes. Safe water was flowing once again in Clipton and beyond.

"Have you finished, Stella?" Alice pointed to my cup. "It's cold now. I can make fresh, if you like. Want a snack?"

"No thanks. I'm getting fat. Lots of good things in the house to eat," I protested. "Help me by not buying so much. You know I can't resist." I got up from the sofa and lethargically walked to the window. Mist clung to the tops of the trees like diaphanous rigging. "How are you and that Sergeant Ball getting along? I see him popping in now and then. Are you encouraging him?"

"Actually, I am." She blushed, and said nothing more.

"I'm glad to hear it."

I went out onto the terrace. Once again the garden was entering dormancy. It was sobering to acknowledge another year was almost over. Time was passing so quickly; I could not keep up. Summer had been shorter than usual because of miserable weather, and I had a lot to do to complete all that was necessary before the season ended. It was maintenance, really. Trees had matured, growing larger than the landscape design could tolerate, and annuals needed pulling out. It was hard work for the gardeners—and me. I became chilled and went back to the house for a jacket.

"Alice, I'm going to potter in the garden for a while."

"Righto, Stella. I have to make a run to town. I'll let you know before I leave."

I zipped up my jacket. It was colder than I anticipated, but I knew I'd soon warm up. Gardening always improved my spirit, no matter what the chore, and I felt uplifted as I filled the wheelbarrow with shears, a spade, and twine. Then I took off to the rose garden where several dozen plants needed attention. Life was pretty wonderful, I told myself as I put on tough working gloves and began to tackle the first bush. Not only was I planning a future with my beloved, but my cherished friend Alice also seemed to be heading in that direction. It was a couple of hours before the cold finally got to me. A door slammed in the distance, announcing Alice must have left on her errand, although I did not hear her call out to me. I stretched my aching back, loaded the tools into the wheelbarrow, and covered them with a pile of cuttings. My hands were protected, but sharp thorns had torn through my jacket sleeves, drawing blood. I dumped everything in the shed, too tired to do otherwise, and made my way to the house. I stopped at the entrance for a moment or two. The peace seemed almost tangible. Clouds tinged with silver hovered in a yellowing sky; in the distance, the opaque moon was waiting as a silent, obscure shadow.

A soaking in a hot bath relaxed me, and I lazily meandered to the kitchen to make a pot of tea. I was filling the kettle when I thought I heard . . . actually, I wasn't sure what. It was a little early for Alice to have returned. My imagination was running amok; however, I continued to listen intently until my ears buzzed with concentration. Was that a footstep or just a floorboard creaking as it compressed at the end of a chilly day? Something seemed out of place. My instinct, my faithful gut, told me I had company. Quickly grabbing a chef's knife from the block on the counter, I turned to face the door. At that very moment, the kettle came to a boil with an ear-shattering whistle. Frantically, I lifted the kettle from the flame.

"The door was open, so I let myself in. Hope you don't mind."

"Margot!" My stomach did a flip.

"We haven't visited in quite a while. I was in the area and thought I'd take a chance to catch you. Please don't let me keep you from your tea. Actually, I'd love a cup myself." She gestured to my hand. "You can put that knife down now, dear. If I startled you, I'm so sorry." I obediently placed the knife back into the block.

"The door was open, you said?"

"Yes, it was ajar." She smiled sweetly. Her thin lips were covered in a red lipstick that had bled into the creases encircling her mouth. "I should have brought a cake or something to go with the tea. Next time."

I was silent, unsure how to respond. The hair on the back of my neck was standing up, and my hands were cold. I poured the boiling water over the tea leaves and went to the cabinet for cups and saucers. "How do you take it, Margot? Milk or lemon?"

"I'll have what you're having, dear." She unbuttoned her coat and sat down at the table. "I've been wanting to talk with you for some time . . . just to make sure there's no misunderstanding between us." She settled herself, stretching her legs and crossing her feet at the ankles. I noticed her knee-length boots were made of very expensive ostrich leather. "When we met at the Petersens' christening, you seemed rather put out when I mentioned your attack. You denied it, but I know otherwise. I told you then that a man had been seen trying to enter your car, and it was not your chauffeur," she persisted.

"Margot, I appreciate your concern, but I was there, remember? No one attacked me. I attended the planning commission meeting, and Reg drove me home. No more excitement than that, I assure you."

She looked hard at me. "You're a foolish woman, Stella Campbell. You've got yourself into something that's none of your business. I know all about you and your detective spying on the farm. You need to take care, my dear."

"That sounds like a warning, Margot. As you seem to know everything, you must know I went to the farm at Simon Belsky's invitation."

"Oh, I do indeed. Perhaps you're thinking of signing up as one of Belsky's students?" She sniggered scornfully, but I avoided the bait.

"Let me remind you that Joe Blake and I worked to restore that building years ago. Naturally, I wanted to see what the students had accomplished." I handed her a cup of tea with milk. "Need I remind you the place has a ghastly past? Cleaning it up will help erase some of that."

She gave a wide smile, showing yellowing teeth. Her eyes were very bright. "I remember very well where and how my husband died. I shall never forget. You came to see me quite often at that time, and showed much kindness." Her tone seeped insincerity. "I miss our little tête-à-têtes, so allow me to reciprocate by giving you some advice." She finished her tea and put the cup down on the table. "I suggest you take care. With your misguided meddling, you are involving yourself in matters that are none of your concern. We wouldn't want any harm to come to you, dear . . . now would we?" She rose from the chair. "I'm glad we had this little chat. Clipton is a small community, so we all need to watch out for each other, don't you agree? Accidents have a way of happening to anyone—just when they are least expected." She buttoned her coat and pulled on black leather gloves. She had deep scarring above one wrist that I noticed for the first time.

"Margot, how is your friend Roger Spencer?" Her face lost colour. "I haven't seen him for quite a while. Did he find another job after being fired by the Building Society?" I waited for a moment, enjoying her discomfort. "As you are so tuned in to this community, you know he stole large sums of money from me—and others. For drugs, apparently."

She suddenly reached out and grabbed my arm, digging her fingers into my flesh. I tried to pull free, but she held on tight. "Don't play games with me, Stella Campbell! Roger Spencer is no friend of mine." Her back stiffened, and she pushed me away. "I'll see myself out." She was gone in a moment.

"Stella? I'm back." Alice came into the kitchen carrying a bag of groceries. "Margot Hughes Young almost knocked me over as she rushed out the door. What was she doing here?" Then she saw my face. "Stella—whatever is it?"

"She just turned up . . . said the door was open. I think she was watching me while I was gardening." I remembered I had spent time upstairs. Had she been in the house while I was bathing? "Could you have left the front door open, Alice? I'm sure you didn't, but—how could she have got in?"

"Of course I didn't leave the door open! Do you think I would be so careless when I knew you were here alone? I made sure I locked the deadbolt. The house was secure, I assure you, Stella. Where were you working? The rose garden?" I nodded. "You wouldn't have seen her from there. The witch—she must have come in through the patio door."

"She told me to be careful—that accidents happen." I looked down at my arm where bruises were developing from the imprint of her gloved hand. "Look, Alice! She means business."

"She put her hands on you? Good gracious, Stella!" Her face turned crimson with anger. "John will give me hell again for leaving you, and he is right to do so. You've got to phone him right away."

The phone rang just at that moment. "Had a break, so thought I'd call my favourite girl."

"I was just about to call you, John."

"Telepathy, that's what it is." I could hear the smile in his voice.

I tried to sound matter-of-fact as I reported Margot's visit. As expected, he gave me an earful. "Show some sense, Stella. The woman was trespassing! Why didn't you throw her out?" He was starting to shout. "I'm based at the Yard and spend all my time worrying about you in Clipton. I can't be split in two like this." He then demanded to talk with Alice. She took his barrage of expletives without comment, although her cheeks were quite pink when she put the phone down. John must have spoken to Sergeant Ball, too, because he promptly showed up at the rectory and took notes on all that had taken place with Margot. When I went to bed that evening, it was difficult to abate my racing thoughts. I sipped on a glass of warm milk, hoping it would help settle me; sadly, it had little effect. I knew Alice was also having difficulty sleeping, not only out of concern for me but because of the double dose of guilt John had laid on her.

John remained at the Yard for another couple of days. When he arrived in Clipton, he lost no time in meeting with Alice and Sergeant Ball in the lounge before talking with me in my bedroom. His whole demeanour reeked of frustration. "Things are coming to a head—for whatever reason, you seem to be becoming more implicated." He put his hands on my shoulders, softening his tone. "You think you're invincible. I can assure you, you are not!" I felt like a teenager being chastised for breaking curfew. I put my head against his shoulder. "You can't get around me that way. Yes, you can," he whispered.

CHAPTER SIXTEEN

John stayed at the rectory for almost a week. I decided it was time to put all the intrigue behind me, and concentrate on the Christmas holiday. Julia and Tim had called earlier to confirm they would be coming. My parents were looking forward to joining us. Five weeks to go before they would all meet John. He went into the village a few times; never did say why. When I asked, he put his finger to the side of his nose and said, "Police business." On his last morning, he asked me to take a walk with him. It was cold, but I hardly noticed with my love at my side. The frost-covered fields looked magical as a delicate sun transformed the icy glitter to diamonds. We came to the equestrian centre outfield, and stopped to watch a small group of horses wrapped in plaid blankets stomping to keep their circulation moving. I put out my hand, clicking my tongue to encourage them to come over to us. Clouds of steam exploded from their large nostrils as they warily walked towards us. They came to the fence and allowed a touch or two, but were too skittish to permit more advances. I turned to John and searched his face for clues to what he had been mulling over in silence for the past thirty minutes. I cleared my throat, wanting to ask what was going through his mind, but was hesitant to break the silence. Unable to hold myself back any longer, I asked the question that had been haunting me for days. I took his hand, and let the words come.

"John, why don't I know anything about your life in London?" He looked startled. "I've never been to your home, never met your family, your friends. Whenever we've been together in London, we stayed at a hotel. I feel excluded, darling. It's as if everything is fine as long as we're in Clipton." There was tightness in my throat, but the words were out, and I couldn't take them back.

He looked down at me, a puzzled frown across his brow. "How can you say such a thing? When I'm away, we talk on the phone all the time. You're right about not meeting my family and friends because I always come to Clipton whenever I have time off. You've never suggested coming to London for longer than a weekend. What's brought this on now?"

"I'm not sure . . . insecurity, mostly. I was thinking if it wasn't for police work, you wouldn't need to come to Clipton, would you?"

"Stella, I don't understand." He drew me close. "I'm here because of you—you are what I want—need. Yes, the slaughterhouse case got me to Clipton, but you are the reason I'm still here—not the investigation. Ball and the local police are quite competent to handle things; they could report to me at the Yard." He looked at me. "Are you having second thoughts about us?"

"I feel we're just drifting, not going anywhere." I was resolute; I had picked my moment to know for sure. "We have odd weeks here and there—and wonderful weekends—other times we see each other only when you can fit me in. I understand Clipton isn't where you would choose to be. You're a Londoner through and through. I've made my life here, but I would change that if—" I couldn't finish.

"I work, Stella. I have a job that I really enjoy. I'm headquartered at New Scotland Yard and can't do anything about that. And we see each other often; have you forgotten I've been here all week? It takes a lot of persuading to get the time I do have in Clipton. I could transfer full-time, I suppose, if that's really what you're asking, but being a local bobby just doesn't appeal to me, frankly." He was getting agitated. "Once this case is closed, I will be given another. It could mean staying in London or going elsewhere. You need to face that, Stella. Crime is universal, and my job will take me where the need is at that particular time." How easily he made his argument.

"Of course I understand your work dictates where you go." I was about to ask, *What if we were married?* but lost my nerve.

"I don't think you do understand. It's far from easy for me. I'm concerned about you when I'm away, and this episode with Hughes Young makes it doubly worrying."

"I don't like feeling this way, John. I'm truly grateful for what we have, and I love you so very much." I meant every word. "I think what I want . . . need to know is, do we have a future together? Can I count on us?" He looked as if I had slapped him.

"I'm counting on us, Stella. You must be thinking otherwise to ask such a question." He stepped back from me. "I know what I want, but that has to be in the future. You need to decide if you want the same thing and are prepared to wait."

I looked away, an ache deep within my chest. What was I doing? This man meant everything to me, and now I was threatening the future I longed for. "John." I wanted him to take me in his arms and make everything all right. "I just want things between us to be better, more settled. Am I really being so unreasonable?" I touched his arm. "When I'm in London, couldn't we take the time to meet for lunch or a drink maybe? You know, be involved away from a hotel. That's really all I'm talking about," I lied.

Without speaking, he stepped away and began to slowly walk back to the rectory. I watched the horses for a few moments longer. With a depth of sadness that crushed my very core, I followed the path but did not catch up with him. Why had I been so stupid, bringing my fears up now? I sounded like a spoiled, petulant brat. I should have taken a breath—waited until . . . when? We had been doing so well, and now I'd ruined everything. The internal tirade continued as I stumbled along and the rectory came into view. I rushed through the front door, rehearsing what I would say to him. Then I saw his overnight bag and briefcase in the hall. Alice was coming out of the lounge, her face showing puzzled concern.

"The inspector's gone. He said Sergeant Ball would pick his things up later. What's happened, Stella? He looked terrible."

"I've just opened my mouth once too often, Alice, and ruined everything, that's all." Tears began to roll down my cheeks. I didn't care; my heartache was agony.

"Oh, Stella. I'm so sorry." She became my surrogate mother again.

I desperately wanted to ask John for forgiveness, and spent a considerable amount of time standing by the phone. I didn't have enough courage to actually dial his number. After a week went by, I could stand it no longer. With nerves at breaking point, I called his office in London.

"Detective Chief Inspector Gailbrath isn't in this afternoon. You can leave a message," the female voice offered politely.

"When do you expect him back?"

"Not until tomorrow. Who is this, please? Who's calling?"

"Oh, just a friend. I'll call back. Thank you." I hung up hastily, hoping he would not get a message that a mysterious female had telephoned. He would surely know who it was. I felt a gnawing inside; it hurt deeply. I went up to my room and looked out on the bleak landscape. Winter was in full season. We had a lot of rain over the past few days, and the ground had reached its saturation limit. I put on a heavy sweater and anorak and made my way down the stairs to the kitchen.

"I have to get out for a while, Alice. I'll stay in the garden. Promise."

"You had better," she said rather crossly.

"I've just got to do something. Huddling in the house is driving me mad," I snapped back.

She stopped what she was doing and gave me her full attention. "You know, dear, if John isn't able to give you all that you want, better to know it now. It will only lead to grief later."

I picked up one of the hot apple turnovers that were just out from the oven. "I'll munch on this to keep warm." I tried to sound upbeat, to reassure my friend, but tears were welling up. "See you in a little while."

Alice was right—it was freezing—once I started walking, however, I knew it was just what I needed. The cold air would clear my mind and push away any dark thoughts. Christmas was around the corner, and I made a mental note to cut the holly and evergreens before the weekend. Beverly and I competed each year in embellishing our homes with elaborate decorations and lights that became the talk of Clipton. It had become a fervent challenge. I felt emotional as I thought about Julia and Tim coming to join me . . . my parents, too. I reassured myself I still had many loving people in my life—*but John, I want you. How do I ask for another chance?*

I absently walked on around the rectory property until I found myself at the side gate. Without hesitating, I went through and took the path to Tythe Farm. I walked quickly. A few things had been nagging at the back of my mind about the slaughterhouse. Someone had always accompanied me there since Sir Ralph had died. I needed time on the property alone, to let my thoughts develop. The house was deserted and the grounds unkempt. Boxwood hedges, once neatly trimmed by Joe, were now unhealthy and overgrown, and the small orchard in which he had taken such pride was in complete disarray. I had not thought of Joe for a long time, but his face came into my mind clearly, as if he was looking back at me. I had lost a wonderful friend when he moved north.

The empty windows of the house were streaked by weather. Obviously, the McKinleys were not good caretakers. It would have broken Joe's heart to see his beloved smallholding in such a sad state. I went straight over to the slaughterhouse. As usual, it was unlocked. The familiar smell of mildew engulfed my nostrils. Thanks to Simon Belsky's students, everything was tidy; only a stepladder remained leaning against one wall.

I sat down in the middle of the floor to let my eyes adjust to the diminishing natural light. John's photographs had exposed certain areas on the walls in various grey tones where there had been recent activity. I squinted to see if I could make out any differences in colour but found none. I got up and made my way to a corner. I thought if I started there and made my way along to the other end, I would have a methodical way to check each brick.

The light was fading fast, urging me to hurry as I made my way along the first wall. I reached up to the brick just above my head and then down to the last one at floor level. If someone were in a rush to pick up illegal drugs, they wouldn't take time to fetch a ladder and climb up. They would want to be straight in and out of the place, so the bricks in question had to be within easy reach. The cold was numbing, but I couldn't give up. I was on the second wall before I came across a loose brick at my eye level. I scraped away the soft plaster holding the brick in place, and yanked it free. Standing on tiptoes, I peered into the opening and saw several small packets. I reached in and took one out, placing it in my pocket. I looked the brick over carefully and saw nothing unusual. Then, as I was about to put it back in place, my thumb felt a slight ridge in a corner on a flat side. Sure enough, it was a number—4, to be exact. I carefully returned the brick and pressed the grout around it. Stepping back to view my effort, I was pleased with my handiwork; one could not tell anything had been disturbed. Thankfully, I noticed I'd covered the 4 with the grout. Quickly, I corrected my blunder.

It was dark outside, and a fine rain was falling steadily. Car headlights swept the farm road as they came towards the house. I threw myself to the ground and held my breath. Doors slammed, and I heard several footsteps on the paved path. The male voices were low, and I thought I heard a word or two of Spanish. Spanish? Oh, I was losing it, all right! The slaughterhouse door creaked as it closed. I lay still, too afraid to risk a dash for it. Then, I thought of Alice waiting at the rectory. Likely, by now, she had the police looking for me. Anxiety gave me courage to take a look over the top of a bush, and I saw a black Mercedes. I wasn't able to see the license plate very well, but the reflected letter L showed clearly—and the numbers 389. A second car was parked behind it. My stomach churned as I crawled away on my knees to the road, thankful now to the McKinleys for the protection of the wall of overgrown shrubbery.

I entered the kitchen and got the expected dressing down from Alice. I gave no explanation . . . just stood in front of her, feeling thoroughly wretched for causing such concern. "I'm truly sorry, Alice."

"Rubbish! You're not sorry." She was furious, ignoring my soaking clothes and mud-covered knees. "Oh, you go along for a while; then, when it suits you, you do exactly what you like."

"Well, stop treating me like a child," I snapped. "I don't need permission from anyone if I want to go out!" My own frustration level was rising, as was my voice.

She took a step abruptly towards me. "Then start behaving like an adult! You're a selfish woman who thinks only of herself." Her eyes narrowed with anger.

I slunk off to my room, feeling totally wretched. I castigated myself harshly over—oh, so many things, until sleep eventually took over and I escaped into a light slumber. It was later, when I was freshening up, that I noticed an odd taste in my mouth and concluded I must have got something on my hands while at the farm, probably from the putty-like grout. Luckily, a thorough brushing of my teeth took care of the bitterness. Luckily, too, the deep feelings we had for each other moved Alice and me forward from frustration to an enjoyable calm evening.

Reg had taken a few days off. Too impatient to wait for his return to drive me, I took the train to London. In my handbag was the small packet I had removed from the slaughterhouse. Dutifully, I had made Alice privy to my discovery, and it was with her blessing I now made my way to an independent laboratory, the address of which I had discovered in the telephone directory. While waiting for an analysis of the substance, I walked along Regent Street admiring the holiday decorations.

"Stella?"

I turned and caught my breath. "Hello."

"What are you doing here?" John broke into a grin. "You look marvellous."

"Thanks. You look good, too." *Oh, John!* I wanted to hold him close, feel his lips on mine. "I'm just doing some holiday shopping." I hoped I sounded detached.

"Of course." He stared at me, searching my face. "I've missed you. Wanted to phone but thought you'd rather not hear from me again." I became tongue-tied. "Stella, am I right? Do you not want to hear from me?" He took a step towards me and grabbed my arm. "It's been hell without you. Will you at least have a coffee with me? Please!"

I couldn't resist. "I'd like that," I stammered.

We said little and sipped on our coffees, glad to have something to do. We were polite in our small talk, having lost the easy comfort we had felt not long ago. I desperately wanted to feel his arms around me, be secure in our love again. I reproached myself in silence. My self-doubts and insecurities had ruined the chance of the life the man I loved deeply had offered me, but my questions concerning his marriage, his career, and life in general had failed to reconcile with his answers, and everything stopped there. John put down his cup and looked at his watch.

"Time to return to the grindstone, I'm afraid." He looked relieved. "It was good to see you again, Stella. I'd like to continue seeing you. Of course, I'll leave that up to you." There was a lump as hard as a rock in my throat that prevented me from replying. He reached over and kissed my cheek and then was gone.

"So, the laboratory confirmed what you thought, Stella? There must be quite a number of addicts in Clipton to make it worthwhile setting up such a scheme." Alice sat across from me on the sofa. "Cocaine is nasty. Ruins your life, and all those around you."

"You sound as if you've had the experience?"

"Not me personally. I had good friends who lost both sons to it. It destroyed not only the boys, but their parents, too. I must say, I've not seen any signs from people we know. Have you?" She threaded a needle with yellow silk, and returned to embroidering a stem of *Genista monspessulana* on the corner of a linen cloth, the fancy name for the common shrub called French Broom.

"Nope! I don't know anything about drugs, so I wouldn't know what to look for. John, of course, told me what he suspected and, now, I've confirmed it for myself. The question is, what to do about it."

"You don't do anything, my girl! It's police work. Just let them deal with it."

"Let them deal with it? You're not serious? I mean, really, we've talked about them dealing with it for years. Three people were murdered, presumably because of the drugs, and the malarkey is still going on. Why?" That was only one of the questions on the endless list, of course.

"Changing the subject, Stella . . . to a sensitive one, unfortunately, but have you decided what to do about John? I didn't know what to say to Ball when he came over yesterday."

"What do you mean? Did he ask you about us?"

"Well, in a roundabout way. He asked if you were expecting John for the weekend. I said it was doubtful."

"Doesn't he know we've broken up? That seems a bit odd when he works with John so closely. Perhaps we need to start asking him a few questions, Alice. Or, more precisely, you asking him questions."

"I'm having lunch with him tomorrow. I'll see what I can do. I agree, Stella. Something is not gelling. I'm to meet Ball in town, which is a change. He usually comes here for a freebie . . . well, not exactly, dear; I know you're picking up the tab."

"You are a silly goose," I laughed.

Alice drove off in her Mini to meet Sergeant Ball after dropping me off at Beverly's home. Little Stella was gaining weight, and her dimples were becoming more pronounced in her chubby face.

"Isn't she like Robert, Stella? He says he doesn't see it, but I think she is the image. Are you like your daddy, darling?" Beverly lifted the baby up above her head, and the little one screamed out in delight. "Well, you've been here long enough, my friend. Start talking to me about your policeman. He's a bloody fool if he's thrown you over. Is it someone else? Is he gay?" She looked so serious, I couldn't help laughing.

"It's nothing like that, Beverly! We just had different ideas about things, that's all. He asked me to be patient, insisting we had a future, but what he could offer me now wasn't enough. I thought it was, then I started to feel I was the one doing all the giving." My words hung in the air without Bev interrupting. "All his commuting back and forth from London didn't help. When he did have time for me, I felt he wasn't totally present. He was the consummate policeman. I didn't realise at the beginning, but the job always came first."

"Didn't you tell him how you felt? I thought you, of all people, would speak up."

"Oh, I tried, believe me, but I made such a hash of it. He just didn't get it, or chose not to—I don't know which. When I brought it up, I sounded like an insecure child. It just came out all wrong. He walked away, packed his bag, and left. No '*let's talk about it, try to work it out.*' He just left." My lip trembled with the sting of the memory. "I bumped into him in London the other day, and my insides turned to jelly. He said he wanted to continue seeing me, but I don't think I can go back now." I felt desperately sad. "It's over."

"Maybe, maybe not. If you still love him and he loves you, there is always a way."

"I would like to think that is true because I do love and miss him dreadfully, but we've lost the magic; I can't believe how quickly it's gone." My voice faltered. "We couldn't even hold a simple conversation for an hour. It hurt so much."

"Stella! Come here, my dear." She held me to her ample bosom as if I was Little Stella, and I was calmed somewhat.

Alice arrived to pick me up. As we drove off, she reported, "I did as you asked, Stella, and questioned Ball about John." She shook her head. "He didn't know you had broken up; said the investigation was proceeding and John would be in Clipton on Thursday. That's only two days away. I told him likely John would be bedding down with him full-time at the hotel now. He didn't seem to be too happy about it."

CHAPTER SEVENTEEN

I returned to London for the rest of the week to visit my parents, and to pressure them not to change their minds about spending Christmas at the rectory. It was a legitimate reason to be out of town when John arrived.

"I'm counting on you coming," I told my mother. "It will only be us, Julia, and Tim. Don't let Daddy talk you out of it."

"He won't, Stella. We told you we'd come. I think Daddy is actually keen on the idea, because he wants to check out the rectory grounds."

"Practically everything is dormant now, Mum. Oh, well, at the very least he'll see that the changes I've made are more in line with the architectural design of the original building. I hope they get his seal of approval."

My mother sat down on the sofa beside me and took my hand. "Darling, are you happy? I mean, really happy? You live alone in that large rambling house in a small community. What keeps you there, particularly now you and John have broken up?"

"I'm quite happy, Mummy. Really! I miss John, of course. It'll take a while to get over him, but I will." How quickly the tears still came.

"You will, Stella. I don't want to pry, darling, but if you need to talk, I'm always here."

"I know. Thank you."

"Why's everyone looking so glum? I hope you haven't forgotten we're going to see *The Mousetrap* play this evening?" My father came into the room carrying the day's newspaper. He exchanged a questioning look with my mother, who nodded ever so slightly. Reassured, he settled down and opened the sports page.

I stood up, struggling to sound stronger in spirit than I felt. "I think I'll take a walk. I won't be long—just need some fresh air."

"I've no argument with you walking, Stella; you just do an awful lot of it, my girl."

"It's my therapy, Dad. I can chatter away nineteen to the dozen, and no one answers me back," I laughed.

"Lunch at noon."

"I won't be late, Mum." I bent and kissed her cheek. "I love you."

"We love you, darling." She placed her hand against my cheek. "Don't you forget it."

I walked over to the greenbelt that backed onto my parents' housing development, my pace slowed by the ache in my chest. I didn't stay long, and returned to my loving parents as their dejected child.

Reg picked me up from Clipton's train station. I slumped down in the back seat of the car with my mother's words still in my head. Perhaps I should sell the rectory and move back to London. When we reached the rectory, Alice was adorning the front door with a large wreath of evergreens.

"Stella! It's so good to have you back."

"It's good to see you, Alice." I caught her look of concern. "I've only been gone a few days. Is everything all right?"

Reg passed by with my suitcase. "She's been counting the hours waiting for you, Stella. You've got two mothers, remember?"

"Away with you now, Reg. I missed her, that's all."

We entered the door together. "Alice!" Mixed evergreens were arranged in a large brass bowl on the hall secretary and gave off a rich woodland smell. Garlands of fresh pine tied with red velvet bows were draped around the banisters to the staircase. "It's lovely!"

"Reg did his share. He'll pick up the tree once you've tagged it." She smiled, happy again.

"I can't thank you both enough!"

"We wanted you to be pleased to be back."

"Of course I'm pleased, Alice. This is my home, and you've made it look beautiful." I knew what she meant though. John's shadow still hovered.

The next couple of days were focused on getting the house decorations finished, and Alice started accumulating items for our family feast. I was on my second trip to the grocer with her detailed list when I bumped into John coming through the exit. He nodded with a polite smile, and I went into the shop feeling utterly despondent. When I returned to the rectory, Sergeant Ball was in the kitchen with Alice. He got up from the table when I entered, a sheepish smile on his face.

"Hello, Sergeant!" I was overly cheerful, hoping to put him at ease. The fragrance of cinnamon filled the room. On the counter were a couple of cooling racks holding iced currant buns. My resistance receded like the mercury in a refrigerator thermostat, and I helped myself. Later, when Sergeant Ball had departed, Alice reported he and John were reluctant roommates. The close camaraderie throughout their many years of working together seemed suddenly absent. "It's all business now, Ball said. He's quite upset about it." Alice frowned. "When working past cases, the two worked as a team—that is, until recently. Now John has become overly civil, and quite secretive about his whereabouts on several occasions. Ball took it for granted John was with you. I soon corrected him on that idea."

I was alone that evening wrapping gifts when a loud banging on the front door interrupted my pensive mood. "What the blazes? Don't knock the door down, I'm coming!" I hurried to open the door, prepared to give somebody a sharp talking-to, but my words stuck in my throat when I looked into Beverly's tear-streaked face. "My dear, whatever is it? Bev?" I reached out for her, and she sobbed against my shoulder. Fear closed my throat. Could something have happened to Robert or the children? *Please, please let them be all right.* She tried to speak but made little sense. I led her into the sitting room and sat her down on the sofa until she gained some control. “Is Robert . . . the kiddies . . . ?”

“Yes, yes, they’re all right. It’s—oh, Stella, I’m so dreadfully sorry—it’s John! He’s dead!”

CHAPTER EIGHTEEN

It took several days before I could face Bev's words, days of sobbing and emotional torture that left my body and mind broken, in spite of Dr Levinton's soporific medication. About a week later, I was being fussed over by a doting Alice, when Reg announced Sergeant Ball wanted to see me. He led a shattered, distraught man into the room, and I choked up at the sight of him.

"Sit by the fire, Sergeant. It's turned so cold again." My voice sounded several octaves higher than normal as I struggled to get the words out. He did as I asked, brushing his hand across his eyes as if trying to wipe away a painful image. "A cup of coffee? Alice just brought a fresh pot in." He nodded acceptance, and a silent Alice filled a cup with the steaming brew.

"Where did you find him, Sergeant?" My question hung heavily in the room. He took a few moments before turning to me.

"In the old slaughterhouse at Tythe Farm. He'd been shot. Judging by the lividity, he'd been dead for fewer than twelve hours." His voice faltered. "Looked like there'd been a fight; his body was considerably bruised." The sergeant was suffering; it was obvious to see. He had lost not only his chief inspector but, more importantly, his friend. He put the untouched coffee on the table. "I understand Mrs Petersen broke the news to you after seeing police activity at the farm." His voice was flat, the professional policeman again, belying the emotion beneath. "She was driving by. It was natural to ask what was going on with all the commotion, but your local constable violated his duty by talking with Mrs Petersen. He's been reprimanded, needless to say."

"She meant well, Sergeant, and he didn't give any detail—only that . . ." I could not complete the sentence. Sergeant Ball's face showed his own agony. "What about Roger? I heard about him later."

"Roger Spencer was found in his flat with what looked like a self-inflicted gunshot wound to his head."

"Will it never end?" I leaned back against the sofa, thoroughly spent.

"I really need to talk with you, Mrs Campbell. I can come back later if you'd prefer."

"No, Sergeant. We can't waste any more time." I sat up straight and turned to face him. "Do you know what John was doing at the farm? Did he go to meet Roger?"

"I don't know, Mrs Campbell. He didn't say much to me over the last few days—just took off without a word. As I told Alice earlier, I thought he was seeing you, so I didn't pry." He cleared his throat, looking markedly uncomfortable. "You know, of course, I shouldn't be saying anything to you, Mrs Campbell, not when we have an investigation going on. It's just I know what you meant to him, what he meant to you." He took out his infamous notebook. "Can you tell me how he seemed the last time you saw him? Was he his usual self or, well, stressed, pressured—you know, different?"

"No, I bumped into him in London. He seemed eager to reconcile. I was the one who was distant. He tried to talk with me, to persuade me to try again, but I cut him off." I looked away with shame. "When I saw him recently at the grocer's, here, in Clipton, we exchanged a glance . . . no words. I take responsibility for that. I gave him no encouragement." My voice faded. The ensuing silence was fraught with raw emotion. My heart cried out for forgiveness; it had been my false pride that denied us a second chance. Would that chance have saved him?

Alice put another log on the fire, stirring it back to life. The room was draped in winter shadows in spite of it being morning.

"Was he alone at that time? Did you see him meet up with anyone?" Sergeant Ball was not giving up.

"No, we passed as I went in the door and he came out. Of course, he could have met with anyone; I wouldn't have known."

"Did you notice anyone who would seem out of place in the shop?"

"Not really. It was crowded with people buying groceries for the Christmas holiday. Margot Hughes Young and Marjory Levinton were chatting by the bakery counter, and Cynthia McKinley was in line at the register. It is, after all, our main market in town."

"Did the inspector have a grocery bag? Had he made purchases?"

I thought for a moment. "Not that I can remember. I think he was empty handed."

"Did the ladies you mention say anything to you?"

"I don't think Cynthia saw me. Marjory and Margot wished me a good morning, but there was no conversation as such. I was in a hurry to get back with the spices Alice needed. If you remember, you were here when I returned, Sergeant."

"Yes, I remember."

"Can't all this wait for a while, Ball? Give her a break?" Alice picked up the coffee tray. "It's nearly time for lunch anyway."

"I'm sorry, Mrs Campbell. As I've said, I can come back."

"No, let's go on, Sergeant."

"As you wish."

Alice rolled her eyes, letting me know she was not happy to be undermined.

"I know I keep repeating myself until I'm blue in the face, Sergeant, but I don't understand why everything, from Sir Ralph's death until now, has taken so long. Don't you have enough officers on the case?" I threw my hands up in despair. "Local police seem to be on a perpetual holiday. John worked out months ago why and how the slaughterhouse was being used. I was with him when he discovered new grout had been placed around some of the bricks. I presume the building was watched after that?" My voice strengthened. "Do you know who was making the drug deals? Sir Ralph was killed when—almost three years ago? Then Steven

Lagerquist and Miller Owens." I suddenly felt very cold. "Now we've lost John and Roger, Sergeant. How can this be? How much longer do we have to endure this nightmare?"

"I'm not at liberty to share police information with you, Mrs Campbell. In spite of what you say, there's been diligence in all our enquiries, and a case has been developed."

"It isn't over, though, is it?"

"Mrs Campbell, please! I don't want to be rude interrupting you, but you must stop all these questions. Please accept my word we are close to the end. That's all I can say at this time."

Alice's look appealed to me, and I withdrew into myself once again.

"The inspector, he . . . John didn't suffer, ma'am. I want you to know that."

"Maybe, but if the police had got off their arses and arrests were made, he might still be alive!"

When Sergeant Ball left the rectory, I watched from the window a stooped, empty man walk to his car. "I'm sorry I was horrid to Ball, Alice. That chap needs a pal to talk to, someone he can confide in. One would think policemen get used to death; this is different, John was his friend."

"We're getting together later. Do you want some lunch or to be left alone?"

"Stay with me; I want to talk. My mind will explode if I don't!" The wind had picked up, attacking two plum trees recently planted to view from the lounge window. In the spring they would be full of lovely pink blossoms. I went back to the sofa and sat down. "What are we missing? There's got to be something right under our noses that we're not seeing." I sighed. "We need to make some notes." I gathered a pen and pad of paper from the desk. "I wish we had a blackboard like detectives use in films." My attempt at levity failed. I wrote on the pad the heading, *Similar factors in all the murders.* Any thought of lunch was gone. The gloom deepened in the room as we turned our minds back to the time when I discovered Sir Ralph. "Acid was the weapon used on him and Steven Lagerquist."

"Mr Owens, too."

"Yes." I wrote down the three names in a column headed *Acid* with the corresponding dates of their deaths. "Sir Ralph died at Tythe Farm in the slaughterhouse, Steven here at the rectory, and Miller in the ditch."

"Joe Blake always thought you were set up to go to the farm the day you found Sir Ralph, Stella. He believed Sir Ralph's death was a mistake."

"Yes, yes . . . I know he and others thought that, but I've never believed anyone wanted to harm me. Joe was the property owner, and would be the one to discover any shady business going on. It would make more sense to bump him off. I had no hold on anyone, and my own life is an open book."

"Perhaps the killer thought Joe had found something and shared the information with you. If you were roughed up, it would be a warning to Joe to keep his mouth shut. Unfortunately, things went too far. Mistake or not, Sir Ralph's death put a stop to additional work."

"That's just it—Joe and I didn't look beyond cleaning up the old building," I insisted.

"Didn't you whitewash the walls?"

"Yes, and we repaired any loose grout. Joe and I would have been nitwits not to have seen anything out of place. There was nothing to arouse our curiosity. It was that old blood and guts on the tile floor that stumped us; that is, until Bev's Robert suggested using the hydrochloric acid. The numbering of the bricks, and what was left behind them, must have been set up after we quit."

"It's too bad Joe moved north."

"Oh, it's so frustrating when all we can do is speculate. And we still don't know why Steven was killed. He was as innocent as anyone could possibly be."

"We may never know, Stella."

"And we'll probably never know what Miller observed at the farm."

"He wasn't found at the farm."

"Yes, Alice, I know!" I replied scornfully. "I bet he was killed at the farm though, and then his body dumped in the ditch. I'm sure his death had nothing to do with the protest against Beverly's father. I can't say I like Sam Euston a whole lot, but he is no killer." I tapped the pen against my teeth as I reconsidered that statement. "No. Bev's daddy is a ruthless, conniving son of a bitch, but not a killer."

Alice turned on the lamps. I glanced at my watch and was surprised to find it close to three o'clock. "We need to stop this! You must be pooped, too." I stretched my arms and legs, encouraging blood to flow. "Let's go out for an early dinner, something simple and fast. What do you think? Can you put off the sergeant?"

"If you're up to it, I'm game. I'll phone Ball now. Do you want Reg to drive?"

"No, give him a break. I'll take the Rover. It'll be good to get a change of scenery." I left the room, calling back, "See you in thirty minutes."

The roads were slick, but we arrived at Michel's Bistro without mishap. The wonderful smell of onion soup wafted through the already crowded room, piquing my appetite the moment we entered. A pretty young hostess informed us there would be a few minutes' wait, so we made our way to the equally crowded bar. Simon Belsky and Ted Nyby were seated at a table chattering amiably with a couple of young men, presumably Simon's students. Ted caught my eye and raised his glass in a salute. "Good evening."

"Ted."

"Stella, I haven't seen you for ages. Please, ladies, come and join us." Simon got up from his chair and stepped forward, indicating the empty chairs next to him.

"Thank you, Simon, but we're just about to be seated. Alice and I are salivating for a bowl of onion soup." I hoped my smile covered the feelings of despair that had overtaken me again; I still couldn't accept that John was gone. Was it really less than two week ago? Thankfully, my name was called, and with a forced cheery goodbye, we followed the hostess to our table. I felt Alice's gaze on me. "What?"

"You know what! Are you up to this? Shall we leave, Stella?"

"No, not at all; it's good to be with other people." Tears welled up as my voice cracked. "I miss him so, Alice. He is everywhere but nowhere."

"Can I take your order now, ladies?" The waiter looked uncomfortable, witnessing my distress. He leaned down close to my ear and whispered. "Is there anything I can do to help, Mrs Campbell?"

"Thank you, Alex, I'm all right. Can we just have a couple more minutes before we order?"

"Of course." He discreetly withdrew.

Alice and I both felt better after a large bowl of scrumptious onion soup topped with a slice of sourdough dripping in melted cheese. We even had a glass apiece of robust ale. "How about some dessert?"

"Oh, Stella, I'm stuffed. Perhaps a little intoxicated too." Merriment brightened her grey eyes. "I'd better have some coffee."

We arrived back at the rectory feeling subdued but grateful for each other's company. Too emotionally drained for anything else, we made ourselves comfortable for the evening and turned on the radio. The news reporter gave brief details of Roger's death, but said nothing about John. Later in my room, I gave in to the anguish I had tried desperately to keep at bay throughout the day. Why had I not encouraged John when we met in London? Had he not said he had hoped we could work things out? What was the matter with me? Why had I denied us a future, denied myself what I really wanted? *Oh, John.* Every muscle in my tense body felt bruised. I finally made my way to the kitchen to get a drink of water. *What will become of me?* I asked the empty room. I had hurt before, but never like this. Then I remembered my family was coming in two weeks for Christmas, and knew it would take every ounce of strength I had to get through it.

"It's going to be all right, my dear girl." Alice appeared behind me and led me back to my room. I slept finally, and awoke to find myself wrapped in her arms. My friend had held me through the night, and I drew consolation from her devotion.

CHAPTER NINETEEN

Alice picked up the phone and talked for a couple of minutes before transferring Julia to me. I was grateful to Alice that I didn't have to go into the latest happenings in Clipton, and Julia was thoughtful enough not to mention anything beyond holiday arrangements. "I'm excited, Mummy. It will be marvellous getting away from the hospital. I'm one of the few lucky ones."

"I'm thrilled it has worked out, Julia. Reg is going to pick up the tree later today. We've tagged a beauty." It took a lot of digging to find any holiday cheer, but talking with my daughter made me aware I needed my family and the house full again. "Alice is a permanent fixture in the kitchen. Oh, the smells coming forth are from heaven." I was suddenly caught up in the moment. "I'm counting the days, Julia."

"Bye, Mummy. I'll phone again. Love you!"

"I love you, my darling child." My children and parents would be with me in ten days, and I was determined to make it a special time. I wandered off to find Reg. We had to get the tree up and decorated, and I had gift shopping to finish. Anything to keep my mind occupied.

It took hours for Alice, Reg, and me to cover the scented fir with crystal balls and whimsical holiday figures. Reg switched on strings of tiny white lights that illuminated the room with their soft glow, and brought out highlights from the ornaments. The sitting room became magical. Glorious Christmas carols playing on the stereo kept us in the appropriate spirit. Our glasses of heavily brandied eggnog were refilled a number of times, increasing the volume of our singalong. I gathered the wrapped gifts from my room and placed them under the sweeping branches of the magnificent tree. It was all coming together. Three very grateful friends sat around the kitchen table that night. I knew my cup runneth over.

I got an early start the next morning, although an extra half an hour in bed would have been appreciated. I had awoken with a throbbing hangover. I drove into town to complete my gift purchases. Dr Levinton drew along side in his sturdy Austin Metro as I parked the Rover.

"How are you, Stella?"

"I'm taking it a day at a time. Keeping busy preparing for the holiday is a big help. My family will be coming the end of next week." I tried to sound enthusiastic, in an attempt to convince him I was progressing. "Don't forget you and your wife are invited to the rectory for a pre-Christmas drink. Check your calendar and let me know. It will be nice to have you as a guest instead of my doctor making a professional call." We both smiled, making an effort over a silly joke.

"I'll ask Marjory to telephone you. In the meantime, keep up whatever you're doing; it suits you."

I nodded. "Will do." I pulled my jacket collar up and walked briskly to the hardware shop. Fred, the owner, was adding tinsel to the display shelves. "A very festive touch, Fred."

"Good morning, Mrs Campbell. Out and about early today." He shook my hand warmly. "What can I get for you?"

"I'll just wander around, if you don't mind. I'm looking for stocking stuffers."

"Take your time." He walked over to help another customer, and I lost myself in filling a basket with torches, batteries, giant clips, compasses, novelty key rings, and so on. Fred packed everything into two sturdy carrier bags, and I took off to the stationers. Alice had mentioned a couple of books she hoped to read, and I wanted to be sure I got copies to put into her stocking. I chose several wallets of useful notelets, and was about to reach for chocolate Father Christmases when I came face to face with

Fiona. She looked sombre in a black coat but a cheery red scarf was wrapped around her neck.

"What a surprise, stranger. How are you, Fiona?" Then I remembered Roger Spencer. "I'm so very sorry about Roger."

She smiled wistfully. "Would you have a cup of coffee with me, Stella?"

"Certainly. When?"

"Now, if possible? It's important."

"Of course. I'll pay for these and then join you."

"Thank you. I'll wait outside."

As I stood in line at the cash register, I realised I had not given much thought to Fiona in all the months since she and Roger were guests at the rectory. What had happened between the two of them? Why had she disappeared? One question led to another, as usual, but the thread was broken when the sales assistant rang up my purchases. Fiona reached for one of the shopping bags as I joined her outside, and we walked together to the Main Street Café. We did not speak until we were seated in a booth at the back of the room.

She leaned forward and placed her hand gently on my arm. "Stella, I want you to listen carefully to what I'm about to tell you. I'm taking you into my confidence because we can help each other."

A waitress came up, and we quickly placed an order for coffee. I looked straight at Fiona and felt my anxiety grow. "Why am I afraid to hear what you're about to say? After all this time you want to talk with me? I've not moved away; you've known where to reach me. Why now?"

The waitress placed the coffee tray on the table, and Fiona poured a cup for each of us. Settling back in her chair, she toyed with a spoon for a couple of moments and then began, her voice almost a whisper. "I'm with New Scotland Yard. I was assigned to Clipton with Detective Chief Inspector Gailbrath—John. I went undercover to investigate the increasing narcotic activity taking over this community. Because of Roger Spencer's cocaine habit, he was seen from the beginning as someone who could be useful.

I moved into an empty flat in his apartment block and made sure our paths crossed. I accepted when he asked me out for a drink, and pretended to confide in him. I told him I was getting over a broken relationship, and needed to be away from London for a while." She paused, taking a moment before continuing. "He was a lonely, needy man, in spite of the opposite image he tried to project, and accepted everything I told him."

I stared, speechless. I looked into Fiona's lovely face, the charming façade that veiled a calculating, probing psyche. "You certainly fooled me. Did Roger learn the truth?"

"No. I'm glad about that. It would have been devastating for him." She hesitated for a moment. "He really loved me."

"How did you end the affair? I assume it was after you got what you wanted from him?" My tone was sharp, spiteful.

"Actually, Stella, I got to really like him. He was considerably older, of course." She looked distressed. "A foolish but decent man, and it was not easy for me to deceive him. It wasn't long before he told me about stealing from the trust, although I didn't know it was your money until later. His drug addiction made him very vulnerable to blackmail, and his life started to spiral down. John told him he knew what was going on, and pressured Roger for information, particularly names. The Yard instructed me to make myself scarce, adding to Roger's growing panic—I told him I'd got a new job and was moving to Paris for a year. He made it complicated by asking me to marry him. Eventually, he seemed to accept the situation, and I left town."

"Are you a detective? Were you John's partner?"

"I'd never worked with the inspector before, and Detective Sergeant Ball wasn't privy to my involvement until recently. I was called in because of my expertise. I'm with the narcotics division. I've been on the force for a good number of years." She suddenly chuckled. "I'm not as young as I appear."

"I can't get my mind around what you're saying. It's too much to take in." A throbbing started up in my left temple. "Why are you telling me this now?"

"I'm telling you because it's what John asked. He wanted to take you into his confidence long ago, but was concerned it would put you in even more danger. You know, of course, we believe you were meant to be the first victim, not Ralph Hughes Young?"

"How do you know it's what John wanted? He had plenty of opportunity to let me know what was going on." My voice broke with emotion. "He was constantly telling me to take care and made my housekeeper promise to look out for me." I was filled with anguish. "I just couldn't believe I was in danger . . . couldn't understand I was a threat to anyone. We went to Tythe Farm and looked around the slaughterhouse together. I thought he would open up to me after that, but he never did. That was one of the clashes that caused the wedge between us. Of course, I understand he couldn't discuss certain aspects of the case with me, but it was more than that. It was as if he was holding back on all levels." I couldn't continue.

Fiona reached over and put her hand over mine. "I'm so sorry, Stella."

"I knew he was under tremendous pressure; my continually asking him why everything was taking so long only added to it." My words faltered. "Why has it, Fiona? Why has it taken so long to bring an end to all this?"

"You've heard ad nauseam that investigations take time, and it is true, particularly when it is as complicated as this case. We've had to proceed extremely carefully because very influential people are involved . . . not only in Clipton, but also overseas. It must seem as if we've been sitting on our hands, but I can tell you we haven't wasted a minute."

"Is it over now, Fiona? Will someone at last be held responsible?"

"Soon, Stella. Very soon, now." The waitress hovered behind me, wondering if we needed more coffee, but I had to get out of the café. My emotions were like a steam press ready to burst, and I stood up. "I have to go—I have to get out." I practically ran out of the café.

"I'll be in touch, Stella," Fiona called after me.

The car's rhythmic windshield wipers gave me a clear view through the cascading snowflakes, but it was still a dangerous drive on the slick road. By the time I got back to the rectory, I was a bundle of nerves. I turned into the driveway, and was perturbed to see footprints in the dusting of snow accumulating on the path leading to the front door. I had no energy left to socialise, and entered the house through the kitchen side door.

I made my way up to my room and burrowed under a comforter. Soon the warmth penetrated my numb body, and I fell into a troubled sleep. When I awoke, I saw it was past two thirty. I stretched, grateful to be warm again, but felt anything but rested. I forced myself to get up and made my way to the top of the stairs, listening for any sound that indicated the unwelcome visitor had returned. All was silent, thankfully. Fighting listlessness, I went downstairs and gazed out onto the patio and beyond. Snow was falling quite heavily. Large feathery flakes coated the landscape like a delicate lace, and created a winter wonderland. It was going to be a white Christmas for sure.

Feeling too lazy to cook dinner, I prepared a sandwich and then filled the time by writing last-minute Christmas cards. Alice was with Sergeant Ball. It was around nine o'clock before I felt a trace of concern, but reassured myself by acknowledging she was not only an adult, she was with a very competent policeman—two things well in her favour. I must confess to relief at hearing a car drive up and a door slam. My urge was to run to open the front door.

"Stella?"

"In the study," I called. She came into the room, her face glowing. "You look like the cat who got the cream," I told her. "Tell me. Did Sergeant Ball propose?"

"Well, not exactly. He did ask if he could court me with that end in mind." She looked happier than I had ever seen her. "Sounds so old-fashioned, doesn't it?" Everything about her was energised. She was beautiful.

"He is truly a gentleman. You said yes, of course! Right?" She nodded shyly. I got up from the desk and hugged her. "I'm so, so happy for you." I kissed her cheek and was surprised to find it wet. "Whatever is it, Alice?"

"It's just I know how hard it is on you, Stella. You were feeling this way such a short time ago, and now . . . everything has changed." She tightened her hold around my waist.

"Don't worry about me. I shall be fine when this whole mess is over, once and for all. To see you so happy is just what I need. By the way, I have some news to tell you. Take your coat off. I'll get us a nightcap."

I relayed my earlier conversation with Fiona. We sat in silence for a while, watching the log in the fireplace discharge showers of embers that glowed like molten lava. It was quite a show.

"You know, it might have been Fiona I heard talking that night when I called the constable out. Remember? I heard voices the night of the Rahn concert. It had to have been her! I don't know with whom she was talking. A man, certainly. I wasn't able to hear what was being said."

"There were only two men who stayed that night: Justin Rahn and Roger Spencer. It certainly wasn't Justin," I insisted. "Fiona and Roger were sharing a room, so why on earth would they meet outside to talk? It must have been someone else."

"It must have been. All this intrigue—it makes one wonder who can be trusted, who really is who they say they are." Alice paused for a moment. "Fancy Fiona making up to Mr Spencer just to snare him. Poor man."

"Poor sucker! She used his drug habit to get to him. It sounds like it may have backfired a little, however. Seems he fell for her, and she got quite fond of him. It would appear a lot of Pandora's Boxes have been opened in the name of love." I looked over at Alice. "Hang on to that chap of yours with both hands." Then I remembered. "Do you know if John found any footprints under the windows from that night you are referring to? He was going to try to make casts."

"I don't know. It was so long after the fact, he likely didn't find any. The gardeners would have worked the beds by that time, and their boots would have destroyed any evidence. I wish I had said something to the constable at the time. It never entered my mind—or his. Pretty lax police work, eh?"

"So it seems," I replied thoughtfully.

"Stella, it just occurred to me—now we know they worked together, could it have been John Fiona was talking with?"

I caught my breath. "I hadn't thought of him. Of course, as they were furtively working together, they had to be extremely careful when they met."

"Perhaps John was questioning us about that night to find out if we suspected Fiona in any way. It would be interesting to know if he had followed through and checked for footprints in the flowerbeds, or if it was all a smoke screen."

"You could be right. Thing is, so what if it was John? Does it matter now, who it was? The pretence is over," I said soberly. "By the way, talking of footprints, someone was here earlier. Did you see them?"

"No, I've been gone since before lunch. How do you know if you were gone, too?"

"They were quite clear in the snow when I arrived back from town . . . a woman's boot, unless we have a very small man running around."

"Perhaps it was someone from the church asking for donations. Last Sunday, Vicar Ken mentioned an upcoming collection." She looked intently at me. "Everyone isn't threatening, Stella. There are still some normal, upright folk in this village, don't forget."

"Yes—yes, you're right, of course." I laughed lightly. "I've got to stop seeing monsters in the shadows." I stretched my back. "It's been quite a day for both of us. I think I'll make it an early night." I got up and made my way to the door. "Do me one favour, Alice. Ask your sweetheart how I can reach Fiona."

"She's here, Stella."

"Good."

Fiona looked lovely as usual, but now I was aware of her true role, I was ill at ease when she entered the lounge. We shook hands formally, and sat down across from each other. "Tea?"

"Yes, please. It is freezing outside. I hate driving under such dangerous conditions." She took the cup from me and sipped appreciatively. "Well, Stella," she asked, "what's on your mind?"

I intended to apologise for walking out on her at the café, and then discuss the mysterious footprints I had discovered outside the rectory a couple of days before, but seeing her looking so confident, so in control, somehow irked me to the point of irrationality. Fully cognisant of being impertinent, I accused her of deviously taking advantage of me while a guest in my home . . . of being used to further a ploy that ended with John's death. Wild allegations spewed out, and my hurt and frustration peaked to the point of ridiculousness. Of course, rationally, I knew she and John were colleagues only. At that moment, though, my jealousy closed my eyes to reality, and I said things that, in retrospect, made me flinch. She sat quietly, her hands folded in her lap, and allowed me to rant. As the words poured from me, she made no defence. At last, my anguish was spent, and I covered my face with my hands, horrified at my outburst.

She came and sat by my side. "I liked John very much. He was a good person and an excellent policeman." Her voice was steady. "I admired him greatly, Stella—that was all. He had no interest in me. Under different circumstances, who knows, but he loved you and only you." I could see she was searching for the right words. "You say I used you—I don't see it like that. I went undercover to do the job I'm trained to do—to find the killer or killers of your friends. Sometimes, I have to do things I don't like, but I will do whatever it takes to bring about justice. You asked many times what the police were doing, why things were not getting resolved; however, our efforts to reassure you were unsuccessful. We're investigating a complicated case, Stella, and security is paramount. For you to be privy to certain information could have devastating consequences. John would never risk your safety."

I looked at her face, so pretty, so young, and wondered at the horrors she must have witnessed during her tenure as an officer of the law. "I have something I need to tell you, Fiona. I should have told Ball ages ago; somehow, I never found the right moment." I shrugged. “I got preoccupied with a painful personal matter.” I described taking one of the small packets I found behind a brick at the slaughterhouse, and the cars and men turning up. “I’ve tried to remember part of the Mercedes plate, but am not so sure now. I think it had 389.”

She stared at me. “You have the audacity to criticise how the investigation is going, but you withhold critical information.” I saw real anger in her eyes. “We know the cars, but have not witnessed them at the farm. You need to make a statement giving as much detail as you can. How many men were there?”

“I didn’t see them, only heard them.”

“Is there anything else you’ve been holding back?”

“No, that’s it, except a lab report confirmed the packet I took from the slaughterhouse contained cocaine.” Then I remembered the accent. “I think I heard Spanish that night.”

“Well, that fits in with our enquiries. Sergeant Ball will take your statement. It’s important, Stella! Please follow through.”

“I will. Forgive me, Fiona. I haven’t been in my right mind. I can’t believe I ever will be again.”

“Time. That’s what it will take, Stella—time.” She leaned towards me. “I am going to tell you something. It is in the utmost confidence because I now believe you deserve to know.” I tried to concentrate on what she said. By the time she was finished, I was on the brink of collapse. Eventually, she stood up. “I must go.” She turned when she reached the door. “I’m leaving Clipton for another assignment, but you know how to reach me if you need to.” I nodded numbly, and then she was gone.

CHAPTER TWENTY

"Yes, yes, Mum, don't fret—I'll be at the station to meet you. Bring lots of warm clothing because the snow is waist high and freezing into blocks of ice. Yes, the rectory is centrally heated and very warm, but if you want to go outside, you will need to be prepared." I was getting frustrated. "No, there is no need to bring food. Alice has taken care of everything." I suddenly figured out this was not what my mother wanted to hear. Christmas dinner was her domain. "Of course, she expects you to do the cooking," I hastily assured her. *Right on, Stella,* I thought smugly. My mother's voice brightened measurably as she went through a list of items absolutely necessary for a perfect stuffing. "We have it all, Mummy. I promise. Yes, even juniper berries." When I hung up the telephone, I could feel excitement mounting about the approaching holiday. The decorations looked wonderful, the food would be delicious, and my beloved family would be together again. Six days to go!

Alice did not take it too well when I announced my mother would reign in the kitchen on Christmas Day. "Mum will be counting on your help, Alice. You were such good collaborators that Christmas Mum taught you how to use tofu. Remember? The two of you had a grand time." I was not absolutely certain, but then I had other things on my mind beyond two women jostling for control over an oven. Alice was pacified somewhat with the news she would have supremacy once again beyond Christmas Day. Dr Levinton and his wife Marjory were taking me up on my invitation to pre-holiday drinks later that evening; Beverly and Robert Petersen, Walter Pearce and his wife, Rita, and Ted Nyby were joining us. I glanced at my watch. "My goodness, is that the time? I have to get ready. I can count on you and Sergeant Ball joining in, Alice? The caterers are taking care of the kitchen."

"I wish you would remember he has a first name."

"Don't reprimand me—you call him Ball. At least I give him his hard-earned title." I raised my eyebrow. "Well?"

"Well what?"

"What is his name? Fred? William?"

"Alistair, actually." She suddenly giggled. "It was the last name I expected. Fred or William was what I had in mind." Laughter exploded from both of us, and we sat on the stairs and hooted. It did us both a lot of good.

The evening started very pleasantly. Everyone wore formal attire for the occasion. The women showed off their new cocktail dresses and expensive jewels; the men in dark suits showed their festive spirit with colourful ties covered in Christmas motifs. Reg ran the bar, and Alice persuaded Alistair to circulate with her and join in the light small talk. It was Robert Petersen who brought up Roger Spencer's death.

"What a shock! Suicide, I believe."

"Poor man . . . we would never have guessed he was in so much trouble. Robert and I saw quite a lot of him at one time. Especially, here, at Stella's," Beverly added.

Ted Nyby got his drink refreshed by Reg and then walked over and stood by me. "From what I heard, it was all about drugs. Poor bugger was hooked up to the gills. It was bad enough he lost his job and his girl, and now, sadly, his life."

"I didn't know he lost his job. You mean he was fired, Ted?"

"Yes, Neil. He ran out of his own money—a considerable sum, I might add—and embezzled from other accounts. As a medical doctor, you know cocaine's not only an expensive habit . . . once it gets its claws into you, you'll do anything for a fix."

"Yes, yes, Ted, I all know about that, but I had no idea. You're right—poor bugger." Neil Levinton put his arm around his wife's shoulders. "I thought I knew everything there was to know about the folks in this parish. Foolish me!"

"Don't be hard on yourself, Neil. What could you have done if you had known?" Marjory Levinton adored her husband.

"I could have done something, perhaps prevented him from ending his life. What an awful waste of a good man."

"Good man? How can you say that, Neil? He was not only a thief but a murderer, too." Walter Pearce's wife glared at the doctor.

"What!" Ted put his glass down with a thud. "Murderer? Who says such a thing? He had a lot of problems, I'll give you that, but he was no murderer, Rita Pearce."

"He killed that inspector, then went home and shot himself. Good thing—saved the expense of a trial." Rita's face was turning very pink. "He could have killed Sir Ralph and those others. He was always around." Her voice rose excitedly. "Don't look so agitated, Ted! Like many in this town, he wasn't who we thought he was!"

"And what do you mean by that, Rita? You've always had a vivid imagination, but you're quite out of line when it comes to Roger. He was a decent, gentle man who tragically had a self-destructive habit—certainly not a murderer." Ted's eyes narrowed with anger. "I'll not stand by and have you sully his name."

"Didn't know you were so close, Ted," she mocked. "How come you're such a champion of Roger Spencer?"

"I knew him from the first day he came to Clipton. Roger worked hard to put this village on the map, raising millions of pounds to get our historical buildings on the National Trust list. I only knew about the drugs when he told me he had taken money." His voice softened. "Poor man had reached bottom and didn't know where to turn. I'm proud he felt he could come to me."

"Now you've brought up the subject, I can tell you Roger made a gallant effort to repay the money he took." Walter Pearce turned to me. "Stella can confirm that."

"Stella? He took *your* money? He did," Rita gloated, "of course he did."

I turned to my banker in fury but held my tongue.

"Rita!" Walter glared at his wife. "That's enough! We certainly don't need any more speculative prattle." His patience was worn thin, and I felt sure the conversation would continue in the privacy of their home. Thankfully, one of the caterers announced dinner at that moment, preventing further conversation. Robert took Bev's arm, and the rest of us followed them into the dining room.

The evening continued in a more pleasant vein; still, Rita's contentious outburst had certainly left a mark on the festivities. She was known for her lack of tact; all the same, the level of her malice this evening was surprising. A spoilt, selfish woman of sixty-plus years, she was tolerated out of respect for Walter. Walter was a friend as well as a faithful banker, but we all knew who wore the trousers in their house. I was relieved when my guests decided to leave earlier than expected. The falling temperature had turned the latest layer of snow dangerously slick. A frigid draught sent me into convulsive shivers as I waited on the porch until the last car headed down the driveway. With relief, I made a dash to my room and changed from my formal togs into something more comfortable. Alice and Alistair were in the kitchen, talking quietly as they put away the extra food left behind by the caterers. Seeing them relaxed and happy together brought remnants of the happiness John and I had known. Alice saw me and smiled. She was radiant.

"Can I get you anything, Stella?"

"No, thanks. I thought I'd give you a hand clearing up. As usual, I'm too late."

"She's always had perfect timing, Alistair! Ever since I've known her." She was joking, of course. "It was a successful evening, Stella. We noticed everyone went away with smiles on their faces."

"That's because they each had a bottle of good champagne tucked under their arm. I think we deserve one, too. I'll get a bottle." In spite of the tension earlier in the evening, I was quite relaxed. "A glass of champagne will give me a chance to wish two very special people a happy future together."

"Oh, who would they be, Mrs Campbell?"

"Get on with you, Sergeant Ball—Alistair. Alice spilled the beans!"

James had Butterfly patiently waiting with a warm blanket tucked under her saddle. I mounted, and with a soft prod from my boot, we ventured down the paths around the equestrian centre that were cleared of snow. It was bitterly cold. Trees moaned eerily under the weight of limbs encased in ice. It was breathtakingly beautiful but deceiving. The horse and I both knew it would have to be a short outing. Steam quickly rose from Butterfly as her body heated, shrouding us both in a ghostly mist. Her harness jingled cheerily, joining the rhythm of her hoofs that seemed to scarcely touch the rock-hard surface beneath us. I became mesmerised, and entered a dreamlike world of silver clouds, rainbows, and sparkling jewels—a picture come alive from the children's book *The Snow Fairy*. Butterfly must have quickened her pace, or perhaps I had urged her on, because I was hunched over with my knees tight against her flanks. I heard the truck's hooter before I heard my name. "Stella! Stella, pull Butterfly in! Good grief, woman, what are you doing?" I don't know how long James had been shouting at me before I came down from fantasy to harsh reality.

Butterfly paced herself as we returned to the centre. I was shamefully aware of lather covering her hide and the tremors passing through her. I hosed her down and rubbed her dry with towels from her tack chest. Steam continued to rise from her, so I covered her with a blanket. She nuzzled my shoulder as if to reassure me she was all right, and I was touched by her gesture.

"Butterfly forgives you, Stella." James was at the stable door. "I'm not sure I do, though."

"I'm terribly sorry, James." I had been reckless putting such a beautiful creature and myself at risk, but it was not as simple as that. All the grief and disappointment I had buried deep inside me over the past several weeks spewed from the pit of my stomach with a ferocious roar. I sat down on the straw-covered floor and bawled like a small child. Forgetting James and Butterfly, I allowed the anguish to pour from me. The horse snorted and gently nudged me as if trying to get me up on my feet. Eventually, James knelt down and drew me to him. He did not say anything, allowing me to purge the accumulated disappointments and sorrow from not only recent events, but from all the years of being alone. After a long while, I lifted my head from James' damp shoulder.

"Can I do anything?"

I shook my head. He pushed my hair back from my face. I looked a sight but was beyond embarrassment.

"Let me drive you home. You can get your car tomorrow." I could only nod. He led me to the truck, and I sat in a stupor until the rectory came into view. He walked round the truck and opened the passenger door to allow me to get out.

"What can I say, James? I'm so sorry . . . I was a fool with Butterfly."

"Yes, you were, but it turned out all right, thankfully. There won't be a next time, so we can forget today. Right? Butterfly is fine. Now you go and take care of you."

"I will. Thank you." I looked into his warm brown eyes. "Merry Christmas, James."

"Merry Christmas, Stella." I waited while he got back into the truck and drove off. At the end of the driveway, he reached out of the cab window and waved. I waved back, and let myself into the house. I was grateful to find it empty so I could have private time to weep some more.

Wrapping gifts was not my favourite pastime; thank goodness, I was near the end. The packages looked very festive under the tree. I had hidden the filled stockings in my room, planning to put them around the fireplace on Christmas Eve. My family would be arriving in two days, and I was pleased to have everything under control, even to the point of ordering fresh strawberries from a company in France that guaranteed delivery on Christmas morning. Yes, I told myself, this was what I need: my family around me to celebrate the most special of all holidays. A food hamper was delivered to the equestrian centre as a peace offering to alleviate my humiliation somewhat, but I knew James would keep his word, and my stupidity would not be mentioned again. I tied red ribbon around the decorated box containing my father's sweater and was satisfied with my handiwork. This was going to be a special Christmas. I could feel it in my bones.

"The doorbell must be out of order. You don't mind I let myself in, do you, Stella?"

Startled, I dropped the roll of ribbon that unravelled across the parquet floor. "Oh, but I do, Margot! This is the second time you've entered my home uninvited." Instinctively alert, I watched her come towards me, and hoped she didn't notice the tremor in my hands.

"That's why I'm here, my dear—to make amends. I've come with a peace offering; after all, it is Christmas." She put an arrangement of red silk poinsettias on the coffee table. She wore a full-length mink coat and matching hat. Her suede boots were wet with snow. I did not ask her to sit down, but she made herself comfortable on the sofa, indicating she intended to stay for a while. She looked thinner; her face appeared to have lined considerably since her last uninvited visit. Was she ill, I wondered? Perhaps the dyed black hair caused her face to look overly pallid.

"A peace offering, Margot?" My voice was steady, belying my impulse to run. "So you admit you implied a threat the last time you barged in on me?"

"Oh, come now, Stella! That's in the past, and I was being a silly old woman. You have to make allowances. Since Ralph's death, I really haven't been myself."

"I haven't time for this nonsense. What is it you want? I'm about to go out," I lied.

"Want? Why, nothing, my dear." She looked around the decorated room. "You've done a very nice job. I'm glad you're celebrating, in spite of losing your inspector. That must have been a shock to you. Still, in one way or another, you do seem to be involved with each of the murders in Clipton. Odd, isn't it?"

I bit my tongue, determined not to react with a torrent of profanities to her malicious goading. I gathered up wrapping paper and ribbons to let her know her time was up. "You're going to have to leave now, Margot. As I said, I'm about to go out."

"You're not being very hospitable. No offer of coffee or something stronger?" She was mocking me.

"I told—"

"Yes, yes—you have to go out."

She made no effort to get up from the sofa, so I sat opposite her, making a show of looking at my watch. "I can give you five minutes."

"Good, that's about all the time I need. I told you before you were getting your nose into things that didn't concern you, but you persisted and look what happened. It cost your inspector his life. Poor Roger Spencer's too."

I felt the blood leave my face. "How dare you say such a thing?" I whined unashamedly, defensive against her hateful accusations.

"Things were perfectly normal 'till you came to Clipton. We were a quiet village where good people lived their lives in comfort and privacy. Thanks to Roger, the Building Society was increasing its funding and, in the name of historic preservation, work was being considered on our older buildings. No one questioned, no one investigated. We went about our business quite happily." Her lips curled in loathing. "Then Miss Prim came into town with all her money and grandeur. But that wasn't enough. She wanted to make her mark, wanted to make a name for herself."

"Joe Blake and I working on the slaughterhouse must have really put the wind up those *good people.*"

She leaned across the coffee table. "Blake leaving Clipton likely saved his neck. He didn't mind leaving you in the thick of it, did he? Who are you to ruin so many lives, Mrs Stella Campbell?" She spat my name out with contempt.

"Ruin lives? By being on the planning commission, I helped improve Clipton, and used a considerable amount of my own money in the process. The civic centre is used extensively, the school is no longer a crumbling shamble, and the townspeople are certainly more involved as a community." I hated reacting to her bait. "Roger Spencer was my friend. It was his very expensive habit that led to his ruin—but you know all about that, of course." My face flushed with anger. "He only embezzled money because he was desperate. You know all about that, too."

"Oh, yes, I know all about that, too. Do go on—you were on a roll. What else did Madam Campbell do to save Clipton?"

I stood up. "I want you to leave right now, or I'll call the police."

"Oh, my goodness, did I touch a nerve? Don't try to intimidate me! You don't know what you're letting yourself in for. Be very careful, Mrs Campbell!"

"Don't underestimate me, Margot. I warn you, I can be a formidable adversary."

"You don't frighten me. Remember, it was you who brought that la-de-da water expert to Clipton to nose around, and look what happened to him. Went over to Tythe Farm and met that Blake. Couldn't do much snooping with the police there; thought he was better than them and went back later. Saw things he shouldn't have and paid a price, didn't he?" I listened, horrified. Margot Hughes Young was a woman of status, the widow of a beloved, respected man. What had happened to turn her into this conniving crone?

"Miller Owens was murdered because he saw something, you say? What could that have been, Margot? What could he have seen? You are so well informed, you must know."

"Oh, my dear," she scoffed, "putting two and two together, are we? What else do you think you know? Come on, tell your Auntie Margot, there's a good girl." She laughed a brittle high note, sending shivers down my spine. I took a step towards her—a reflex that took us both by surprise. "Get out! Get out of my home *now!"* I went to the sitting-room door and held it open.

"You are quite ill mannered, Campbell; however, you'll have other chances to show me hospitality, I'm sure." She gathered up her gloves and handbag, and picked up the poinsettias. "You don't deserve these." I barely gave her a chance to step out before

I slammed the front door after her. Not only was I angry, I was afraid.

"What the blazes? Alice!"

"Sorry, my dear, I didn't mean to alarm you." She gripped my arm. "I followed that bitch in and was listening at the door. I overheard everything. You have a witness now. We must call Alistair."

Alistair was all business when he arrived at the rectory, giving only a polite nod to Alice when she opened the door to him. He wasted no time before questioning me about Margot's visit.

"It's a pity you couldn't have made her talk more, Mrs Campbell. You know, drawn things out of her, particularly as Alice was listening. Of course, you didn't know that at the time. That being said, the Hughes Young woman certainly implicated herself by her threatening tone." He was very much the policeman as he wrote in his notebook. "I think it's time the police called on Mrs Hughes Young. Fiona will be happy to oblige."

"Fiona? She's back in Clipton?"

"Yes, ma'am, by my special request. She knows the case well enough to replace John. It took some doing with the Yard, but when one of our own is lost, it becomes personal, you see." He got up from the chair, putting his notebook and pen into a briefcase. "I don't suppose you'll be getting any more unexpected visitors with your family arriving in a couple of days. All the same—"

"Yes, Alistair," I interrupted, "I know—be careful, Mrs Campbell."

"Um . . . right." He gave a polite salute and followed Alice out of the room. Alice returned scowling.

"He's upset, Stella—really upset. Oh, by the way, Fiona's name is Richardson. She's a detective inspector with narcotics. Alistair says she is very good at her job. Let's hope, eh? Then perhaps we can all wake up from this frightful dream."

Intense sadness overwhelmed me. So much deception, and now this encounter with Margot was the final straw. The room closed in on me. "I need some fresh air," I exclaimed—my habitual reaction whenever the level of stress became too much.

"It's absolutely unfit for man or beast out there." Alice stared at me in disbelief. "Where are you thinking of going?"

"Oh . . . around the garden." I shrugged. "I need to get out of here." I grabbed my coat from the hallstand. "Don't worry; I'll be alert," I called out. I opened the front door and stepped out into the squall of freezing sleet. I quickly donned the gloves and hat I found in my coat pockets, and made a beeline to the greenhouse. The snow came almost up to my knees, making it difficult going. Pretty soon I was gasping for breath. It occurred to me about then that I was being quite ridiculous and very entertaining for Alice, if she was watching.

The greenhouse looked lovely; the panes of glass were covered in a coating of thin, translucent ice. It took a great deal of effort to free the door. By the time I was through, my gloves were soaking wet, and I switched on the lights with fingers that were bloodless. The humid temperature inside the building was high enough to keep tender plants safe until spring; however, veins of frost had managed to creep in, etching intricate patterns that shimmered in the artificial light. I walked between the counters that were laden with row after row of geraniums, perennials, shrubs, and seedlings. With luck, the young plants would survive the severe weather, and again blossom into a profusion of colour. Terra cotta pots were stacked at the end of the structure next to bags of chicken manure, compost, and fertilisers. The harsh world outside disappeared from my mind. Feeling invigorated, I took a broom and started to sweep up remnants of soil spilt between the counters, happy to be busy in an atmosphere I loved. I emptied the dustpan in the bin and returned the broom to its station, conceding it was time I got back to the house. I was surprised it was later than I thought, for daylight was fading as I slid and stumbled my way back to the house.

"That was just what the doctor ordered," I called to Alice as I took off my coat and wet boots. "Brrr. It's jolly cold, though!" I went into the kitchen. It was empty. I went to the foot of the stairs and called out. "Alice?" Probably taking a nap, I assumed, and returned to the kitchen and warmed some milk for a hot chocolate. I was washing the mug when she showed up. "Hey, you! I was beginning to wonder where you were."

"I was reading and nodded off." She looked at the clock on the wall. "My goodness, I slept far too long. What would you like for dinner, dear?"

"Actually, I'm not at all hungry. Let me make you something. Something easy, that is." I smiled at her. "I can open a tin of soup. Tempted?"

"Soup would be fine." She sat down at the table, yawning. "How long were you out in that appalling weather? You must have been frozen!"

"I pottered around in the greenhouse. It wasn't that bad once I got there. Getting there was a bit rough, though. I hope the trains keep running. It will be a disaster if no one can get out of London. I'll be so disappointed if the kids can't make it." I opened a tin of tomato soup and poured the contents into a saucepan. While it warmed, I chopped up a few fresh basil leaves to sprinkle on top. It smelled wonderful. The doorbell rang, interrupting our domestic bliss.

"Now, who can that be?" Alice was gone before I could protest.

It was Fiona. "Sorry to come so late in the day, Stella. Alistair is on his way. We wanted you to know we've just arrested Margot Hughes Young before the local rag prints it all over its front page."

Later, the four of us relaxed in the lounge. A blizzard roared outside, sending waves of snowflakes against the windows. Christmas Eve was the next day, and it was still uncertain if my family would make it to Clipton. The village's one snowplough would not be enough to clear such appalling conditions. The grandfather clock in the hall chimed seven. It was going to be a long evening.

Fiona began to outline the day's events. "You both understand what we say must not go beyond this room? We've broken police protocol a number of times by confiding in you, and we must rely on your word you will honour our trust." Alice nodded in

Alistair's direction. Fiona continued. "Because of Hughes Young's unwelcome visit today, Stella, we decided it was time to move in on her." Fiona's manner became more professional. "I used my own car—didn't want to let on I was with the police. The house was being watched, so we knew she was home. She was surprised to see me, of course, but affable, inviting me in right away."

"Are you sure she didn't know you were with the police? She seems to know everything going on in Clipton, including when I'm alone in the rectory."

"She certainly makes a point of being informed, Stella. Fortunately she believed Roger and I really were in a meaningful relationship, even accepting it ultimately led nowhere. That was lucky because it gave me freedom to do some manipulating. Judging from her initial reaction when she saw me standing on her doorstep, I'd say she genuinely thought I'd taken a job in Paris. Roger must have told her about my ploy to break up with him. Her first question was to ask if I'd returned for Roger's funeral. I told her I had." Fiona looked away for a moment. "The coroner's office released his body a couple of days ago." Talking about Roger was, obviously, far from easy for her. Had she loved Roger after all? I guessed at least a little.

"Fiona was wired," Alistair announced.

"Alistair, you sound like a cop in an American film," Alice chortled.

"He's right. We needed to record every word of the conversation." Fiona was unsmiling. "That Hughes Young woman is a cunning old girl. Anyway, one thing led to another, and I got around to asking how well she knew Roger. She spoke quite freely, said she had known him since he first came to Clipton ten years or so ago. She and Sir Ralph saw him both socially and professionally quite regularly. Sir Ralph donated a large sum annually to the Building Society, and Roger handled its trust money very effectively."

"Fiona, would you like to take a short break?" She looked drained.

"Thank you, Stella, but I'm almost through. Margot seemed genuinely fond of Roger, in spite of the squabbles you witnessed, Stella. Even acknowledged his drug problem. I asked if she knew who his dealer was, where he got the stuff. She clammed up immediately, so I tried another tactic. I told her I was a user, and needed a supply for the Christmas holiday." It was a relief to see Fiona smile. "I thought the woman was going to collapse when I told her it was one of the things Roger and I had in common."

"She believed you?"

"I was rather astonished that she did. She said she couldn't help me but, after a moment, gave me a telephone number. Later, she offered coffee, and while she was in the kitchen, I called out I needed to use the toilet. It's upstairs, so I made a detour to her bedroom instead."

"Weren't you scared to death, Fiona? I hope you had your gun."

"Alice! You've been reading too much fiction," Alistair said. That was my thought, too.

"Well, I knew I had to be quick, and luck was on my side," Fiona continued. "A personal telephone book was on the dresser, along with a file folder. I took the book; obviously the folder was too large. I took the contents instead, folding them and putting them inside my jacket. I had to rush to flush the toilet, and got back downstairs just as she appeared with the tray." Fiona looked seriously at Alice. "No gun was necessary!"

"Now you're laughing at me."

"A little." Fiona smiled for the first time. "I was eager to leave but had to have the coffee after she'd taken the trouble to make it. She asked if I had seen you, Stella. I said I expected to see you at the funeral, but had no intention of calling on you—we had nothing in common now Roger was gone. She seemed to like hearing that, and let her guard down a bit. Said you were a bloody snob. Of course, I agreed." Her eyes twinkled. "I had to get out of the house as soon as possible, so I voiced concern about the storm. I was worried she'd hear the papers rustling under my jacket when I put on my coat. Like a good hostess, she saw me out. At the front door, she took an envelope from her cardigan pocket and pushed it into my hand—said it was just a little something for the holiday. Before I knew what was happening, she gave me a hug and was gone, slamming the door behind her."

"You didn't arrest her?" Alice sounded incredulous.

Alistair answered. "No, not then. I was hiding in Fiona's car, and never felt so cold in my life! Managed to take pictures of Hughes Young at the door passing the envelope to Fiona. Back at the hotel, we played the tape recorder. There wasn't much we could use. The pictures were better—they clearly show Hughes Young handing the envelope to Fiona. I kept the camera on Fiona making her way to the car. That way, we have a record she didn't exchange the envelope or anything. The last picture was of her putting the envelope into a bag, which I sealed." He grinned at Alice. "When we got back to the station, Fiona opened her Christmas present. Inside the envelope were two tiny packets of—guess, Alice?"

"Cocaine?"

"Cocaine! We had her! Fiona and I went back together and arrested Hughes Young for possession. You should have seen her face when Fiona flashed her badge."

"Did you call the telephone number Margot gave Fiona?" I asked him.

"No. We passed it on to Fiona's pals in narcotics."

CHAPTER TWENTY-ONE

Christmas Eve was not what anyone could have predicted. Blue and white squad cars raced around town, their sirens blasting away any holiday cheer. Tythe Farm was encircled by yellow police tape fluttering from rods, and completely off limits to the public. A few hardy locals observed the activity through binoculars, their fascination heightened enough to endure the foul weather. The McKinleys were handcuffed and led from the house, then quickly driven off in an unmarked car. Alice reported on all the excitement when she returned from helping the vicar with final touches for the evening's candlelight service. She was full of exuberance. "That's what love does to you," I told her. Instead of laughing at me, she hugged me.

"I look the way you did when you were with John." We both knew she had spoken the truth.

I stayed close to the phone all day, hoping Julia would manage to get through from London. Many phone lines had snapped under the weight of ice, and roads from the city were reported impassable. My wonderful Christmas plans were at risk of disappearing. Restlessly, I wandered around the empty house. Eventually, I sat at the piano and forced my fingers to work the keys, but it was a futile exercise. My heart was not in it.

Christmas morning arrived, giving the town a gift that sent everyone searching for their cameras. Exquisitely lovely in hazy sunlight, an enchanted landscape reached out to a cloudless blue horizon. Snow families with coal eyes and carrot noses smiled toothlessly, their stick arms a roost for energetic hedge sparrows and red-breasted robins. From the new church steeple, two giant bells pealed joyfully through the crystal air. Alice and I stood at the kitchen window. "It's too lovely; it almost hurts." I knew what she meant. Our tranquillity was rudely interrupted by a whirling noise that grew in intensity. Flurries of powdered snow were whipped up as if in a giant blender.

"What on earth?" In utter amazement, we watched a helicopter come into view, flying low over the garden, and coming to rest in the field across from the rectory property. The door swung open and two duffle bags were tossed onto the snow. Then my son jumped out. Keeping low, he helped my mother and then my father. Julia quickly followed, slamming the door shut behind her. Alice and I were speechless. Without further thought, we ran out to greet them. Although coatless and in slippers, we simply could not hold back. "This is unbelievable! What an incredible surprise!" I was so happy I felt I would burst.

"Well, we're in a bit of a shock too, I can tell you," my father gasped. "We got a call last evening from your friend Detective Inspector Richardson. A police helicopter was heading to Clipton this morning, and she said she'd be happy to give us a lift. Several major roads in London were ploughed, so we were able to drive to a hangar at Heathrow Airport, and meet the lovely woman there." My father's eyes twinkled. "And I mean lovely!" I grabbed his arm and led him through the front door. Tim followed, leading my mother.

Julia squealed in delight. "Oh, Mummy, the house looks amazing!" She was quick to notice the ornaments on the tree that she and Tim had made when they were young children—my prized possessions. The papier-mâché had held up, but the glitter and sequins had not done so well. All the same, they were displayed prominently at eye level.

Once the bags were unpacked and everyone had freshened up, we gathered in the lounge. Alice disappeared into the kitchen. "Make yourselves at home. Alice will only be a moment with something hot to drink. I couldn't believe it, Daddy . . . a helicopter?"

"We still can't believe it, Stella. We could never have gone beyond the major highway," he said, shaking his head. "The snow is so deep, one doesn't realise its impact without a bird's eye view. There were abandoned vehicles everywhere. You should have seen Mother's face when we took off—I thought her eyes were coming out of her head!"

"You can talk, Stan Sullivan. You were practically dribbling with excitement!" my mother retorted, indignantly.

I excused myself, and went into the kitchen to give Alice a hand setting up tea with traditional hot mince pies. She was a happy woman again. The weeks of preparation had not been wasted after all. We were going to have that traditional Christmas as planned, including a dinner with all the trimmings.

"We owe Fiona a big thank you. What an amazing thing she's done for us, Alice. Poor girl, having to be on duty today of all days—I wonder if she has any family?"

"I'll find out everything when Alistair gets here. I could phone him now, if you like?"

"Please do. I want to invite her to dinner, if she's free. I don't like to think of her alone in a hotel room. What could be so urgent it couldn't have waited until after Christmas?"

"I don't think police officers have the luxury of holidays. Once they take the oath, it's a twenty-four-hours, seven-days-a-week commitment. That's why a lot of marriages end in divorce."

"How come you know so much about such things?"

"Alistair and I have been talking."

I did not press her; she was arriving at a crossroads, and I was not going to do or say anything that could influence her direction. I loaded up the refreshment cart and pushed it into the lounge where my parents and children were dozing. I owed their presence to Fiona, and would not forget it. "Wakey, wakey. Tea's up," I announced happily.

Alice was able to reach Alistair on the telephone, and he agreed to bring Fiona with him for dinner. My mother disappeared into the kitchen and did not reappear until it was time for her to change her clothes. Alice set the formal dining table with white linen, and lit the scores of candles we had placed around the room. It looked enchanting. When she heard the doorbell, she practically ran to open the door. Alistair and Fiona were dressed up for the occasion, he in a dark grey suit, white shirt, and red tie, and she in a black wool dress with delicate beading around the collar and cuffs. Tim watched her like a hawk, and I noticed Alice held on to her sergeant's arm quite tightly.

"How can I possible thank you enough, Fiona? I always believed Father Christmas arrived in a sleigh, not a helicopter!"

"I'm happy it worked out, Stella. It was the only way we were going to get to Clipton ourselves, and there was plenty of room to spare. I remember you saying where your parents lived, and your maiden name is on file. Being a clever detective, I managed to contact them." She grinned impishly, nodding to my mother, now her devoted fan. "This lousy weather has caused absolute chaos!"

With all the devastating events over the past few years, I had begun a habit of saying prayers. When I called out to my god, my mind held no image but I did feel comforted. My prayers that night changed. Instead of begging for salvation, I gave thanks. The people most important to me were safe and close by. The blessings of Christmas are many; I was convinced I had received every one.

The following day, Boxing Day, was a day to relax in. No more panic shopping for Christmas gifts, no more worrying about food, et cetera. Although snow was banked on either side, the road was clear, and we ventured out for a walk. It was still rather slippery, so Mum decided to return to the house with Alice and Dad. Tim and Julia continued on like Spartans, dragging me along with them. They sparred like aggravating teenagers, but my pleasure reached its limit when snowballs rained down on me, and icy slush got under my coat collar. "What beasts!" Of course, I threw my own arsenal back at them. Eventually, the cold got to us, and we turned back, singing "I'm Dreaming of a White Christmas" at the top of our voices. As the rectory came into view, Tim suddenly became serious, "From the half-finished sentences and innuendoes you exchanged with Fiona and Alistair after dinner last night, something serious is going on. Why are the police still here?"

"Are you in danger, Mummy?"

"Absolutely not, Julia. I will concede there's been an investigation going on ever since Sir Ralph Hughes Young died some time before Miller. Things became more complicated when it was discovered a drug cartel was involved. Fiona's with the narcotic division at New Scotland Yard and Alistair is a detective sergeant who worked with John." I paused, alarmed I had inadvertently opened the door to more questions by bringing up John's name. I steeled myself as I felt Julia's hand tighten on my arm.

"Where's John now? What happened between you two?"

"You don't need to answer that, Mum. Julia, you're out of bounds."

"I wasn't prying, Tim! I just wondered. I expected him to be with you for Christmas, Mummy. That's all."

Frantically, I tried to think of something to say, but my mind refused to cooperate. I had thought—foolishly, I now acknowledged—that Alice had explained the situation when Julia first phoned about Christmas holiday arrangements. John's body had just been found. I should have confirmed my assumption with Alice. "Almost home. This chill is piercing," I said, and quickened my pace, catching Tim's glare directed at his sister.

Lunch was waiting for us. It is amazing how much time revolves around preparing and consuming food. After watching the Andy Williams' Christmas special on television for a while, we all dozed off—only to be awakened by Alice with afternoon tea. I tried to avoid Julia. Alas, it was only a temporary respite. She came to my room just as I was getting into bed that evening. It had been a long day, and I was worn out.

"Mummy?" She called through the door. How I wanted not to answer!

"Yes, Julia, come in."

She lay down on the bed by my feet, grabbing a pillow to make herself comfortable. "I'm not trying to pry, really, but what happened between you and your detective? Did you break up? Tim and I thought you were talking about a future together."

"At one time, we were. It just didn't work out."

"You look so sad, Mum. Did he break your heart?" Her large eyes questioned, wanting to probe in a place I did not want to go.

"A bit at first. I'm all right now. Life goes on, as they say."

"Where is he?"

"Gone."

"Gone? Just like that? What a prig!"

"Julia, I'm not going to talk about it." My tone convinced her, and she rolled on her back and stared up at the ceiling. "Tell me about the hospital. Have you met anyone special there?"

"I've seen a doctor a couple of times. He's really nice—in urology. We're not serious or anything; there isn't much time for romance. By the time I get off duty and crack the books, all I can think about is sleep, not the availability of men."

"Is Tim seeing anyone?"

"Not really. You know he can't make a commitment to a job, let alone to a woman." She laughed. "Don't worry, old lady; you'll get your grandchildren."

I laughed too. "You read me like a book." I reached out my arms, and she came to me. Her hair smelled of shampoo, and I buried my face in her ebony tresses. "You know, of course, Alice is seeing Alistair. It's serious. I'm waiting for them to make an announcement."

"They are so sweet together." Julia lifted her head and looked at me. "What will you do without her? Obviously, they won't live here."

"Actually, darling, I haven't given it too much thought. I'll worry about it when it happens." I gave an exaggerated yawn. "My, I'm tired! You must be too, sweetheart. Let's call it a night, eh?"

"Can I stay with you?" That was the last thing I wanted, but I heard myself say, "Jump in," and pulled the sheet back for her.

"That detective's a darn fool, Mum!"

"Go to sleep, Julia."

In the morning, I left my inquisitive daughter still sleeping and made my way to the kitchen. Although my mother must have been as tired as the rest of us, I suspected she would be working the stove at full throttle. I was right.

"Good morning, Mum." I kissed her cheek. "Did you sleep at all?"

"I did—like a baby. Your father's walking around the garden. I can't imagine what he can see under all that snow. You've done a remarkable job with this place, darling. He is so proud—we both are. You've accomplished a great deal for a single woman." She gestured to the coffee pot. "It's fresh."

I took a mug from the cabinet and filled it. "Just what I need."

"Stella, I want to talk with you before your father gets back. I want you to tell me exactly what's going on in Clipton."

"What do you mean?" More questions; my mood nose-dived.

"Parents are supposed to be there for their children when they are in trouble. Alice didn't say much, but I overheard her talking with Alistair—something about more arrests being made. I asked her if John was still on the case, and she went all funny on me. Said I should talk with you. I thought my question was reasonable, but it seemed to put her on the spot. Even Alistair looked uncomfortable."

"Mum, I know you mean well, I just don't want to go into it now. Please . . . I'll tell you everything another time, I promise. Please let it go." I could say no more.

"Oh, Stella! Whatever is it, dear? You can tell your mother. You can tell me anything—you know that, surely?" She came and sat at the table next to me. "My darling girl."

I collected myself and slowly, reluctantly, began to tell my mother the whole story, from Sir Ralph's murder to John being found dead. She sat very still. When we heard voices coming down the stairs, she put her finger to her lips. "Get yourself dressed. We're having breakfast in town—just the two of us. Everyone else can fend for themselves, darling." She wiped my tears away with a napkin. "I'm going to find your father and explain, or he will be worried."

Feeling utterly weary, I did as I was told. Luckily, Julia was no longer in my room, and I hurriedly pulled on warm clothes and a parka. The Rover's engine was running when I met up with my mother. "Daddy got the car started. Doesn't like these road conditions. I promised we'd be careful."

"That's fine, Mum." I got in the driver's seat, and we headed towards town. "Dad must have thought you'd gone mad, leaving when you were in the middle of getting breakfast for everyone."

"He doesn't give a hoot about such things. He wanted to come along, but I thought it would be better if it were just the two of us. He'll do anything for you, Stella. That man's got a big crush on his little girl." We arrived at the café and were surprised to find the parking lot quite full.

"Do you have a booth at the back?" Mum asked. The waitress nodded and led us to one by the kitchen doors. Mum looked dismayed. "Oh, this is awful. There'll be no privacy here."

The waitress smiled reassuringly. "It's the only one available, or you'll have at least a fifteen-minute wait. Staff coming in or out of those doors can't hear a word, and other customers avoid the area all together. You'll have total privacy." Mother accepted graciously. We ordered muffins and fruit, but coffee was needed at once.

When the waitress moved on, Mother leaned closer to me. "This Roger Spencer who was found shot—do you believe it was suicide?" I did not respond. "Seems a bit too tidy to me . . . he shoots John and then drives all the way back to his place to do himself in. Why? He could have just as well done the deed there, in the slaughterhouse."

"You're full of surprises, Mum. You're not thinking of joining the police force?" I smiled, but my heart was not in it. "I did think it odd when Fiona first told me. Perhaps he panicked and instinctively went back to his flat. At least, for John it was quick. Roger suffered. Apparently, the bullet didn't kill him immediately. Forensics showed he bled to death." I said the words but felt intense sadness.

"Didn't you say they fought?"

"That's what I was told. John had a lot of bruising." I stirred my coffee distractedly. "Alistair said John had become quite enigmatic, not talking much and leaving without saying where he was going. Alistair was quite upset—they had worked together for years and became very close. He put it down to John seeing me, so he didn't say anything."

"He didn't know you had broken up?"

"No. Another mystery. If things had been normal, John would have confided in Alistair." I sighed deeply. "Nothing makes sense. I have so many questions . . . maybe there simply aren't any answers."

"There are, dear; we just have to find them." She reached out and took my hand. "What about you, Stella? What is going on inside of you? You talk about the Clipton secrets, but not about you. You're holding your feelings too close to yourself—like a koala bear holds its baby. Nothing can pry it away."

I stared at her with wide eyes. "Mother! What a strange analogy!"

She stared back, and then chortled, surprising me again. "I suppose it is, but you know what I mean, darling. A koala mother has to let the baby go before it gets too big, or she becomes overwhelmed by its weight. You need to let your baby go, too, Stella."

"I will, eventually. Right now, I can only think about John in an abstract way. If I let myself feel, I won't be able to function."

"I'm here when you're ready."

How grateful I was for parents who not only loved me unconditionally, but also knew when to back off. I turned the conversation away from me. "We knew ages ago that the drugs were picked up from the slaughterhouse. I found a couple of packets behind a brick just like the packets Margot Hughes Young gave to Fiona. I presumed money was left in their place, but John said payment would be made up front, before any drug was supplied. Roger was heavily in debt over his addiction, and that was the impetus behind him helping himself to my money. I can't imagine him going to the farm each time to get his supply.

Maybe that's why he visited Margot so often? She appears to have had her own stash."

"Her name keeps coming up. Do you think John was a user?"

"John? No."

"How would you know, Stella? I read an article written for parents of adolescents about signs to look for; you know the kind of thing: 'Does your teenager have a constant runny nose and pink eyes?' There was something about sores, too, but I wouldn't necessarily connect such symptoms to only drug addiction. Why did John go to meet this Roger?"

"Who knows? Perhaps Roger had some information that was helpful to the case—trying to pay back his debt to society for not being quite as upstanding as we all thought. I don't know why they'd meet at the slaughterhouse, either."

The waitress brought our order. "Private enough, ladies?"

"Perfect," Mum replied.

We ate in silence, engrossed in our own thoughts. After a second cup of coffee, Mum picked up the bill and left a generous tip under the saltshaker. "Better get back. Everyone will be wondering what's happened to us." As we walked out of the café, Mother linked her arm through mine. "Everything's going to be all right, Stella. You'll get through this painful time, and come out stronger and better for it."

"Stronger? Perhaps, Mum. Better? I'm not so sure."

We arrived at the rectory to see two blue and white police patrol cars parked in the driveway. "Now what?" I reluctantly turned off the car ignition.

"Oh, look—it's Fiona," Mother said happily. "Don't assume it is police business. She may have come with news about getting us home."

"I thought you were staying for at least a couple of more days, Mum?"

"We really should get home, but it will, of course, depend on the trains running again." She got out of the car and called out, "Fiona! Fiona!"

Fiona was smiling as she came to meet us, reassuring me she had not come with any alarming news. "You naughty girls! Everyone was wondering where you'd run off to."

"We decided to have a mother-daughter breakfast . . . just the two of us." My mother beamed. "Do you have any word about getting back to London?"

Fiona smiled back at my mother; a mutual fondness was developing between them. "You can go back any time, Dixie. The lines have been cleared and trains are running again, if somewhat behind schedule." She turned to me. "Actually, I came about another matter."

"Now, why did I suspect that? What is it, this time?"

"Your greenhouse, Stella. I'd like to have a crew search it—with your permission, of course." Astonished, I nodded my consent. She went to a patrol car, and four men got out, quickly removing bags and equipment from the car boot. "Stella, will you walk with me for a few minutes?"

"Mum, you'd better go inside and do some explaining about our jaunt." I tried to sound light, ignoring her questioning frown. I felt a twinge of unease as Fiona fell in step beside me, and together we walked around the side of the house.

"It's too frigid to be out here, so I'll get to it quickly. We got a tip that narcotics are hidden in the greenhouse."

"You've got to be joking! I was in the greenhouse only a couple of days ago. There's nothing there, I can assure you."

"One would hope, but we have to rule it out. Perhaps you didn't look in the right places. It could take a couple of days for my chaps to do a thorough job. I'm sorry about that."

I stared at her. "Fiona, let's stop all this pussyfooting around. You give me scraps of information that only increases my frustration. Tell me exactly what's going on—please."

"I've been very up front, actually, Stella." Her gaze was steady. "You know about the arrest of Margot Hughes Young for possession and supplying cocaine to me. She could have made bail, but, as it turned out, she requested police protection in exchange for vital information. We made a deal, and sent her to London. That's why we needed the helicopter—to get her out of Clipton and in a secured facility as soon as possible. The local bobbies are no match for the thugs she's been hanging around." She sighed with obvious frustration. "Because you don't see anything happening, it doesn't mean we're twiddling our thumbs! Another week, it could well be over, and we'll all be grateful for it." I looked at her and wondered how she dealt with all the death and mayhem her work involved. "I have to go. I'll try to come by tomorrow." We each went our own way without further exchange.

On her return the following day, Fiona reported that several bags in the greenhouse were, in fact, full of marijuana—not compost as marked. No cocaine was found. Crime scene investigators invaded the property for several days, causing much excitement for my father. In spite of the chill factor, he stood obediently outside the yellow tape marking off the greenhouse and surrounding area, speculating and enthusiastically conversing with the small army of men going methodically about their business. He became a surrogate father figure to them, although a couple were close to his own age, and trekked back and forth loaded with thermoses and snacks. "Those poor coppers should be home with their families, not freezing their arses off out there." White boxes containing samples for impending assessment were whisked away in vans that slid along the treacherous roads. Alistair became the one-track minded policeman again, permitting himself only snatched moments with a sulking Alice. Arrests were made in town. Suspected traffickers of narcotics had been living inconspicuously in the midst of us, after all. I knew none of them except for a couple who were casual acquaintances. No charges were filed against the McKinleys. Rumour had it they relocated to Canada.

Fiona seemed more relaxed on her next visit, and more willing to talk as she sat across from me at the kitchen table. "Roger's flat was often used to meet with buyers. He would hand over the brick numbers written on paper so that no words were exchanged—a safety measure should his place be bugged by any opposition."

"That sounds a very dangerous arrangement for Roger." I was sceptical. "It has to be the riskiest system I've ever heard of. Did Roger swallow the paper afterwards—or the buyer?"

"Stella! Do stop! I'm trying to fill you in. Don't keep interrupting."

"Sorry. Go on."

"The exchange was made, and Roger delivered the money to Margot Hughes Young, who, after pocketing a percentage for herself, made sure the rest was given to the suppliers."

"Did Sir Ralph get suspicious? Is that why he was killed?"

She hesitated before answering. "We understand a number of people were suspicious of the extra money his wife was flaunting. Conveniently, Margot's wealthy aunt had died, and Margot let it be known she had inherited the old woman's estate. Her explanation was never questioned, but we later found she was never mentioned in the aunt's will."

"Sir Ralph, Miller, and Steven were murdered in such a vile way." I shuddered involuntarily. "What could it have been that made them such a risk?"

"It's regrettable you discovered in the most personal way how dangerous hydrochloric acid can be."

"Regrettable? Regrettable, indeed, Fiona." I felt disproportionate offence at that remark, but let it go. "Do you know who ran the scheme? Who was at the top?" I asked even though I knew there would be no response.

Fiona grimaced. "I can assure you, the pieces *are* coming together. We just need to be a hundred per cent sure of ourselves—can't afford to make a mistake, not now." She got up from the table. "Well, must be on my way."

I walked with her to the door. Feeling somewhat rebuffed, I watched her drive away.

Fiona Richardson was indeed a unique young woman. We never referred to the day a couple of months before, when she had come to the rectory at my request. I had ranted in a jealous outburst, hinting that she and John had more than a professional connection. She had waited patiently while I vented to the point of exhaustion, and then made an announcement that swept the ground from under me:

"John has a son, the result of a one-night stand. His name is Nicholas. He must be about twenty-three now." Her words struck me dumb. "He was raised by John's parents and, by all accounts, is a very personable young man."

"What happened to his mother?" I squeezed out.

"Her first reaction was to abort, but John managed to persuade her to go full term and give up the child to him. She agreed . . . for a payment that took all his savings. John's parents raised the boy with pride and without regret."

"A son! Why wouldn't John have told me?" I looked at her in wonder. "A child would never have come between us. He must have known that!"

"I'm sure he did, Stella."

"Why would he tell you and not me?"

"He had to tell someone because the job was becoming more dangerous—dangerous for him. He couldn't tell you. As I said before, any information you were privy to created a huge risk to him, especially as he had created an undercover identity to infiltrate the traffickers. He told me only after I gave my word never to tell another soul—unless something happened to him." She shook her head sadly. "Something happened to him."

The taxi disappeared around the corner and sped off to the train station. Services had resumed again. My parents and children had stayed a couple of extra days but decided to return to London. Another storm was forecast in the near future, and they were reluctant to chance any further delay. I was rather relieved to see them go, frankly. I had much to think about.

I wandered aimlessly around the house. I had meant to call on Beverly and the children but had left it too late. She would be coping with dinner, so I decided to pop over the next morning. I had not seen the Petersens since before Christmas. I put a record on the turntable. Frank Sinatra crooned my favourite, "It Had to Be You"; the melancholy words suited my mood. I drifted into the kitchen to make a snack of cheese and crackers. I sang along with Frank, . . . *for all your faults, I love you still* . . . and the knot at the base of my neck began to loosen. Dusk was coming in quickly, and I switched on the lamps, flooding the kitchen in bright light. I studied the woman mirrored in the glass of the cabinet door. She showed suffering; it startled me, for I was convinced I had carried the deception of hiding my feelings to the outside world very well.

After a luxurious soaking in the bathtub, I propped myself up in bed and tried to catch up on some reading. I must have dozed off before making much progress. When I awoke, it was a little after two in the morning. I turned the bedside lamp off and was settling myself to sleep out the remainder of the night when I became aware of muffled sounds inside the house. I was unconcerned—until I remembered Alice was with Alistair at the Retreat hotel. Then my imagination went wild. *Please don't throw acid on me.* An indelible image of the horrific consequences had never left me. I slipped out of bed and crept to the door. The sounds were coming closer. My hands were trembling uncontrollably, preventing me from turning the key in the lock. Terrified, I looked for something to protect myself with. Gratefully, I grabbed the heavy silver candlestick on the dressing table, the Christmas gift from Julia and Tim. The door handle turned. I pressed myself against the wall as the door slowly opened and a figure entered the room. My eyes were adjusted to the darkness, and I saw it was a man. Time seemed to stand still as I watched him go up to my bed and raise his hand. Impulsively, I rushed forward and, with all my strength, struck him with the candlestick. He keeled over without a sound. My own legs gave out, and I found myself falling on the figure splayed out on top of the rug. Wild with fear, I looked upon a face that seemed vaguely familiar—but it could not be. Somehow, I scrambled to my feet and ran out of the room. Fortunately, I had the presence of mind to lock the door behind me.

Once downstairs, I telephoned the police, praying there would be no delays. I could hear the frantic assault to the door to my room. My knees were shaking so, I sat on the stairs with a butcher knife in my hand, and waited. At last, I heard cars on the driveway, and rushed to let the police in. Alistair was the first through the door, and a couple of uniformed officers quickly followed behind.

"He's locked in my room." I held out the key to Alistair.

"Good girl. Stay down here." He handed the key to an officer, and then gently led me out of the hallway into the kitchen. "Make some tea or something. I'll be back."

"Be careful. Alice would never forgive me." He nodded, and disappeared through the door. There was a lot of scuffling, a few shouts, and heavy steps on the stairs. I filled the kettle with water and placed it on the stove. After a minute or two, Alistair came in with my dressing gown over his arm. I had forgotten I was wearing only my nightdress, and gratefully covered myself.

"Did you recognise who that was, Stella?"

"It was dark, but I'm sure I know him—it just can't be, though! He's dead!" I rubbed my fingers against my brow. "What's happening to me, Alistair? I must be losing my mind. Sir Ralph is dead!"

I felt his arm around me. "Take it easy, now. That chap certainly resembles Sir Ralph. We'll get a positive identification at the station. I phoned Alice. She's on her way to stay with you." He released me and turned the whistling kettle off. Pouring the boiling water into the teapot, he asked, "Got any biscuits?" His smile removed the strain from his face. "You did very well tonight, Stella. I don't want to think what could have happened if you hadn't kept your wits about you." He poured milk and sugar into two mugs.

"I don't take sugar, Alistair."

"You do tonight. I want you to eat a couple of biscuits, too. All right?"

"If you insist," I mumbled.

When Alice arrived, I fell into a troubled sleep on the sofa. When I awoke, I was covered in a blanket and she was sitting in an armchair across from me. Her eyes were shadowed with fatigue.

"Good morning," I croaked from a bone-dry throat.

"Good morning, dear. No need to disturb yourself. You've had a terrible shock. Rest is what you need." I became aware of heavy rain that sounded like grit being thrown against the windows, and I shivered. "It's been raining all night." She tucked the blanket around me. "Washed away all the snow that was left on the ground." She sat next to me. "Alistair is still here. He can't say enough about you, Stella. He's become president of your fan club." She looked down at her hands and was still for a moment. "If anything had happened to you, I don't know what I'd have done." We held on to each other, trying not to think of the unthinkable.

Fiona joined us for breakfast. It was toast, really. Food was the last thing we had on our minds. She kept us in suspense—one could say played with us, and only when she had finished her last mouthful did she address the question uppermost in our thoughts. "I know you are most impatient to hear who it was last night. Well, Stella—you were quite right. Sir Ralph Hughes Young is alive and kicking. His fingerprints proved it. He must have thought paying you a visit was worth the risk of blowing his cover. It's not unusual that a foolish decision helps us get our man."

"Obviously, he meant to hurt Stella!" Alice's voice cracked. "Perhaps kill her?" She asked the question I dared not; it was the primary one I held in my own mind.

"He has said very little so far, but I don't think he was interested in making a social call. Stella is safe, Alice. He won't harm anyone where he's going," Fiona assured. The fluttering in my chest subsided a little.

"That's not the point, Fiona! Why haven't the police had Stella and the house under surveillance? You've said over and over she was at risk." Alice pushed.

"We tried, I can assure you, but Stella has a habit of slipping off whenever she feels like it."

"That's no excuse! You'd expect it of our local police, but not New Scotland Yard. It's bloody poor police work."

"The truth is, we've not had the manpower. We've been stretched to the limit. John's concern for your safety was always uppermost in his mind, Stella." Alistair did not look happy making such a statement. "He repeatedly asked you to make certain you were accompanied whenever you went out. For some reason, you practically put your thumb to your nose when he stressed you used common sense."

"Alistair! Don't talk to Stella like that!"

"It was his priority, and you both know it, Alice. We did our best."

"You are absolutely right, Alistair. I used poor judgement. For some reason, I never accepted I could be in danger. Yes, there were occasions when I felt vulnerable, but my stubborn streak kicked in. I don't know what I wanted to prove; perhaps that I couldn't be pushed around." I looked at him sheepishly. "I've been a fool. Worse than that . . . my stupidity caused John so much unnecessary anguish, and look where it led him." My heart ached as I reflected on the pain I had caused, not only John, but many others.

"Well, it's water under the bridge now. Thankfully, you're safe and sound," Alice said.

"Yes. Let's move on, please." I looked at Fiona. "Where has Sir Ralph been all this time? I was utterly stunned when I saw his face. He looks different. His hair is gone and other things are changed. I knew who it was, though, even in the darkness."

"If it is Hughes Young, that leaves the question who was in the slaughterhouse?"

"Yes, indeed, Alice. I was the clever one who foolishly identified the poor chap as Sir Ralph."

"Don't be hard on yourself, Stella. It was a logical mistake," she said. Nevertheless, I was culpable.

"The body you found was that of a seasonal farm worker, someone who roamed around from farm to farm picking crops, doing odd jobs, and so on. Margot Hughes Young roped him in when he turned up at the house asking for work. He was the perfect victim—no one would miss a casual labourer, and he had a similar physique to Sir Ralph. Poor blighter was killed, and then dressed in Sir Ralph's clothes. Hydrochloric acid was poured onto his face so there would be no way to identify him except through his clothing, and you did exactly that, Stella. The unfortunate man was set up from the moment those two vultures set eyes on him."

"Where has Sir Ralph been hiding all this time?"

"Actually, he's been right here in town. He disguised himself, thanks to a little plastic surgery. His wife and Roger wangled him the job as watchman on the school site when it was being renovated. Gave himself the name of Edwards—Stanley Edwards. Once that job was completed, he just became assimilated into the village." Fiona's laugh was without amusement. "The grand master of Clipton's drug trafficking extravaganza has been right under our noses."

I recalled seeing Margot with the watchman when I went over to the school to complain about the messy condition of the site. "I saw Edwards a number of times. He worked on the town hall renovation as well as the school. I never suspected a thing."

"Why would you? He spoke with a Buckinghamshire drawl, his eyebrows were thinned, his head shaved. The beard helped, too. You—we—were just not looking."

"It's odd I would think of Sir Ralph when all I could see was a shadow of a figure in my room. I suppose the essence of him remains in spite of his disguise. It's unbelievable."

"He and his infamous wife met with Roger at those renovation locations on a regular basis." Fiona's voice faltered. "They deliberately got Roger hooked on cocaine, and then made him their patsy. He was a sweet man, just weak." She looked down at her hands, and I knew she was recalling better days for both of them.

"Did Roger kill John?"

"Roger didn't shoot himself, Stella. Forensics proved that. You can't kill yourself and then get up and sit in a chair at your desk. The whole scene was fabricated. His body was positioned to look like suicide. Blood splatters and powder residue from the gun didn't match up, either."

"I asked about John, Fiona. Not Roger."

She looked questioningly at me, betraying that she had drifted in her focus. "Of course—John. Sorry. They did fight, but we've confirmed Roger was in his flat at the time of John's death."

I nodded, not trusting myself to speak. She went on to explain the police had known from the beginning that the body in the slaughterhouse did not match up to Sir Ralph, mainly because the deceased had calloused hands and very large feet. "Sir Ralph had never done a hard day's work in his life, and his shoe size was an average ten. The timing of Edward's arrival in Clipton was suspect too, according to John's notes. He had quite a file that he had kept hidden. Only his superintendent knew about it. Unfortunately, there was just too much risk if it got out."

"Alistair was puzzled why John didn't share his suspicions with him," Alice broke in. Then she saw Fiona's questioning stare, and sheepishly added, "Alistair mentioned it inadvertently when he was feeling rather depressed."

"I nagged John constantly," I declared glumly. "Instead of trusting and supporting him, I let him down when he needed me the most."

"Don't do this to yourself, Stella. Concentrate on the time you had together when things were good. It is no use going over and over what you should have, could have, done differently." Fiona sounded as if she had learned that lesson the hard way.

"Fiona's right, Stella. Nothing can be changed now," Alice said.

"Police officers are a unique breed—doesn't matter if it's a man or a woman, the job comes first—it has to. It can make the personal cost very high. Relationships are too often casualties of such dedication." Fiona touched my arm. "You and John gave it your best. Let it go, Stella." I said I would try.

The next couple of days were surreal. I took Butterfly out for a ride. We took our time. The snow was gone after torrential downpours but the land was rock hard. A few remaining leaves clinging to sapless limbs were brown and brittle. The birds were silent except for a couple of rooks noisily chastising a red fox on the prowl in the distance. The splendid fellow was likely looking for a female, for this was their mating season. I could feel Butterfly's increasing energy under me, reflecting my own vitality. The rhythm of the pace was hypnotic, clearing my mind and restoring my body. I felt light, graceful, flying on ethereal wings as rider and mount became one. It took time for me to come down from such a liberating high, but I had learned my lesson well. I was not going to repeat my previous mistake and put this beautiful creature at risk. Both feet were securely on the ground when I stabled my noble steed. James watched me loosen a bale of fresh alfalfa and fill Butterfly's feedbag.

"You're spoiling that filly. She'll be asking for room service next." He asked if I had a good holiday, and I reciprocated with the same question. We were awkward, too polite. Perhaps it was residue from our last meeting when I had my tearful breakdown. Eventually I left the barn, calling out, "See you later."

My parents telephoned several times to thank me for my hospitality and, more especially, to enquire about the well-being of their daughter—still a gullible girl in their eyes. Of course they were blissfully unaware of Sir Ralph's visit, and I reassured them that all was well. A bowl of beautiful spring flowers arrived from Julia and Tim, reminding me not only what was on the horizon season-wise, but of time passing into a future where my heart would be healed and a sun would warm me again. I breathed in the heavenly perfume of the blooms, and felt hope.

CHAPTER TWENTY-TWO

"Robert and I are leaving for Savoie at the weekend. Do come over, Stella. I haven't seen you since Christmas," Beverly bellyached.

"Lucky blighters. I haven't skied in France since I was married. Lunch will be wonderful. See you in half an hour."

Bev looked lovely in the palest blue angora twin set, black wool slacks, and two-inch-high heels. Any weight gained from having Little Stella had completely gone. My new grey gabardine pantsuit was rather dowdy by comparison, and I mentally made a note to choose livelier colours for future purchases. "I've missed you," she said, pulling me into the house.

"Likewise. Now we've got over the niceties, show me the grub." We laughed, happy to be in each other's company once again. A tray of tiny sandwiches and gooey pastries was in the centre of the coffee table.

"Nothing formal, just munchies while we catch up. All right?"

"Absolutely."

Blanchard, the butler, appeared with coffee and a decanter of Cointreau. He moved unobtrusively, pausing for a moment to ensure things were in order before disappearing as silently as he had come. Beverly poured black coffee into two fine porcelain cups, adding a shot of the golden liqueur in each. The heat from the coffee released the orange concentrate from the Cointreau. She handed me a cup. "It is a little early, but why not?" I took a sip. It was delicious.

"Stella, if you don't want to talk about John, I respect that. I do want to say, however, if there is anything Robert or I can do, you know you can count on us." She took a bite from a salmon and cucumber finger-sandwich to give me a moment before I responded.

"I'd rather not—not now, anyway."

"Understood." She gave no indication of emotion except for a slight twitch at the left corner of her mouth. "Now, let me tell you all about the latest boring escapades my darling kiddies have gotten into." She caught my eye and smiled affectionately. I felt very close to her in that moment.

Later, Robert and the children arrived from skating on the frozen pond.

"It was really well organised, darling." Robert kissed Beverly's brow.

"We had hot chocolate, Mummy, and saw a lot of our friends there," Sarah reported. At that moment Little Stella decided to make her grand entrance in Nanny's arms. I was thrilled to have the chubby fourteen-month-old placed on my lap.

"Oh my, how lovely she is." I looked at Sarah. "She is just the image of her big sister." The little girl beamed. "Are you going to stay with Granny and Grandpa while Mummy and Daddy are away in France?"

"Yes. It will be lots of fun."

"I don't think you can wait for Daddy and me to leave, Sarah," Beverly teased. "You will get so spoiled, I don't know what we will do with you."

"Will your father see them?"

"Oh, you can bet on it. He and Robert's father compete to be the most favourite grandfather of all time."

"Grandpa is teaching me chess," Robbie announced. "I do get rather mixed up with all the different pieces, and how each one can move." He frowned, recalling his confusion. "He is very patient with me."

"I had a terrible time learning, but I love the game now." He leaned against me, at ease. "Someday we'll play together."

Robert tousled his son's hair. "Let's leave Auntie Stella and Mummy to talk while we raid the kitchen. Come along. You must be hungry."

Beverly lovingly watched her family leave the room. Their blathering echoed through the house, giving it life. It was good to be in a normal household. No intrigue, no questions—only doting parents focused on taking care of their beloved children. Little Stella started complaining, and tried to wriggle out of my arms.

"She wants to show you how well she walks, Stella," Bev said proudly. I helped the little one down from my lap. Before I could stop her, she made a beeline for the tray. "No, darling!" Laughing, Bev salvaged a squashed slice of cake from her daughter's chubby fist. "I'll take her to Nanny." Holding tightly on to her mother's hand, the toddler walked, if a little precariously, out of the room. Beverly returned within moments. "She's getting more teeth, poor little mite. It's painful growing them and painful when we lose them."

I looked at my watch. "Bev, I'd better be going. I stayed longer than I intended."

She looked sharply at me. "What have you to go back to? You're free to do exactly as you wish without having to account to anyone for your whereabouts. You're lucky, Stella."

"Funny, I was just thinking how lucky you are, Bev."

She helped me into my coat. "Take care of yourself. I'll call you when we get back."

"How long will you be away?"

"Two weeks. I always dread going, but once we're in the car and on our way to the airport, I buck up. Robert can't wait. The snow conditions are supposed to be perfect." She smiled rather wistfully. "Even if they weren't, Robert would go. He sees going to France as another way to escape from hibernating in this small hamlet."

"He hasn't settled any better?"

"No. He never will. He's a big-city chap, and will remain one. Perhaps he's right. With all that's happened in Clipton, living in the country may not be such a good idea."

"Cheer up, my dear. Forget all about this place and concentrate on your darling husband." I kissed her on both cheeks. "I'll miss you while you're away, so call me the moment you get back."

"I will." She waited at the door, giving a last wave before I turned the corner.

I was feeling extremely downcast by the time I got back to the rectory. I was conscious of the silence in the house. Alice was gone more and more, and I expected her to announce any time when that would be a permanent arrangement. Alistair had presented her with a stunning emerald-cut diamond ring, and was looking into retirement benefits. In spite of my own plight, I felt genuine happiness for my dear friend. Once she announced the wedding date, I would do all I could to make it a grand occasion. A wedding was something to look forward to, and I decided to accompany further contemplation with a cup of tea.

I replaced the receiver and ran up the stairs to my room to change. Constable Bob said to be at the police station around ten thirty. I didn't have much time. Old sweats had practically become a uniform, unless demands dictated I tidy myself up. It sounded as if I needed to make an effort for this occasion. Over the years, I had encouraged Alice to become more fashion conscious, but recently I had let myself go badly. Hastily, I dressed in a pair of wool slacks, a turtleneck sweater, and my pea coat and slipped my feet into a pair of brogues. A hurried brush through my hair, a smear of lipstick, and I was ready. The fifteen-minute drive to the station was uneventful, although my blood pressure must have been sky-high.

"Morning, ma'am. Everyone's in here." The constable led me to a door marked Private. He knocked before opening it, and then stepped back to allow me to pass. The room was furnished with a long table surrounded by several grey upholstered chairs in which Fiona, Alistair, and three uniformed police officers sat.

"Good morning, Mrs Campbell." A tall, slim man in his forties came towards me, his hand outstretched. "I'm Chief Superintendent Farnam. Thank you for coming on such short notice." He gestured to a seat at the table. A couple of flasks, presumably of coffee, were in the centre of the table with a small stack of Styrofoam cups. A packet of shortbread was opened, scattering crumbs that left grease spots on the polished wood. Fiona motioned towards one of the flasks.

"No, thanks." I sat down, feeling oddly out of place. What could these professional investigators possibly want with me?

"Mrs Campbell, I have a particular interest in the Clipton case because of the brutal demise of one of the officers who came under my jurisdiction—Detective Chief Inspector John Gailbrath. My staff informed me you have been through quite an ordeal yourself, and have many questions. I can assure you it has been a trying time for the law, too. New Scotland Yard's law enforcement is often put in dangerous situations, particularly in clandestine operations. Nevertheless, it is required to be unwavering in its efforts to protect the public from those involved in diabolical illicit acts. In this particular case, it meant not just local criminals, but cartels supplying illegal drugs from the Continent. Our investigations involved cooperation from Interpol, the safe integration of our men into various operating factions, and gaining the confidence of local perpetrators. All that takes time, Mrs Campbell . . . a lot of time." He was articulate, yet detached. "During the next couple of days, those whom we believe have broken the laws of this land will be taken into custody. It will then be up to the Central Criminal Court to decide their fate." His eyes met mine and I saw understanding. "Detective Sergeant Ball and Detective Inspector Richardson tell me you were a special friend of DCI Gailbrath." I nodded. "We owe him a great debt, Mrs Campbell. He worked tirelessly throughout his career to make a safer world for all of us." Suddenly overwhelmed, I looked away to avoid his gaze. A cup of coffee was placed in front of me—I do not know by whom—but my hand was shaking so much, I made no attempt to pick it up. "Mrs Campbell—may I call you Stella?" He did not wait for me to respond. "I wanted to personally meet you, Stella, to assure you John was nothing short of a hero. Putting himself in great jeopardy, he infiltrated the local cells and obtained critical data that led to the case breaking open." I felt his hand on my shoulder. "We are all proud to have known him."

"Yes," I managed to whisper. I got up from the chair and started to walk towards the door.

Fiona called out. "Stella, I'll drive you home." She looked concerned. I shook my head, desperately wanting to be alone—to again cast condemnation on myself for turning away from a man who had only asked me to believe in him. Doubt had been the saboteur. My insecurity of not accepting we had enough had suffocated our chance of a life together, a life I wanted so deeply, but was too fearful to claim.

I drove erratically with my foot pressed hard against the accelerator until the tyres could hold the road no longer, and the car skidded off the slick surface. The car bumped along the ditch for a few yards before coming to an abrupt stop, causing me to hit my head forcibly on the steering wheel. I stared unseeing through the windshield. I do not know how long I sat there, perhaps an hour, perhaps longer. I remember Fiona helping me out to the police car, and driving me back to the rectory. She didn't say anything, just wiped my face from time to time with a damp tissue as I cried myself to the verge of collapse.

CHAPTER TWENTY-THREE

"Easter Saturday," Alice announced happily. She looked less matronly in a new dress of a youthful yellow. "We've already talked to Vicar Ken."

"I'm delighted for you both!" Shamefully, I was a little envious, too. "You'll allow me to have the reception here, of course."

"Thank you, Stella. We were hoping you'd say that." Relief flooded her face. "The alternative was a shindig at the Retreat's banquet room. Not quite what we wanted."

"That's taken care of then. Where are you going for your honeymoon?"

Alistair, sporting a new haircut, was markedly uncomfortable as he cleared his throat. He took a moment before answering. "We were thinking of Paris . . . well, Alice was."

"Or Rome. He's such an old stick in the mud—wants to go to the Cotswolds." She clenched her hands at her sides, determined to have her way. "It has to be somewhere special. It is our honeymoon, after all."

Trying for an affable truce on such a sensitive subject, I went to the refrigerator and took out a bottle of champagne. Alistair managed to pop the cork without too much spillage, and filled the three flutes I had set out from the cabinet. I raised my glass and toasted the happy couple. "To my dearest friend and her betrothed."

They drove away, disappearing into the advancing dusk. I switched on the television news, mostly to fill the void I felt with sound, rather than to catch up with current affairs. The world news reported conflict, hunger, and disease. I turned the channels and came across a French film that was about to start. I settled on the sofa, and allowed myself to escape into the wonders of Africa through the English subtitles. By the time *Fin* appeared on the screen, I had become fidgety. I had always wanted to go to East Africa, particularly to see the wild animals in Kenya's Marsabit National Park and climb Mount Kilimanjaro in Tanzania. The names were so exotic, and conjured up the beautiful images I remembered seeing as a child in heavy bound books. It took a moment or two for the idea to form, and I resisted at first. Travelling alone had no appeal. I showered and settled in bed. Before falling asleep, I had my mind made up. I would sell the rectory and travel. The first place on my agenda would be East Africa.

I drove over to the Petersens' to review what bedding plants needed replacing around the property. The formal driveway to their home needed brightening up, too. I made notes for the gardeners, who would deal with such things the next day. Beverly caught me just as I was about to drive off. Accepting a welcomed cup of coffee in the kitchen, I decided to break the news of my impending life changes.

"Stella, you can't!"

"Oh, Bev, I can." I laughed. "There is absolutely nothing in Clipton for me anymore. If I stay, I see only a bleak, empty future."

"Well, thanks. That makes me feel really good!" She wrinkled her nose, mocking me.

"Silly—you know what I mean. We'll always be friends, no matter where I end up. You're the sister I never had—and I love you as such. It's different for you; you have Robert and the children. Julia and Tim have long left the nest, and are living the lives *they* have chosen. When my parents pass, I'll be without anyone. That's not a very appealing scenario to contemplate."

"Is it safe for a woman to go traipsing around the world alone? Sounds rather dubious to me." She thought for a moment and then smiled broadly. "You can join a singles travel club. You know—it's a way to meet people, especially men."

"Now you're being absurd. Men my age only want young girls. *All* men only want young girls." We both laughed, allowing the levity to distract from my earlier announcement.

"When do you intend to do all this?"

"I will wait until after Alice's wedding."

"Stella, I can't bear it . . . what will I do without you? You understand me. Robert and my father haven't a clue!" She threw herself at me. "Dear girl, you're breaking my heart."

When I returned to the rectory, Alice was at the desk in the library writing out lists. "I only have you and your family to invite to the wedding on my side, Stella. Alistair has quite a large family, most of whom expect to attend. It looks like about thirty to thirty-five people in all. Will that be too many?"

"Too many? You must invite everyone you wish, Alice. This house can accommodate a larger number comfortably. And, of course, there are the three guest rooms, if anyone needs to stay." I tried to encourage her. "Don't worry about anything; it's going to be perfect. I promise—just perfect!"

"Alistair's brother and sisters want to keep to tradition—you know, the groom's family responsibility of paying for the flowers and hired cars. I have my savings for the luncheon, Stella. I don't expect you to pay for anything. Allowing us to have the reception here is most generous of you. We will need nothing more."

I stepped back; her words felt like a physical blow. "Are you serious? You're not going to allow me, your closest friend, to give you your wedding?" I felt disproportionate hurt. She got up from the desk and came towards me, but I backed away. "No, Alice. You must, of course, have it the way you want." Our eyes locked for a moment before I turned and quickly walked out of the room.

We avoided each other for the rest of the day, and around six I was relieved to hear the front door close behind her. I still felt the sting of Alice's rejection. There must be a misunderstanding. I resolved to sort it out as soon as possible. We were family.

It was the following day before our paths crossed again. I saw her from the window as she unloaded her car, and I went out to give her a hand, hoping it would break the ice.

"Those look exciting," I said, gesturing to the half dozen or so silver foil boxes she was piling up on the driveway.

"Don't they! I only have to add a ribbon." She was obviously pleased with herself.

"Alice, please don't shut me out."

She froze, about to gather carrier bags decorated with expensive store logos. Slowly she turned to face me. "Shut you out? I think the shoe is on the other foot."

"What do you mean?" Shocked, I looked questioningly at her. "What have I done?"

"Done? Just quit, that's what you've done. Selling the rectory and running out of town, just like that . . . didn't even talk to me about it."

"Alice!"

"Don't Alice me, Stella. Obviously you feel you can confide in Beverly Petersen . . . tell her about your plans for Africa. Why would you talk to me? We've only been friends for a million years."

"Oh, Alice. You, of all people, must understand I need to get out of Clipton. Now you and Alistair are getting married, there's nothing to keep me here. I have so many painful memories." I took her hands and was grateful she did not pull away. "The rectory is too large for one person; it needs a family to keep it alive. Everywhere I look, I see John. And I can't allow myself to even think about Miller and Steven."

"Of course, I understand. It must be dreadful." She looked on the verge of tears. "I phoned Beverly to check when you would be coming home, and she told me about your plans. It was quite a shock, I can tell you."

"I regret she told you before I had a chance to explain myself. I have to get away, Alice, or I'll go mad."

"Now you've explained, I understand, Stella. I'm always here for you. Always."

"I know that. I had only just made up my mind about moving, and Bev was the first person I saw. I just blurted it out. Perhaps we're both being overly sensitive. You must know I didn't mean to hurt you."

She nodded. I was relieved to see a smile. "Will you go shopping with me for my dress?" she asked, rather tentatively.

"You bet I will!" My eyes unexpectedly misted. "We'll have a day in London."

I helped her gather up the boxes and bags, and we went into the rectory, much relieved the painful episode was over.

My plan to move from Clipton began to take on momentum. I talked with my parents; to my surprise, they supported the idea completely. "Get a flat, here, in London, Stella. You've always been happy in the big city. There's so much more life. And you'll be near Julia and Tim." My mother almost convinced me; nevertheless I was uncertain where I wanted to settle. I contacted a travel agent to enquire about a safari to Africa, and was given a whole itinerary over the phone. Excited, but with more than a little apprehension, I asked for details to be mailed to me. It was a powerful feeling knowing I could actually make such a trip; but having a travel partner would have made it more appealing.

I drove into town and talked with Ted Nyby about putting the rectory on the market.

"I'm sorry to see you go. You will be missed, Stella."

"Thanks, Ted. I've made good friends here, but I really do need to move on."

"I understand, my dear." He shook his head in sympathy. "Losing that good man of yours was tragic."

"If you could keep your eyes and ears open to any possible interest in the property, I'd appreciate it." I ignored his last remark.

"I'll be happy to."

I walked quickly away, avoiding another discussion about my loss. It seemed to be the topic of conversation wherever I went. I was relieved to drive back to the rectory, away from prying eyes and further questions. Fiona and Alistair were coming for dinner that evening, and their company would be welcome.

Without appetite, I toyed with the food on my plate. I regretted that it annoyed Alice no end. She had given time and effort to the pasta dish, knowing it would be a meal we could all enjoy whether vegetarian or meat lover. I managed another forkful before giving up.

"So, Stella, you seem to have your plans worked out," Fiona said, having no obvious trouble tucking into the food on her plate. "I envy you."

"You do?" I was surprised. "I still have a lot to iron out—where to go once the rectory is sold, what to do with the rest of my life."

"Won't you continue with your landscaping business? You made a difference to Clipton. With your reputation, I would think you'd have little trouble building a clientele in London."

"Thank you for that, Fiona." I paused. "There are so many people who'd love to be in my shoes—no responsibilities, no money worries. I am very fortunate."

"Yes, that's all very well, but you have to remember there are people, several actually, who care what you decide." I searched Alice's face and saw genuine concern. "Don't look at me like that, Stella," she scolded me. "If you live abroad, I'll never see you again."

"Alice, I promise you, wherever I end up, that will not happen. We'll see so much of each other, poor Alistair will think he's got a second wife!"

"Oh no!" he protested, good-naturedly.

"Surely I don't need to remind you, Alistair, that Stella's been through a great ordeal since coming to Clipton." She put emphasis on *great*. "Locals here aren't all that welcoming. It took a long time before they accepted her."

"Why a post-mortem now? Please, Alice, let's not do this," I implored, but she was on a roll.

"It was partly through Stella's efforts and money that Clipton is what it is today, a lovely restored hamlet. There are major changes—not only to the buildings. Hundreds of trees have been planted and median landscaping put in along Main Street. It's all Stella's work—and what thanks does she get? Heartache!"

"I appreciate your advocacy, but many others were involved. Right now, I'm looking forward to a new beginning."

"I know you are, Stella. Before you can do that, you have to put the past to rest first. Then you really can move on with your life. For years, you and I have speculated over what happened in Clipton, and now you deserve to have the answers." She turned to Alistair. "Tell Stella what you told me." He looked decidedly uncomfortable. "Go on, Alistair. You too, Fiona. I think Stella needs to know the whole truth about what's really been happening in this idyllic little village." Her tone was sarcastic. "Alistair?"

I looked at her, puzzled by her insistence. We were all silent for a moment, uncertain of where we were heading. She suggested we move to the lounge. The three of us dutifully followed her lead.

"So—start at the beginning, Alistair."

He looked at me, clearing his throat. "Well, I think you know pretty much all there is to know, Stella." He looked beseechingly at Fiona, who seemed unwilling to interrupt, and he reluctantly proceeded without her help. "The case is now in the hands of the prosecutors, and we believe it's strong enough to bring certain individuals to trial."

"Are you sure you want Alistair to go on? It could be upsetting, Stella," Fiona said.

"Please proceed, Alistair," I encouraged. "I don't know what you have to say. I thought we'd already talked ourselves to distraction over Clipton's dark side. If Alice is right . . . there is more, I do need to put this part of my life to rest, once and for all."

He gazed at me before he settled back in an easy chair. "I'll summarise from the beginning; if you have questions, Fiona and I will do our best to answer them. Fair enough?"

"Absolutely." I did not take my eyes from his face.

"Over three years ago, you discovered a body in the slaughterhouse at Tythe Farm. It was assumed to be Sir Ralph Hughes Young. Then, several months later, Miller Owens was found in a ditch. The modus operandi was identical: strangulation, then dousing with hydrochloric acid. He was a guest in your house, as was Steven Lagerquist, who was murdered in a bedroom, here, at the rectory."

"Good grief, Alistair. We know all that."

Ignoring Alice, he continued, "Inspector Gailbrath had been investigating drug trafficking in Clipton for a few months before the first murder took place. When you discovered the body, the inspector was directed to expand his enquiries." Alistair looked at me to assess my reaction. I nodded for him to go on.

"Just say John, Alistair." Alice was becoming more agitated. Fiona reached over and took her hand to quiet her.

"Let him go on, Alice."

"The circumstances were suspicious and, after some probing, John was convinced you had put yourself in danger. He was right. The Hughes Youngs had used the empty rectory extensively for their sordid activities. When you bought the property, that upset the apple cart, as they say, and they hurriedly found an alternative." Alistair looked grim.

"And the alternative was the slaughterhouse?"

"Exactly! It seemed the perfect place—going unnoticed right under everyone's nose. When you got involved in renovating the building with Mr Blake, they really got annoyed with you." He grew quiet.

"It wasn't you per se, Stella; the trafficking was established long before you arrived in Clipton." Did Fiona really think she was making me feel better with those words? "You just happened to hamper their plans quite innocently for the second time. It was Sir Ralph who came up with the idea of faking his own death—thought it would scare you and Joe Blake off. His wife had the honour of throwing the acid on the poor substitute. She was rather careless and got some of the stuff on her arm. It left quite a nasty scar."

"Yes, I saw her arm when she came over to the rectory the first time. Was I set up to find the body?"

"Sir Ralph made sure you saw him earlier that morning, and knew you would testify to that. At one point, he had the idea the police would suspect you as the responsible party, because it was your supply of hydrochloric acid that was used. Of course, you had no motive." Fiona leaned towards me. "Stella, do you want to go on with this?" She stole a look at Alistair.

"I do."

"Fiona, neither you nor Alistair have said anything we don't already know. You both talk as if you're writing a report. It's ridiculous."

I ignored Alice, knowing her protest was out of concern for me. "Sir Ralph wasn't very smart if he thought his death would prevent Joe and me continuing with our project. Once the police released the property, Joe went straight back to work. I helped for a while longer, but my interest had gone out of it."

"The Hughes Youngs were not concerned with Joe Blake." Fiona grimaced. "They thought him a numbskull, apparently. For reasons known only to her, you were the one who got in Margot's craw and she couldn't let go. She admitted you were being watched. Even confirmed you were followed when you left the station after Miller Owens' remains were handed over to his family."

"Who killed Miller?" I heard myself ask.

"Roger Spencer—at the farm; then he dumped the body in the ditch," Alistair broke in, glancing at Fiona, but she showed no sign of emotion. "He and Joe Blake were there earlier. They left after a short while; presumably, because there was nothing of interest to Owens. Then Owens went back alone. At that time, he overheard Roger and Sir Ralph talking. That was his death sentence."

My mouth was completely dry, making it difficult to articulate. "What about Camrose? What could she possibly have done to them—a sweet dog who was friendly to everyone?"

"Apparently, there was concern she would lead you to them. They believed that retrievers had the same talent to track as bloodhounds."

"What despicable people." I grimaced, remembering my devoted dog's beaten body in the tool shed.

Alice got up and closed the drapes against the dark night. We watched her, grateful for a break in the sorrowful dialogue. She looked at her watch. "It's getting late. Can we continue this tomorrow? Stella?"

"I'd rather get it over with now, if everyone is agreeable. Of course, I understand you two have to work tomorrow."

"We do have an early start, but if you wish, we can stay a little longer." Fiona looked questioningly at Alistair. "All right with you?"

"Yes," Alistair agreed.

I needed to go on, get everything out in the open, however painful it might prove to be. "Why did Steven Lagerquist have to die? He was no threat to anyone. He graciously accompanied me to the farm to look for Miller; that was all."

"It was a warning to scare you off, let you know you weren't safe, even in your own home." Alistair's brow furrowed. "How did Mrs Hughes Young put it? 'He was a casualty of war,' if I remember correctly." Alistair scowled with contempt. "I've been in the force a long time, and I've not met anyone quite as callous as that madam."

We were locked within our own thoughts for a moment before Alice voiced another question. "Has Simon Belsky anything to do with this debacle? He made the slaughterhouse his students' project. A perfect cover if he was up to no good. And what about his sister and brother-in-law? They bought the farm from Joe."

"We've checked out Belsky and his students. They are quite legit. In fact, he was the one who reported the loose bricks and numbers to John. The students did a good job—too good, because they soon worked out the system. Belsky got them back to York, post haste."

"I don't understand. John told me about the numbers when he got the lab report on the grout around the bricks. I didn't even know he was in contact with Simon."

"Perhaps it slipped John's mind. Belsky had his own ideas about what was going on, and met with John a couple of times."

"Why didn't he mention it to me?"

"Who knows, Stella? There are still many unanswered questions. We may never get all the tees crossed. Belsky's sister was drawn into the intrigue, unfortunately, through blackmail." Alistair sounded all in. He was too sapped to hide it.

I sat in a stupor. Who could have possibly guessed such gruesome affairs were going on? To an outsider, lovely Clipton seemed the epitome of a law-abiding community. I had been deliriously happy when I first settled in the rectory. I now knew I had no choice but to move on while some remnant of life remained within me. "It seems I've brought bad luck to many of those who've known me. Poor Michael. What could Cynthia have done that allowed Margot to get her fangs into her? She seemed rather a dull individual."

"Something to do with her academic achievements. They weren't exactly what she presented and, if the truth came out, her husband's career could be ruined. Her brother's also. When Michael found out—I understand his wife told him herself once she knew the game was up—he went after merciless Margot; however, he was quickly and rather brutally put in his place. He got another beating when she found out he approached you, Stella." Alistair paused. "Well, they're free of it all now, and back in Canada."

"What about the supplier—the cartel?" I asked. "Did the Hughes Youngs run the show or follow orders? I understood from John the drugs came in from the Continent, mainly France."

"The Hughes Youngs took orders from a French supplier by the name of Henri—"

"I think we should leave it at that, Alistair," Fiona interrupted. "There are still loose ends that need tying up by Interpol." Fiona looked at me. "This Henri is quite a monster. I'm glad he is someone else's problem."

"The whole thing is just unbelievable! All this has been going on right under our ruddy noses!" Alice said, getting up stiffly from her chair. "Sorry, Stella, I've had enough for one night. If you will excuse me, I'm going up to bed." She yawned. Alistair went to her and led her out of the room.

"You must be exhausted too, Fiona. I appreciate you and Alistair staying on and going over everything with me. My mind is a complete jumble—it will take some time to digest everything I've heard tonight." Alistair returned wearing his overcoat. He had Fiona's coat over his arm. I stood up and embraced them both. "Thank you—thank you for everything. You've been wonderful to me, and I'll not forget it." Alistair helped Fiona into her coat. They exchanged a warm smile, a smile between genuine friends who had shared both good and not-so-good experiences together.

"Well, we'll be off then. I'll phone in the morning, Stella. Alice and I have some more wedding details to go over," Alistair said pleasantly. I saw them out and locked the front door. I was so weary I didn't bother making it to bed, and curled up in the armchair, falling asleep immediately.

I awoke around three in the morning. The log in the fireplace had become a fine grey ash. I wrapped a shawl around me, not because I was chilled; it was for comfort. I walked over to the window and looked out. The quarter moon was a luminous scythe against a backdrop filled with brilliant stars. In the distance, I could make out the shapes of the many trees and shrubs I had planted over my years at the rectory. I began to feel wistful. I stood in the silence for several moments. Struggling emotionally, my befuddled thoughts cleared and I faced what had been tormenting me, not just for the past hours, but for a long time. I sighed nervously. I was heading in a direction I had unconsciously resisted. Sitting back in my chair, I held my feelings tightly at bay as I went over everything I knew about New Scotland Yard's Detective Chief Inspector John Gailbrath.

CHAPTER TWENTY-FOUR

London is a wonderful, cosmopolitan city. When Reg brought the car to a stop outside the Dorchester Hotel on tree-lined Park Lane, I felt my spirits rise to a level I had not known for many months. Perhaps my parents were right; maybe I did belong in London? The rectory was on the market; sadly, there was little interest from buyers. The scandalous headlines in the newspapers had made Clipton out to be a snake pit. Nevertheless, I had a room in an excellent hotel for a whole week, and I intended erasing everything connected to Clipton from my mind.

There was plenty to do in my favourite city to ensure I did just that. I had a wonderful lunch with Julia, who looked asleep on her feet. "If I'm not working ridiculous hours, I'm studying for exams," she said. She was not complaining. She was in love with her work, proving she was her father's daughter all right. She had always been a pretty girl, but now her features were taking on a maturity that caused even me to take a second glance. She was becoming beautiful.

"Don't forget there is a world beyond medicine, darling. Have some fun."

Following my own advice, I made use of glorious Hyde Park across from the Dorchester by taking brisk early-morning walks, stopping at the Serpentine Café for a cup of coffee on the way back. One day, I rode the London Eye, and felt a swell of pride as the capsule slowly rose high over the River Thames, revealing a panorama that included Buckingham Palace, the Houses of Parliament, and St Paul's Cathedral. Over the Millennium Bridge was Waterloo Station from where you could catch an express train to Paris. At ground level, one would never know the breath-taking vista. A visit to the London Museum gobbled up another full day. On my last day, Reg took me in the car to Bond Street, and good-naturedly helped me choose wedding gifts for Alice and Alistair. That evening, he joined my parents and me for a delectable dinner in the hotel's King Room Restaurant. Regretfully, I had not seen my son, Tim, but was happy enough to speak to him on the telephone, and hear encouraging reports about him from my father.

"You don't need to worry. I agree he's taking his time with settling on a career, but he'll find what he is looking for. Be patient, dear."

"I will, Daddy. I've learned a good deal over the last few years, and appreciation of my family is at the top of the list."

As Reg guided the car up the drive to the rectory, a beaming Alice was waiting to greet us. "Welcome home, Stella. I've missed you!"

"Liar! You couldn't wait to see the back of me so Alistair could move in," I chided, grinning.

"Oh, dear . . . I thought I'd got away with it."

Reg took my bags up to my room before joining us on the patio for a glass of delicious lemon and barley cordial. It was a warm, sticky afternoon, and the garden was a blaze of colour.

"I love this place," I confessed. "If only I could pick everything up and move it out of Clipton! That would be ideal."

"Well, actually, you could if you really wanted to. Would cost an arm and a leg, of course," Reg said, helping himself to a refill of refreshment.

"True. I have to decide where to go first. I have to make up my mind before I leave for Africa; otherwise I may have to stay out there! Perhaps I'll become a game warden." Alice raised her eyebrows at me. "Only kidding, Alice," I tittered.

"While you were in London, one realtor came for a walk through, but he had no clients with him. You may not be able to sell, and then you'll just have to remain here."

"Alice, the rectory has been a wonderful place to live in over the years, and there are many things I will miss dreadfully. As much as it grieves me, I have to move on. There are too many ghosts."

She studied me for a moment. "I suppose Reg will have to find another job?"

"Reg and I have already talked about that, and he knows I will do everything I can to find another position for him. If I live in London, a car will be more trouble than it's worth. Reg's a Londoner; he understands. Actually, he got a taste of it recently, poor chap. Public transportation will suit me fine." I tucked my hair behind my ear and casually asked, "Any other news, Alice?"

"You're referring to the Clipton horrors, of course. Well, actually, there really isn't. Alistair and Fiona have been going back and forth to London. Alistair said they have significant evidence against those beasts arrested, and the Crown, as the prosecuting party, will be handling the criminal proceedings. Eventually, they'll get to that step, but we know not to hold our breath."

"So—case closed for us?"

"Not exactly. It's just about to begin another chapter. We will all be called as witnesses at the trials. That means you also, Reg. I understand lawyers will be contacting us for depositions quite soon."

Reg rolled his eyes. "Blimey, I don't want to be a copper's nark."

"Don't be daft! You'll be giving evidence under oath, not going behind someone's back to gossip." Alice got up from the chaise longue and gathered the glassware onto a tray. "I'll take care of these while you unpack, Stella. And you, Reg, take care of the car."

"Yes, your majesty." Reg bowed low, then went off to follow orders.

On the morning of the wedding, I went to the stables for a short ride on Butterfly. James came along, riding on a magnificent piebald. He said he envied my upcoming African trip. "Always fancied going around the Cape. I live far from the water now, but love the sea. I come from a long line of sailors. When my father died, he left his yacht to my brother and me, and we sail whenever the opportunity presents itself."

"I never knew, James. Why do you live inland?"

"Duty and my pocketbook. I inherited my father's horses. The stables where he had them housed for years was closing, so I had an agent put out feelers for my own place. He found that Clipton's equestrian property was available. It was a good set-up. I knew I could make a success of it, if I kept on budget. Property on the Isle of Wight is out of my reach!"

"Is that where you're from?"

"Yes. It seems a long way from here, doesn't it? Clipton has been good to me, though, and I've made a pretty good profit. With luck, I'll eventually be able to afford a place on the coast, perhaps in Bournmouth. I'm always checking the properties available around that area."

When we returned to the stables, he insisted on taking care of Butterfly for me so I could hurry back to the rectory and get ready for the wedding. We felt a mutual friendliness, and warmly hugged each other before I drove off. I was grateful there was no sign of the aloofness I had felt at our last encounter. Perhaps I had imagined it. "I wish you all the best, Stella."

"You, too, James."

I felt a twinge of excitement as I drove up to the rectory. The caterer's van was in the driveway and the house was a hive of activity. I cheerfully greeted a couple of the strangers taking over my home, and ran up to my room to get out of the rank jodhpurs that were getting smellier by the minute. Looking utterly bewildered, Alice bumped into me on the landing.

"Hey there," I said, kissing her rather flushed cheek. "What are you in such a hurry about? You're supposed to make yourself scarce this morning, so everyone else can get their work done."

"Oh, Stella. I'm going absolutely crazy. There must be something I can do."

"Come and keep me company while I shower and change." I tucked my arm through hers and led her into my room. "The kitchen is out of bounds now the caterer is here. Go onto the balcony and watch Reg and his crew setting up the chairs for the ceremony." Luckily, he would be out of earshot and would be able to get the work done without her input—others could say her interference. "The sun is predicted to break through this heavy cloud cover around noon . . . perfect timing for the two o'clock ceremony in the garden, don't you think?"

"What time is it, now?" She was actually trembling.

"Alice, sit down. I'm going to get you a glass of something to settle your nerves." I hurried down to the lounge and poured a small brandy. On my way back to my room, I saw Beverly and waved. "Thank you so much for helping with the flowers, Bev. Alice is a wreck, so I've got her trapped in my room. I'll see you in a little while."

"Don't worry about me, Stella. I was born for this." She pointed to the chaos surrounding her; enormous containers full of fresh flowers seemed to be everywhere. "The florist delivered the table pieces first, so they are in place. Now he and I are about to set up the formal arrangements." She blew me a kiss. "I'm in my element."

Alice had wrapped herself up in a blanket and was resting on my bed. "Here you are. Drink this while I take care of my ablutions." I handed her the glass of brandy and then switched on the radio, moving the dial to a classical music channel. "Just try to relax, Alice. You'll only make your face all splotchy."

"Oh, thanks a lot! That's all I need, on top of everything else!" She pulled a face but smiled. "Thank you, my sweet Stella. Thank you for everything." I nodded, smiling back, and then hurried into the bathroom.

Later, we took a walk together through the house, checking the flowers. Alice had chosen deep pink tulips and white lilac for the formal arrangements, and their perfume filled the air. Small centrepieces of pink roses and blue hyacinths decorated each reception table.

"Everything looks so lovely, Alice." I led her to the garden where an archway of roses and lilac had been erected on the terrace. A white rose boutonnière was placed on each guest's chair.

"It's exactly how I planned, Stella. It's perfect."

"You deserve the very best."

"Hey, you two!" We turned to see a man hurrying towards us.

"Joe Blake—of all people! What are you doing here?"

"I received a fancy invitation to a very posh do, and it gave this address." I ran up and threw myself at him. "Joe!" I held on to him, secure in his familiarity.

He grasped my hand and turned to Alice. "You look wonderful, ms-bride-to-be. Your copper's a very lucky bloke."

"I'm so happy you made it, Joe." He opened his arms, and she joined us in a huddle. Genuine joy ran through each of us.

"You're going to have to entertain yourself while we ladies get dolled up, Joe. There's a ton to eat in the kitchen. If you're very nice, perhaps Reg will pour you a glass of champagne or two."

"Reg is still here?"

"Yes; not for much longer, alas. The rectory is on the market, and I'll not need his services. I'm on the lookout for him, though. There's a chance the Petersens will take him."

"They'd be fools not to. Then, of course, they know that!" He patted Alice on the shoulder. "We'll talk later. I don't want to be blamed for your eyebrows being on upside down because I held you up."

"Right!" Alice and I quickly made our way to our rooms. The hairdresser had arrived, and I was first in the chair.

Guests were mingling, and the caterer's staff circulated with trays of canapés and flutes of champagne. The decibels of sound from amiable small talk increased dramatically as the guests drank. Kenneth Wickam Foxwell arrived on his motorbike. Clipton outsiders were amazed to see him enter in studded leathers, and then transform himself into an imposing minister of the cloth, complete with starched vestments and a large, well-worn bible. "It's like a scene from a 007 film," a pretty guest gushed. "Remember Sean Connery stepping out of overalls and wearing a dapper evening suit underneath?" I looked down from the upstairs landing and watched Joe in deep conversation with Reg and Vicar Ken. They had a lot of catching up to do; so did he and I. I went down to join them.

My parents, Julia, and Tim arrived later than expected . . . thankfully, before the ceremony began. Mother wore a plum-coloured print dress and Dad a light-grey suit complete with waistcoat. They seemed to have made the transition quite comfortably from their usual casual togs. I was proud to introduce my family to the other guests. When Tim saw Joe, his face lit up. Joe had been a special friend to my entire family. Then Tim saw Fiona, and his eyes became even brighter. He quickly excused himself, and made a direct line to her side.

After a few minutes of small talk with my parents, Joe said, "If you'll excuse me, I'd like a word with madam, here." Mother beamed as he led me to a quiet corner. "I'm only in Clipton for the night. I go back to Cumberland tomorrow afternoon. Will you have breakfast or an early lunch with me? There's a lot to talk about, and I don't know when I'll see you again."

I looked into his kind eyes, aware of deepening lines crossing his weathered brow. Several years had gone by for both of us, and I wondered at the changes he saw in me. His thick hair was completely grey now and neatly cut. He was in excellent physical shape. The dark suit fitted him perfectly, and he seemed taller than I remembered.

"I'm completely at your service, sir." I reached up and kissed his cheek. "You must know that."

"Good. I'll pick you up at seven in the morning."

"Seven? Be reasonable!"

"I'm only teasing," he laughed, "You say what time. I don't want to waste a minute."

"Why don't we eat here? If you are willing to take the risk, I'll scramble some eggs. By the way, where are you staying? The Retreat?"

"Unfortunately, yes. It isn't what it used to be. I'll take you up on your offer of eggs. I have good insurance." There was a hint of sparkle in his eyes.

"Come at seven thirty."

"Right!"

Alistair's brother Daniel interrupted further banter by making an announcement. "Ladies and gentlemen, your attention, please. If you will make your way to the garden, we can get ready for why we are all here, the marriage of Alice and Alistair."

"My goodness, is it that time already? Excuse me, Joe, I must finish dressing and give Alice a hand." I hurriedly made my way up to her room and barged through the door, almost colliding with her.

"Alice, forgive me. Time just ran away." I stopped blathering and stared at her. She looked back at me. Belying its expense, her dress of cream silk was simple yet beautifully tailored. She wore my gift of pearls and matching earring, and carried a posy of wonderful Gertrude Jekyll pink roses. "I've never seen you looking lovelier."

"Well? Aren't you going to say anything about the hat?" Her curls were tamed by a picture hat in an outrageous shocking pink.

"Absolutely! It's gorgeous! Really, Alice! Alistair is going to have heart failure when he sees you."

"You don't look so bad yourself, actually. I prefer you in green but can't have you looking more glamorous than the bride."

"This is nice, though," I looked down at my blue shift. "Even if I do feel like one of those hyacinths!" We burst into uncontrolled laughter. A knock on the door reminded us we had things to do. It was Reg.

"Ready?"

"Almost. I just have to grab my gloves and flowers." I ran to my room and quickly returned. Alice took Reg's arm, and we made our way down the stairs.

Vicar Ken was waiting patiently. When he saw Alice, he gave an admiring wolf whistle. "You look stunning, Alice." She did, indeed. He led the way through the garden with Alice and Reg following. I brought up the rear, trying to keep pace in time to the quintet's interpretation of Tchaikovsky's "Romeo and Juliet". Alistair's expression was one of utter bliss as he watched his wife-to-be walking towards him. The ceremony climaxed with their exchange of touchingly expressed hopes for the future. Following comedic speeches and several glasses of excellent champagne, the guests were treated to a delectable meal.

It was well into the evening before the guests considered leaving, and I gratefully kicked off my new shoes as the front door closed for the last time. Tim had driven Julia back to London earlier. Upon my urging, my parents agreed to stay the night. My mother came and joined me. She rested her stocking feet on the ottoman. "Ah, that's better."

"I'm so happy with how the day turned out. Worth a little foot discomfort, eh, Mummy?"

"Oh, yes, darling—a perfect day . . . except for all this mess to deal with." She gestured to the many glasses and dishes scattered around.

"Mum, you are not to touch a thing! The caterer will clean up."

"I must do something, Stella. The place is a wreck."

"Go up to bed and get a good night's rest. Daddy was worn out; I know you must be."

"Well . . . if you're sure." She hesitated, reluctant to leave me. "I can stay and keep you company, if you like."

"Stop worrying about me, Mum." I smiled, warmed by her devotion. "I'm feeling better than I have in a long time." I was surprised by my words as much as my mother, but they were true. At last, I was beginning to accept there was a future for me, and I intended to claim it.

"Your father and I have been waiting to hear that for some time, darling." She plodded over and kissed the top of my head. "Goodnight, dear!"

"Sleep well, Mum."

I remained curled up on the sofa and thought over the glorious day. Everything had gone like clockwork. Reg drove Alice and Alistair to Clipton's tiny private airport to fly to London's Heathrow, where they were going to catch a flight to Paris. Alice had won over Alistair in the end, and his dream of fishing in the Cotswolds was for another day.

It had been a pleasant surprise seeing Joe again. Alice had confessed some time ago that she had kept in touch with him after he moved to Cumberland, and apparently telephoned on a regular basis. When she informed him John had come on the scene, however, the calls had become less frequent. I asked her why she had kept their contact such a secret, she replied, "I'm not sure why, really, Stella. When Joe asked you to go to Cumberland with him and you turned him down, it was a bit awkward. If you're thinking I told him tales out of school, you're quite wrong. We just chatted about day-to-day things." Of course, I didn't believe a word.

I heard a quiet cough and looked up. My father stood in the doorway, saving me from further reflection.

"I thought you would be in bed by now. It's past midnight, you know?"

"Couldn't you sleep either, Dad?"

"Oh, I have no trouble getting off; it's all the trips to the bathroom that prevent me from sleeping through the night." He shook his head and lamented, "It's very trying getting old."

"Dear Dad . . . you're not in nappies yet." I stretched and yawned. My father turned off the lamps, and we made our way up the stairs together.

I awoke before the alarm went off at six, showered, and threw on a pair of jeans and a plaid wool shirt. The catering company had done an excellent job of cleaning up, leaving no sign of the bedlam from the day before. I wrote a note to enclose with my cheque, thanking them for going above expectations, and then I quickly set the kitchen table, got the egg whites beaten, mushrooms sliced, and cheese grated. Coffee was brewing before my mother joined me.

"You've got an early start, Stella. Can I help?"

"Would you grill the tomatoes? Those rolls need heating, too, please."

"This is all rather impressive for Daddy and me. Are you expecting others?" She was coy, all right!

"You know very well Joe is coming." I noticed she was uncomfortable and needed reassurance. "You and Dad are more than welcome to join us. I'm sure Joe would like that." My father came in rubbing his forehead. "Hangover, Daddy?"

"I certainly have, and it's a brute!" The effort to speak caused him to wince.

"The coffee is just about done, Stan." My mother disappeared for a few moments and returned with a bottle of aspirin. "Take a couple with a bite to eat, and then lie down. I don't want to miss our train home, dear."

"I'll be fine by then, Dix." His words didn't correspond with his rather greenish skin tone. Mother put a large mug of coffee in front of him along with two aspirin and a slice of dry toast. Obediently, he swallowed the pills with a gulp of coffee and bit into the bread. He had learned well over the years to follow his wife's instructions without complaint.

The doorbell rang. "There's Joe." I hurried out. I opened the door and whispered, "My mother and father are here."

"I'm a little disappointed. I wanted us to talk." He came into the house and took off his overcoat. Underneath, he wore a navy polo shirt and jeans that made him seem younger somehow. He followed me into the kitchen. "Well, good morning to you two!" He hugged my mother and then saw my father. "You need a hair from the dog that bit you, Stan."

Mother was appalled. "No—no, he doesn't! He doesn't need any more booze. We've got a train to catch."

"All right, but it always works for me." Joe sat down at the table and helped himself to a cup of coffee. "I'm leaving town myself this afternoon. What time is your train, Dixie? I'll give you both a lift to the station."

"Ten thirty, Joe. By the looks of Stan, I don't think we can make it." She turned to my father. "Stan, you look awful. You should go and lie down, dear."

"Yes, Daddy, please rest. Reg will drive you home. A train is out of the question."

"That would be grand, Stella. I think I will put my head down for a while." Mother followed him out of the kitchen, her arm around his waist.

"You come from special people, Stella."

"Yes. I know that very well." I went to the stove and lit a flame under the skillet. I turned to him. "Joe, it's been so long. Tell me what you've been up to all this time." I tried to sound interested but casual.

"Yes, it has been a long time. Well . . . I've been busy making a success of the ranch." He hesitated before continuing. "I had hoped it would have been different, that we'd be doing it together. Regretfully, I left out the most important part . . . I wasn't the man for you. You've had a bad time of it, I hear. Lost the man you did love."

"I loved him very much. It has been a long road with many turns since you left Clipton. You know about the drug trafficking, and the involvement of the Hughes Youngs, of course." My shoulders sagged. "I want to go away and forget it all."

"You have to face it first, lass. I know a little of what happened. I understand the police expect to put the villains in prison for a lot of years." He came up and stood by my side while I whisked cream into the eggs. He tucked a loose strand of my hair behind my ear. "Still have your hair in your eyes." He smiled. "Seems I was always trying to push it back."

"It has a mind of its own—just like me, eh?"

"You can say that again!" I could feel the tension in him at my side; however, I wasn't prepared for his next statement. "I still love you, Stella. I always will." I poured the eggs into the hot pan, unable to respond. The silence was overwhelming as I struggled for words. "I don't mean to embarrass you. I don't know why I said anything." He shrugged. "Must be being back in Clipton."

He smiled and touched my shoulder. "Please don't be awkward with me. We're friends . . . the best, remember? I don't want to spoil that."

"The very best, Joe."

I outdid myself, providing a breakfast that was not only tasty, it looked good, and we both ate with a hearty appetite. My mother joined us, and we exchanged insignificant small talk until Joe announced it was time for him to leave.

"It's been like old times. I've enjoyed seeing everyone again but don't miss Clipton at all." Although he was smiling, I could see he was disappointed we had so little time alone. "Thanks for breakfast. You look wonderful, Stella. I think I've told you that already."

"Hopefully you won't leave it so long before you make another visit, Joe," Mother said.

"Perhaps, Dixie. I don't get away when the stables are full. Horses can be demanding buggers."

"You know what they say about all work and no play, Joe? Don't let that happen to you." My mother hugged him for a long moment. "Keep in touch. We'd love you to visit us in London. Remember, that's a standing invitation."

"I will, Dix. My best to Stan, and have a safe journey home." He looked at me for a brief moment. "And you, Stella, have a wonderful life. You deserve it." Before I could respond, he was gone.

"Stella, you were so aloof. That poor man," Mother reprimanded me. "He came all this way not just for Alice's wedding, and you know it."

"Mum, please don't! I'm happy to see Joe . . . but you know how I feel." My words trailed off as my mood plummeted.

"What's going on? Where's Joe?" My father, still looking a bit off colour around the gills, came into the kitchen.

"Nothing, Dad. Joe had to leave, and Mum thinks I was mean to him."

"Dix, stay out of it. It's her life."

"I know, Stan, but it's an unfulfilled life, and she knows it." She walked up to him. "I'm glad you're feeling better, dear. We can go home now."

"I'll call Reg to bring the car round when you're ready." How empty the house would soon be.

CHAPTER TWENTY-FIVE

I absently put a record on the turntable without bothering to switch it on, and wandered around the house, eventually making my way into Alice's now-vacant room. She and Alistair had moved her things to their new home in the Chelsea area by the River Thames. It was a pretty two-story brick house with green shutters. Alistair had built window boxes that we had fun planting with brilliant red geraniums. I touched the chair where she used to sit reading the latest bestseller before going to bed. The outline of her shape still remained in the soft cushions. *Be happy, Alice,* I whispered into the stillness. The sharp ring of the telephone broke into my morose state of mind, startling me.

"Hello?"

"Stella, it's Fiona. At the wedding, you asked me to call you. You have more questions?"

"Fiona! Yes, thanks for getting back to me. I still have a few concerning John." There was silence at the other end of the line, and, for a moment I thought the connection was broken. "Fiona? Are you still there?"

"Yes, Stella. What is it you want to know? I thought Alistair and I had gone over everything with you—more than a few times, actually." She sounded impatient, and my anxiety increased.

"Yes—yes, of course, but I did some checking myself and came across information that was inconsistent with what John had told me." Again there was silence. "Fiona?"

"I'm sorry, Stella. I don't know what you want from me."

"I want to know if you will help me. My questions are quite straightforward, and the answers should be, also." I was becoming defensive. "Will you help me?" I asked again. There was reluctance in her voice as she agreed to try. "I'll not to waste your time, Fiona." I took a breath and began. "When John and I first started seeing each other, he told me he had been married for four years. He was using cocaine. His wife tried it only once, and it resulted in her death. That devastating experience brought him to his senses, and he quit cold turkey." I paused, remembering how grief-stricken he had looked when he described the incident. "I bring up the story because I would have thought, to be accepted as a candidate for the police force, drug addiction was strictly a no-no. I was surprised he rose through the ranks so easily. Again, I accepted his word, thinking the good old boys in blue gave an errant man another chance."

"Stella, where is this going? All you're doing is raking over things long past. What good will it do?"

"Please bear with me . . . then I really can put everything behind me and move on." I heard her exasperated breath through the phone. "Am I wrong? Can a drug addict whose wife's death was attributed to drugs become a police officer? It seems to me New Scotland Yard would be taking a huge risk."

"It all depends on the circumstances, and who is willing to stick his neck out. John was highly regarded, so promotions would have been in order. He passed all exams, was terrific on locations, did detailed detective work—"

I couldn't hold back and blurted out, "Wouldn't it have been prudent to keep an extra eye on him in case he relapsed?"

"Stella, what exactly are you getting at?"

"I don't believe the story. I don't believe his wife died the way he said she did. I think the police would have gone over every detail of her death. Supposedly, she choked on her own vomit; if it were true, it would have to be established by the coroner and posted in public records. I could find nothing." The words rushed out. "I couldn't find any record of his marriage, either. If it isn't true, why did he tell me such a blatant fabrication?"

"He never talked to me about a wife or how he joined the police force."

"Isn't that a bit strange? Doesn't that sort of thing come up during friendly chitchat between colleagues? I think you know he joined the force with a clean record and, as you say, soon earned the respect of everyone who knew him." I waited, hoping she would confess . . . to something.

"So?"

"So why did he cook up the rubbish he fed me? Talk to me, Fiona. I'm trying to bring everything to a close, but the door refuses to shut while I still have these questions. I sincerely loved John. I'm not trying to blacken his name or anything, I'm just trying to make sense of the time we had together."

"Will you be in this afternoon?"

"Yes."

"I'll see you around two." She hung up.

She arrived exactly at two, and followed me into the lounge. "Can I get you anything—coffee, tea . . . a glass of juice or something?"

"No, nothing. Let's just get this over." Fiona had a deep frown on her lovely face. As usual, she was well dressed; the pale, honey-coloured suit brought out highlights in her blond hair. She sat down in a chair and crossed her long legs. "I'll tell you everything I know. Perhaps, then, you will be satisfied." Her tone was emotionless, professional. I sat opposite her and kept silent. "John Gailbrath was on the case for some time, but not making progress. He decided to put out the story he had a drug addiction to set himself up—the same story he told you, including about a wife, except he made sure it was known he was still a user. He kept that little detail from you. If anyone snooped around, it would seem reasonable you thought he was clean now. It was for your safety. He did love you, Stella; he hoped when it was all over he would be able to explain, and you would understand the reasons for his deception."

"Is the story of him having a son really true?" I clutched my hands together to steady the developing tremor.

"It is—the result of a one-night stand, as I've already told you. No wife, no lover, just sex." She went on. "He thought—and the department agreed—those he wanted to reach would be highly interested to know he had a weak spot, an Achilles' heel. They bought it, and he played the role of their lackey very convincingly. He did everything they asked—within reason, of course—and his reward was not money; it was cocaine. He had researched the drug's affects with professionals in the field and talked about addictive behaviour with druggies inside."

"Inside?"

"Prison. He was very thorough and convincingly duplicated the behaviour he saw, enough to persuade any doubter he was on the level."

"Oh, Fiona!"

"Don't Fiona me, Stella. This is what you asked for." Her tone was sharp, unsympathetic. "Eventually, Margot Hughes Young introduced John to an important member of the cartel, a Mexican by the name of Alfredo Rodriquez. Based on her conviction, Rodriquez took John into his confidence. John then made several drug drops at the slaughterhouse after retrieving consignments from Mexico through Marseille, France. That's why he was gone so much. He was useful—could short-cut customs just by flashing his badge and pulling rank. He had no qualms about strong-arming those who didn't conform. Apparently, he could be quite vicious. He learned about Sir Ralph's hoax on one of the occasions when he took payoff money to the Hughes Youngs' house. It was quite a shock to see the old man alive and kicking when he was supposed to be dust. Forensics was able to acquire the urn with the cremated ashes from Sir Ralph's bogus columbarium niche, and proved some other poor blighter played that role. You were, by the way, set up to find the body." She got up from the chair and paced around the room, emotion building in her voice. "To make it short and sweet, Stella, John's weakness wasn't drugs at all—it was you! He learned you were going to be, shall we say, made to disappear, and he frantically tried to find out when and other details. He discovered from Roger that Margot intended to kill you herself. She had decided you were getting too nosy, particularly after you were seen snooping around the slaughterhouse on your own."

"Someone was there? I didn't see a soul."

"There was always someone around, Stella. Every move you made was noted by them, including you taking a packet of cocaine from behind one of the bricks. When Margot learned about that, she wasted no time in setting up your *accident* with a loser whose very existence revolved around getting high." Fiona stopped herself, remembering something. "I believe Alice reported seeing Margot with him some time ago."

"Yes, she mentioned it to me."

"Because of John's diligence, that young man had little chance of following through with his orders, and was quickly arrested. John found out about an alternative plan to get to you, and panicked. He got careless—made the mistake of alerting Alistair one too many times—and brought suspicion on himself. He was watched very closely after that. That's why he didn't put up much of a fight when you separated. It put a safe distance between the two of you. Over time, he and Roger established a level of reliance between them. Unfortunately, John was overheard talking with Roger about you while they were setting up a drug drop at the slaughterhouse." Fiona paused. When she continued, her voice was emotionless, flat. "A couple of nasty pieces of work beat him to death. Then, just to make sure, they shot him. Roger was shot, too, and his body taken to his flat to make it look like suicide. You only get one chance when big money—I'm talking about millions and millions of pounds—and influential, high-ranking thugs are involved." She looked at me with eyes bright with hostility. "I believe you have it *all* now, Stella."

Feeling utterly ashamed, I turned away, and she left without another word.

CHAPTER TWENTY-SIX

"Your trip will help, dear. Take your mind off everything." Mother meant well. She was referring to the safari in Africa—at least that was where I told my family I was going, but I had to punish, not reward myself. I deserved no respite from the self-loathing eating away at my soul. I felt in a trance, carrying through with the lie right up until the departure date. Reg drove me to Heathrow Airport and walked with me to the entrance of the boarding area—even hugged me as he wished me a safe trip—but I never boarded the plane. My name was not even on the passenger list. Instead, I stood in the middle of the teeming terminal; a wealthy, gutless woman, so fragile, she was on the brink of shattering like a piece of brittle glass. Uncertain of my next move, I waited for a few minutes, then walked to a taxi rank and gave a street address in Earl's Court.

The amiable driver asked, "What number, miss?"

"Wherever there's a rental sign."

The bed-sitter was small. A sagging single bed, a grungy dresser, and a chair completed its furnishings. In one corner was a two-ringed gas range set on top of a curtain-draped counter. The sink was filthy. "I'll take it."

"A month in advance and one month's security deposit," the dishevelled landlord demanded.

"I'll give you cash."

I stayed holed up for several days, getting out of the lumpy bed only for trips to the communal bathroom along the landing. Deranged, I prayed to a god I hoped was real, and begged for mercy. The Benadryl did its work well. I remained semi-conscious, although my nightmares caused me to scream aloud until my neighbour banged on the wall, yelling for me to cut it out. Eventually, I reached the point where I could stand my own stench no longer, and stepped into the grubby bathtub. The hot water helped soothe my cramped muscles that had held me in a foetal position for days. My mind began to clear, and hunger forced me to walk to the corner shop for groceries. It took effort in my weakened state, but it was worth it for I felt surprisingly better after swallowing some broth and crackers. A few days later, I was strong enough to walk around familiar streets, and came across the coffee shop where Geoff and I first met. I went in and ordered a cappuccino.

Reg picked me up from Heathrow after I telephoned him with the flight arrival time. I got the information from Sud Afrikan's arrival and departure line. He looked at me for a couple of moments, and then opened the car door without saying a word. As soon as we arrived at the rectory, I telephoned my parents. My mother picked up after the fourth ring.

"Yes, it was wonderful, Mum. Much more than I imagined." I hated lying, particularly to my mother, but I continued the farce.

"You've been gone much longer than we expected. You should have let your father and me know, Stella. We were worried."

"I only extended for a couple of weeks. Anyway, I'm back now, and I'll call you again in a few days." I replaced the receiver. Although delighted I had returned safely, Tim and Julia were quite disappointed my bag of souvenirs was lost in flight. My deception ate at me. I had to face my family with the truth, soon.

Alice and Alistair were settled in their charming house. When I dutifully made contact, they insisted I spend the first available weekend with them. "You can show us all your photographs," Alice said.

"I haven't got them processed."

"Then get on with it."

"I have some good news." I was happy to change the subject. "The estate agent called. A couple are interested in buying the rectory. Keep your fingers crossed they take it."

"Stella?"

"Yes?"

"Are you all right, my dear? You sound, well . . . odd."

"What on earth do you mean? Of course I'm fine."

"Call us when you're free to come. No excuses. We'll be expecting you."

"I will. My love to Alistair." I was distraught when I hung up. It is quite true: one lie always leads to another.

A different couple came with the realtor that afternoon, and showed genuine interest in the rectory. To my delight, they were keen gardeners. After enthusiastically touring the grounds, they announced the property was exactly what they had been looking for. They appeared to be in their mid-thirties. Rather young to be so financially robust, yet acknowledged my price without a blink of an eye. I was assured of a final answer within a few days. I stood at the front porch and watched them drive off, and then took a slow stroll around the whole estate, stopping occasionally to take in a particularly pleasing view. It had been a major challenge to develop the landscape and bring life back to the old place. The profound satisfaction I had felt in creating such a home for myself still remained. I was content when I returned to the house, and found Beverly waiting on the patio, watching me.

"What a pleasant surprise, Bev. I was going to give you a call later."

"Fibber! But that's okay." She looked me up and down, a deep furrow in her forehead. "You look terrible, Stella. What's happened to you? You're as thin as a rake. You didn't make it to Africa, did you?"

"I don't want to talk about it—not now, Bev. It has taken a while, but I assure you I'm all right." I led her into the kitchen.

"You're all skin and bones, Stella. Listen, my dear, what happened to John wasn't your fault. The quicker you get that into your thick skull, the better."

"Beverly, please. I can't—won't listen to any more!" I tried to turn away as she caught my arm.

"Punishing yourself isn't the answer, Stella. Don't you see? You must live the very best life—for John. Then his wasn't wasted." If her lip trembled a little, her voice was defiant. "He would be counting on it."

I eventually made it to Chelsea, as promised. It was a month later than I anticipated, to my chagrin; however, I was able to accomplish several things on my to-do list during those extra weeks.

"I've sold the rectory," I announced with much relief. "Escrow will close in ninety days, so I'd better get off my derriere and sort out where I'm going."

"Look at property in Chelsea. Then I'll have you close by," Alice urged. "It's very central, and there are some lovely places on the market. We can look around this weekend."

"I was thinking of renting until I had a clear idea of what I wanted to do. It's such a big decision, and likely will be the last place I will ever live. I've already looked at a flat in Kensington by Hyde Park. It's small, cheerful, and close to everything I could possibly want. I'll put my furniture in storage for the time being."

"You haven't much time to get everything organised. A ninety-day escrow will fly by."

"Yes; however, if it is necessary, the buyers are willing to let me stay longer for a reasonable rent. I'm glad it's the younger couple taking the house. They have small children and several dogs! Bev and Robert will love that." I was warmed by the idea. "The old place will get a new lease on life. It's time for a change."

"Will you keep your landscaping business going? Can you, from London?"

"Oh, yes. It's probably better for me, actually. A London address perhaps sounds more successful than one in the country. Frankly, Alice, I'm uncertain about many things just now. I may even go into the horse business with James." I laughed as Alice's eyes opened very wide, indeed. "He needs some capital, and I am a source he might consider. Don't look so shocked. I'm open to anything at the moment."

"Talking of horses, have you heard from Joe?"

"There was a phone message from him while I was away. I didn't call back because I've really nothing to say."

"Stella, he is your friend."

"It's a little more complicated than that, Alice. He still has feelings for me that I can't reciprocate. It's much better this way. Now, don't look at me like that!" Fortunately, Alistair joined us, and the conversation shifted gears.

When I first arrived at the Chelsea home, Alistair had opened the door. He seemed taken aback seeing me on the doorstep with my overnight bag, and I thought perhaps I had the weekend date mixed up. "Alistair, is everything all right? You were expecting me?"

"Oh—yes, of course, yes. Welcome, Stella." He stood back and let me pass. "Alice is in the sitting room. Alice—it's Stella."

"My dear!" She came rushing out of the room and warmly embraced me. "I'm so glad to see you." I watched the joyful expression on her face change to one of alarm. "Look at you. You're a complete wreck. Where have you been hiding yourself, Stella? It certainly wasn't Africa."

"Let the poor girl sit down, Alice."

"She's not a girl, Alistair, she's a grown woman, and old enough not to play silly games!" She put her face close to mine and glared. "Well, you've got some explaining to do." I saw her expression soften just a fraction.

It was a relief to confess. My two friends sat across from me without saying a word until I had finished. Then Alice let me have it.

"How could you? Going off on your own like that . . . what a sham, telling everyone you'd gone to Africa. It's beyond belief! You have family and friends who love you. Didn't you think we deserved the truth?"

"Try to understand. It was what I had to do—get away from everyone who knew me. I could only purge the pain and remorse from me if I was completely alone. I couldn't do it in Clipton." I smiled at her, trying to alleviate her distress. "I'm really all right, Alice. I came back because I'm all right now." She nodded weakly. Alistair coughed a couple of times before saying rather gruffly, "I'll put the kettle on for tea." That British prescription again, and I was grateful.

Thankfully, once the confrontation was behind us, we settled peacefully and had a delightful couple of days together. Alice brought out several books borrowed from the local library that were full of glorious coloured photographs of plants suitable for a cottage garden. My advice was sought for the design.

"Lots of peonies and tall hollyhocks. The birds and insects will love them." Alice was in ecstasy. "I wish the ground was large enough for a small pond, but I can't have everything, I suppose."

"You can, if you keep it simple. I'll draw up a couple of examples."

"How wonderful. Alistair can build it." He remained silent. He was learning to accept there was a honey-do list in his life now.

On my last morning before returning to Clipton, the phone range. Alistair was at New Scotland Yard, and Alice was busy loading the washing machine. "Get that, please, Stella," she called.

"Hello, the Ball residence."

"Are either of them there?" It was a male voice.

"It isn't convenient just now. May I take a message?"

"Who is this? Is this Stella Campbell herself?" The voice was slightly teasing.

"It is. You know me?" The voice was familiar.

"I know you, Stella Campbell." He chuckled at my discomfort. "It's Joe Blake."

"Joe! I'm sorry. I haven't heard your voice on the telephone for so long. Our recent conversations were extremely limited, you may remember."

"I do remember, very well. So . . . how was Africa? Did you climb to the top of Mount Kilimanjaro? The view must have been spectacular. I hope you took lots of photographs."

Alice stood in front of me and mouthed, "Who is it?"

"Joe, Alice is here now. Let me hand you over. Nice talking with you. Take care." I handed the receiver to her and went into the garden, reluctant to eavesdrop. Soon, Alice called me back to the kitchen. Her face was animated as she reported on Joe's business savvy.

"That stud ranch of his is getting recognition all over the world. He is a rich man—a very rich man. Now all he needs is a nice woman to spend all that money on." She leaned towards me. "Stella, you couldn't have a better friend than that man. He adores you."

"I know how good he is! We were very close at one time, but we've both moved on."

"You may have . . . he hasn't. He has invited Alistair and me up to the ranch and wants you to join us. Believe me, my dear, he knows you have no romantic interest in him. He would like to rekindle your friendship. That is all, I promise."

"I've got the rectory to deal with and all that packing. There's no way I'll have the time. Thank you for thinking of me, but I have to say no." The subject did not come up again, and soon we were chattering like two old nest hens. Then it was time for me to leave. I hugged her gratefully before setting off in a taxi for the train station.

All in all, it had been a successful visit: I had cleansed myself of the shame I felt over the fictitious African trip, and was comforted by the understanding generously shown to me. I was fortunate, indeed, to have such beloved friends. While I waited for the train, my thoughts turned to Joe Blake and his invitation to visit Cumberland. Under different circumstances, it would, of course, have been pleasant to see his ranch. We had an easy-going relationship before he moved away, and had been so close, that each knew what the other was about to say, before the words were actually spoken. The train was running late, but I didn't care. I no longer had pressing matters to deal with, and was heading towards a simplified, if somewhat solitary, life by desire. I sat down on the platform bench. A young woman with four small children joined me. I listened with pleasure to their happy chatter, and reminisced over my own motherhood. "They talk constantly all day. I hope they aren't bothering you?" The woman became aware her son was kicking my overnight bag. "Stop that, Paul. Say sorry to the lady." The cherub looked at me with eyes the colour of cinnamon. "Sorry." I smiled and pushed the bag under the seat. The train eventually made its way into the station, and the mother ushered her noisy brood into a carriage. As I made myself comfortable in a seat by a window, uncertainty overcame me. For all my outward bravado in front of family and friends, I had moments when an unknown future did not seem quite so appealing, after all.

It was with great difficulty I said goodbye to my many friends in Clipton. James rode over on Buddy to thank me for the cheque I had left on his desk when I took my last ride on Butterfly. "I believe in your plans, James. I know you will do well; you have your heart set on it."

He shook my hand warmly. "Thank you, Stella. I won't let you down."

"I'm counting on it," I replied.

Bev and Robert walked over to the rectory on my last evening, and we had a drink together. There were no goodbyes in their case; we expected to see a lot of each other in the future. Ted Nyby, Dr Levinton, and Vicar Ken all dropped by to wish me good luck. Lastly, I closed my account with Walter Pearce's bank and transferred the funds to a local branch in Kensington.

"All right, Reg. Let's get out of here." I was tearing up. I had promised myself I would not look back at the rectory, but I couldn't help myself. I watched the graceful building fade from my view as the car gathered speed.

"That old house is getting a new life, and so are you, Stella. It's a new chapter for a lot of us." Reg winked at me in the rear-view mirror. "It's going to be a good one, guaranteed."

I had taken a short lease on the flat in Kensington, furnishing it rather sparsely, and then had the rest of the furniture and most of my personal belongings put in storage. Reg drove me back and forth between Clipton and the flat as I got settled in, and he made me promise to call him if I needed anything in the future. "I made sure that it would be all right with the Petersens because you are still my priority, Stella. They told me it wouldn't be any problem."

"Thanks, Reg. I'll remember that!" Loneliness was a heavy weight in my chest.

CHAPTER TWENTY-SEVEN

The year passed quickly and then another. I became comfortable in my small flat. I advertised my landscaping services, and contracts gradually picked up after a rather slow start. The first couple of months dragged by; the only enquiry came from a private home in Hampstead Heath. A small conservatory was required. The job held little interest for me, although I was pleased my name was among those being considered. I did not exactly hibernate but, certainly, my life slowed considerably.

The Petersens would call when they came to London, and we had delicious dinners on Robert's company card. Little Stella had become a rather intense kindergartener. We continued to spent happy times together at every opportunity her parents would allow. Fiona married a successful solicitor, and retired from the Yard before their first child was born. I'm godmother to their second son. I also saw quite a lot of my family who, after a stiff reprimand, forgave me for my deception about Africa. Alice and Alistair, of course, intended to be regular visitors. They were inquisitive about the flat; however, once they saw its size, there was little insistence for further visits.

"You can't swing a cat in here, Stella," Alice complained.

"But I don't want to swing a cat in here," I replied.

I loved taking walks in Kensington Gardens and Hyde Park and spent enjoyable hours wandering in all the museums along the Cromwell Road. I lived a different life than the one in Clipton; I was on my way to finding myself again, and discovered I was happy.

"I can't believe it's our second anniversary already. How can it be two years?"

"Tell me about it, Alice. I just renewed my lease for another twelve months. Remember I was only going to stay temporarily until I found a new house?" We talked pleasantly, and were on one of our several phone calls made each week.

"You have pots of money, Stella. You've got to start spending some."

"Alice! My pots of money, as you call them"—I tried to mimic her—"are all tied up in a trust for Tim and Julia, and I pay all my parents' expenses." I laughed to myself. I was wealthy, of course, and had everything I could possibly need. Charities received generous donations on a regular basis; other than that, the pounds, shillings, and pence kept growing in my accounts. "I know, let me spend a few quid on your anniversary gift. What would you like from this old skinflint?"

"I'd like you to come to our party. Alistair put in to have the time off, so we can celebrate in style. You have no excuses, so we shall expect you . . . oh, and we'd like a supply of table linens, preferably with monograms. Cotton is the gift for the second year, I discovered."

"I'll be there; you can count on it. By the way, when is Alistair actually going through with his retirement?"

"Who knows? He just loves that bloody job so much. Says he's going to give notice, then can't quite go through with it. Actually, I don't really mind. It's not easy living with a man twenty-four hours a day, is it?"

"He'll know when it's the right time. Well, Alice, I've got to go—got to get a gift for a pushy couple I know."

"I'd prefer heavy linen. Cotton creases so easily." We hung up. Nothing more needed to be said. Right?

The house looked enchanting. Small lights were wrapped around the trees, and coloured Chinese lanterns hung from the portico. Voices and music drifted from the back garden. The taxi driver helped me unload a case of champagne and my overnight bag. He looked at his generous tip twice before folding the notes and putting them in his waistcoat pocket. I caught the eye of a waiter and solicited his help getting the bottles into the refrigerator, and then made my way up to the room I would be using for the night.

It was the first party I would be attending in a long, long time, and it had been fun to shop, not only for the gift Alice had requested, but also a new dress. In a Sloan Street boutique, the assistant steered me away from a grey silk. "It drains the colour from your face, and is too matronly, madam." She looked at me for a moment before disappearing. When she came back, she had a floral sundress in peach tones over her arm. "This is better. Much more with it."

"I was thinking of something a little more formal, actually. Spaghetti straps are a bit young for me, don't you think?"

"Not at all. You've got good shoulders. Try it on, at least."

The moment I put the dress over my head, I knew the girl was right. I felt completely different as I happily looked at every angle of myself in the dressing-room mirror. The peach colour added a healthy glow to my skin and did, indeed, make me feel younger.

"I'll take it," I said with enthusiasm.

"A light wrap in a pale olive green would be good—and a pair of sandals in the same colour." The assistant promptly disappeared. Within a few moments, she returned carrying both items. When I was all dressed up, she nodded her approval. "You look completely different, madam—you look lovely." I really believed she wasn't just cajoling me.

Beverly Petersen was the first to see me when I entered the garden. "Well, look at you!" I actually blushed. Soon, Alice was at my elbow, pushing a drink into my hand and introducing me to other guests; one couple also had a daughter in medicine, and we happily commiserated. I was confident as I circulated and engaged in light conversations. An advertising executive talked about his garden-nursery account. He thought I could be useful on an upcoming photographic session, and asked me to give him a call. "You'll be paid, of course," he said, handing me his business card.

I was thrilled, and intended to follow through. We continued to make small talk about other possible work until I felt a hand on my arm. Turning, I looked up at Joe Blake.

"Hello. I didn't know you were in London."

"I've been coming down quite often, lately. Luckily, this trip coincided with the happy couple's wedding anniversary." His grey eyes were clear against his tanned face. He looked at my empty glass. "Can I get you another drink?"

"Please." I excused myself from my companions and walked with Joe over to the bar. "Dry martini with a twist."

"Make that two," he said to the barman. "So, young lady, what have you been up to since we last saw each other? That was a long time ago—at Alice and Alistair's wedding—and here we are at the second anniversary. Unbelievable, eh?"

"It certainly is, although I haven't quite severed the emotional cord to Clipton. I keep busy, working a little here and there. I see my family quite a lot, and volunteer at St George's Hospital at Hyde Park Corner. It's where my daughter practices."

"I remember Julia well, Stella. I was once a part of your family's life, too."

"I'm sorry, Joe. I wasn't sure you would remember where Julia worked, that's all." We sipped our drinks, feeling awkward. "Tell me about your ranch. How many horses do you have now?"

"We have eight excellent stallions, and ship semen regularly. When the time is right, the mare is brought to the ranch and a selected stallion services her. Then it's an anxious wait for everyone. With luck, the outcome is fruitful; the foal gets the best characteristics from both parents, and everyone is happy. It sounds easy but, believe me, it is very complicated, and takes lots of speculation and prayer to get the desired result. Word is out we have a high successful rate, so business is booming."

"I watched a documentary on the television about stud ranching. I was totally captivated."

"You should come up for a visit. You may actually enjoy yourself." He nudged me, grinning. "I'm only asking you to think about it," he teased. I smiled back. The tension between us was ebbing. I snatched a peek at him while sipping my drink, and conceded this man had once been my soul mate, someone I had thought would be in my life for ever. Circumstances beyond our control had changed all that. We strolled leisurely to the end of the garden and sat on a bench under a large green umbrella. It was pleasant to be in his company again.

"Joe?"

"Mm?"

"I'm sorry for being so reticent. It's been difficult for me to move beyond the last few years."

"Don't you think I know that, lass? Remember, Alice and I have kept in touch. I know what went on in Clipton, and blame myself for involving you in the slaughterhouse in the first place. I've felt culpable ever since. All that nonsense going on under my nose, and I hadn't a clue. Drugs! Murder! It's unbelievable!" He stretched his arm along the back of the bench. It seemed natural for me to rest against it. "I was just a simple farmer enjoying the friendship of a very special woman." He moved his arm to my shoulder, drawing me close. "Alice told me how you suffered. I wanted to snatch you away from it all. Then you became involved with John Gailbrath, and I had to keep out of it. These years have been very hard on me, Stella. I walked away, leaving you to face everything alone. Can you forgive me?"

"There's nothing to forgive, Joe. You weren't responsible for what happened!" I reached out and touched his arm. "I'm not the person you knew, Joe. I have to learn to trust again, to allow myself to be vulnerable." I laughed nervously. "I don't know if I have enough time to work through all the sadness, but I'm trying."

He nodded. "You have time, Stella. You'll find your spark again." He suddenly laughed. "From the way you look right now, I'd say you've found it or are a bloody good actress."

"You like this dress?" I asked, grateful for the change of subject.

"I like this dress! I like you!" He became serious. "I'm here for you, Stella . . . always have been. Don't shut me out again. Let's see where it takes us. Will you give me that?"

I studied his strong hands holding mine. They were tanned, callused—hands that were not afraid of hard work but they knew tenderness, too. I looked up, and an overwhelming feeling of affection for him ran through me. I saw the emotion in his eyes as his lips tenderly brushed my cheek. I blushed, surprised by wanting more. "Yes, Joe, I'll give you that."

"My train leaves in a couple of hours. Come with me," he said simply.

We looked at each other for a long moment. With his hand holding mine, we went to find Alice and Alistair to make our excuses.